WYCAAN MASTER: BOOK TWO

# THE FIRST DECREE

*A Novel*

## ALON SHALEV

Tourmaline Books
Berkeley, California

The First Decree
Wycaan Master, Book 2
Copyright © 2013 Alon Shalev

Tourmaline Books, Berkeley, California
http://www.tourmalinebooks.com

ISBN: 978-0-9884428-4-9

LCCN: 2012950789

First Edition: February, 2013

This book contains an excerpt from the forthcoming book *Wycaan Master Book 3 - Ashbar* by Alon Shalev. This excerpt has been set for this edition and may not reflect the final content of the forthcoming edition.

Published in the United States of America

# DEDICATION

Each summer for three years, a family gathered around a campfire, deep in the ancient redwood forests, to hear the story told. A 9 year-old boy sat with eyes wide open and, together with the ancient trees, bore witness to the tales of Odessiya and the summoning of the Wycaan Masters.

To my son, Asif, who makes friends and builds his own alliances. Who is as brave, strong-minded, and creative as the legendary dwarves of Odessiya. And who, between large yawns late at night, kept this story as honest and true as he is.

# ACKNOWLEDGEMENTS

- To Monica Buntin, my editor, for once again making sense of an awful lot of words.

- To William Kenney, my book cover artist, for your amazing ability to continually transform my jumbled ideas into such beautiful pieces of art.

- To Jeny Lyn Ruelo and her team at The Fast Fingers, for the interior design and formatting, always willing to guide and help me.

# PROLOGUE

*W*hen history inscribes what transpired after the fall of the Great Alliance, let it include a chapter about the dwarves. For though men and elves will dominate its pages, the story of those who dwell underground must not be forgotten.

It was I, King Hothen the Elder, who led his surviving dwarf warriors from the battlefield. Our numbers were small and prospects harrowing. We left our dead — including my own father, King Goldenore — to the vultures and the crows. I knew only that I must keep our people alive. Dwarves are brave warriors, and our battalions fought in the fiercest encounters. So it was that as the piles of bodies grew, many — too many — were of noble dwarves.

I instructed our leaders to hold faith, for as he lay on the battlefield, precariously balanced between life and the great halls of our ancestors, the Wycaan Master Perridor shared with me a vision. The Wycaans, he revealed, were massacred but not obliterated.

"Hold fast to our ways," he whispered. "Bide your time in the shadows underground where the greedy eyes of men cannot see. Rebuild our nation and wait. For I promise: A Wycaan will come to lead you. And though he will not be of our race, he will find friendship among the dwarves and help you return to your rightful place."

With our armies decimated, I led our people to a deep cave, far away, and there we built mighty Hothengold. The first law passed was one of survival, known as the First Decree. It stated that, following the great treachery, no man, elf or other – save dwarves – were allowed under the mountains. Those who wandered our way fell to our axes, and the great dwarf nation drifted out of sight and mind of even the most ambitious emperors.

In time, as our numbers beginning to rise, I sent out the leaders of the six clans, ordering them to secure other such underground fortresses and seek mining opportunities, as only we understand.

But hearken to my words, noble dwarves. The land of Odessiya will never heal until the races unite. Whether by promise or blade, the Alliance will one day rise again, and the dwarf nation will, once again, take its rightful place at the council of the great races.

Until then, my people, I counsel patience, a trait not often found among dwarves. Let us grow our clans and our wealth away from the eyes of the empire, but let us never forget. Be vigilant, be patient, and wait the coming of the Wycaan.

These are the last words of Hothen the Elder, High King of the Dwarves.

From the Chronicles of King Hothen the Elder.

# ONE

"**W**ake, young master. Danger approaches and we must talk. Oh, I am so sorry to stir you from such deep slumber."

Seanchai groaned as he wrenched himself from a rich dream. He tried to hold onto it as one places a marker in a book, but it was already gone. He focused instead on reorienting himself.

"What? It's dark out. Ethrain? What's happening?"

"Sire, join me outside so as not to disturb the others."

Seanchai glanced over at Rhoddan. The big elf's rumbling snores might have shaken the walls of flimsier huts. In the corner his human friend, Shayth, twitched and muttered as he fought demons of his past that assailed his subconscious every night.

Wrapping his cloak around himself and grabbing his thin, curved Win Dao swords, Seanchai joined the old elf outside. The village elder pressed a steaming cup into Seanchai's hands. The hot tea stilled the Wycaan's shivering body, and his senses sharpened as the potent drink took effect.

"What is it, Ethrain, my friend?" Seanchai asked after a moment.

"You know my village, though small and poor, takes great pride in giving you shelter, Wycaan. We are honored to provide you with time to rest and heal, to feed you and mend your clothes. We will share stories about your visit for generations."

Seanchai nodded. "It is I and my friends who are grateful. You have offered us much when you have little for yourselves. I wish I could give something back."

"No, no, that would be wrong, Wycaan. But listen to me now, for I have not woken you without cause. I fear for the safety of our village, and, as leader, it falls to me to make whatever decision I feel I must to protect our humble home."

The wrinkled elf sighed as he shuffled back and forth in front of Seanchai. His body was bent and he leaned heavily on a staff, shaking his head. "The villages of Tripoguard and Selvestus both gave you shelter, and both were destroyed for harboring you after you left. This I have heard from yourself and others."

"It is so," Seanchai said. "And there have been three others since we fled Galbrieth. General Tarlach himself hunts us, and his troops destroy anything in their path that reveals our scent. I warned you of all this before you took us in."

"Indeed you did, my Lord Wycaan. Still, we are many leagues from these villages and far from the roads that armies travel upon. But you must understand: we are two months from our harvests. Our fields, scant though they might be, are key to our survival over the long winter months, and we must harvest in peace. A few hours ago one of our young traders returned. He reported troop movements coming this way."

Seanchai gasped. "Are you sure?"

"Yes. Their advanced sixers have already reached the mountain pass ten leagues from here, and there they stopped."

Seanchai frowned. He knew the army split its troop units into groups of six, and that these small units could move fast and often undetected. He considered how close they might be.

A female voice spoke from behind him. "They may well leave the main highway and come in this direction. Scouts and rangers will surely be sent."

Seanchai reached out an arm. Ilana slid into his embrace, taking his mug and sipping the tea.

"I will bring you another cup," Ethrain offered, but Ilana raised her hand to stop him.

"We must leave, Seanchai. There are many elders and *calhei* living here. With our people's decimated numbers, we cannot afford to put any young in danger."

Seanchai nodded. "I'll wake the others and we'll pack. Can you work on a route?"

"I will gather supplies for you, Wycaan – as much as we can spare," Ethrain said.

"No," Seanchai insisted. "You must keep your food reserves for yourselves. Hide them away from the village just in case. We'll hunt and forage as we go."

"Then I humbly request that you leave while it is still dark," the old elf said.

"Why?" Ilana asked, raising a thin eyebrow.

Ethrain looked at the ground. "When my people hear that I sent the Wycaan away, they will be very angry with me. I will probably lose my position as leader. It is best that you go while the village sleeps."

"Surely they will understand?" Ilana protested.

"Yes, they will. My logic is sound. But everyone in this village would gladly die for Seanchai." He looked up at the big elf and smiled. "You have brought us such pride. I never thought I'd live to see the day . . ."

"There is nothing smart in dying without reason," Seanchai declared. "Nothing will be served by your village being destroyed." He stood tall, his huge body towering over the elder, his voice deepening. "Tell your people that these are the words of Seanchai, the Wycaan. Tell them that I hold you in high esteem as a wise leader, Ethrain. Tell them that my only regret at leaving so soon is that I cannot learn more from your experience and leadership."

"You honor me so, Wycaan."

"You will tell them what I said?" Seanchai pressed.

"Every word." The village leader's voice shook with emotion.

"I thank you, then. Keep me in your prayers and tell the villagers to wait for my word."

"It will be done, Wycaan. Come, Ilana. Let me suggest a good route."

Ilana glanced at Seanchai, not needing to express her thoughts for him to understand. How could she decide on a route when he had no plan? Two months of running from village to village was not bringing down the Empire or uniting the races.

Seanchai sighed. The memory of his teacher and her death were still fresh two months after the event. Mhari's crushed body lay under the huge stones of the Galbrieth fortress. Without the guidance of a Wycaan Master, he was still the young, confused elf he had been when he had fled his parents' village.

He entered their hut and shook Shayth awake.

"Wake the others and pack. We need to leave now."

Seanchai did not wait for a response. He went back outside and filled his lungs with the crisp morning air. Mhari had given him instructions in anticipation of Seanchai continuing without her. She had told him to go to the Forest of Markwin and study with the Elves of the West. These mythical elves were often the heroes of fairytales told to eager young *calhei* by their parents.

Rhoddan staggered out from the hut, threw his bags down on the ground, and disappeared into the trees. When he returned, he jokingly addressed Seanchai: "Hey, snowflake, do you want me to pack up your stuff, too?" Rhoddan was still not used to Seanchai's white Wycaan hair, since he had barely seen Seanchai since the ceremony, which changed his hair color so dramatically.

Seanchai nodded instead of laughing. "Thanks," he said, and stalked into the woods.

He could feel Rhoddan's gaze on his back as he retreated, stopping to lean on a tree and inhale deeply. He was evidently out of tears. He had tried to allow only Ilana to see the depth of his grief, but they all knew.

Rhoddan would lay down his life for Seanchai without a moment's hesitation, but would also chide Seanchai for not taking the loss like a warrior. Shayth had seen so much killing, had killed so many himself, that his skin was too thick to allow emotion to pierce it. Maugwen, the young human who had escaped with them, avoided Seanchai when she could and looked terrified every time he spoke to her. Beautiful, dark-skinned Sellia, a graceful hunter and warrior, was tough, and Seanchai was loath to show any weakness in her presence.

Only Ilana. Only she would be allowed to see his shields come down. It was Ilana who reminded him who he really was under his Wycaan skin, and she loved him in spite of his weakness.

Footsteps approached – hers. He turned and forced a smile.

"We must leave," she said, reaching out to stroke his cheek. "Come."

And he followed her, as he knew he always would.

# TWO

General Tarlach stood at the junction of two main roads, right at the edge of a trading village. He felt the heat from the burning thatch, heard the screams and pleas of the peasants, but he was indifferent. At his feet lay the female leader, a withered old elfe who had tried to convince him that the white-haired elf and his party had forced the village to host them.

The elfe's protestations had fallen on deaf ears, and soon, her body lay lifeless on the ground. It was a pathetic village, Tarlach thought – a dozen rickety huts with emaciated animals wandering aimlessly. The people had all been old and sick. The empire would be cleansed by this day's actions.

General Tarlach spat at the corpse as he reflected on the past two months. The day after he had sent word to the Emperor, describing the raid on Galbrieth and the prisoners' escape, he had set out to catch and kill the elf and his motley band. And, Tarlach conceded to himself, he had unfinished business with Shayth, the Emperor's nephew.

He would risk losing his own head if he did not return with the elf's. Surely the Emperor would punish him for what had happened at Galbrieth. He would not hesitate to mete out such punishment to one of his own officers.

Shayth had gotten under his skin and made him careless. He had sheltered the boy after his parents' tragic demise, allowed him to grow in his own house alongside his son, Ahad. But until their confrontation at Galbrieth, Tarlach had no idea that Shayth knew how his parents had died, or that his uncle, the Emperor, had engineered it. Now he understood why Shayth had disappeared and why the confused, hurt boy had left such a violent trail in his wake.

Tarlach wondered if his own family was now in danger. Would the Emperor punish them for his incompetence? He had been an exemplary officer and had risen through the ranks as a loyal servant to the Emperor. But a man who kills his own brother and sister-in-law is capable of anything, and Tarlach's wife and son lived in the city, very near the palace.

Approaching voices caught his attention, and he shook his head to clear it. The two men were clad in green and brown, carrying knives and short swords instead of wearing the red armor and weapons of the army. These rangers were trackers and spies who served whoever paid well. General Tarlach did not begrudge the money, for they were the best. They could walk for miles and track renegades for days, drawing near enough to hear even whispered conversations.

"My Lord," one said, his head bowed. "They set off toward the mountains. There are several villages there. We'll try each one, but we should also bolster the troops at Cliftean Pass. If they plan to go beyond the Western borders of Odessiya, they must travel through the pass."

"How long ago did they leave this village?"

"It is hard to say," the other ranger, a younger man, answered. "They are good at concealing tracks."

"But not good enough to fool you?" Tarlach queried.

"No sir, but maybe . . ." The ranger stopped.

"What is it, man?"

"I'm just guessing, sir, but I wonder if it might perhaps be a lack of experience. Do you know if seasoned men run with them?"

Tarlach had turned his back to them assuming the conversation at an end, but this ranger interested him and he hesitated. "It's a young group, as far as we have gleaned from the villagers who have met them."

"Sir?"

Tarlach turned around. Usually when he dismissed his soldiers, they gladly scampered away. These rangers were respectful, but not fearful of him.

The young ranger continued. "So far, they've zigzagged without a clear destination. My friend is right to suggest strengthening the guard at Cliftean Pass, but we can't be sure they will head west."

Tarlach raised an eyebrow. "Yet that is the general direction so far, is it not?"

"Yes, sir," the youngster replied without dropping his gaze. "However, if they had a clear destination, then they would have struck a straighter course westward. If it were me, I'd already have been through the pass by now, as that is the most dangerous area in which to engage or avoid an enemy."

"You're suggesting they are running wildly, maybe panicking?"

"You *did* say they are young, sir."

"Yes, I did. What is your name?"

"Jermona, sir."

"You are young, yourself, are you not?"

"I have been a ranger for three years, sir," he said puffing out his chest. "But as soon as I could walk, I accompanied my father and his brother, and learned from them. My entire family has been rangers for generations."

"My young friend speaks freely, sir," the other interjected apologetically. "He is enthusiastic and conscientious – maybe a little too enthusiastic."

He attempted a nervous laugh, but Tarlach's face remained hard.

"Yes, he is young and speaks freer than one of his station should," Tarlach replied. "Jermona, accompany the officers to my command tent. You will attend my meeting and listen. Do not address the officers, but when we ride, you will share your impressions with me.

"The value of your insight just might lie in your exuberance. Those we chase are also all young and enthusiastic, like yourself."

Tarlach nodded curtly to the older ranger. "Rest and eat something. We will move on within the hour." He then turned to his assistant who, as always, lingered eagerly nearby. "Bortand, let the soldiers stand down. Call the officers to my tent."

Bortand bowed and walked away, calling out orders in his high, squeaky voice. Tarlach stepped over the dead village elder. Then he glanced around and, assured that he was alone, turned, swore, and kicked her lifeless body.

They were marching again. Heeding the advice of his rangers, General Tarlach sent troops up into the pass with instructions to lie in wait. There were a handful of sentries stationed there already, and they would maintain their regiment. Three more sixers he directed to different villages on a broad trajectory, while the rangers led the bulk of his army to the village nearest the pass.

A call went up from behind. Three horsemen – messengers from the Emperor – galloped furiously up from the rear, leaving a thick cloud of dust in their wake. Tarlach signaled for the column to keep riding. Bortand and a sixer held back to wait.

A short while later, Bortand rode up alongside the general. Tarlach turned and smiled.

"Why are you red and puffing, my rotund friend? It is your horse that is bearing the weight."

Bortand did not smile as he usually would. "You have a scroll from the, um, Emperor, my lord. It is sealed. You alone must open it."

Tarlach glanced at his assistant and saw his frown. Bortand might be chronically out of shape, but his mind was as sharp as any. Tarlach took the scroll and maneuvered his horse to the side of the path. Another sixer of well-built troops, each wearing a special blue insignia on his uniform, surrounded him at a discreet distance.

Tarlach pulled a knife from his boot and cut through the wax seal bearing the Emperor's insignia.

*You have never failed me until now, Tarlach, and I trust you will not fail me again. As you are aware, the elf and his companions must not pass through our Western boundaries or find what lies beyond, lest they discover what we have long kept secret. This must not happen.*

*Kill the elves. Bring me my nephew if you can. Otherwise, kill him, too. I trust your judgment on this matter.*

*Your wife is well and sends her love. Ahad is close by. I watch over them. Serve me well, as always.*

Tarlach read the parchment a second and third time. Then he folded it carefully and put it into his saddlebag. He silently resumed his position at the head of the line and though his expression remained unchanged, he quickened the pace of his army.

# THREE

Ilana led as they walked in heavy silence. She felt the weight of the dawn mist closing in all around her and shivered as the damp dew seeped through her clothes. It was still two hours from sunrise, and the gray pallor matched the group's collective mood.

They walked parallel to a path through a wood so as not to chance meeting someone on the road or leave an obvious trail of footprints. She heard Maugwen behind her trip twice on roots and small stones. Ilana had not consulted Seanchai about the direction. She headed west, distancing them from Galbrieth, clinging to the belief that he should seek out the Elves of the West as Mhari had instructed him. Moving in this direction also gave a sense of purpose to Sellia and Rhoddan who were becoming increasingly frustrated with Seanchai, though they hid it from him. She wondered how long they would hold back.

Ilana fretted about Seanchai. She had not expected him to be the same young elf she had known before his time with Mhari, but there was still a vulnerable uncertainty about him that let her know he was still struggling with his journey and powers. He had had to grow up fast. Too fast, really, but who didn't in these dangerous times? Still, he had likely lost his parents and entire village, seen his teacher die, and, by his own hand, taken many lives. He had great power, more than he was probably aware of. But she knew he wore his responsibility as a burden, as he struggled to take charge of himself without Mhari's guidance. The only time his face did not seem harrowed was when he meditated or trained with his swords.

Since they had fled the garrison of Galbrieth, Ilana and Seanchai had found only a few brief opportunities to be alone. In these precious moments, he allowed himself to mourn, to relax, and to let his thick armoring down. Only in her arms did he feel safe, illusion though it was. The truth was that he was an animal hunted by the Emperor, the most powerful man in all the lands. The odds were against him – against them all.

"Tsst!" The warning came from Sellia, on Ilana's right.

As one, they dropped to a crouch, a move Rhoddan had drilled into them. But Sellia made no attempt to conceal herself as she approached Ilana. She bent down when she reached Ilana and hissed in her ear.

"You're not concentrating, Ilana." Sellia's voice was harsh. "We're following you. If there's danger in front of us, you must be the first to sense it. Keep your mind clear of everything else while you guide us."

Ilana nodded. She knew Sellia was right. She signaled for them to rise and continue.

For the next three hours, their path rose steadily. Gwen, unaccustomed to such rigorous travel, was clearly tiring. Ilana announced a break after the young girl stumbled one too many times. Shayth and Rhoddan unpacked some bread, cheese, and fruit.

Seanchai glared at his friends. "You took food from the village? They have nothing and already gave us too much. I refused supplies when Ethrain offered."

"And snubbing his generosity insulted him," Rhoddan answered without looking up. "It is a great honor for them to sacrifice for you."

"We have little time to hunt or forage," Shayth added. "You serve them best by putting distance between us and the village."

Seanchai turned his back on them and saw Sellia standing apart from the group. She had an arrow noched as she scanned their perimeter. He walked over.

"Go eat," he said. "I'll keep watch."

She looked at him, her rich brown eyes locking into his, her tone clipped. "I'm sorry for your loss, Seanchai. I'm sure Mhari was special. But you need to move on."

"I *am* moving on," he snapped. "Haven't you noticed? All I seem to *do* is move on."

She didn't flinch at his sarcasm. Instead, she spoke to him firmly while she took the arrow from her bow and returned it to her quiver. "I'm not as sweet as your girlfriend, but I care for you, and I care for them." She nodded toward the others. "I want to be sympathetic, but this isn't the time. Listen to me, Seanchai. You serve no one by wandering around, hiding. We'll all follow you to the ends of the earth, but you need to decide where we're going and why."

"Go eat," Seanchai replied, turning his back to look out around them.

Several minutes later, he heard a hushed argument behind him. He walked over to the group and addressed Gwen, who sat slightly apart from the others.

"Maugwen?" he said. "Would you please stand guard for a while?"

She nodded and rose.

"Eat," Sellia said and tore off a hunk of bread for him.

He sat and chewed for a short while and then looked up. "What lies ahead of us?"

Ilana drew a map in the dust. "If we keep heading west, then we will reach the Cliftean Pass. It is half a day's walk from here, but . . ."

"But what?"

"It seems too obvious," Shayth said. "Tarlach will surely have troops there by now. There was probably always a military presence, but he must have reinforced them the moment we started heading west."

"Why *are* we heading west, Wycaan?" Sellia asked, her brow furrowing as her mind raced forward. "What's out there that he doesn't want you to reach?"

Seanchai stared at her, thinking, and then glanced back toward Gwen. The diminutive girl stood with her back to them, but was definitely within earshot. Seanchai still wasn't comfortable with her presence. Only Ilana seemed to feel bonded to her.

"Help," he murmured. "Maybe."

"Maybe?" Shayth snorted.

"Maybe," Seanchai said, glancing again at Gwen. "I can't . . . I can't be sure. I'm not supposed to reveal who is there and . . ."

"And?" Ilana looked concerned.

"And I can't be sure they will help us, if they even exist."

"Mhari told you to travel to this place?" Shayth asked.

"Yes, but she wasn't . . . there were things she wouldn't share with me."

"But you think we should head there?" Ilana persisted.

Seanchai shrugged and his voice was soft. "It was Mhari's instruction."

"You don't sound too convinced." Sellia crossed her arms.

"It was Mhari's instruction," Seanchai repeated, his voice stronger now. "Let's get through the pass if we can. I'm done talking."

They packed up and moved off. As the sun rose in the sky, they began to climb steeper terrain. After stopping twice to remove their cloaks and drink from a stream, they reached a ridge around midday. Ilana signaled for them to approach it with care.

They crawled to the top of the ridge and gazed across a winding plain into a narrow gorge, where they counted eight soldiers. Ilana assumed there would be at least another four sleeping – two sixers in total. She glanced around once more before signaling everyone to retreat. When they had safely disappeared under the cover of trees, Ilana realized that Seanchai had stayed on the ridge. She turned back, but Sellia gently touched her arm and shook her head.

It was a while before Seanchai returned, rubbing his forehead and frowning.

"Were you scrying?" Rhoddan asked.

Seanchai nodded.

"What's scrying?" Gwen asked.

"In this case, it's the ability to see great distances and make out what is there," Ilana explained.

"Neat," she said and then looked at Seanchai. "It hurts you to do it? To scry?"

Seanchai nodded. "It'll pass," he said and sipped some water. "But we won't."

"We can take them," said Rhoddan. "I could do with some exercise."

"No, we can't," Seanchai replied. "Those soldiers are bait. It's a trap. There are many more hidden inside the pass, including, I think, pictorians."

"Pictorians?" Gwen asked.

"You don't want to know," Shayth replied. "They are big and horned. Some are eight feet tall. They are strong, ill-tempered, and probably eat little girls for snacks."

"Shayth!" Ilana glared at him.

"We're going that way," Seanchai pointed north to a range of unwelcoming peaks about to be enveloped in cloud.

"What's there?"

"I'm not sure, but I felt a power in those mountains."

"I think you're right," Gwen agreed, her eyes fixed on the mountains. She sounded uncharacteristically confident.

They all looked at her with clear skepticism, and then at Seanchai. He was smiling at her.

"I'm glad," he said. "I value your instincts, Maugwen."

# FOUR

Jermona was very pleased with himself when General Tarlach took his advice and sent troop reinforcements to guard the pass. The young ranger had said the group wouldn't fight if there were enough soldiers, and the general added four sixers of pictorians to ensure they wouldn't try.

General Tarlach had instructed Jermona to join the rangers tracking the elves and to be given the point position, the one who gets closest to glean information. The young ranger was thrilled with how things were working out. He was currently following them at a comfortable distance, but would get closer under the cover of the forest ahead of them.

The tall, muscular, white-haired elf was clearly the leader. When he spoke they all seemed to listen, though Jermona could see that he was moody. The pretty young elfe obviously was his consort, as she seemed to be the one who placated him. The two other elves, a slender, toned male and a beautiful, black elfe, were obviously guards. He carried an assortment of blades and she had a long, red elf bow.

Jermona had gathered vague details about them all as he watched, but it was the humans that particularly intrigued him. This was the first time he had seen the Emperor's nephew, the infamous criminal. They said he was as stealthy as a ranger, but Jermona doubted this. His father always said rangers were born into their families. Shayth was probably just being tolerated because of who he was. He wondered whether General Tarlach knew who the young girl was, as she had not been mentioned when he had been briefed.

Two things intrigued Jermona as he watched them all interact. First, they were all more or less his age and completely unencumbered by older people ordering them about or griping about their inexperience. He reckoned that kind of freedom must be fun, and wondered whether the other rangers would respect him more if he got close with the general.

The second thing was that these were elves and humans working together, and the elves were not subservient. They were at least equal, or, in the case of the white-haired one, in charge. Jermona had only known elves who had been beaten down and submissive. They appeared to be a simple, harmless folk – pitiful, really. But these elves were clearly different. He had heard about the rescue and escape from Galbrieth at the Emperor's birthday celebration. The white-haired elf and the dark-skinned elfe had rescued the others just as they were about to be executed.

He shook his head. How could a bunch of elves launch an attack on a garrison in broad daylight, much less bring down a large portion of its massive walls? They had clearly been outnumbered by the army, and were still successful.

Jermona wondered what it would be like to have people go through so much trouble to rescue him. The rangers had a strict code: if you were captured, you were expected to either try and escape, or kill yourself. A ranger never revealed the secrets of his people or trade. But then, rangers were very rarely caught. They could melt into the shadows while the captors were focused on the people the rangers worked for.

The group was heading north with the leader and his consort leading the way. The dark elfe walked on one side, ever alert. He would have to be careful of her. Elves were purported to have good vision and she looked like she knew how to use her bow. The other elf walked on the opposite side with the young girl alongside him. The Emperor's nephew brought up the rear.

As the point tracker, Jermona would routinely meet up with the other rangers to pass on information for them to relay to General Tarlach. He smiled to himself at the prospect of sending the older rangers to do this. This job would certainly elevate his rank and importance. He had done well to speak out to the general.

He was happy when, in the late afternoon, they entered the forest. He would keep his distance as they set up camp and move closer after dark. If they were foolish enough to light a fire, they would have little vision beyond its light and he could hide close by and listen.

He hoped to hear something substantial to report to General Tarlach and curry further favor, but more than that, Jermona was genuinely curious about this group and how they functioned.

Seanchai and Ilana walked a little way ahead of the others so they could talk alone. Now that he felt a sense of purpose heading north, Seanchai felt better, though he was apprehensive about the power he had felt ahead. The mountains loomed up in front of them; there would be some serious climbing.

He caught Ilana glancing at him. "What is it?"

"Nothing, really," she said, sighing involuntarily. "I'm thinking I might spend the rest of my life criss-crossing Odessiya with you, never quite sure where we are going from day to day."

"Mhari said that this was the life of a Wycaan; that even when we have a just and civil society, there will always be need for our services."

"To fight?"

"No," Seanchai replied. "I want to learn more about using this power for good. I dream about creating a school for healers, somewhere far from any city. It will have a forest and mountains and lake nearby. It needs to be remote enough that only the most motivated will come."

"That's nice," Ilana said. "But what about the sick? How will they get to you if your academy is so isolated? Who will you practice on?"

Seanchai nodded. "Good point. Let me take the next few hundred miles to ponder this."

She laughed, and he took her hand.

"We might end up walking from one end of the kingdom to the other and back, but, like you said, at least we'll do it together. It was so hard being separated from you, especially knowing you were in prison."

She squeezed his hand when his voice wavered. After a few moments of silence, Seanchai asked, "Did you know I would come?"

"Yes," she said, "but I hoped you wouldn't. It was reckless."

"I had to."

"I know," she grinned. "Rhoddan and Shayth mean a lot to you."

"They most certainly do," he replied and laughed. "And I got to meet Maugwen."

"It was nice what you said to her back then, about trusting her intuition."

"It's the truth," he replied.

Ilana looked at him. "Is there something I don't know?"

"What *don't* you know?"

She pushed him playfully. "Seriously. You never complain about her slowing us down. Why?"

"Maybe I'm a nice elf," he shrugged.

"No," she replied. "I mean, you are a nice elf – maybe too nice – and always see the best in people. But I think there's more." She waited expectantly.

Seanchai glanced behind to ensure they could not be heard.

"Mhari and I did some serious scrying. We traveled to Galbrieth and followed your energy trail. When I found you in the jail cells, I felt hers. It was very powerful; much different from other humans. I didn't think much of it until we had finished and Mhari mentioned it. She, too, had felt it."

Ilana couldn't help glancing back at Gwen, who smiled and waved. Ilana recalled their girl-talks in the dungeons, where Gwen had promised Ilana that her beau would come rescue her. She had been right.

"Gwen's okay," she said. "She helped me through a terrible time."

"Yes," Seanchai replied, his voice distant. "But I will call her Maugwen, for a time will come when she will demand it of us."

By midafternoon, the group had entered a forest. Seanchai the wood elf was thrilled. He smelled the moss and the decomposing leaves and relished the trees' energy. He couldn't wait to stop for the night and practice his meditation exercises as one with the forest. He was almost giddy with joy, but this was replaced with growing unease. Abruptly he stopped, and his suddenness halted the group.

"Something's not right," he warned quietly. "We should proceed with care."

Sellia and Shayth silently took position on either side of the others, bows noched at the ready. Rhoddan fell back, drawing his knives.

Gwen whimpered, and Ilana put a protective arm around her. "It's okay, I think. Something spooked Seanchai and we don't want to take a chance, that's all. It's probably nothing. Maybe a wolf or other predator."

Gwen glanced at Ilana's free hand, clutching her own long knife. "Thanks," Gwen whispered, "but he's right." Ilana caught Seanchai's eye at this admission.

They skulked down the path, alert, until Seanchai paused and stared to his left. He dropped his bags and cloak and turned to Gwen. "Please stay with the supplies."

She nodded and suppressed another whimper. The others fell in behind Seanchai, who moved quickly and furtively, but almost immediately disappearing out of their sight. When they caught up to him, he was facing a pack of wolfheids, the half-human, half-wolf creatures warped by dark magic.

The wolfheids crouched, snarling, at the edge of a wide circle with two exits. Nearby, a wagon was overturned, its riders cowering behind it. Two bodies lay still on the ground.

Seanchai poised with one sword in front for defense and the other high above his head. Two wolfheids emerged from the pack circling him from different sides. Seanchai didn't move until a third wolfheid sprung from atop a rock to his left. The other two sprung as well.

The Wycaan jumped into the air and twisted. The higher sword went straight through one wolfheid's neck, severing head from body. Carrying this momentum he struck the other two airborne creatures, one with each sword.

Arrows twanged as Shayth and Sellia's arrows felled two more wolfheids. The rest of the pack had seen enough, and as one, turned and fled into the trees. Seanchai approached the overturned wagon, disheveled and breathing heavily. No one moved from behind it.

Ilana walked into the clearing and loudly asked Seanchai to put away his swords, which were dripping with blood and gore. He wiped and sheathed them sheepishly.

Ilana approached the wagon. "Come on out. We won't harm you."

There were whispers and scuffling behind the wagon before two short, rather stout people cautiously emerged. The larger one had his long hair tied back and sported a long beard. The other had similar long hair and looked possibly female and definitely old.

Sellia spoke. "I'll fetch Gwen. She might be of help here."

Ilana stepped forward and addressed them as she would speak to scared children. "It's okay, little ones. Do not be afraid."

"Little ones?" the biggest growled deeply.

"Please excuse my friends." Shayth approached, grinning widely, his hands outstretched to his sides, with his palms facing the survivors in the universal sign of peace. "They don't mean to be rude. They've never met dwarves."

# FIVE

J ermona's mouth fell open. He was so shocked at what he had just witnessed that he barely recovered quickly enough to hide himself when the dark-skinned elfe passed him on her way back to where they had left their packs with the human girl.

Wow. The white-haired elf had just taken down three full-grown wolfheids in a single, smooth movement. It had been over in seconds. Jermona had also taken note of how efficiently the dark-skinned elfe and the Emperor's nephew had felled two more, but that big elf, that . . . *special one* . . . now he understood why people were calling him that.

So this was what it was all about? *This* is why General Tarlach himself led a full battalion to capture a young, scrawny, fairly inexperienced bunch of elves and humans? The elf moved so fast and with such precision. Jermona had felt his power from his hiding place a good twenty yards away. While the young ranger had heard of warriors who fought with two swords, he had never seen one.

He sunk lower in the bush where he was hiding as he heard the dark-skinned elfe and the young girl approaching. They were carrying a number of bags and talking about what had just happened. The girl was almost toppling over under the weight of her load.

". . . and he really killed three of those beasts by himself?"

"That's what I told you, twice already."

"He was amazing when he rescued us. So were you, Sellia. I've never seen a woman fight like that."

"Well, I'm hardly a woman," the one called Sellia replied, arching an eyebrow.

"I'm so sorry. I didn't mean . . . you know. I'm learning not to think of elves and humans differently. This is still new to me."

"I understand," Sellia replied. "Sounds like you've been hanging round Ilana and Rhoddan for too long."

"Rhoddan," the girl almost purred. "Did he kill any?"

"Do you have a crush on Rhoddan?" Sellia asked, and Jermona could see bright white teeth gleaming as she smiled. He wondered if the girl had been thrown in jail because of her attraction to an elf.

"Of course not," the girl replied. "He's an elf and I'm a human."

"Yes, but you're trying to forget that we're different, right?"

A giggle escaped the young girl, then, right as they left Jermona's hearing range, he heard her say, "He is very brave, though, isn't he?"

Sellia laughed loudly. "Ah, Gwen. You're right. We really aren't that different."

Jermona was so absorbed in the group's conversation with the dwarves that he jumped when a nut hit his cheek. He turned in the direction it came from and saw another ranger motioning him over. They joined three others who had gathered out of sight and earshot from the travelers. The oldest addressed Jermona in a deep voice.

"You've done well, Jermona. You're a credit to your father's training."

"Thank you, Uncle," Jermona replied proudly. "You also taught me."

"I did, and I'm very proud of you, too, though I don't approve of you currying the favor of General Tarlach. He's a harsh and violent man. Get close if you want, but always be ready to escape if you have to. Do you hear?"

Jermona nodded and received a pat on the head. "Good," the man continued. "Now, what can you tell us?"

Jermona quickly recounted what he had seen and learned about the individuals and group dynamic. The other rangers clearly thought he was embellishing when he described the fight with the wolfheids, and flat-out didn't believe him when he mentioned the dwarves.

"Ain't no dwarves this far north," one said.

"Are you sure, Jermona? Could they just be heavy-set kids?"

"With beards and axes?" Jermona retorted, rather annoyed that he was being questioned like this. General Tarlach would not have asked such questions.

One of the rangers turned to Jermona's uncle. "With all due respect to Jermona, I'd like to scout ahead and confirm what he's said."

"Why, Jan?" Jermona snapped, and then lowered his head in contrition after his uncle glared at him.

"Because," Jan said testily, "*I'm* the one going back to convey your report to the venerable general. Like your uncle said, you don't make mistakes with General Tarlach. Before I go, let me replenish your supplies with my own. I can replace them at the camp..You said the elves are heading into those mountains?"

"Yes."

"Do you know why?" Jermona shook his head and Jan looked at the others. "Does *anyone* know what's in those mountains?"

They all shook their heads, and then Jermona's uncle spoke. "But if dwarves, who live hundreds of miles away, are interested in these mountains, there's something important there. Of that, I'm sure.

"Jan. Head back to the general and report what you've heard after you've verified its accuracy to your satisfaction. Jermona, you'll continue to track the elves, yes? That's what you want?"

Jermona nodded.

"Good," his uncle said. "Hortat, Synus and I will be nearby, so keep leaving signs. Hortat, I would like you to scout ahead. We need to know what's waiting for us in those mountains and tell the general as soon as we find out."

"Aye," Hortat replied.

Jan left them after he had given some small brown cloth bags to Jermona. "The others can forage," he had explained, "but if you're the point man, you shouldn't have to worry about food as you shadow them."

Jermona's uncle put his brown-gloved hand on the young ranger's shoulder. "You've done very well, my nephew, but I caution you. Don't get overly confident, and don't underestimate the Wycaan. I don't fancy the chances of even the best ranger against him."

"You think he's that good?" Jermona asked.

His uncle stared at him with an awed, faraway expression. "Remind me sometime to tell you stories of when our people served the Wycaans, long ago."

"*We* served *elves*?" Jermona scoffed. "I don't think so."

"We worked closely with the Wycaans, Jermona, regardless of their race. Human, dwarf, or elf – it didn't matter. It was considered a great honor."

Jermona gaped at him, but his uncle just patted his shoulder. "Just be very careful, Jermona. I would hate for anything to happen to you. Go now."

# SIX

"Dwarves? They're *dwarves*?" Seanchai asked excitedly, hopping from one foot to the other. "Do they speak Odessiyan?"

"I believe these dwarves do, judging by the expressions on their faces," Shayth replied, running a hand through his spiky hair, "and they're standing right in front of you, so I suggest you address them directly."

Seanchai turned to face the dwarves, realizing that this was his first encounter with a race he needed to persuade to join the Alliance if he had even the remotest chance of defeating the Emperor. He may not have started out on the right foot, though he hoped chasing off the wolfheids would help them forget his lack of tact.

"I'm sorry," he said meeting the eyes of each dwarf. "This is all new to me. As my friend said, I've never met dwarves before."

"Well," said the bearded one, folding his arms across his chest. "Yeh have us at a disadvantage. I can see yeh ears are pointed, but everything else about yeh is different from anything I've ever seen."

"I am Seanchai, son of Seantai. I am an elf and a Wycaan warrior."

"Indeed. A Wycaan, yeh say?" He did not seem impressed. "Well, now that's all clear, I thank yeh and yeh friends for saving us." He moved to the two dwarves lying still and checked for pulses. Then he stood up and sighed. "May I request that yeh help us turn the wagon up straight and put our friends inside? We'll honor them when it is safe."

"Where are you going?" Ilana asked. "I haven't heard of dwarves traveling this far north."

They shuffled their feet. Then the male said: "It's best we don't say."

"What!" Shayth growled. "He just saved your lives–"

"Shayth!" Seanchai interrupted without turning from the dwarves. "We'll help you," he said to the male. "Then we'll escort you to your mining camp in the mountains. But please, where I come from, it's polite to share names."

He paused, but kept his gaze fixated on the bearded dwarf, who thought for a moment before bowing low.

"Mah name is Ballendir and this is Ophera. I truly thank yeh for coming to our aid. This is an inhospitable land, but that's no excuse for a dwarf to forget his manners. But tell me how yeh know we're heading to a mine in the mountains." He coughed. "Uhh . . . if indeed we are?"

"A Wycaan has many talents," Seanchai said. "We can fight, we can breathe underwater, and we can be very observant."

He walked to the back of the wagon and withdrew a pickaxe protruding out of a split crate.

The others laughed, and the dwarves shuffled their feet, apparently mildly embarrassed at their lack of covertness. The tension eased once Rhoddan organized everyone to help empty the wagon and stack the crates.

While they worked, Seanchai crouched by one of the bodies – a female. He removed the chain mail and poked around, feeling for wounds and broken bones. Ballendir and Ophera watched suspiciously as they helped right their wagon.

Seanchai put his palms on her chest and closed his eyes. He could feel a very faint and erratic heartbeat and began to summon energy from the ground to help him. Gradually, a wave of warmth moved through him into the wounded dwarfe.

"Bring me her bedroll, a towel if you have one, and water."

Seanchai moved to the second body, but the blood pooled around its waist didn't give him much hope. He touched the cold skin, frowned, and slowly pulled the fallen dwarf's cloak up to cover him.

He checked the injured dwarfe again. Her pulse was still aberrant, but Seanchai thought it might be just a bit stronger. He put his hand on her forehead; it was scalding. He thought of his mother, a world away and in another lifetime. She was a healer and would have known what to do. Seanchai recalled at least that he shouldn't bring down the fever, but needed to hydrate her.

Ballendir brought the bedding and helped Seanchai gently wrap it around the wounded dwarfe. The towel he wet and used to drip water into her mouth. Ballendir took over.

"She went down hard," the dwarf said. "I checked quickly, but I never felt a pulse."

"I'm not sure she'll make it either, my friend. I can continue to strengthen her along the way, but I'm not an experienced healer."

"Maybe we best leave her here then," the dwarf said gravely.

"Why?"

"I appreciate yeh help, Master Wycaan, but if we can only sustain her with yeh presence, then we have a problem."

"What?"

"Yeh're right, we're going into the mountains. At some point yeh won't be allowed to stay with us."

"I can help you take her to your camp," Seanchai said. "Then I will leave, if that is your wish."

"Yeh don't understand," Ballendir said, shaking his head.

"He speaks of the First Decree," Shayth said. "They won't let someone who is not dwarf enter their caverns. For thousands of years they have held this iron-cast rule."

"Aye, the First Decree," Ballendir repeated solemnly.

"You can't just leave this dwarfe to die," Seanchai breathed deeply to control himself. "Are you not beholden of each other?"

Ballendir's cheeks flushed. "We are. We value the life of another dwarf very highly. And I value the life of mah sister above all. She is mah blood, and blood of mah clan, as we say."

"And at one time you allowed the other races in?" Seanchai asked.

"Aye, before the great betrayal. Our legends tell how elves, men and dwarves once lived together. It's a long story. I will tell you when we rest tonight."

"You allowed the other races to enter your boundaries," Seanchai persisted. "Once, in a bygone age?"

"That's correct."

"Good. Then that settles it. I'll keep your sister alive and bring her to your camp."

"What?"

Seanchai stood straight, forcing the dwarf to look up. "I am a Wycaan, Ballendir. I come bearing a message for your people. That bygone age you spoke of is being resurrected." His gaze intensified. "Together, we will reforge the Alliance and the dwarves will once again take their rightful place in society."

Ballendir stared at him in disbelief. Then a grim smile stretched across his face. "Perhaps yeh need to tell mah what a Wycaan is, exactly."

# SEVEN

Geneeral Tarlach reached the Cliftean Pass and felt a wave of relief when he found that the elves had not engaged the forces there. As long as they stayed within the borders of Odessiya, Tarlach believed he could find them. He instructed his troops to set up camp to rest for a day.

They had been chasing the renegades now for two months and, though these were battle-hardened troops, he saw no need to push them further. He sent some of the sentries at the pass out to hunt. They would enjoy the change of routine and give the battalion a well-deserved treat of fresh meat.

Tarlach slept for a few hours and then went to the kitchens. The cook had his back to the entrance and didn't look up from his steaming pots. His deep voice boomed, "When I have food ready, you'll know it, and then you can come eat with everyone else. Who do you think you are? Even the general himself wouldn't dare sneak into the kitchens while the meal is still being prepared."

Tarlach smiled, tempted to reveal himself. But he feared the big cook might have a heart attack when he realized at whom he was yelling. Tarlach didn't want to lose such an important member of his staff.

Back outside, he found Bortand, his assistant, waiting patiently. He seemed to know instinctively when the general was around. Tarlach rued the day he would have to find someone to replace him.

"How did you know where to find me, my friend?"

"Why, my good general," Bortand replied. "You, um, assume I came looking for you?" He rubbed his ample belly. "Life on the road can be challenging for one with, um, my . . . appetite."

Tarlach laughed. "It's good you're here. The fresh air and exercise will help you lose some weight. And anyhow, while I admire your considerable talents, I fear they will not be enough to get you past that cook."

Bortand looked between the kitchen tent and General Tarlach. He frowned. "Sir, would you like me to get some food for the both of us and bring it to your tent?"

"A flawless strategy, Bortand," the general laughed, "but I'll wait until the soldiers eat. Go forage for yourself if you wish, and then join me when you're ready. I shall stroll around the camp for a while."

"I can wait, sir. You're right; a gentle stroll will be, um, good for me." He patted his stomach again.

Tarlach knew his troops did not enjoy his meandering. When he was younger, he had maintained a good rapport with many of his soldiers. They appreciated his jokes and his concern for their families and themselves. He had bound them to him, and they had been ready and willing to die for him. Many of them, in fact, had.

Now they stiffened when he came into sight. They laughed overenthusiastically at his jokes and answered his questions very formally. Where his leadership had once divined the respect and compassion of camaraderie, it now met only with the harsh rigidity of fear.

As it should be, he figured, but still, that fellowship was something he missed. Perhaps that was why the young ranger, who showed no trepidation, had interested him so. As he and Bortand walked the grounds, soldiers sprung to attention and came out of their tents as soon as they heard he was approaching. He wanted them to rest, so he led Bortand away from the camp to a cluster of trees nearby.

They had barely sat down when they saw a horse galloping toward the camp. On its back rode a ranger. The rangers fascinated him. They did not cower to his command, or even that of the Emperor, though they always showed both great respect. They considered themselves a free people roving the lands. They never mentioned ranger villages, but surely there were ranger women and children? He hadn't questioned them because they fulfilled an important need, and they did it extremely well.

As the ranger dismounted and strode briskly over to the general, Tarlach called to a soldier, who scampered over. "Go the kitchens. Tell the cook I require food for the ranger brought here. Whatever he has right now will suffice. And he should send some ale."

"I will bring it back myself, my lord." The soldier saluted and ran toward the kitchen tent just as the ranger reached Tarlach and Bortand.

Tarlach considered this ranger to be the leader, though there was another also older than the rest.

"My lord," the man said and bowed his head full of thick, gray-streaked hair. "May I submit my report?"

"Sit down, man," the general said, offering a place along the log. "What news do you bring?"

"Thank you. As I think you know, sir, the traitors moved north when they reached the pass. As you ordered, Jermona is the point tracker."

"How's the boy doing?"

"Though he's young, he is well-trained. And he takes his responsibilities very seriously."

"And you trust him as your point tracker?"

"Yes sir, Jermona is good enough to be point. He has done well and, besides, there are always two or three close behind him, ready to take over if needed."

Tarlach stroked his chin. "What if I told you to now put a more experienced man at point?"

"Sir?" The ranger frowned. "Is there a problem? I understood it was your desire that Jermona took point. Have we not been of adequate service?"

"Adequate?" He snorted. "Don't belittle yourself or your men. You're excellent at your job. I hold you all in high esteem. Yes, I had requested him at point. I was just wondering . . . do not read anything into it. I truly value your service."

The ranger bowed his head again, lower this time. "Thank you, General Tarlach. I have worked for you now for ten years and hold you in high esteem, as well."

"I am pleased to hear it. Here come the refreshments. We will have a proper meal soon. Take a few bites for now to satiate your hunger, and then give me your report."

# EIGHT

Seanchai was surprised at the sheer amount of crates and boxes and how heavy it all was as he helped right and repack the overturned cart. Ballendir and Ophera, the old dwarfe, shuffled nervously, anxious not to reveal what they were carrying.

When the wagon was ready and Ballendir's wounded sister safely secured with Maugwen watching over her, they began to move north. Two mules pulled the cart; their harnesses had prevented them from trying to flee the wolfheids, a fact that had probably saved their lives.

Seanchai couldn't believe he was in the company of dwarves, and it gave him a needed sense of purpose in his journey. Though he was not following Mhari's instruction, he was at least doing something constructive. He was intimidated by the idea of the Elves of the West, not because he feared their existence, but because he wondered how he would fare among their practiced, concentrated power.

Seanchai felt strongly he was on the right course. He looked around at his small collective. Ilana and Ballendir walked just behind him, discussing the route. The others had spread to both sides and behind, wary and silent.

Rhoddan had clearly been physically tortured and his wounds, though fading, were still visible. He had refused to discuss them with Seanchai, bearing it alone as he felt a warrior should. Shayth bore no

visible wounds but something had clearly happened. He had asked
Shayth what Tarlach had done but his friend was as closed as ever.

Ilana called to him. "We'll make camp in a couple hours. It'll take
at least another day to enter the Bordan Mountains, and we must
consider Ellendir."

"Ellendir?"

"Mah sister," Ballendir explained. "*En* be the name of our family
and *dir* the name of our clan. It's a rich vocabulary, which gets lost
in translation." He hesitated and then said: "I'm glad yeh're coming
with us."

Seanchai looked at him, befuddled. "You trust me?"

"I didn't say that exactly. But whatever else yeh are, Seanchai,
yeh're a healer. In dwarf culture, healers are considered an almost
priestly class. Ilana told me how yeh see yehself as a healer not a
warrior. In the short time that I have known yeh I have seen both
sides. This speaks to me. Also . . . bah, I talk too much. Yeh must
excuse me. Mah people will tell yeh that I'm very opinionated and
speak mah mind too freely."

Seanchai smiled at him. "I'm glad you share your thoughts,
Ballendir. I hope you can help me understand your people better."

The old dwarfe snorted from her place on the cart, and then
recoiled under Ballendir's glare.

"Ophera scoffs because she knows mah so well. Yeh should
probably take everything I tell yeh with a pinch of gold."

"Like what?" Seanchai asked.

"Aaah, later. Mah answer would not be short. Over dinner,
perhaps."

Seanchai realized that he had not eaten since the morning. "Well,
now's as good a time as any to break for a meal," he said.

They all laughed, but, as Seanchai was not the only one hungry, they stopped in a clearing a short while later, away from the path.

Seanchai and Ilana lowered Ellendir off the wagon and began their Ryku. Seanchai sensed Ballendir behind them, no doubt watching for any movement from his sister as they channeled earth energy into her body.

Afterward, Seanchai sat and watched Ophera light a small fire and hang a cauldron over it. She worked without saying a word, eyes always cast downwards. Soon, the aroma of cooking vegetables permeated the campsite.

Maugwen helped prepare the broth. She added what remained of the rabbits from the previous day and also produced some bread, which excited the dwarfe. Seanchai felt uncomfortable with Ophera's clearly subordinate role and, after he had eaten his stew, took the pot and began to clean it.

An agitated conversation ensued in Dwarfish between Ophera and Ballendir. Finally, Ballendir nodded and turned to Seanchai.

"We'd rather yeh not clean the dishes. Yeh're our guest, and we feel it to be impolite."

Seanchai started to object, but Ilana caught his attention and shook her head ever so slightly. Perplexed, he turned to the dwarfe.

"I mean no offense, but I need to make tea with my herbs. The drink is for Ellendir and me. It gives energy and helps to stimulate the body. In her case, it will help to replenish her blood supply."

Ophera looked to Ballendir, who managed to either sum up what the Wycaan had said in a few words or just told her to acquiesce. She rose, took the pot away from Seanchai, and cleaned it. Then she poured some water in, looking for Seanchai to signal how much.

"Thank you, but I would prefer to add the herbs and stir," he said.

"Why?" Ballendir asked.

"Firstly, I want to ensure the right amount and secondly, it mustn't boil."

Another furious exchange ensued until Ballendir stopped it with a sharp word. Ophera plopped on a tree stump and crossed her arms. She glared at Seanchai, who felt bad.

He took a small pouch and added three pinches of herbs to the water. He wasn't sure how much to give Ellendir, as he was completely ignorant about dwarf physiology. He could take his own and dilute the rest, he decided. When Ophera handed him a wooden spoon, he took it but immediately handed it back as a peace offering.

"Would you stir? I'm very tired and would appreciate the help. Please make sure it doesn't boil."

Ophera nodded stiffly. She approached the task with utmost seriousness, and Seanchai went back to sit with Ballendir.

"Now perhaps you'll tell me what makes you different from other dwarves, and why the dwarf nation seeks isolation."

"Gladly," Ballendir said. "But first we should light our pipes. Perhaps I can interest yeh in some testleweed? It grows near our mountain range back in the East."

"To smoke?" Seanchai asked, looking to his friends for help and receiving only amused grins. "I've never–"

"Really?" Ballendir raised two bushy eyebrows. "Is this something that only dwarves and men do?"

"Elves smoke pipe weed," Ilana said.

"Well, now," Ballendir mused. "I see I have a lot to teach yeh, young Wycaan."

# NÎNE

General Tarlach listened carefully as the ranger described each individual in the party and recalled the decision to head north. Tarlach wanted to know more about the human girl, but the ranger knew no more than her name and physical appearance.

At the mention of dwarves, however, Tarlach started. How many dwarves? What clothes were they wearing? Could the rangers tell what clan they belonged to? He asked a dozen more questions to no avail.

"You should have sent a more experienced scout," Tarlach snarled, knowing that it had been his decision to send Jermona. "Dwarves always like to show their clan colors. I need to know which clan is thinking of moving so far north right under my nose."

"My lord," the ranger replied evenly. "I went myself to confirm that they were indeed dwarves. I can assure you they were not wearing clan regalia."

General Tarlach abruptly stood and looked away. Dwarves. Why? He turned back to the ranger and asked the same questions again and received exactly the same answers. Finally, he dismissed the ranger.

"Do not leave the camp. I will have new orders for you." The ranger nodded once and left.

Tarlach gazed at a nearby hill without seeing it. He sighed, deep in thought, and looked over at Bortand, who was hovering close.

"Why, my friend?" he asked. "Dwarves do not travel above ground if they can help it. Why are they on the move?"

"My general," Bortand began. "First, um, we should remember that this is a small group. They could be an advance scouting party or simply running away for politics, love, a gem feud. This might also explain the lack of insignia."

Tarlach nodded slowly. "Yes, that makes sense. If they were transporting anything of worth, then there would be a lot more of them."

"Unless, of course, they hoped to travel, um, unnoticed."

The general nodded again and stood abruptly. "Come. This is very disturbing and we must deal with it quickly."

Bortand was shuffling to keep up with the general. "Why does it disturb you so? They don't seem to me of any, um, significance."

"Because we don't want the Wycaan to get in with the dwarves," Tarlach replied without looking. "If he is isolated from the races, there's little damage he can do."

"You worry this elf will forge an, um, alliance among the races?"

"It has happened before, Bortand, and now this elf's group includes humans, elves and dwarves. History has a nasty habit of repeating itself."

"Yes, sir. Indeed, it does."

"And the Emperor, my friend, has a keen interest in history."

Jermona kept his distance from the party until they set up camp for the night and lit a fire. The shadows cast by the flames provided a perfect cloak for him and the fire ensured the party would have no night vision. He settled behind a good-sized rock, making sure he was situated where they wouldn't see him if they left the fire. He was eager to hear their conversation.

The dwarf, Ballendir, was very talkative, but would not reveal their mission or details about their journey. This dismayed Jermona because he knew once the general heard about the dwarves, he would ask about this before anything else. He listened as they discussed their wounded dwarfe companion and the herbal mix the big elfe was preparing as they ate.

After they finished dinner, a pungent smell reached Jermona. At the sound of choked coughing, he peeked around to look. The huge elf, Seanchai they called him, was holding a pipe and gasping for air. His bright red face was a sharp contrast to his white-blond hair. The others were laughing at him and Jermona wondered whether Seanchai would draw his blades and reassert his authority. But he seemed to take it in good humor.

The dwarf counseled Seanchai on how to smoke the pipe. Jermona knew from his travels that elves used it ceremoniously and that humans and dwarves smoked frequently, especially in the taverns. Ranger youth were only allowed to smoke pipes when they came of age, and he had not been interested.

While they smoked, the dwarf told a story. Jermona listened intently. He had heard it before, but from a very different perspective.

Many soldiers had already tucked into their meals by the time General Tarlach joined them for dinner. The remnants of two wild pigs roasted over an open pit, and the cook had set a table with vegetables, bread and ale. It had been a long time since they had enjoyed hot, fresh meat.

Three soldiers rose from the table nearest the cooking pit and offered the general their table. He nodded and considered inviting them to join him. It would terrify them, he realized, and anyway, he needed to talk with the ranger.

He looked around but couldn't see the ranger at any of the tables. He turned to Bortand, intending to instruct him to bring the ranger, but Bortand was already seated, bent over a full plate of steaming meat. Tarlach laughed at the sight and called for a soldier to find the scout.

While he waited, he took a plate; helped himself to some meat, vegetables and bread; and joined Bortand at the table. Just as he sat down, the cook bustled out of his tent and presented a large oval tray to the general.

"One of the hunters caught a pheasant, my lord," he said.

"Thank you," Tarlach said, barely glancing up. "And please, compliment the hunters."

The cook bowed as he walked away. Tarlach dug his fork into the pheasant and took a large portion. Then he signaled to Bortand who delicately and expertly sliced off some choice parts.

The ranger appeared, eyes puffed up and curly, gray hair dripping with water.

"I woke you?" the general asked.

"It is of no consequence," the ranger replied, eyeing the pheasant but not moving to take any.

After swallowing his bite, the general invited the ranger to join them. "The pheasant is particularly good," he remarked.

After the ranger had filled his plate, Tarlach leaned forward. "I want you to replace the young ranger. Take him out of the tracking group." He purposely stopped to gauge the ranger's reaction and was impressed when the man's tanned face remained impassive.

"I have a special task for the boy. I want him to reveal himself and join the group as a spy. He can tell them that he's running away from life as a ranger."

"Why would he be heading north?" Bortand asked, his mouth full. "Excuse me," he said as he swallowed. "We need a reason for him to be going in that direction."

Tarlach pondered this.

"How about because he's heading to a village beyond the mountains where our people live?" the ranger suggested. "He doesn't need to reveal a name. We closely guard where our people live, as you know. It'll be an expected response. And I think it makes more sense if he says he is running from the Emperor's service."

Tarlach eyed the ranger carefully. Was there a basis for that statement? He wouldn't be able to pry anything from the experienced ranger, either way. This mission had suddenly become more interesting. The general smiled slowly.

"I have another idea," he said. "I know how to make it look genuine."

# TEN

"So," Seanchai said when his coughing fit was under control. "How do you smoke this thing?"

He held the pipe at arm's length like something that might bite at the slightest provocation. The others were gathered around the campfire and trying to stop laughing, except for Ophera, who tended Ballendir's sister.

"The first thing yeh need to do," Ballendir explained, "is to treat it nice, like a good companion. Yeh just attacked it like it was a wolfheid. Light it slowly; breathe small, sharp breaths; and then take a smooth draw once there's an even burn. This weed is supposed to help yeh relax, not choke yeh."

Another round of laughter followed, and Seanchai realized that, surrounded by his friends, he felt more at ease than he had since, well – since he could remember. Ballendir seemed quite a character. He wondered if all dwarves were like him, as he puffed apprehensively.

"You don't have to smoke that," Ilana said. "It's just a male thing, and I'm sure it can't be good for you."

"Not so, lass," Ballendir protested. "Female dwarves smoke and share equally in every other part of our lives. Mah clan's leader's a female," he said as he turned to Seanchai, "and don't ever underestimate a dwarfe in battle."

Ballendir inhaled at length. "And we no longer use plants that are addictive and eat yeh body from the inside. Horrible memories I have of mah dear grandparents' generation and the hellsbane they smoked. But our herbalists found weeds that can be smoked without evil effects and even have medicinal properties. This one helps yeh relax and is usually smoked in the evenings, or by very angry dwarves."

He laughed at his own joke, though the others just smiled and Ophera, who had now joined them, rolled her eyes.

"Tell me about your herbalists?" Seanchai requested after a moment.

"We used to get help from the elves when we ventured above ground more often, but once we buried ourselves in the caves, we needed to become self-sufficient. We only went above ground to hunt and forage, and maintain our natural eyesight. Now we mainly use plants that grow underground or in little light. Thankfully, the rich mineral deposits in the rocks enrich the properties of these herbs."

"Do you use a lot of mushrooms?"

"Aye, we do," Ballendir answered. "Do yeh have an interest in herbs?"

Seanchai began to tell about his mother, but Ilana interjected and smoothly changed the subject so Seanchai wouldn't have to think about the family he had left behind. Seanchai smiled at her gratefully and Ballendir, oblivious to what had happened, obliged her request to tell them why the dwarves had gone underground.

"Aye, I was just about to get to that," Ballendir said, putting his pipe down and resting his hands on his belly.

The old dwarfe snipped at Ballendir in Dwarfish.

"Ophera wants yeh to know that mah opinion on what I'm about to tell yeh isn't our general clan view, or that of most of the dwarf nation." He nodded to the old dwarfe with exaggerated respect.

"How so?" Ilana asked.

"Well, I think it's wrong we isolated ourselves. I think it was a mistake to go underground and ignore the plight of those above ground. The First Decree was the first mistake."

Ophera inhaled noisily and continued to stare into the fire.

"Start from the beginning," Rhoddan requested. "Tell us how it happened."

Ballendir took a deep breath and a sip of ale. He furrowed his brow as he began. "Yeh all know of the Great Alliance, do yeh not?"

"I don't," Maugwen spoke for the first time. "A what?"

Ballendir smiled at her. "An alliance is when an agreement is struck between individuals or groups. The Great Alliance was among all the races and allowed for many generations of peace and prosperity.

"We dwarves lived mainly in the mountains, but some moved to the city to conduct business and stayed because they enjoyed the culture and the way of life. There were also dwarves on the High Council and they, of course, required other dwarves in their court."

"Dwarves were leaders, not humans?" Maugwen asked, surprised.

"The leadership rotated among the races," Seanchai answered. "It went from man to elf to dwarf and then back again."

"Elves too?" Maugwen said without thinking. "Sorry," she whispered.

"It's not you," Shayth said, snapping a twig. "We were brought up to think that we're the superior race."

Ballendir nodded. "The High Council sent out expeditions beyond our boundaries. The dwarves represented a small part of these expeditions, because we found plenty of bounty in the bowels of Odessiya. It was men who desired to discover new races and new lands. And it was their downfall.

"The expeditions discovered wealth in the lands beyond and built their industry on the backs of slaves. Often these slaves were dwarves for we're the finest miners They say over thirty thousand dwarves were taken to these other lands and put to work.

"When it was discovered, a terrible war ensued. But the humans had done more in secret than just gather wealth. They either conscripted or bribed pictorians and wild men to join them, so when civil war erupted, they invaded with massive armies."

He paused to gulp his ale, a pained expression on his face. Ophera stared vacantly into the fire.

"Yeh must remember that ten thousand years of peace and prosperity had passed. We had become lax in training our people to fight and while the gems in the axe handles were shiny, their blades were dull.

"Many dwarves answered the call to war to fight for those enslaved in the faraway lands. We marched to join the battles on the Great Plains, to honor the accords of the Alliance."

Ballendir took another swig from his cup before continuing harshly. "And our people were massacred. We aren't bred for fighting on open plains, and we learned a devastating lesson. Our leaders took us deep underground and there we reclaimed the dwarf way of battle and protecting ourselves.

"Yeh want to reforge the Alliance?" He stared at Seanchai. "Yeh better have a powerful argument if yeh hope to persuade the dwarf nation to come above-ground again."

# ELEVEN

A had skulked through the streets of the capital, his cloak wrapped around him and his hood over his head. Even the son of the great General Tarlach should not be on the streets this late at night.

He kept to the sidewalks, darting through the dim range of the flame-flickering street lamps. It was chilly, and the promise of winter had all sensible folk indoors. He was glad he was not going to school tomorrow.

His class would be on a field trip to Carparian Lake to study its rich and diverse plant and animal life, but he had been denied permission to join them. His mother refused to tell him why he could not go, and he had begun to suspect that she might not know herself.

What he *did* know is that for at least the last week, someone was following him. Being the son of an important general, his first thought was that maybe someone might try to kidnap him, to extort money or secrets from his father. But when he had gone to army security, the officer he spoke with had condescendingly told him that he was paranoid.

He had left angry and embarrassed. At fifteen, he was badly equipped to deal with such people. If his father was around, he would have them snapping to attention, but his father rarely came back to the capital these days.

Ahad would have liked to spend more time elsewhere in Galbrieth, where the mountains and caves offered fascinating specimens of plants and interesting animal species. But there was no school in the region for one of his class, and he was an excellent student. For his own future, Ahad and his mother stayed in the capital.

His friends at school had heard whispers of something afoot in Galbrieth. His father had lost a great battle but was now chasing the enemy and cutting them down.

But tonight, Ahad walked the dark streets because he had received a cryptic message from one of his father's closest friends. It was only seven words: *Turnsen Square. Midday. The butcher's leanest cut.*

When Ahad was eleven years old, his father had told him a secret he was never to share with anyone. His father was part of a secret society of officers who would always look out for each other and their families.

The message was a code. "The leanest cut" meant he was being called for something urgent. The butcher on Turnsen Square was actually a tavern near Market Square, and "midday" meant one hour past midnight.

Several times a year, his father would walk him there, often during the night, to keep his memory fresh. Otherwise, they never spoke about it unless his father was going away. Then he would extol his son to study hard and take care of his mother, gather him in his arms and hug him. Pulling him close, his father would always whisper, *"Remember: the leanest cut."*

Ahad hadn't given this exercise much thought in quite awhile. At first, being trusted with such secret information made him feel terribly important, but as the years passed, he began to think of it as one of his father's eccentricities. He loved and admired his father, a great hero of Odessiya, but Ahad was a scholar, and his path would not lead to the battlefield.

Ahad stopped at a corner and doubled over, pretending to cough uncontrollably while glancing behind him. Whoever was tracking him expected him to be sound asleep in his bed, but they may have seen him leave. Once sure he was alone, he ducked into the tavern and walked to the designated table in the far corner.

A uniformed man sat there with his cap pulled low over his face. Ahad's heart sped up as he approached the man, swallowed, and bent over the table.

"What do you recommend from the menu tonight?" he asked.

"The beef," the man murmured. "It has the leanest cut."

Had anything else been suggested, Ahad would have fled. He sighed in relief as he sat down. This was exciting and terrifying, all at once. A serving woman approached, and the man immediately ordered ale for his friend. He clearly had no intention of letting Ahad speak to anyone else. After the ale arrived, the man leaned forward.

"I come bearing a message from your father," he said, his voice low.

"How is he?" Ahad asked politely.

The man frowned. "This isn't a social call," he hissed. "Just listen and ask questions that are relevant."

Ahad was thankful it was dark and the man could not see his cheeks flush from the rebuke. Not trusting himself to say anything more, he just nodded.

"What I'm about to tell you is for your ears alone. Understand?"

Ahad nodded again.

"*Just you*, understand?"

"I understand," Ahad snapped.

"Things don't fare well for your father. He instructs you to prepare a small bag with garments you can layer for different weather, your traveling cloak, and a few supplies that can withstand time and the elements. Wear your good boots. Only bring necessities, for you might have to carry them a long way. Do you understand?"

Ahad again nodded and the man continued. "Keep the bag hidden. Let no one know about it, ever. Keep yourself in shape. You are a student and your father is proud of you, but do not neglect your body. You may be called to travel a great distance.

"A man may come and invite you on a trip." The man leaned even further forward. "He must tell you that the trip is to see the Alagorian storks migrate."

"The Alagorian storks are extinct," Ahad replied, his academic mind taking over.

"I'm not interested in your studies, boy," the man glanced around the nearly empty, smoky room. "Ask him in what direction the storks fly. He should answer south."

"A safety mechanism?"

"Yes," the man answered. "Good. If any of us are compromised, we will give a different direction."

"So if I'm told a different direction?" Ahad felt a chill inside.

"Go with him, but know you must escape when an opportunity arises. Best wait until you are out of the city and preferably have a horse. Wait for the night. Offer to share the guard duty, and then flee."

"Where to?"

"At that point, it probably won't matter."

Ahad lifted his tankard and took a great gulp. The soldier continued.

"Your father thinks that if someone wanted to get to you, they would suggest you join them on a field trip, but beware of any type of ruse. You train with the army, no?"

"All students are required to—"

"Then it could be a cadet exercise or something related. That is why we're being so specific. Now repeat everything back to me."

Satisfied that Ahad understood, the man began to rise. Ahad put his hand out.

"I have a question," the boy said, struggling to settle his voice.

The man sat back down and sighed impatiently. "What?"

"You said one bag and not to tell anyone. What about my mother?"

"You are correct," the man said. "One bag."

# TWELVE

Ballendir and Seanchai sat in companionable silence as the embers began to smolder. They had moved out of the light of the campfire to guard and talk without disturbing Rhoddan's thundering snores. Ballendir perched on a rock, meaty legs dangling, smoking his pipe. His eyes darted to trace any sound of nocturnal life in the forest.

Seanchai had just finished guard duty and was resting against a tree trunk. They had been traveling with the dwarves for two days, and Seanchai enjoyed Ballendir's company. He had peppered the dwarf with questions and found Ballendir very willing to share the history and customs of his people.

But tonight, Seanchai felt uneasy, though he couldn't pinpoint exactly why. He thought perhaps it was because they were about to enter the Bordan mountain range, where he would have to address the dwarf clan that he now believed lived there.

"Why don't yeh sleep, lad?" Ballendir asked. "What troubles yeh?"

"I'm nervous about meeting your people," Seanchai replied. "I've never served in an ambassadorial role before. I'm not sure that I understand the politics of any race."

Ballendir nodded through his pipe smoke. "Aye. And dwarves know how to play politics. Yeh'll find it very challenging."

"I'm glad that I have you with me, my friend."

The dwarf laughed. "I'm not sure how much of an asset I am."

"Why not?"

"I told yeh. In mah clan, I'm seen as a bit of a . . ." he scratched his beard, "a bit of a free thinker."

"A free thinker?"

"Well, more likely, a troublemaker." They both laughed.

"You still haven't told me why you are out here," Seanchai hedged.

"Aye, that is correct."

"In fact, you haven't told me much about what to expect when we enter the mountains, either."

"That is also correct. Never think that just because the forest is quiet that yeh are alone. The trees have ears and excellent hearing."

They both stared at each other, realizing the forest had gone terribly quiet. Seanchai's unease grew, and he loosened the straps that secured his swords in their sheaths. He thought he was being paranoid until he saw Ballendir's face.

"Wake the others, laddie," the dwarf whispered, slipping down from the rock and hiding his pipe underneath it. He crouched behind the rock, axe in hand.

The faint sound of running footsteps quickened Seanchai's silent gait. He first woke Shayth, then Rhoddan. He kicked earth over the fire as he passed it. Just as he grasped Ilana's shoulder to jostle her awake, he heard the cries of a chase. The pursuit was getting closer, and Seanchai positioned himself near Ballendir between his friends and the forest.

Shouts and snapping branches got louder. A human ran into their camp, passing Seanchai and Ballendir in his haste. He stopped, panting heavily and almost toppling over from his forward momentum. He glanced around at the wagon and those who were quickly rising from their blankets.

"What the . . . chasing me," he gasped. "They're—"

He didn't get any further. Two huge pictorians charged into the clearing. They, too, stopped in surprise. One roared with pain as Sellia shot him in the forehead. As he staggered backwards, Seanchai slit his neck from behind with both swords.

Ballendir cried out and charged the second, who turned at the sound. Seanchai thought the giant actually failed to see the dwarf, who was a good three feet shorter than him. Ballendir brought him to one knee with an axe behind the kneecap.

Wounded, the pictorian was still quick enough to block a second blow. Sellia quickly put an arrow through his throat, and as he collapsed, Ballendir turned to her.

"Would yeh mind? I was in the middle of taking this one down, mah'self. How rude."

They all chuckled nervously, except the boy, who was standing with his hands on his knees and panting.

"You'll . . . get your . . . chance. There are . . . another five and . . . a ranger."

Rhoddan quickly assumed control. He sent Ophera and Maugwen to hide under the wagon.

"We need to lead them away from Ellendir," he called, his voice deep and authoritative. "Let's retreat to the path we were on and then back toward the mountains. Sellia, hide here and see if you can pick off the ranger. He might try and creep up on Seanchai or the boy."

The boy drew a short sword. "I'm with you," he said to Rhoddan, though his sword shook.

They moved to the left as five more pictorians entered the open space. These soldiers were more prepared to meet combat and had their massive broadswords and battleaxes ready. The company fell back to the road, drawing the pictorians away from the wagon.

Once on the path's smoother surface, Seanchai turned to face the biggest soldier, who towered over him at eight feet tall. Everyone watched as the pictorian swung his huge blade around. Seanchai caught it between his swords but instead of blocking the attack, Seanchai allowed the weapon's path to continue, twisting the pictorian and presenting himself with an opportunity for a wide kick in the pictorian's waist.

His foot smashed into a dense bone, and he hopped back, howling with pain. The pictorians laughed and his adversary once again raised his sword and swung. Seanchai attempted the catch-and-kick maneuver again, this time aiming higher and connecting with the pictorian's neck.

He staggered from the blow and never had a chance to recover as one of Seanchai's swords plunged into his neck and the other through the giant's chest. Seanchai whirled round, ready for more, and stopped as he realized everyone had been fixated on his fight with the beast. This lasted only a moment more as Ballendir and Ilana took on one pictorian, Rhoddan and the boy another, and a third leapt at Shayth.

"It is time, traitor prince," the soldier roared, but where his sword intended to contact Shayth's skull, there was only air.

Shayth had ducked around a small tree and now stabbed into the confused beast's side. The pictorian struggled for a moment but straightened and prepared to pounce. Shayth crouched, his blade up and ready. But as the soldier lunged forward, Seanchai slammed into his huge back with amazing speed plunging him helplessly onto Shayth's broadsword.

"Help Ilana," Seanchai pointed and Shayth saw him turn swiftly and strike a smaller pictorian, his double blades a deadly blur. Then he turned to help Ballendir and the boy, who were retreating down the path, clearly on the defensive.

As Seanchai ran toward them, the pictorian sent both Ballendir and the boy flying with a swing from his huge axe. Ballendir hit a tree trunk and staggered to his feet. He shook his head but had difficulty refocusing on the advancing creature. The boy was also rising slowly but saw what happened next.

The pictorian picked up speed as he charged the dwarf, but did not make it to his target before being lifted off the ground and smashed, headfirst, into the think tree trunk. The whole tree creaked from the impact, and the unconscious pictorian fell on Ballendir, who collapsed under the giant's weight. Seanchai pulled the huge creature off his friend, striking a killing blow to ensure he wouldn't rise again.

"I was just about to take him, too," Ballendir pouted.

"I know you were, but I need you to help the others," Seanchai replied, spinning around to hide an emerging grin, just in time to see the final pictorian fall beneath Shayth's sword and Ilana's long knife.

"I could have taken him," Ballendir muttered again.

Seanchai did not reply, but ran to Rhoddan, who lay on the path, rubbing his head.

"Are you okay?"

"Yes," Rhoddan replied. "I need a shield. Blocking a pictorian with your head is not a smart idea."

They all turned to the boy, who stood with his mouth gaping open, his breathing heavy, and his eyes almost popping as he stared at Seanchai.

Seanchai, still panting, approached him and asked, "Who are you?"

"Jermona," the boy said, his voice full of wonder. "Who are *you?*"

# THIRTEEN

T he day started badly for Ahad. He had thought to sleep in since he had not been allowed to join his classmates on a field trip. A servant woke him and announced that Ahad was expected at breakfast with his mother.

Sitting opposite her on the terrace was torture. He kept thinking of the last words from the messenger in the tavern: *One bag*. Ahad's father was making plans to save him, but not his mother – not the woman who had stayed strong and loyal to the general whether he was home or, more often, away.

A ray of sunshine pierced through the trees, bathing her head in an angelic glow. Despite the streaks of gray in her hair and the occasional worry line on her face, she was still a beautiful woman. Ahad was sure the respect she commanded in the court circles was not just because she was the wife of the great General Tarlach.

"What do you plan to do today?" she asked him as she sipped her mint tea.

"Go to the lab at school. I'm allowed access and will do some of my own experiments."

"You promise not to blow up anything?" she asked, flashing a lovely smile. "I'm going to a meeting to plan an event for children of lost soldiers. I'll be back after midday. If you like, we can go for a walk together."

Ahad didn't answer.

"You don't need to decide now," his mother said. "I'll be here. If you get lost in your science world, I'll understand."

Ahad just nodded. He had no intention of going to the school. When he had returned home in the early hours of the morning, he had been unable to fall asleep and instead spent a while deciding what to pack in his bag. He would buy a few things in the market today and then go visit his grandfather. It had been some time since he had, but maybe the old man would have some answers.

The market was a small, bustling neighborhood, now sprawling outside the inner castle walls. It was not hard for a boy to disappear here. In fact, he had favored this place for hide-and-seek with friends for that reason, much to the chagrin of the stall owners and merchants. Of course, the son of the great General Tarlach would only receive a mild rebuke.

Ahad had methodically divided his list into three sections. He planned to go out once a week on different days for three weeks, this time buying some clothes and new boots. Next week, he would purchase a few compact items for the road, such as a flint to light fires. These were nothing that a young man wouldn't want to procure for a field trip. Finally, he would buy weapons. That might prove more complicated, and he needed to figure out how to do this.

As he strolled through the market, he watched to see if he was being followed. He was, of course, but this would not spoil his plans for now. He would definitely need to find a solution on the third trip.

Ahad had soon finished shopping, having learned to tell merchants that his selections were presents for his father. He usually ended up trying to pay more than the absurd prices the merchants wanted.

*"It was an honor to sell something to General Tarlach's son. Please tell the general where you bought it. Long live the Emperor."*

Ahad made his way out beyond the town walls to a small cottage, one of several that backed up to the forest. He knocked on the door and waited. He could hear shuffling inside.

He had bought a bag of lemons and some sweet drovas honey. It was expensive and very restorative. The old, bent man who came to the door would certainly appreciate it.

"Ahad, my favorite grandson," the old man beamed as he extended two spindly arms.

"I'm your only grandson, papa," Ahad replied, and hugged the old man. "I've brought you some lemons and honey. I'll make some lemonade to cool us."

"That's a grand idea, my boy," the old man said as he turned around laboriously. "You make the drinks and bring them outside. I'll wait in my sun chair, if you don't mind."

Ahad returned with a ceramic jug and two goblets. "Papa, where's your helper?"

"She's gone to the market to buy food for her family. She'll be back to make me lunch later."

"Is there anyone else here?"

The old man heard the edge in his grandson's voice and looked up. Like his son, he had spent his career in the army, and though his body was frail, his mind was not. "No, no," he said, keeping Ahad's gaze. "But still, perhaps we shall drink a bit and then you can help me walk out to see my garden. I would like to check if the gardener knows what he's doing."

He nodded in the direction of a cherry tree near the fence. The message was clear. Here they could be overheard, but over there no spy could hide within earshot.

They chatted as they sipped their cool drinks. Ahad told his grandfather that he was upset not to be allowed to participate in the school trip and the old man nodded. Ahad hoped he was taking in what *wasn't* being said as much as what was.

"How's your mother doing?"

"She keeps busy. I'm not often at home and–"

"– and when you are home, you bury yourself in your studies. I've heard, and I'm very proud of you, as is your father."

"She worries about him, too. My father hasn't written as often of late. He's very busy, it seems, and we don't even know when he'll return home to visit."

The old man nodded and finished his drink, a few drops dribbling down his chin.

"Let us walk. I want to show you my garden."

It took them ten minutes to reach the cherry tree. Ahad could have walked it in less than one if he had gone alone, and he felt impatient. As soon as the old man was seated and caught his breath, he looked around.

"See my beautiful garden?" He extended his arm and spoke louder than needed. "Look at all the land around us. Is it not beautiful?"

Ahad was being told to scan well and see if anyone was watching them. They were alone. The man following him was probably waiting in the shade outside the front of the house.

"I'm worried for my father," Ahad said quietly. "Do you . . . do you hear anything?"

"Twice a week a young man comes here and takes me to the Officer's Club. There I chat with my friends, all of us old, senile warriors whose deeds grow greater as our minds dim.

"Our sons, when they visit from the field, accompany us, and this way we all remain informed of what is happening. I always eat lunch there. I like the beef. The cook makes a dish from the leanest cut." The old man paused a moment, meeting Ahab's eyes and nodding slightly to let Ahad know that he had seen what his grandson was looking for.

"Those involved in politics often find that they're vulnerable not only to the enemy, but to their ruler and the powerful overseers who rank in the Emperor's court. You never show them weakness – only respect and loyalty.

"Your father, though, is vulnerable to something else."

"What?"

"Do you remember when you were younger, maybe ten years ago, and your parents took another boy into your house?"

"Shayth? Yes. He was wild even then. We were friends at first, but he changed and was angry all the time. One day, he just disappeared."

"Your father values loyalty above all else, Ahad. It is why the Emperor trusts him, why your mother loves him, why his soldiers bind themselves to him, and . . ." the old man shook his head, "why he is in terrible peril."

"What does this have to do with Shayth? My father couldn't have been very loyal to him if he let the boy disappear."

The old man shook his head. "Your father was very loyal to Shayth's father. Learn about Shayth, but be careful who you ask."

Ahad thought of his mother's offer to go for a walk today. It suddenly seemed like a very good idea.

"Grandfather, let me help you back to the house. I need to go soon."

As the old man stood up, he grabbed Ahab's arm for support. His wrinkled face came in close. "Did you make yourself a shopping list?"

Ahad nodded.

"There are some things that you will not be able to buy without arousing suspicion. Allow your grandfather, an old but distinguished warrior, the honor of passing on his tools of the trade to his only grandson."

Ahad stared at him.

"If someone asks where you got them, there is no need to lie, but keep it discreet if you can. Next time you come to visit me, bring a bigger bag. Fill it with vegetables from your mother's garden and some of your thick science books. I will enjoy the vegetables, but not the books."

"Thank you, papa," Ahad whispered. "I don't know what to say."

"In these situations, I find it is always best not to say more than you have to. Visit me again soon. Maybe at the end of the week?"

"I will," Ahad promised.

"Watch yourself. I only have one son and one grandson. It is the sad legacy of the warrior. You are a hero when you win, but heroism is so fragile in the face of defeat. It is a terrible punishment to grow old when your family needs you."

# FOURTEEN

"Where did you—" Seanchai began, but Rhoddan stopped him.

"The boy said a ranger was with the pictorians."

Seanchai pushed past Shayth and ran back to the camp. The wagon looked untouched.

"Sellia?" he called.

"I'm here," she said, leaping gracefully from a tree branch.

"The ranger?"

"He didn't come."

Seanchai turned and ran back to the boy. "What direction would he go to report back?"

The boy pointed south and Seanchai took off. When he returned to the camp two hours later, the others were gathered around the relit fire. Only Rhoddan seemed to have been able to fall back to sleep and snored obliviously. Seanchai stared at his close friend as he caught his breath. Rhoddan was impressive in many ways.

"Did you catch him?" Ilana asked.

Seanchai shook his head and kicked a stone. "He can't be quicker than me. I must have gone in the wrong direction."

"Don't take it so hard," Shayth said. "He's a ranger. He probably didn't try to outrun you. They make their living by being stealthy."

"And I should have sensed him when I scryed." Seanchai rubbed his head and then turned back to Shayth. "Anyway, what's a ranger?"

"Ask him," Shayth nodded to Jermona. "You're one, too, aren't you?"

Jermona nodded and then bent his head. "Not a very good one, apparently. I couldn't lose the pictorians."

"What happened?" Ilana asked, much more empathetic than Shayth.

"I don't want to talk about it," the boy said and turned his back on them. He rested his head on hands that rested on his knees.

"You will if you want to stay with us," Shayth said, his voice still sharp.

"Shayth," Ilana admonished him.

But Ballendir cut in firmly. "I'm afraid Shayth's right. This changes everything."

Seanchai grinned. "Ballendir, my friend. They send you off on some secret mission, and you return with half an army."

"What mission?" Ballendir glared at him. "And anyway, you six kids hardly constitute half an army." He muttered something irritatedly in Dwarfish that Seanchai was glad he couldn't understand. Ophera did, though, and she replied to Ballendir sharply. He sighed and nodded, then turned to Seanchai. "Ophera said that from what she's seen, she wouldn't like to confront yeh with only half an army. I have to agree."

He walked over to Jermona. "Listen, son. If we're to stay together then we need to know who yeh are and why they're after yeh."

Jermona jerked away. "Who said I want to join you?" He paused and took a deep breath. "I'm very grateful that you took out that sixer. You saved my life, okay? But that doesn't mean I have to share everything with you."

He stood up and paced a bit. Five sets of eyes followed him. When he turned to them, his voice was young and soft. "Can I stay tonight?"

Seanchai rose early to do his exercises. When he finished and opened his eyes, the boy was sitting on a rock, watching. Seanchai stretched and sighed.

"Does that help you with your powers?" the boy asked.

"Yes," Seanchai replied quietly. "Jermona, please tell me what a ranger is?"

The young boy answered with pride about his father and uncle, careful not to reveal names, and then he spoke about his apprenticeship. Ilana came over and listened, too. When Jermona finished, she invited them back to camp to eat.

"We need to pack up and keep moving," she said. "The ranger will have gone for help."

"Come on," Seanchai said to Jermona. "Are you hungry?"

"Always," Jermona said and smiled.

Back at the camp, there was a thick broth bubbling in a pot. Seanchai went to check on Ellendir. She looked pale, he thought, though he figured living underground would do that as much as anything.

He took his pouch of danseng root and picked up a small pot to make Mhari's strength-building tea. At the fireplace, Ophera grabbed the bag of herbs and gave Seanchai a warning glare.

"I need to—" he began, but she just raised a small pot of water that had already boiled and put a large pinch of dried roots into it.

She stirred and covered the pot but did not return it to the embers, choosing a place near the fire where it was close enough to stay warm.

"She knows her herbs?" Seanchai asked Ballendir, who looked on, smoking his pipe. "She knows to identify that this is a root and needs to brew."

"Aye, she has served mah family for many decades. She loves Ellendir like a daughter. She appreciates yeh healing efforts."

"And how does she feel about you?"

Ballendir called out to the dwarfe, who replied with something curt that needed no translation. Seanchai laughed.

"Are yeh still sure you want me to represent yeh?" Ballendir asked.

"I would be honored," Seanchai beamed. "It says something that a servant can joke with you."

"She is no servant," Ballendir said, his tone stern. "Though there is hierarchy in a clan, there is no slavery or anything like that. She could walk away tomorrow if she wished . . . and stay despite my wishes."

He snickered at his joke as the dwarfe brought Seanchai his tea. "Thank you," he said and she nodded. He wondered why she never spoke to him or in Odessiyan when she clearly understood. She kept to herself and Seanchai respected that, but his instinct told him that she was listening and watching keenly.

"How do we handle the boy?" Seanchai asked. "I don't want to let him go off by himself. It seems cruel."

Ballendir inhaled his pipe deeply. "Seanchai. He's a ranger. They're crafty, skillful and, above all, mercenaries. He might be a pup, but don't let yeh guard down. I'm not sure, at this point, if I prefer to have him in mah sights. If we let him loose, I wouldn't know if he was tracking us."

"Do you have an idea of what we'll do when we enter the mountains? We need to decide and move."

Ballendir nodded and called everyone around. "We're going to enter the Bordan Mountains today. I'll guide yeh to a small valley with a lake. There we'll leave yeh. If yeh stay there, we might return. If yeh move on, that's fine. If yeh get chased out, good luck."

There was silence for a while. Seanchai stared at Ballendir. "That's it?"

"Did I tell yeh that I'm well-known in mah clan as a master strategist?" he asked with a smile. "Ophera and I will take the wagon and mah sister. You alone may join us."

"What? What about my friends?"

"If yeh welcomed, then we'll return to fetch them."

"And if I'm not welcomed?"

Ballendir puffed his pipe and apprehension flicked across his face. "Then, my friend, if yeh have any chance of escaping it'll be by yehself."

"They might try to kill him?" Ilana asked.

"I'd say there's a pretty good chance of that." Ballendir replied from behind a thick cloud of smoke. "I warned yeh of The First Decree."

"And you would let them?"

Ballendir's face hardened. "Yeh don't understand dwarf culture, Ilana. If they decide to kill him, mah axe will be the first to swing."

Seanchai glanced over at the old dwarfe, who was cleaning up breakfast. She returned his gaze with a toothy smile. He was sure she understood this conversation much better than he did.

# FIFTEEN

A had reentered the city and walked home. One hand held his purchases and the other was thrust into his pocket, fist clenched. He knew he was being followed. By now, he could sense the man's presence.

Once inside his house, he went quickly to his room and packed his wares into a backpack. He had bought a fine, hooded cloak. It was thick and would serve as an extra blanket. He added two pairs of heavy trousers and a pair of stout walking boots. Then he took the new boots out and replaced them with the pair he was wearing. He would need to break in the new stiff leather, and he ought do it now since he had no idea how long he had.

His mother returned and found him sitting at the table in the kitchen, his head buried in a book about plant life. What she failed to notice was the map inside the book that he was memorizing. Next to the book was a sandwich with a single bite missing, and a flagon of mead.

"Is that all you're eating?" his mother asked, and then looked at the cook.

"Not my fault, milady," the large woman said, wiping her hands on her apron. "I try to tempt him, I do. Now, if I could put my stew into a book, he'd devour it, no mistake."

Ahad's mother laughed and ran her hand through her son's unruly curls.

"Hello, mum," he said and looked up. "I could do with that walk if you're still offering."

His mother beamed. "I'll be ready in ten minutes . . . assuming you finish that sandwich."

"I'm sorry you didn't go on the field trip with your classmates," Ahad's mother said as they strolled through the gardens. "I know how much it would've meant to you."

Ahad nodded and glanced around. Tall stone walls enclosed their grounds, and his father would have guards patrolling. No soldier would want to be the one who allowed an assassin or robber to get by. But after a few minutes of observation, Ahad decided there were no sentries near.

"Mother," he took her arm. "We're alone now, and I need to know some things. It wasn't your decision that I not go on the school trip, right?"

She didn't answer. When he told her that was as good as a yes for him, she didn't argue.

"If anything happened to father, what would you do?"

"Why do you ask, dear?"

"Please, just answer. What would you do if something happened to father?"

She frowned. "I'm not sure I like where these questions—"

Ahad stopped and pulled her around to face him. He looked at her intently. "I need answers, and I think you're the safest person for me to ask. But I could go find someone else if you prefer."

He knew he shouldn't speak to his mother so sharply, but he held her eyes and refused to back down. His mother stared at him for another moment.

"Someone has said something to you," she stated. "Someone has gotten to you, frightened you."

"No one has frightened me," he corrected. "Little frightens me."

He looked at his feet when he realized this was a stupid thing to say to his own mother. "Please," he pleaded. "Answer my questions."

She began walking again and he kept pace. "It would depend how old you are. If you were still at home, then I would stay here. We would have enough money, and the Emperor would probably look after us. If you were grown, I would return home to Lake Merydyth."

"Why?"

"This is not my city. I fell in love with a dashing young army officer and moved to the capital to be with him. But most of my friends and all my family are there."

"Why don't we ever visit your family?"

"Your father doesn't get on with them." She looked around and lowered her voice. "They aren't great supporters of the Emperor. It was once a source of contention between your father and me. I go to see them once or twice a year without him or you. It's better that way."

Ahad nodded. His mind was reeling. So his father assumed that if she needed to flee, she already had a plan? He wondered if she could walk away from her own son. Suddenly he wasn't sure.

"Tell me about Shayth," he requested.

"Shayth? Why?"

"Because I need to know."

"Shayth is the Emperor's nephew. His father, Prince Shindell, and your father were best friends. They went through the academy together and fought side-by-side in countless campaigns. They had a very special bond.

"When you and Shayth were born, both fathers wanted to bring you together. Of course, they were always in battle or on a mission. So I took you to the palace and, in time, forged a friendship with Shayth's mother."

They had reached the pagoda on the edge of the Tarlach estate. The view was beautiful and they sat for a moment, each deep in thought. Eventually, Ahad broke the silence.

"Why did Shayth come to live with us? What happened to his parents?"

His mother turned slowly, eyes full of tears. "Both of his parents died, within days of each other. Your father was on a mission with Prince Shindell when he was killed. Your father felt responsible, and asked the Emperor if he could take Shayth into our house. He was heir to the throne. The Emperor had no children back then."

"How did they die, and in such quick succession?"

His mother stood and paced, biting one of her long fingernails. "I stood here many times with your father discussing that exact question. He made me swear not to share my theories or his fears." She turned to Ahad. "After you, my son, I love your father, as I did the first day I met him. I will keep my word to him."

"Why did Shayth run away? Why didn't you go after him?"

"So many questions," she sighed. "When the Emperor's new wife bore a son, Shayth was no longer the heir."

She hesitated, but Ahad was ahead of her.

"He fled? He thought he was in danger?"

She nodded, her back to him now, arms crossed tightly over her chest. Ahad's mind was reeling.

"How would a nine-year-old boy know all this?"

No answer.

"One of you told him. One of you told him to flee."

His mother swung round, her eyes blazing. "No," she snapped, and then caught herself. "We would never do that. I think he overheard us talking, out here probably, and made his own decision."

"Why didn't father go after him?" Ahad stood, agitated.

"I can't answer that," his mother said. She put her arms around him and drew him close. "There are many rumors being spread right now. But what I know is your father caught Shayth near Galbrieth," she whispered. "The Emperor issued a declaration to execute him in the garrison of Galbrieth on his birthday. Shayth escaped two months ago."

"How? How would anyone escape from that fortress?"

"That is the question many are asking, including, I am sure, the Emperor himself."

"Father is in danger?"

"Maybe." She hugged him tighter and whispered in his ear. "And if he is, then we are, too."

# SIXTEEN

It began to rain as they entered the Bordan Mountains. The peaks were engulfed in thick cloud and they were quickly drenched and miserable. Their progress was slow on the wet, slippery rock.

"Does it rain a lot?" Maugwen asked Ballendir as he helped her up from a fall.

"Oh, no," he said, almost cheerfully. "Just most of the year. In the summer it can get quite pleasant for a few days."

"But . . . it's summer now." Ilana said.

They all stared at the dwarf. He shrugged, unfazed.

"How can you live in a place like this?" Sellia asked.

"Yeh hardly notice it after a while," Ballendir replied, and then grinned. "Of course, it helps when yeh live underground."

They all laughed through their discomfort. At one point, the wagon wheels spun in the soggy ground and needed to be pushed. When the wagon started forward, Rhoddan slipped in mud. His elfish swear elicited cackles from Ophera.

"Does she understand any languages other than Dwarvish and Odessiyan?" Seanchai asked Ballendir.

"Not that I know of," he replied. "But I think the lad expressed himself pretty clearly. Aah, let's take this path. The lake is not far now."

The path gently descended and soon the lake appeared, as dull as the surrounding mountains and the sky above them. The path hugged the lake on the left for a short while before jutting away toward a tall ledge. There was ample space to camp and escape the rain underneath it.

"I thought this was here," Ballendir said proudly. "It'll serve yeh well. Collect some wood and dry it. Yeh have fresh water, fish to catch, and a beautiful view. This could become quite a vacation spot with a little imagination."

They all stared out at the mass of gray.

"It *is* dry, at least," Ilana admitted.

"Ballendir?" Rhoddan was still standing at the entrance. "Is there another way out of here if we get attacked from the way we came?"

Ballendir asked Ophera as everyone watched expectantly.

"She asked if yeh all know how to swim."

While everyone unloaded food and dry wood from the wagon to leave at the campsite, Seanchai focused his healing energy on a still-unconscious Ellendir. He worried about her and what might happen once they arrived at the dwarf camp.

When he finished, he got down from the wagon and saw an argument was beginning. He hurried over.

"You can't keep me here. Am I your prisoner now?" Jermona was the only one standing up, and his short sword was unsheathed, jerking erratically at whoever spoke.

"Put it away," Seanchai said, his voice quiet but firm.

The young ranger half-heartedly pointed his blade at Seanchai, who knew he had no real intention of attacking.

"I'm not goi-"

"First, sheath your blade," Seanchai roared. "We saved your life. Put it away."

Jermona contemplated for a moment before doing as he was told. "I want to go. If they do come after me – and they still might – I need to be gone."

Ballendir spoke. "He's a ranger. Once he's out of sight, he can track us the rest of the way. It's out of the question."

"Then let him go first," Maugwen suggested.

"No. He could hide and wait to follow us. Either he swears to stay with yeh, or I'll bind him."

"Then I *am* your prisoner," Jermona argued.

Seanchai knew everyone was waiting for his decision, as they had ever since they had fled Galbrieth. He couldn't believe how things had changed in the year or so since he left his village. He was annoyed with himself for not settling this in the forest.

"Come with me," he said to Jermona and led him away.

They sat on rocks at the other end of the camp. Seanchai leaned in closely.

"I cannot share with you where we're going because, in truth, I don't know. We're both fugitives from the Emperor's army. It seems a shame that we quarrel or use force against each other.

"I serve a greater good. I have been given gifts, talents – powers, if you will – and I have the opportunity to overthrow this oppressive regime and free all those who are enslaved or beaten down. Do you understand?"

Jermona nodded, and Seanchai felt he had the boy's full attention.

"Whatever happens next is vital. I need Ballendir and whoever else lives in these mountains to trust me."

"You don't know who is here?"

"No."

"It could be just a small family of renegade dwarves hiding out."

"I hope not." Seanchai didn't reveal that he had felt a pull of power long before he had met Ballendir. "Either way, I think you're safer here than on your own."

"Why?"

"I've been through many battles with the people you see over there. Shayth is ruthless with both sword and bow. Rhoddan is a warrior in every sense of the word. Sellia moves without a trace, and her arrows never miss. They are all honorable and will protect you if you stay. And they are my friends. I will not go far from them."

"What about Ilana and the little human? You didn't mention them."

"Maugwen doesn't fight, but I feel there's something special about her. I have yet to discover what it is. I'm not, in truth, bound to her like I am to the others. She's new to our party."

"And Ilana?"

"She is brave, smart, and an excellent guide. She's just as likely to talk her way out of a difficult situation, as she is to fight. But if she needs to fight, she is relentless."

Jermona was smiling.

"What's so funny?" Seanchai asked.

"I think you forgot to mention that you would defeat half an army to protect her," Jermona laughed.

Seanchai smiled. "*Half* an army? You're wrong, my friend. I would waylay an *entire* army to save her."

They both laughed.

"I like that you're all so bonded to each other," Jermona said as he glanced back at the others. "I've never seen this."

Seanchai smiled again. "Then you'll stay?"

"I'll stay," Jermona agreed.

Jermona did stay . . . until the middle of the night when, while on guard duty, he met the rangers who had been tracking them. Though he provided a thorough and detailed report, he did not feel the pride that had accompanied him when he had begun this mission.

Upon his return to the campsite, everyone seemed to be asleep. Seanchai and the dwarves had left several hours ago. Jermona missed the big elf, but knew that as long as Ilana was here, Seanchai would be back. There were four other rangers out there tracking Seanchai and the dwarves. They would discover what secrets these miserable mountains concealed and help the general set whatever trap he devised.

Jermona could settle back for now and relax. He would emerge a hero no matter what happened. But right now, this didn't please him. He woke Shayth to guard and lay down, his hands folded behind his head, and stared into the dark. He wasn't feeling so good about himself anymore.

# SEVENTEEN

G eneral Tarlach stared out of his tent. Everything about this land was gray. The sky held rain-swollen clouds, and a thick fog stretched down the mountainsides. The ground was nothing more than puddles and churned mud.

He walked toward the big mess tent. He was anxious: anxious to keep moving, anxious to finish the upstart elf, anxious to catch Shayth, and anxious to return to the Emperor's good graces.

He was worried for his family. He looked westward, knowing that troop reinforcements should arrive any day and that his fellow officer would bring word from the capital.

Halfway across the camp, a scurrying Bortand joined him, balancing a leather case probably packed with important documents. They didn't talk, each turned inward from the damp chill.

The thirty men already inside the mess tent sprung from their benches as their general entered. Tarlach immediately motioned for them to sit and settled in the area partitioned off for him and his officers.

His table was quickly piled up with eggs, meat, bread and cheese. A plate was set before him, and a steaming cup of hot tea placed by his right hand. He looked up to thank the lad who had been so attentive, but he had already melted into the shadows.

He filled his plate and sipped the tea, watching Bortand wolf down his own breakfast before he began his daily report. Despite three weeks of travel, Bortand's waistline hadn't slimmed one bit.

A rustle at the partition drew Tarlach's attention. A ranger stood there, water dripping from his hood and cloak.

"Dry yourself off in the kitchen," Tarlach said. "Then come and eat with me."

A few minutes later, the man took a seat opposite the general, next to Bortand. He had a mug with tea, but nothing else.

"Not hungry?" Tarlach asked.

The man shrugged. "You should hear my report first. That is my duty."

"As you wish," the general nodded. "I'm listening."

"Jermona successfully joined the group. He walks with them now for three days."

"He was chased as I suggested?"

"Yes, by a sixer of pictorians. He ran right into their camp."

"A sixer of pictorians? You were confident the elf could deal with them?"

"Yes, but the others are very good, too. There is a dark-skinned elfe who is quick with her bow, and the other two elves wield their knives with skill and passion."

"You failed to mention the Emperor's nephew." Frown lines tightened Tarlach's face.

"I-He is there and fights . . . very competently."

The general glared at him. "You think I prefer not to hear about Shayth?"

The ranger met his stare and replied calmly. "It is rumored that the boy is a sensitive subject for you."

"Such assumptions are beyond the scope of your, um, reporting responsibilities," Bortand retorted hastily.

"My apologies." The ranger lowered his eyes and said no more.

The silence extended, and the ranger scooped some food onto his plate. Tarlach recognized that this might be a rebellious response, in that if Tarlach wanted more information, he would have to relent. These rangers had a stubborn independence about them that both worried and intrigued him.

"You are right," he said to the ranger, deciding to be conciliatory. "Shayth lived in my house as a boy. His father and I were very close. It saddens me to see the path he has taken, but, as an officer, there is no room for such sentimentalities. When we attack them, we will kill him if we cannot take him alive. It will upset me, but not change or influence my decisions. Please continue."

The ranger finished his mouthful and drank it down. He had barely picked at his food.

"They have entered the Bordan Mountains. The wounded dwarf is supposedly still in bad shape. Jermona has not seen her but the elf tends to her several times a day."

"What does he do? Is he a healer?"

"Jermona doesn't know, but each time he leaves her after a session, the elf seems to want or need a drink. Jermona suspects that it is something energetic and therefore tires him."

"Interesting. Go on."

"The main party camps by a lake in the southern mountains. The dwarves left them there and have since continued north with the white-haired elf. Four rangers track them, as Jermona must now stay with the company. Some of the group are already suspicious of him, especially the Emperor's nephew."

"Then why don't they send him on his, um, way?" Bortand asked.

Tarlach answered. "If they're suspicious of him, letting him go means he can track the dwarves."

"Exactly, my lord," the ranger continued. "We have told him not to initiate contact with us again for now. We will signal him when we have need. The place where they camp is secluded, so it won't be easy for them to flee if you choose to attack."

General Tarlach nodded.

"As for the dwarves and elf still moving, we're concerned that if there is a colony, there will be guards out scouting routinely," the ranger continued. "It might prove more difficult to track them as closely as we can in the forests or on the plains. Dwarves know how to track in the mountains almost as well as rangers."

*Almost?* Tarlach thought. Out loud, he asked, "Do you have any doubt there is a colony?"

"No, sir. Not if they are receiving supplies."

Tarlach looked up to see a soldier he did not recognize standing at the partition. Bortand rose, went over to him, whispered something, and returned.

"He is the, um, advance from General Shiftan's brigade, my general. I sent him to eat while he waits for us."

General Tarlach nodded and turned back to the ranger.

"Continue as you are doing. Try and ascertain where and how large the dwarf camp is. When our troops are ready to enter the mountain range, you will meet us there. I expect enough intelligence to promptly plan an attack.

"Please take your food to the main area. I wish to talk with the messenger who has just arrived."

"Thank you, General Tarlach." The ranger bowed his head and rose.

"Good work, as always," Tarlach said, but didn't look up.

The young soldier entered and stood before General Tarlach, stiff as a plank of wood.

"At ease, man," Tarlach said as he took a bite of bread and cheese. "Have you eaten?"

"A bit, sir. I will eat again when you dismiss me."

"What news, then?"

My lord, General Shiftan is two days away. He brings a brigade of soldiers in three regiments, one each of men, pictorians, and dwarves."

"Dwarves?" Bortand dropped his heaped fork. "I didn't know . . ." His voice trailed off as he saw that his superior was not surprised.

"I ordered them," General Tarlach replied. "Long have we suspected that one day we might have to fight the dwarves. What better way, if we are to confront them on mountains or underground, than to engage them in battle with other dwarves?"

"So, we're planning for, um, battle?" Bortand asked.

General Tarlach's reply was swift and clear. "No. We are wiping them out."

# EIGHTEEN

Sellia crouched behind a sharp rock to stare out over the plains, seeking relief from the biting wind. She was restless and hated these mountains. It was nice, despite the cold, to be able to see open land. Sellia had grown up under near-constant sunshine, and had started to wonder if there even *was* a sun in this godforsaken place.

Sellia had been swept along with this expedition. At first, the idea was just to help Seanchai rescue Rhoddan and especially Ilana, who had grown up with Sellia in Uncle's camp.

But she was drawn to Seanchai. He was bonded with Ilana and, in truth, she was happy for the elfe who was like her little sister. Being so strong and vigorous, Sellia had only once met an elf that was her equal. He was long dead and she still single. It wasn't easy these days to find someone compatible – and now, she admitted to herself, to find someone comparable to Seanchai.

But this was not bothering her. She was not happy that the young ranger had joined them so easily. She didn't trust him and didn't like the fact that they were camping in a place with no exit. When he had joined them, the boy had said there was another ranger. If that were true, then the Emperor's troops would know by now that they had entered the Bordan Mountains.

She saw the dust cloud to the south. The column of soldiers confirmed what the young ranger had said. But then, as she scanned westward, she saw another unmistakable column of dust. There were two armies coming, both converging at their single exit route.

Sellia put her bow across her shoulder and scrambled nimbly down the mountainside. They still had two – maybe three – days, but she was anxious to leave this depressing, gray country.

Her return to the camp went unnoticed. Everyone stood around the cooking pot engrossed in an argument took place. Sellia drew an arrow, strung her bow, and shot the mountain goat cooking on the spit.

Everyone jumped back defensively as she approached. "There are troops approaching, still a couple of days away, but I don't want them to hear the row you're all cooking up. You might frighten them away."

They went quiet and she told them to sit. She was the oldest here and self-appointed leader in Seanchai's absence. "What's happening?"

Rhoddan spoke. "The boy went off during the night. I don't trust him."

From their body language, it was clear that Shayth and Rhoddan were angry with Jermona. Ilana's cheeks were flushed and Sellia assumed her friend was the one defending the young ranger.

"Well it's a moot point," Sellia said. "We must leave. We can kill him or set him free, but we need to move."

"You would *kill* him?" Maugwen's eyes were wide.

Sellia gave her a look and saw from the frightened expression on the girl's face that she knew the answer.

"We are *not* killing him," said Ilana, fists on her hips and her tone quietly firm. "We are better than that."

The young ranger sat motionless. He looked very young, but not frightened.

"We need to decide where to go," Sellia said, looking at Ilana. "We need to leave and somehow manage to be where Seanchai will be able to find us."

"Perhaps we should split up?" Everyone looked at Rhoddan. "Some of us can head south and lead them away from here. The others can find another, more secure place in these mountains to wait for Seanchai."

"Who goes?" Shayth asked.

There was silence. Sellia thought that everyone wanted to go and yet couldn't leave Seanchai. Then she caught the boy glancing to the side. She moved off in the other direction.

"Where are you going?" Rhoddan asked.

"Call of nature," she replied without looking back. "Want to come?" She smiled, knowing that Rhoddan was blushing. It had become her favorite pastime.

She slid behind some rocks, took her bow from her shoulder and noched an arrow. She moved higher, wanting to surprise from above whoever was watching them.

She moved slowly, ensuring that every step was silent. She heard him before she saw him. She rose above him and tensed her bow.

"If I lose sight of your hands, I'll shoot you," she said calmly.

The man didn't appear scared. He spread his arms to his side. "I am a ranger, not a soldier."

"Whatever you are," she said, "you are my prisoner."

The man shook his head. "I don't think so."

Sellia felt the sharp blow to her head but not the impact when she hit the ground.

"Over there!" Rhoddan cried and they all turned.

Ilana immediately saw the two men running deftly up the mountainside and grabbed her weapons.

"Don't bother," Jermona said, the only one who had not moved. "They're rangers. You won't catch them."

Ilana's sharp vision saw her friend slumped over a rock. She moved forward cautiously, darting from cover to cover. But no one else threatened her, and she was soon at Sellia's side. Rhoddan helped her carry Sellia back to camp.

As they lay her down, Ilana looked up at Shayth. "Is that necessary?"

Shayth had an arrow aimed at Jermona. "What were they doing?" he growled. "Planning to kill us?"

"Rangers are not assassins," Jermona replied, trying to keep his voice calm. "They were probably trying to discover our plans."

"You saw them," Shayth said. "Why didn't you warn us?"

"One of them is my uncle."

"As soon as Sellia is ready, we move," Rhoddan said. "Prepare your belongings. Ilana, Shayth, please help me with Sellia. You," he pointed at Jermona, "if you move from that rock, one of these fine archers will shoot you. They are both very good. Shall we bet who kills you first?"

"How will I receive my winnings if I bet right?"

Rhoddan shrugged. "Good point. Just don't move."

Once it was just the three of them, they hunched over Sellia to inspect the wound. It was clearly swelling, but not bleeding badly.

"She'll have a headache and a bump, but not much more." Ilana said. " It could have been worse."

"Rangers are extremely proficient," Shayth said. "They aren't violent unless they have to be. If they'd wanted to kill her, they would have. Ilana? Do you understand what we need to do?"

"Move north," she replied begrudgingly.

"Yes. We must go further into the mountain range and hope to lead them away from Seanchai. He won't know where we are heading."

Ilana sighed.

"I'm sorry to be leaving him, too," Rhoddan murmured. "I know how you feel."

Ilana stared at him and fought to suppress tears. It would be easier for her to stay here and fight an army than leave without Seanchai. She knew that Rhoddan loved Seanchai in his own way, but he was wrong: he had no idea how she felt.

# NINETEEN

Seanchai was miserably wet. The rain had seeped into every nook and cranny, and within an hour of leaving the lake, he was completely soaked through. But more than that, he was leaving Ilana and the others again. Ballendir assured him they were not going far, so she would be nearby, but it was still hard. He would be underground, almost in a different world.

He had become used to walking together, waking with her next to him, having her scent near him. He realized separating from her would only get more difficult.

He was also tired. Ellendir was improving, but slowly. He was channeling increasingly larger amounts of energy to keep her alive, and it was taking its toll on him. He didn't want to increase his dosage of the danseng tea for fear of using up his already dwindling supplies. He would have no chance to seek out the elusive herb anytime soon.

They walked for several hours without stopping, an apprehensive Ballendir glancing more and more frequently at Seanchai as they neared their destination.

They left the path and began walking downwards on a track that quickly narrowed to little more than the wagon's width. Smooth rocks, reaching at least eighteen feet high, rose on either side of them. Seanchai admired the defensive capabilities of the passage.

When they reached the mountainside, Ophera turned the horses that had pulled the cart down the wider of two paths. A dwarf appeared. He stared at Seanchai as he silently took the reins. Ballendir turned to Seanchai.

"Would yeh lift mah sister out of the cart and follow mah." He turned toward the narrower of the two paths and then back to Seanchai. "And please, Wycaan, no questions for now."

Seanchai nodded, mirroring the gravity he heard in Ballendir's voice. He lifted the unconscious dwarfe and followed Ballendir through a tunnel so low and narrow that he was forced to turn sideways and squeeze through. Ophera followed closely behind him.

The path turned sharply several times and Seanchai realized that this stone maze would be impossible for human, elf or pictorian soldiers to penetrate. When they finally emerged from the tunnel, Seanchai turned back to face the rock front and stretch his cramped muscles.

He was met by easily a hundred dwarves wielding arrows and spears. He noted that their weapons were thicker and heavier than those of elves, but he didn't doubt they were just as effective.

"Try not to kill anyone," Ballendir growled under his breath to Seanchai. Then he raised his stout arms and addressed the gathering. "The elf is with mah. He has kept mah sister from death."

There was a shuffle and a few older dwarves pushed through the crowd. Their attire bore symbols and jewels, leading Seanchai to assume these were the clan leaders. One moved toward Seanchai and reached to touch Ellendir. He turned and called something in Dwarfish. A stretcher appeared and she was quickly carried away.

"Where are—" Seanchai began.

"No questions," Ballendir hissed.

An old dwarfe, wearing a white cloak over shiny chain mail, turned to Ballendir. Her voice was deep and rich.

"He is not one of us, Ballendir. Why did you break the First Decree, a solemn and irrevocable oath?"

Ballendir cleared his throat. Seanchai could see his friend was intimidated.

"Clan Chief Rothendir," he said, bowing his head. "This elf saved our lives. He defeated a pack of wolfheids almost single-handedly, and then a sixer of pictorians."

There was a murmur among the crowd.

"You saw this with your own eyes?" Rothendir asked.

"I did," Ballendir's voice was getting stronger. "As did she."

Everyone's stare turned to Ophera, who wrapped herself tightly in her cloak.

Ballendir continued. "And he has kept Ellendir alive all this time, administering energy to her several times a day."

The clan's leader glanced at Ophera who again nodded, and then stared at Seanchai. Still, she addressed Ballendir. "How? Does he possess stones?"

"No. He has no need of them. He wields energy through his body."

Again a murmur circled the cavern. The clan chief stared at Ballendir for what seemed like ages. When she spoke, her voice was firm and resonated off the cave walls.

"Ballendir, son of Truendir and Balltir. Will you be the first to yield the axe?"

Seanchai tensed. He didn't fancy his chances in a cramped room with a hundred angry and armed dwarves. He glanced at his friend. He certainly didn't want to harm Ballendir.

"Aye, mah lady," Ballendir did not hesitate.

"Very well," the clan's chief sighed. She looked up at Seanchai. "You will stay in the outer caverns for now, and will be guarded at all times.

"Ballendir pays you a great honor. He has brought you underground and offered his axe to defend you. Should you attack us, steal from us, or try to escape, his life will be forfeit. For now, go rest. We will eat with the council and hear your story this very evening."

"Thank you," Seanchai said and bowed because it seemed the right thing to do. "Does Ellendir require my help?"

"No. She's in good hands. Our stones are strong."

The cavern emptied, with the exception of four guards who stood in pairs at each entrance as Ballendir led Seanchai through one of them.

"When you say you'll be the first to swing the axe," Seanchai said, "you mean in my defense?"

"Aye. Dwarves do not easily accept guests, even other dwarves. But when they do, they'll defend them with their lives. It is a honor system, dwarf values."

"Thank you," Seanchai said to Ballendir. "I appreciate your trust and your willingness to ensure my safety."

"Safety?" Ballendir's face was full of surprise. "Yeh not safe. All I have ensured is that neither am I."

"Well, that doesn't sound like the smartest of moves." Seanchai couldn't help laughing.

"I already told yeh," Ballendir smiled. "Among mah clan, I'm considered quite the strategic thinker."

# TWENTY

As General Tarlach led his army out of the forest, he smiled to himself at the sight of a second company from the west waiting down in the valley before them. Though all soldiers wore the red and black armor of the empire, it was an odd complement of troops.

Six sixers of pictorians brought up the rear. They were loyal and solitary, but brutal. Tarlach corrected himself mentally: it wasn't so much that they were solitary, but that everyone else kept their distance.

In the middle was a mass of dwarves. Tarlach had requested at least three hundred, and he could make out six different regimental banners. If there were indeed the normal sixty soldiers in each regiment, then there were considerably more than he had requested.

He was impressed. Though the idea of training dwarves for the army was his, the credit for creating the program fell to General Shiftan, whose garrison was nearer dwarf populations and further from the eyes of others in the Empire.

Leading the dwarves and pictorians were two battalions of men, and then General Shiftan's command. Shiftan and Tarlach went back as far as the academy. They were part of an elite group of officers who pushed their way through the army's ranks. In their younger days, they had been a brotherhood led by Prince Shindell, the Emperor's brother, more famous for their partying than their feats in battle. But that had soon changed.

After Prince Shindell's death, the group had unofficially dispersed, but the bond was always there, and always strong. Tarlach spurred his horse ahead, excited to see his friend and anxious for news from home.

But he would have to wait for the latter. Shiftan came forward with six guards and his administrator. Bortand and six of his own guard were just as surely right behind Tarlach.

"Well met, General Tarlach," Shiftan said, saluting and smiling.

"Well met indeed, my friend," Tarlach replied, returning the salute. "You've brought a fine party with you."

"We are at your service. I think we're glad to leave the garrison, are we not, men?"

Heads nodded and murmured agreement.

"We're a couple of hours away from where my scouts have established a base camp. We shall talk there."

"Are we entering the mountains today?" Shiftan asked.

"No," Tarlach replied. "We'll camp at their base, spend tomorrow resting and strategizing, and attack the day after."

"Is there a danger of attack if we are that close and concede height to our enemies?"

"No. My scouts have established a perimeter on the first high ridge. But if you would like your scouts to go ahead, one of mine can take them."

"Your scouts are all rangers, no?"

"They are." Tarlach gestured to one sitting on a horse just behind his guards.

General Shiftan and the ranger nodded to each other. "If they're rangers, then I'm at ease. Lead on with your forces, General. May I suggest we dine tonight with our officers and catch up? My cooks have fresh meat with them and make the leanest cuts. There is much for us to discuss."

General Tarlach nodded. "I look forward to it. Until tonight, then."

The keenest observer might have wondered at the single spasm in Tarlach's left hand, but it was voluntary, and its intention understood only by his old friend: *Leanest cut. Message received.*

General Tarlach knew the guard on the evening sentry shift. He was an experienced and competent soldier, having faced the enemies of the empire without fear. He would probably prefer to face them again rather than the two figures that emerged out of the darkness and walked toward him.

The soldier snapped to attention. "General Tarlach, sir." He saluted and, seeing the other's insignia, said, "General . . . ?"

"This is General Shiftan," Tarlach said.

The soldier saluted again. "General Shiftan, sir. My cousin served with you until last year."

"He was with me in the Korfican campaign?" Shiftan inquired cordially.

"Yes, sir," the soldier replied, and Tarlach wasn't the only one impressed.

"Is he . . . ?"

"He was wounded, sir, and is back in Galbrieth. His wife just gave birth, sir."

"What is his name?" General Shiftan asked, now genuinely interested.

"Jiftmore, sir. Anderman Jiftmore."

"Please send him my congratulations. Is he able to work?"

"Yes, sir. He can't follow his father into blacksmithing because of the shoulder wound, sir, but he has service in a good family's house. And his army pension helps, sir."

"Good man," the general replied. "Have you eaten yet?"

"No, sir. But my shift is over soon. My friends will keep food for me."

"Go eat now," General Tarlach interceded. "You are relieved. Tell the next guard to stay in the mess tent. He will be sent for."

"Relieved, sir?" The man looked perplexed, no doubt wondering if this was a test.

"Do you doubt the ability of two of the Emperor's generals to fulfill your guard duty?" General Tarlach raised an eyebrow.

The man gulped, and Tarlach tried not to laugh. "Run along, man. There is roast duck, and it is better hot."

The man half saluted, half thanked him, and scampered away.

Shiftan sighed. "Do you remember the first days of the academy? We were scared, enthusiastic, and so arrogant. When did we become so intimidating, my friend?"

"When the stakes rose," Tarlach said, his eyes following the soldier's trail. "How was your leave in the capital? How are your wife and daughters? They must be fine, young women already."

"Indeed. I have doubled the guard around them. I would slaughter every young man in the capital if I could."

They both laughed. Shiftan glanced around and lowered his voice.

"I met with him. He understands. I know he visits with your father. That is a good sign, no?"

Tarlach nodded. "What are the rumors at the club?"

"That it would be wise if you brought this episode to an end, and quickly."

"Thank you."

"Are you worried about what is happening here?" Shiftan asked, concerned.

Tarlach didn't answer and instead took a swig from the flask he carried.

"What is it, Tarlach? I have seen you face hordes of savages, battalions of well-trained soldiers. What do you fear?"

"I fear nothing," Tarlach barked, and then stopped, surprised at his own venom. "Excuse me."

"Is it the Emperor's nephew? You don't have to worry. Let me handle him for you, old friend."

"Thank you, I'd prefer you did when the time comes. But it's not him."

"The elf company? They are youngsters, I hear."

Tarlach shook his head. "Do you remember the stories of the white-haired ones?"

"Yes. I used to beg my father to tell me stories of them. Great servants of the ancient Emperors who went on unbelievable quests and performed acts of heroism."

He laughed, momentarily lost in his childhood memories. Then he turned inquisitively when he realized there was a point to Tarlach's question.

"What is it, my friend?"

"The leader of this group is a white-haired one."

"What? Those were tales for children." Shiftan shrugged.

"No. They were memories, preserved through the passage of stories from generation to generation."

"You are saying this boy—"

"Elf," Tarlach corrected.

"You are saying that this young elf is a Wycaan Master?"

"Not a Master yet. His training was interrupted. He must not be allowed to become a Master. This is why the Emperor is on my back." He turned to face his friend. "This Wycaan elfling has the potential to bring down the empire."

"Does he know that?" Shiftan frowned.

"I hope not. And he must never be allowed to explore the full extent of his power."

# TWENTY ONE

Sellia crouched on a ledge, looking down at the army camp. Next to her, Shayth swore under his breath. She had wanted to come and estimate how many soldiers were down on the plains and, though the blow to her head had healed, the group had insisted someone go with her. She chose Shayth because of his stealth and silence.

She sighed. When she had first broached the idea that they should not stay by the lake, where they would be vulnerable to attack, she had seen Ilana's pained expression and was concerned that she wouldn't be heeded. But while she had been unconscious from the ranger attack, the others had apparently had a similar conversation. Tomorrow, they would move on. She turned to leave, but stopped when she heard Shayth gasp. He was still staring at the approaching army.

"What is it?" she asked.

"That's a lot of soldiers for a few . . ." his voice trailed off as he squinted into the distance. "Sellia, elves have better vision than humans, right?"

"Sure," she replied.

He pointed. "Can you make out the pictorians at the back on the right?"

"Yes," she replied. "Why?"

"And you see the humans in front near the banners?"

"Sure."

"There is a group between them. I was thinking how small they look compared to the pictorians, but now that I—"

"Dwarves!" she exclaimed. "They're dwarves."

"I wasn't aware that dwarves served in the Emperor's armies," Shayth said grimly. "I wonder if they have been trained secretly. Specifically."

They stared at each other.

"This changes everything," Sellia whispered. "We need to get back to the others."

"Why does this change everything?" Maugwen asked.

"We thought they were after us," Rhoddan replied, despondent. "We thought we could lead them away from here, away from Seanchai."

"And?"

"They haven't come for us," Ilana answered. "They've come for the dwarves. We've led them here. If the Emperor's dwarves can breach the defenses, Ballendir's people will be trapped. And so will . . ."

"What can we do?" Maugwen asked, her face suddenly pale.

"I-I don't know," Ilana answered.

"I can lead you all out of here," Jermona said. "Perhaps they will follow."

No one answered.

"You must trust me," he said louder. "I am a ranger."

Shayth whirled round and grabbed his collar, pulling him close so their noses were almost touching. "Whatever noble values you think your people hold, you're nothing more than highly-skilled and well-paid mercenaries."

"We kill nobody," Jermona protested. "They just proved that with Sellia."

"You don't shoot the arrow or stab with the sword, but you help an evil dictator massacre and oppress an entire land. And you do it for money."

Jermona's voice broke as he protested. "The Emperor is—"

"—is a murderer. He murdered his own brother and sister-in-law."

"They were pr—"

"They were my parents," Shayth's face flushed red and his voice increased in ferocity, freezing everyone in place. "Who's been paying you and your people for your services?"

"G-general Tarlach. He is a—"

"He is the man who betrayed me, who stood by while my parents — one of them his best friend — were murdered. And he continues to serve that very same murderer." Shayth tightened his grip on Jermona's shirt. "What were you going to tell me about him?"

The young ranger just stood there, hushed and helpless. It was Rhoddan who put a firm hand on Shayth's arm. Shayth glared at him, but Rhoddan didn't waiver.

"It's getting dark," Rhoddan murmured to Shayth. "Would you please take the first shift?"

Shayth slowly let go of Jermona, who slumped down on the rock behind him. Then Shayth picked up his bow and stalked off.

"We rise early," Rhoddan said. "Everyone either pack up or help cook these rabbits that Sellia caught. It might be the last hot meal for a while."

He took his knife out and went to the fire pit. Sellia joined him. She was smiling wryly.

"That was impressive," she said.

"What was?" Rhoddan had an embarrassing habit of blushing whenever Sellia spoke to him. He hoped the growing darkness concealed it this time.

"I'm not sure anyone else could stare him down."

"Ilana has," he said. "She grew close to him when they came to rescue me in Galbrieth. He has been through a lot — too much for someone who has not seen out two decades."

"You feel close to him, too, I think."

"I have fought alongside him. I would happily die alongside him."

Sellia laughed. "Ever the warrior, Rhoddan. Ever the warrior."

"AAAATAAACK!" The scream from Shayth was accompanied by the cries of men falling.

Ilana kicked out the fire and then ran towards the attack. Sellia grabbed her bow and threw her quiver over her shoulders, then tied Jermona's hands and feet.

"I can help," he protested.

"No, you can't." She glared at him before turning to Maugwen, who stood rigid with fear. She gave the girl a small, sharp knife from her boot. "Guard him. If he tries to speak, stuff something in his mouth. If he tries to escape, kill him."

Maugwen's eyes widened.

"Sellia," Jermona said. "If this is the advance, then they might have come for me."

"To kill you, or to rescue you?"

Good question, he thought.

Sellia left them and joined Rhoddan in his battle with two soldiers. She noched an arrow and shot the one closest through the neck. The other turned toward her, giving Rhoddan the opportunity to parry the soldier's swing and stab him under the breastplate. Sellia moved on and landed arrows in the pair Ilana was fending off.

A horn blew, and the two or three soldiers still standing scurried to retreat. Shayth roared and charged, but Ilana cried out to him.

"Stop, Shayth! You don't know what's there."

Rhoddan grabbed him as he passed, and Sellia drew her bow at the last retreating soldier. She hit him, but he managed to keep running. She cursed. Ilana reached them.

"That was feeble," she said.

"No," Shayth panted, his adrenaline still racing. "They know how many we are. They know that Seanchai and the dwarves have gone, and maybe even that Jermona is still alive, if they even care. I think they achieved their goals."

"Let's get some sleep," Rhoddan said. "We'll double the guard and move out before dawn."

"No," said a deep voice from behind. "I don't think yeh will."

They all spun, reaching for their weapons. Before them stood three dwarves, stout and covered with armor, their axes still sheathed.

"We're from Ballendir's clan and been sent to take yeh to a safer place," one said. "Our clan council thought we should move yeh before the advance arrived. I regret that we showed up late to the party."

# TWENTY TWO

Seanchai slept deeply, so when Ballendir came to wake him just an hour or so into his slumber, he was hard-pressed to rise. The little cave was barely large enough for the straw bedding. He sat up, and Ballendir crouched next to him. He glanced back at the guards.

"Move to the other side there, lads. Yeh can still see him, but I must council the Wycaan in private."

The guards obliged without a word, and Ballendir turned so that his back was to them.

"This isn't going to be easy, mah friend. I have broken the First Decree, an iron law by bringing yeh here. I have also given up the secrecy that we have held here for decades. Neither is appreciated."

He shifted his weight into a more comfortable crouch.

"Dwarves put great value in history and tradition. We don't change fast, and we don't appreciate young dwarves with new ideas."

"Is that also your claim to fame?" Seanchai asked, smiling.

Ballendir sidestepped this remark, too focused to veer off track. "This is about yeh learning fast how dwarves think. They aren't happy with yeh and what yeh've done, and so far, yeh haven't addressed them.

"Take it slow, Seanchai, and don't lose yeh temper. But yeh must stand firm. Do yeh know what yeh want from us?"

"Your allegiance. If I can recruit the free elves and the humans, I want the dwarves to stand with us."

"What will we get for that? Why should we risk our lives?"

"To be free. To be able to live above ground if you want, and to trade freely."

Ballendir frowned. "We're not in the same position as the elves. Most of our people are free. Yeh'll need to refine this point."

A shuffle outside signaled that they had company. Ballendir straightened up. Seanchai stood, as well, and promptly banged his head on the low ceiling.

"Ouch!"

The others laughed good-naturedly.

"Ballendir has been coaching yeh?" asked the dwarf who now stood before them.

Seanchai glanced at his friend and then back to the other dwarf. "Yes, he has, and I value his guidance."

"It's good that you listen to advice. Come. We're ready for yeh."

They followed a corridor that turned into another cavern. This one was brightly lit and decorated with shields and axes. The walls were also covered with woven materials and a big, silver horn.

In the middle of the cavern was a table fashioned from a round, smooth slab of rock. It was a shiny gray, and Seanchai couldn't help from running a hand over it. This was met with a cough and raised eyebrows from Ballendir. Seanchai removed his hand. The table had twelve smoothed edges for place settings. In front of each setting was a carved rock cube meant for sitting. When Seanchai sat, he felt more like he was squatting.

The council members' hair and beards ranged from gray to white, and their faces were lined with age. Ballendir sat next to Seanchai, and opposite them was Ophera. She met Seanchai's eyes momentarily before looking away.

Seanchai suddenly noticed that everyone else was staring at him. He smiled and squirmed in his seat.

"You are young," said a heavyset dwarf to Ophera's left. "Young and far from home."

"Indeed," Seanchai said, not sure how to continue.

He didn't have to. A flurry of activity followed as dwarves poured into the cavern, laden with trays of food. Seanchai felt his stomach rumble. But as he surveyed the food, he saw a lot of dark, heavy meat.

The dwarves began to pile up their plates, and a hum rose. Only Seanchai and the Ophera did not take food. She rose and came behind him and Ballendir. She whispered into the dwarf's ear and Ballendir stopped eating and turned to his guest.

"Excuse mah manners, Seanchai. I haven't seen such a feast as this in months. I thought yeh eat meat?"

"I do," Seanchai said. "But only the white meat of fish and bird."

"Yeh ate rabbits when we were traveling. Was that because yeh had no choice?"

Seanchai nodded and Ballendir relayed this to Ophera. She took Seanchai's plate and filled it with vegetables and something that looked like meat. She then signaled to a dwarf standing by the door and whispered in his ear. He disappeared and soon returned with some cheese and bread. This he set down near Seanchai.

"Thank you," Seanchai said to Ophera.

"Those," Ballendir pointed to the dark food on Seanchai's plate, "are pertroba mushrooms. They help to build yeh body and muscles. Those red ones are . . . I don't know how to translate it; something like 'steak imitator.' Taste it. Yeh won't believe it's not from a mighty beast."

"You eat a lot of mushrooms because you live underground?"

A redheaded dwarf on Seanchai's other side answered. "We use mushrooms for many things. The variety of species we have are good not only as food, but for medicine, poisons, and even dyes."

"Poisons?"

"Didn't yeh mother warn yeh not to eat mushrooms yeh can't identify?"

Seanchai nodded, saddened by the thought of his mother and whether or not she even lived. Ophera said something quietly, and the redheaded dwarf nodded.

"I'm sorry. Did I bring up painful memories?"

"Yes," Seanchai replied, "but not about mushrooms."

When the food was finished, the clan chief called out, and the dishes were removed. Bread and cheese were left, and flagons of ale were brought in. Many of the dwarves – Ballendir included – took out pipes.

Rothendir, the clan chief, turned to Seanchai. "Do yeh not smoke?"

Seanchai grimaced. "Ballendir has taught me, but I have no pipe."

The dwarves all stared at him as though he had told them he lacked an arm. They shook their heads in disbelief, and Rothendir turned to Ballendir.

"I assume you plan to rectify this?" she said sternly.

Ballendir nodded. "We've been a little distracted," he offered, but it was clearly not enough.

"The ale is good for me, thank you," assured Seanchai. "Please do not worry–"

"He will need a tall stem for one of his size," Rothendir continued, looking critically at Ballendir.

"He's an elf and should have an elf pipe." The red-haired dwarf added.

Again, they all nodded. Seanchai was feeling impatient and, as he gulped the ale, a little lightheaded. He put his pewter cup down rather too hard, and the room went silent. He looked around, knowing he had their attention and that he had to make it count.

"We need to talk," he said firmly.

# TWENTY THREE

S eanchai rose from his seat and surveyed the dwarves sitting around the great stone table. He resisted the urge to stretch his cramped muscles.

"My name is Seanchai, son of Seantai. I fled my home in Mothian Wood when the Emperor's army came to conscript me. I have powers, as Ballendir has said, or, rather, I serve as a channel – a conduit, if you will – for the energy in the earth and all around us. I possess the ability to channel this energy. It is how I kept Ellendir alive.

"Many humans and elves worked together to send me on a dangerous journey to a great teacher, Mhari, who trained me to understand and use these powers. Before her teachings were complete, my friends – those we left nearby – were captured by the Emperor's army. I went to Galbrieth, a large garrison that houses General Tarlach's troops. There, together with my Master and Tutan allies, I rescued them from public execution, and we brought down one side of the Galbrieth fortress.

"You see that my hair is white, yet I am young. My body is toned as a warrior, yet as has been pointed out, I am still a *calhei* – a young elf."

Seanchai paused, took a sip of ale, and looked around the table.

"Let me tell you a story. Once upon a time, there was a great alliance; a bond among all races. That alliance lasted for more than ten thousand years and was a time of prosperity and friendship. I'm sure your race has stories of this time, much like humans and elves."

He paused to look at each of them and was met with nods of acknowledgement.

"The guardians of the Alliance were Wycaans. They came from each race and were trained to wield the power of energy. They were teachers, healers, and warriors. In my time with Mhari, I went through a transformation, and had a vision of the Alliance being rebuilt. I dream about it at night, seeing what I hope is a possibility for the future.

"I ask you to join me to help reforge the Alliance and stand against an evil despot who subjugates all our people."

"Our people are not oppressed," one dwarf said. "We live under our mountains as free dwarves."

There was a murmur of agreement.

"Underground," Seanchai said, his tone flat.

"Yes," the same dwarf said. "We are dwarves. Dwarves live underground."

"I have seen, in my visions, the city of Dur-Rhustan," Seanchai replied, and there was a murmur around the table. "I have seen dwarves living in the great city, serving as rulers of the land in their turn. I have no qualms with a dwarf who chooses to live underground. That is, one who *truly* chooses to live underground.

"But when a dwarf lives underground in secret, when the famed hospitality of your race is not extended to all who pass, when dwarves rarely come above ground to trade in the light, when they scurry around in secret," he pointed at Ballendir, "then I suspect there is a thin line between *living* underground and *hiding* underground. When the First Decree is the first welcome, then I question your claim to be free."

There was a murmur again, distinctly less pleasant than before, but Seanchai held up his hand.

"There may or may not be dwarves who live in servitude to the Emperor. I don't know. But I do know that if your people *tried* to live above ground, they would have a hard time, as we elves and many humans do.

"And I think you know it, which is why you go to such great lengths to keep your people safe and out of the Emperor's line of vision. But I wonder: what if the Emperor discovered that there were dwarves living here and elsewhere, not acknowledging his rule and not paying his taxes? What if, once the Emperor defeats the final remnants of the rebellion, he begins to look for a new enemy to conquer?"

He returned to his seat and took another sip of ale, careful just to wet his throat.

"The way I see it, you have two choices: You can join the Alliance and stand together with the rest of the dwarf nation, the free men, and the elves. Or, you can sit in the dark, watch from the shadows, and wait. But know that you will be called to fight eventually. Your decision isn't about whether or not to fight; it is about when and with whom. Think well upon how you will fare if you stand alone?"

Several discussions broke out at once. The clan's chief banged her pewter mug on the table, and the room fell into silence. One dwarf stood.

"We should not listen to his words. Our nation is spread throughout Odessiya. Our people live in well-fortified caverns. Only another dwarf could break through our defenses."

"Really?" Seanchai asked. "How can you be so sure?"

"You saw how small our tunnels are, how they curve. They won't allow anyone bigger than a dwarf to fight."

"So they blow the tunnels up," the elf shrugged.

The dwarf slapped his hand on the rock he was sitting in. "These are dense rocks. You need to know what you're doing. You need to understand stone. Only a dwarf . . ."

He trailed off, and they all watched as Seanchai stood and stared at the rock cube he had been sitting on. It *was* heavy and dense, but he used his training to leverage his weight against the ground. He picked up the stone cube and put it on the beautiful table, which solicited murmurs of surprise from many and a groan of despair from Ballendir. Seanchai laid his hand on the rock and closed his eyes. He began his breathing.

"Are you planning to chop it?" sneered the dwarf who had been arguing with Seanchai. "I will summon our healer to put your hand back together."

Some laughed, but most just stared at Seanchai. He opened his eyes and looked around. When he addressed those directly in front of him, he scarcely recognized his own voice. "Please step away from the table and stand behind me."

Only Ophera followed his advice. She was sitting directly opposite him. Ballendir also rose, though he was standing next to Seanchai. Seanchai's body was suffused in warmth, and his palms vibrated. He moved his hands behind him and shifted his weight to his back foot. Then he pushed his hands forward, shifting momentum to his front foot – it was a blur to everyone watching.

The cube flew across the table and straight into the opposing wall, smashing to bits on impact. Many of the dwarves dove for cover. Seanchai calmly walked around and picked up a small slab. As the dwarves stared at him, he tore it apart with his bare hands. Then he turned and inspected the dent and cracks in the wall.

"Sorry about that," he said, tossing a small rock in his hand. "You're right; it really is a very dense rock."

He returned to where his seat used to be and was wondering whether he could request another cube to sit on when he saw that a breathless dwarf had entered the cavern. He was whispering furiously into the clan chief's ear.

After a moment, Rothendir looked around and announced, "There is an army assembling in the valley. Already they have sent scouting parties into the mountains." She looked at Seanchai. "We have moved your friends for their own safety."

Seanchai suppressed a desire to ask if they were unharmed. Rothendir had not finished.

"There are many men and a host of pictorians."

"I'd like to see them trolls try and enter our seams," said the dwarf who had objected before, more out of bravado than actual confidence.

"The pictorians will not enter the tunnels," Rothendir replied evenly, her voice taut. "Many dwarves march in their ranks."

The room erupted into cries of disbelief. Seanchai could only watch as the volume grew. Then he noticed Ballendir stand and smash his pewter down on the table. Instantly the room went quiet.

"Our Lady, the Priestess of Hothengold," he announced, "wishes to speak."

All eyes in the cavern moved to Ophera.

# TWENTY FOUR

Seanchai leaned against the cavern wall and watched the council settle down. He had a distinct feeling that with the arrival of this news, he was no longer a participant in the conversation. He had made his request and the dwarves had to make their own decision now.

He looked across at Ophera, whom he thought until just recently was a servant to Ballendir's family. Bringing her here must have been the mission Ballendir wouldn't acknowledge.

When she spoke, her soft voice resonated through the cavern. She had his and the dwarves' absolute attention. More dwarves entered and stood against the walls to listen to their spiritual leader.

"Many, many years ago, our clan brought me here to be your guide. Throughout our long and proud history, the priestesses have served our people with teaching, healing, and guidance. In the richest of times, we served as the foundation of renaissance. In the darkest of times, our counsel has kept the dwarf nation alive."

She glanced at Seanchai. "Now heed my words. I have observed this young elf both as a warrior and a healer. I have seen him dispense of pictorians and wolfheids with swords and raw power – energy that he yielded without the use of stones. Even in the greatest intensity of battle, I saw how he looked out for his friends. And, despite leaving the battlefield exhausted, he always came straight over to help heal my acolyte, Ellendir, expending whatever energy he had left to keep her alive. He is driven by friendship and principles.

"Our people have a rich history, but never was it richer than when we lived at one with our neighbors in the days of the Great Alliance, when the Wycaan Masters were the stewards of the land of Odessiya. Of this I have read and also seen in dream quests. I know it to be true."

She looked around the room, challenging any who might disagree. Her voice grew stronger.

"Long have our people lived away from the light of the empire. We justify our isolation from the races because of the great betrayal and excuse ourselves because neither this despotic Emperor nor his fathers before him were directly hurting us.

"Yet now we hear that this Emperor has conscripted dwarves and trained them to fight other dwarves. A conscript is a slave, and our people are no longer safe above or below the earth."

There was a murmur and nodding of heads.

"It is true that we have built formidable defenses here. But we designed these defenses to fight man and pictorian. Do we stand and fight fellow dwarves who serve against their will? Has that ever been a part of our proud history?"

Again, she scanned the room, seeing a mix of discord and confusion.

"We will prepare for battle, even as we also prepare to leave. We shall engage the enemy, for we must ascertain that a dwarf will indeed raise axe against another dwarf on the orders of a human ruler.

"The young who have trained for war will test their mettle alongside the elders. The families will begin to evacuate." She looked over at Seanchai. "You and your friends will stay and fight alongside us. It is important that you prove your loyalty."

Seanchai nodded.

"We will gradually collapse the mountain. The young soldiers and the elf's company will flee through the tunnels of the Great Low Way, along the serpent's trail, to the capital at Hothengold. Ballendir, you will lead them. I will tend to Ellendir as best I can."

The dwarf nodded, though Seanchai could feel his sadness.

"Tonight we will send five of our swiftest messengers out to each of the great clans, telling of what has transpired and summoning them to the capital."

"Do you think they will come, Mother?" the red-haired dwarf asked.

"We will declare a Clansfelt," she said coldly, and her face hardened. "It is binding to all."

Now the buzz grew louder.

"But one has not been called for over fifty years!" someone exclaimed in amazement.

"Indeed," Ophera replied patiently. "It has been far too long. But a decision must be made, and it involves all the clans." She stared at Seanchai. "If we are to answer the call of the Wycaan, it must be with the strength and unity of the entire dwarf nation."

General Tarlach strode into his command tent, thankful to be out of the incessant rain that hadn't ceased once since they arrived in the valley below the Bordan Mountains. General Shiftan had offered to lead the raid against Shayth and the elf's company to determine where the dwarves were and what they were facing for the full-blown battle. If the confrontation had escalated, Shiftan would be on-hand to kill Shayth.

Now, as he waited to receive a report from this raid, Tarlach was pretty sure he was ready to kill the boy himself. His wife and son were in danger, as was the flawless military reputation he had worked so hard to build. But he was secretly grateful that Shiftan was willing to deal with Shayth. He was a good friend.

When the general entered, half a dozen officers snapped to attention. He found Shiftan and a ranger crouching over a map that was fast becoming a model as soldiers built paths and ridges.

"General Shiftan," Tarlach said.

His friend straightened up. "Aah, General Tarlach. This is Mialano, my chief ranger. He has been with me for three years now. Mialano, if you please?"

"General Tarlach, sir. We attacked the camp as planned, engaging the enemy with two human sixers. General Shiftan and I observed from this point, along with two other sixers ready to fight." His finger touched the map. "Two additional rangers were at the point of contact, though they did not engage the enemy directly.

"We were quickly able to ascertain that the lead elf and the dwarves had already left the camp. With two others, I followed their trail.

"We tracked them to the dwarf stronghold, but could see no way in without being detected. I believe that it will be difficult for humans to enter and impossible for pictorians. I have rangers scouting the mountain to determine if there are additional entrances."

"Very good," Tarlach replied. "General Shiftan, what are your recommendations?"

"We must first attack with the dwarves," General Shiftan said. "It will be a devastating blow for those inside, who likely built their defenses narrow enough only to impede humans and pictorians. We will try and take the outer defenses with our dwarves. Once we reach bigger caverns, we can send in our men and pictorians.

"I have a few additional surprises, General Tarlach. We have brought explosives – enough to cave in the outer defenses – and a team of dwarves who specialize in this work. Once we have opened up the narrow tunnels, they will feel the full strength of our forces."

"When shall we attack?"

"The rangers brought back rock samples. Our scientists need to examine them to decide what type and strength of explosive is required. They are doing that now and will pack several explosive packages for us. I suggest we plan to attack at dawn in two days."

"How much explosives have you brought with you?" General Tarlach asked, intrigued.

Shiftan smiled. "I wanted to ensure we had more than enough. If you prefer, we can just flatten the mountain altogether."

The tent rang with laughter and, for a few moments, Tarlach could no longer hear the rain pounding on the tent.

# TWENTY FIVE

Dwarves bustled around Seanchai, each busy with a task. Everyone but him, that was. He stood in the first cavern, waiting and wishing he had something constructive to do. Ballendir had told Seanchai his friends would meet him there.

He had visited Ellendir earlier, but the healers would not let him help on Ophera's instruction.

"Conserve and build up your energy," the priestess had said. "You will need every last bit of it in the coming weeks."

Seanchai wandered aimlessly and restlessly about the cavern. He ran to help a young dwarf who dropped a barrel full of small, round rocks.

"Not you, sire," the young dwarf said reverently. "The priestess won't allow it."

"Seanchai! Seanchai!"

Seanchai's annoyance disappeared as his heart leapt. Ilana fell into his arms and he held her tight, inhaling her fragrance. She pulled away from him, blushing. He felt only slightly repentant.

"My name is Rhoddan; I don't believe we've been introduced." Rhoddan stood there, formally offering a hand.

Seanchai grinned and embraced his friend, both of them laughing. Then he turned to Shayth, who pointed his bow at Seanchai.

"Don't even think about it," Shayth threatened, eyes smiling.

Immediately, a number of axes suddenly appeared precariously close to Shayth, not noticing that there was no arrow noched in his bow.

"He's joking," Seanchai said, and the axes dropped with a collective sigh of relief. Seanchai couldn't resist a jab: "Anyway, he's a lousy aim. He would have missed me from that distance."

The cavern reverberated with laughter, easing the heavy tension permeating the place.

"Hey. Need I remind you that *my* aim is true?" said a female voice from behind as Seanchai led them all to the adjacent cavern.

Seanchai turned to see beautiful, dark Sellia, hands on arched hips, and a bump on her head.

His smile vanished. "What happened?"

"We'll tell you inside," she said.

"Seems like you've made yourself a few friends," Shayth patted his shoulders. "Why doesn't that surprise me?"

But they didn't get to talk for long, because Ballendir entered with the priestess.

"Welcome, one and all," he said. "Excuse mah briskness. Seanchai, the priestess wants to take yeh deeper into our home. I will stay and bring yeh friends up-to-date."

"The priestess?" Shayth's question expressed the surprise on each of their faces.

"Like I said," Ballendir grinned. "I'll bring yeh up-to-date."

Ophera pointed to Ilana.

"You share a special bond with the Wycaan," she said softly. "You may join us."

Seanchai and Ilana followed her through a series of tunnels deeper into the mountain. The priestess walked slowly but surely, leaning on a staff that Seanchai hadn't ever seen her use before. He wondered if it was ceremonial.

They turned through a narrow corridor into a cave full of raised beds, some occupied. Seanchai saw Ellendir and went to her. Her eyes were open, and she smiled feebly when she saw him. She struggled to raise a hand, and Seanchai gently took it. With considerable effort, she opened her mouth to speak.

"Conserve yeh energy, mah child," a large, matronly dwarfe said from the other side of the bed. "Yeh want the elf to know that yeh appreciate his healing. I'm sure he knows."

Seanchai nodded, but this did not appease Ellendir. She shook her head. Seanchai bent over her, and she whispered slowly, forcing each word out.

"Thank . . . yeh . . . for . . . returning . . . the priestess . . . to mah . . . people."

"You are welcome for that, as well," Seanchai said. "Be strong, so that you may continue to serve her and your clan."

Ellendir smiled and breathed easier. The priestess took Seanchai's arm and gently guided him into the next room. Seanchai gaped – it was an apothecary. He stared at bunches of herbs hanging from the low ceiling, bound and drying. Along one wall was a huge wooden cabinet with hundreds of small drawers. On a large stone table, there were herbs at different stages of preparation and Seanchai picked up a mortar and pestle, thinking of his mother.

"I wish we had time to teach you our ways and plants," Ophera said. "But I do have something for you." She turned and called to another elf, who gave her a small leather pouch. "Thank you," she said, and handed the pouch to Seanchai.

"The herb you drink is known to us. We call it ruzakil, or 'old dwarf on the mountain'. I saw that your supplies are running low. It does not grow around here, but hopefully you will be able to find some in Hothengold.

"What we *do* have here is a mushroom that we dry and slice." She patted the pouch. "Do not let it go to powder, for you must not ingest the mushroom itself, only drink it as a tea. It is called Kombuqua, or 'old dwarf under the mountain'. It's similar to ruzakil . . . especially in the taste, I'm afraid."

"You're very generous," Seanchai replied.

"I am very practical. I need you to be at your peak. Come, I have two more surprises for you."

She took Seanchai and Ilana down a steep staircase that hugged a wall. It was very damp, and Seanchai noticed that there was fungus on the wall glowing red. They used its light to guide their way. At the bottom was a small lake.

"I think you know what to do here," she said. "You are not the first Wycaan to sense the power under the mountain. This is what drew you here, no?"

Seanchai's mouth dropped open as he gazed at the lay lake.

"Go into the water," she said. "We will sit here with our backs to you. It is the most privacy I can offer."

Seanchai walked to the lake's edge. He hadn't felt energy like this since he was in the cavern with Mhari for his transformation. He stripped off his clothes and walked into the freezing water until he was completely submerged. He gave himself up to the water, feeling it flow through his body, relaxing and invigorating him at the same time.

When he came out of the lake, he dried off with his shirt. Even in this simple act, his muscles were stretched and powerful. He touched the skin of his face and found it taut and smooth. As he approached the women, he saw Ilana's awed expression. He felt good.

As he drew closer, however, he saw her eyes were red. Ophera had an arm around her. Now, as he sat with them, they separated and watched him.

Seanchai looked at the old priestess. "You said other Wycaans have used this pool. Have you seen them yourself?"

"I am very old," she said, nodding. "Older than I look, I hope."

"Who were they? Were they elves, dwarves, humans?"

"I met your Master," she said. "A beautiful woman in her youth. I grieve for her and your loss. But the one I remember most dearly was my mate for a short while. He was badly wounded and feared to be taken alive by the Emperor at the time. If he is still alive, I do not know. It is difficult being the mate of a Wycaan." She patted Ilana's hand.

"Is that what you were talking about? Is that why Ilana was crying?"

"So many questions. Can two females not bond? Ah, we have so little time. This is my third and final gift to you."

She reached under her cloak and produced another leather pouch. From it, she carefully spilled out several stones onto her lap. "We dwarves wield our energy through stones. These are mine. Now, Wycaan, I give them to you. That is, all but one."

"I can't take them. Especially not now."

"I plan to collapse the mountain, Seanchai, once the general's army is inside. I will be under it, as I have been for most of my life. Ellendir will take my place, and she already has her stones. I have planned a way for her to live, but I will not share it, so don't ask. Please," she raised a hand to stem his attempted objections, "there is no time, and I am content with my decision.

"You will learn the power of these rocks in due time. But these are a pair." She gave one smooth, green stone to Ilana and the other to Seanchai. "Guard these well. No Wycaan and his mate have ever been able to stay together in times of strife. Their stories are full of romance, but often have tragic endings, I'm sorry to say."

"What do these stones do?" Ilana asked.

"When you are separated, even at opposite ends of Odessiya, the stones will help you find each other."

"Thank you," Ilana said and hugged her.

"Thank you," Seanchai echoed. "How do they work?"

The old priestess raised her head from Ilana's shoulder. "I don't know. I've never used them."

"What?" said Ilana. "If you were the mate of this Wycaan dwarf—"

"He made me swear not to use them to find him."

"Why?" Seanchai asked.

Ophera gazed at him for a moment, pained, and then sighed. "Because he truly loved me."

# TWENTY SIX

The first wave attacked at dawn. The horn of Zu'Reisin was blown, its long, deep notes reverberated through the tunnels. The battle of Bordan had begun.

Seanchai leaped from his bedding, quickly packed his bags, and swung his dual sword harness around his body in one smooth, well-practiced movement. Next to him, Ilana and Shayth were similarly preparing.

Rhoddan and Sellia were sleeping with an advance unit at the perimeter where the guards rotated. Maugwen had left with the families and elderly dwarves. She had been reluctant to leave, but Rhoddan was adamant that she would be of little use in a fight and might endanger the rest of the company when they retreated. Speed and endurance was their only chance for survival.

Seanchai worried about his own usefulness fighting in these narrow tunnels. He was trained to swing his swords, which required space.

Ballendir stood in the corridor outside their cave, barking orders and directing dwarves to various positions. He watched Ilana and Shayth run past him.

"Where's the other human? Where's the ranger lad?" he asked.

"I let him go," Seanchai replied.

Ballendir shook his head in disbelief. "Why?"

"I won't force Jermona to fight with us. It would make us no better than the Emperor, conscripting and forcing people to fight their neighbors. I don't want him in a position where he has to choose sides.

"If he is telling the truth, then he will flee to his ranger village. If he is a spy, as you all think, then he will be where we can see him."

"And then yeh can kill him?"

Seanchai nodded.

"I'm glad to know that," Ballendir said and smiled. But then his grin disappeared. "Seanchai, yeh'll need to be ruthless. This is going to be close-contact fighting: slashing and stabbing. Do yeh understand? Yeh have knives, no? Let mah see them."

Seanchai showed Ballendir his long and short elf knives. It had been a while since he had used them, but Rhoddan had made him constantly sharpen them. He took a deep breath. "Let's go. Your people should see us at the helm."

"Seanchai," Ballendir squeezed his arm. "Ma people need to see yah as a leader in battle. Be loud, yeh understand? They will follow yah, as will I."

The first to come were broad, stocky dwarves, covered with chain metal and bearing the red and black of the Emperor. Resistance archers, including Shayth and Sellia, cut them down from above as they filed through the narrow gorge to the cave entrance. When the archers' arrows were exhausted, they hurled rocks down with surprising accuracy. Seanchai watched, yelling encouragement, as the remaining troops in the first wave retreated.

They were quickly replaced by a second wave holding their shields above their heads in a solid, interlacing cover. Arrows and rocks alike were ineffective and bounced off the shields. The larger rocks knocked several soldiers to their knees, creating a hole for the archers' arrows, but it wasn't enough.

Seanchai watched, knowing that this group would reach their ground troops. He turned to send a messenger to Ballendir and saw several soldiers surreptitiously scaling up the side of the mountain. Two were already on the ridge preparing to spring on the archers.

"Shayth!" he cried. "Draw your sword. We must hold this ridge as long as possible."

As he was out in the open, Seanchai drew his swords and charged with Shayth only a few paces behind him. They threw the first few soldiers off the ledge and engaged two pictorians who had scrambled up the steep incline onto the plateau. Seanchai ducked under one's massive broadsword and stabbed the huge creature in the side between his armor plating.

As he pushed the giant over the rock face, Seanchai gasped. The whole mountainside was a mass of human and pictorian soldiers.

"Sellia," he yelled. "Get them back. No, get them over here with whatever rocks are left."

The dwarves scurried over and threw the remaining rocks onto the soldiers climbing. It would buy only a little more time. Another horn blew and a dwarf grabbed Seanchai's arm.

"We must go back. They want to close the gates."

Seanchai turned and called out. "Follow me to the entrance." Then he grabbed the dwarf who had just spoken to him. "Do you know the best way?"

The dwarf nodded tersely and set off with Seanchai close behind. Seanchai glanced back as Sellia and Shayth shot their remaining arrows at the soldiers climbing the ridge.

As they approached the entrance back into the mountain, they encountered enemy dwarves and humans who had lowered their shields to advance.

"Archers!" Seanchai cried.

A dozen dwarves pushed to the front and brought down several rows of the enemy before their supplies of arrows were exhausted.

"Axes!" They pulled their bows over their shoulders and drew their axes.

"With me," Seanchai commanded, and raised his swords. Battle cries left their lips as they charged into the thick.

The soldiers, now surrounded, fell quickly and Seanchai led his troops back into the mountain.

Once behind the gate, clanking chains quickly lowered the heavy iron grate. Several dwarves pulled levers on both sides, releasing huge rocks that rolled down on either side of the gate to reinforce it.

Seanchai helped escort two wounded dwarves inside and passed them to the care of the healers. Ilana, Ballendir, and Rothendir joined Seanchai, Shayth, and Sellia.

"How did yeh fare?" Ballendir asked.

"We couldn't hold as long as we'd hoped," Seanchai replied, panting for breath. "There must be thousands swarming the mountainside."

"How did *yeh* fight?" Ballendir asked.

"It was all out in the open."

"He was very authoritative," Sellia said. "What's in that mushroom tea you've been giving him?"

They all laughed and Ballendir gave Seanchai an approving nod.

"The dwarves on the opposing side?" They all turned when Ophera spoke from behind them. "Was there any remorse or hesitation in their fighting?"

"No," said the soldier who had guided them in from outside. "They were disciplined and determined soldiers of the Empire. They did all that was expected of them."

"There are many out there," Sellia said. "I don't know how long we can hold."

"Just a little longer," the priestess answered. "We must give those who evacuated a little more time."

"Let them come!" someone cried. "It doesn't matter how many they are. They have many obstacles to break through and even then, they can only come one dwarf at a time!"

The dwarves raised their axes and cheered. But a large explosion sent many to the ground. A second explosion was quickly followed by a third. Dust and sunlight beamed through the reinforcements around the gate.

Shayth looked at the priestess and smiled grimly. "Exactly how much time do you need?"

# TWENTY SEVEN

Ophera didn't flinch. She turned to Ballendir, who looked just as shocked as everyone else.

"Back to the second hall." When he didn't respond, she slapped Ballendir's arm to jar him out of his daze. "Call them back to the second hall." She turned to grab Ilana's shoulder and addressed her more gently. "Help me back, Ilana."

By this time, Ballendir had come out of his stupor and was barking orders, keeping archers up on rock ledges as the last line of defense while the rest of the clan retreated. He called to Seanchai.

"Get back, elf. We need to keep you safe."

Seanchai frowned.

"He's not very good at leaving friends behind," Rhoddan said from his other side, a wry smile on his face.

"It's incredibly annoying," Shayth said, drawing his own bow. "Get used to it."

"And infectious, I think," Ballendir observed. "Let's have some fun while the others retreat."

The first enemy dwarves that appeared through the dust didn't get a chance to absorb the uncommon sight as dwarf, elf and human confronted them in a unified front. Gradually, humans replaced dwarves and several pictorians dragged themselves through. The dwarf colony was soon reeling before such overwhelming numbers.

From behind Ballendir, Seanchai and the others came a cry to fall back, followed by a blast of the horn.

Once through the arch to the second cavern, another iron gate slammed down heavily, the chains that held it whirling through the air. More boulders were released on either side.

"They dare to use explosives in our mountain!" cried Rothendir.

Then she smiled and nodded to two dwarves up on a ledge. They pushed down on a lever as everyone covered their ears. Seanchai copied them and braced himself for what was next, but the bang was startling and echoed throughout the corridors, cave walls, and in his ears.

Rothendir instructed her clan excitedly, "Take new positions! We defend the second hall."

Dwarves scurried all around. Ballendir signaled for Seanchai's crew to follow him to a higher ledge. On the way he grabbed a bundle of arrows and threw them to Shayth. Sellia was behind them and grabbed another. She turned to Seanchai.

"Bring a couple more. I would hate to suddenly have nothing to do."

Seanchai grinned in spite of himself. His friends seemed remarkably calm. Perhaps this was all under control. Then a string of explosions reached them from the outside.

"Why so far away?" Seanchai asked.

"Must be widening the tunnels," Ballendir replied, furrowing his brow. "They need the room to get more troops through."

Tense silence fell heavy, and broke when they heard scrambling sounds from just outside the gate. A thundering explosion blew the gate to smithereens, and soldiers poured through while the flash blinded Seanchai and the others.

Ballendir called a hail of arrows down upon the soldiers. Sellia shot arrow after arrow in rapid succession, reloading her bow just as fast as Seanchai could pass them to her.

A gasp erupted as the still-standing soldiers made room for a huge creature. The troll hulked in on all fours but then rose on two feet, towering many feet above the stubby dwarves, its thick, gray, leathery muscles lending power to the huge club it brandished. It didn't seem to care who its target was, and the Emperor's soldiers retreated warily behind it.

Sellia and Shayth were the first to react, though their arrows barely pierced its tough skin. It looked up, saw the company on the ledge, and roared as it charged them.

Seanchai felt a wave of panic but steadied himself with a deep breath. "The eyes," he yelled. "Shoot for the eyes!"

Sellia answered the call immediately, hitting the troll's left eye and sending it roaring backward. It flailed and pulled the arrow out, along with its eye. It resumed its advance, rolling its head and baying for revenge.

"Shayth," Sellia yelled. "Shoot the other eye."

The troll was ready for it this time, though, and batted Shayth's arrow away. Sellia moved next to him and fired a second arrow. The troll could not react in time. It fell, crushing two soldiers underneath its massive weight.

Seanchai leapt down from the ledge, almost fifteen feet. He cut through the four remaining human soldiers before leaping on and stabbing the fallen troll. The troll thrashed in pain and sent Seanchai rolling off of him. It tried to rise but collapsed, lifeless.

A cheer went up from the clan, but died quickly as two more trolls entered the cavern. Ballendir echoed Seanchai's earlier order to aim for the eyes. The troll nearest Seanchai staggered under the barrage, giving Seanchai an opening to jump onto his back and slice with his sword. He then jumped off the falling troll but landed too close to the third one.

Seanchai rolled to avoid its club, but hit his head on a rock in the process. He shook the dizzy feeling, but the troll didn't bother raising his club now that Seanchai was on the ground. A massive foot kicked out and sent Seanchai flying into a wall, his swords flying from his hands.

Now the troll advanced on him, club high above its head. Seanchai tried to summon power, but was weakened and the troll barely staggered.

Ilana climbed down behind the troll, trying to gather Seanchai's swords, but was too far away to help. Suddenly, though his sight was fuzzy and his ears ringing, Seanchai heard a clear voice inside his head.

*"The blue stone, Seanchai. Channel your power through the
blue stone."*

Seanchai reached blindly to the pouch and instinctively drew the blue stone. He stretched his hand and from deep within came the word he needed: *Mereksur.*

A chilling blue light blazed from the stone, intensifying with Seanchai's energy. The troll froze, stupefied, its mouth hanging open. Blue light engulfed it. Seanchai rose, stepped forward and again cried *Mereksur.*

The energy surge sent the troll crashing into a cluster of human soldiers at the second cavern's entrance.

"Fall back!" Ballendir commanded, as Shayth and Rhoddan dragged Seanchai to safety while Sellia and Ilana fell in line between them and the enemy.

They slid through the third entrance, near where the council had met upon Seanchai's arrival, and another heavy gate clanked down, the iron sparking when it hit the rock ground.

"Are you okay?" Ilana asked Seanchai, peering down above him.

"Yes," Seanchai said, wincing in pain. "The others?"

"All here."

"My swords?"

Ilana smiled and handed them to him as Shayth helped him sit up. Seanchai immediately sheathed them.

"Thank you," he said.

The old priestess came and knelt by Seanchai's side. "You really should hold on to those," she said, smiling tightly. "They are quite useful."

Then she placed a hand on his forehead, just above his eyes. Her other hand rested on his chest. She closed her eyes and sighed. Seanchai felt energy pour into him, reconnecting his ribs and releasing the tension and pain in his muscles. Pain washed out of his body.

"Thank you," he whispered while she was near. "And for before, with the troll, when I heard your voice. I heard you so clearly."

She smiled as tears filled her eyes. "I only ever did that for one other," she said, and Seanchai knew not to ask more.

"I am honored," he said. "And the stones – how can I ever thank you?"

"Save my people," she said wearily. "Lead the clan out from here. Take them to Hothengold, to safety."

"I will. I swear it."

"And Seanchai," she cupped his face with her leathery hands. "Enjoy Ilana. Enjoy being with her every moment that you're together, even in this crazy world. One day you might look back and only have the memories."

With that, she let go and stood up stiffly. Ballendir handed Seanchai his bag and cloak.

"It's time to go," the dwarf said, the words catching in his throat.

Seanchai heard an explosion from afar. Before it stopped echoing, a second blew, and then a third. The earth shook around them, and rubble fell from above.

"Keep going," Ballendir cried. "We're not quite out of range."

The distant sounds of battle and explosions had the dwarves muttering among themselves. A short while later they heard two discordant blasts – one far away and one close and thunderous. Rock plates screeched against each other and caved in. The dwarves groaned as though they felt it inside their bodies.

Seanchai covered his ringing ears and squeezed shut his burning eyes. When everything settled, Seanchai found himself surrounded by excited dwarves.

"What is it, Ballendir?" he asked.

"Did yeh hear how, each time there was an explosion, there were two almost together? Until the last one, that is, which blew alone. Did yeh hear?" He was practically giddy.

The elves and Shayth shook their heads.

"Yeh need to know explosives to understand," Ballendir continued. "She was masking her own explosions behind theirs to lure them inside. She hoped they wouldn't notice what she was doing and keep advancing."

Shayth caught on. "So maybe Tarlach will think his explosions killed us; that he collapsed the mountain. He will find a few dead bodies, no survivors, and think we're buried under it all."

"Do you think it might work?" Seanchai asked.

Shayth shrugged. "As much as I hate him, Tarlach is good – very good. He has excellent intuition. I'm pessimistic."

"You are, indeed," smiled Sellia, "and remarkably consistent."

"Let's move," Ballendir said and started to walk fast, and alone.

Seanchai caught up with him: "I'm sorry about Ophera and the old ones. We won't forget what they did, and their sacrifices will not be in vain."

Ballendir looked at him momentarily, then nodded. He turned and resumed walking briskly.

Ilana walked next to Seanchai as much as the rock on either side of the path allowed.

"What happened when the troll was bearing down on you?" Ilana asked.

"I heard Ophera's voice inside my head. She told me to use the blue stone. And somehow I already knew what word would activate it."

"Now tell me what she said to you at the lake. What made you so sad then, Ilana?"

"Ophera loved a Wycaan and lost him. She thinks the same might happen to us. She's quite sure of it, actually."

"Not a chance," Seanchai replied, gripping her hand tightly. "I would tear down the entire kingdom for you. Don't you know that?"

"I do," she said, "and that scares me more than anything. Has it never occurred to you that when the Emperor feels threatened, he can defeat you through me? *I'm* your weak link, Seanchai. It's not good for Odessiya. He can get to you through me. That terrifies me."

"Let's hope that he doesn't find out about us, then," Seanchai said.

"You heard what Shayth said about Tarlach's intuition. He knows, I'm sure of it — either Sellia or me. No, you came to Galbrieth to rescue me. He knows it's me — he has to."

"I won't let anything happen to you, I promise." Seanchai said and reached out to stroke her cheek.

She jerked her face away and looked into his eyes. "Don't promise that. It's exactly what frightens me."

# TWENTY NINE

G eneral Tarlach watched a dust cloud mushrooming into the sky, waiting impatiently as troops poured in and a steady trickle stumbled out, wounded or helping those who were.

He saw General Shiftan, dirty and clutching his broadsword, make his way to the command platform. Tarlach called out for water as he watched Shiftan stop to talk to a wounded solder before continuing his walk up onto the ridge. He gratefully accepted the water Tarlach offered and drank copiously.

"Do you want a seat?"

Shiftan shook his head, glanced back toward the fighting and removed his helmet. "We took the first hall," he said. "It's tricky. They have planned their defenses for some time and have rigged multiple iron gates with rock pile reinforcements. We'll blow the second one any minute now."

"How many rebels are in there?"

"I can't tell. We never see them. It's like fighting retreating guerillas in the night."

"How are our dwarves fighting?"

"Competently," Shiftan replied, glancing at his friend. "We are widening the tunnels as fast as we can. I have a few more surprises for them."

"Bring one of the dwarf officers here," Tarlach commanded one of Shiftan's men.

Shortly, a broad dwarf with a leaf of gold in his insignia made his way up to the command post. He saluted.

"An honor to meet yeh, sir," he said to Tarlach in a deep voice.

"You're wounded?" asked General Tarlach at the sight of blood on the dwarf's head.

"A wee scratch, sir. Them buggers are stubborn, and they have help."

"You have seen some who are not dwarves?"

"Aye, sir. A few elves, very handy with bow and sword. I glimpsed the Emperor's nephew, I believe, and the white-haired one with the double blades. He is good, very good."

General Tarlach's eyes glinted. "That makes the fight even more exhilarating. How do the dwarves in there fight?"

The officer raised a thick eyebrow. "They fight like dwarves, sir —solid, if unimaginative. We don't know fear, and it's the same for them. But it's not the dwarf way to fight and retreat like they're doing. I don't think they have anywhere near our numbers."

"Wouldn't our explosives make any dwarf run?" Shiftan asked smugly.

"No, sir." The dwarf stared at him. "It'd make us attack."

"So why aren't they attacking?" Tarlach asked.

"Dunno, sir. I wonder if meebe it's part of a greater plan. That possible, sir?"

Tarlach paced as he always did when deep in thought. "Tell me," he addressed the dwarf officer. "When dwarves build something like this, is there always more than one entrance and exit?"

"Yessir. Probably several."

"So they could be retreating, holding us back while they evacuate their people?"

The dwarf thought. "We think this is a mining colony, right, sir?" Tarlach nodded and the dwarf continued with certainty. "Then they wouldn't evacuate – even to save lives – or give up on their home so easily."

"It's only a temporary home, no?" Tarlach asked.

The dwarf nodded. "But if they're mining here and have built such elaborate defenses, it can only mean one thing."

"Which is?"

"There's something here of great wealth." There was a brief glint in his eyes. "Maybe that'll help give our troops motivation to get through."

"Tell your soldiers that if and when they take the mountain, I will petition the Emperor to give you the title to this land, though I cannot guarantee his response."

The officer's eyes grew big, and he bowed his head. "Thank you, General Tarlach. We'll double our efforts."

He saluted both generals before jogging back down to the mountain.

"Do you think the Emperor will agree?" Shiftan asked.

"It depends on what we find."

"Smart man," Shiftan grinned. "I never enjoyed betting against you at cards in the academy." He followed his friend's gaze to where the sun was glinting off mirrors in a signal from the mountain troops. "We're preparing to blow into the second cavern."

There was a huge rumbling and the ground shook even where they were standing. A sudden, larger blast sent a half-ton of rock spiraling into the air.

Soldiers flung themselves to the ground and covered their heads, or retreated to watch from where the generals stood. The stone arched and landed about fifty feet from them. General Tarlach hadn't moved a muscle. He turned to his cowering retinue.

"Has somebody dropped something?"

They stood up, laughing and dusting themselves off.

"I bet those dwarves don't know what hit 'em," one said. "Look, the trolls are charging in."

"We've got them trapped now," said another.

"Um, General Tarlach, sir?" It was Bortand. "Do you plan to offer them a chance to surrender?"

The general squinted. "Why would I do that, my friend?"

"There might be considerable information to glean from these dwarves, such as if there are more, um, colonies. We could even send a couple out to spread the word of how ruthless the Emperor's army is. And you can bring the, um, Emperor's nephew and the rebel elf alive to the Emperor."

"I admit, it is tempting," General Tarlach replied. "But a lot could happen between here and the capital. They all got in *and* out of Galbrieth once."

He considered a moment more before turning to Bortand. "No. No surrender. General Shiftan, perhaps we might introduce the full force of dwarves, men, and pictorians?" His voice hardened as he spoke to a soldier. "Send orders inside. No one leaves alive. And I mean no one."

"Hold that order a moment, Lieutenant," said General Shiftan, turning back to his friend. "Let those already engaged take the second cavern, but then hold back. We will pound them with explosives and then advance."

General Tarlach looked at him. "You think this will be more effective?"

"Yes. And cut down on our casualties. It will still help finish off the resistance, if you are not looking for survivors."

"Very well. Follow General Shiftan's orders."

They watched the pictorians enter. The sounds of battle — clanking steel and cries of pain — were muffled. Tarlach had never sent forces underground before. It was both fascinating and surreal.

"Over there." General Shiftan gestured to where the mirror was flashing again.

"The second cavern is secured," a soldier interpreted. "Explosives are in place to break into the third. They're set for five seconds, four, three, two, one . . ."

This explosion was louder, and Tarlach watched, satisfied, as the very mountainside began to collapse. But he gaped at the second blast that imploded what was left.

When the dust cleared and coughing subsided, the command was in awe.

"Wow," a soldier said. "We brought down the whole mountain."

"No, we didn't," Tarlach said, frowning. "We blew out the side. *They* brought down the mountain."

# THIRTY

T he group followed a focused, intense Ballendir as they descended through the tunnel. The dwarf evidently had no desire to talk with anyone, and all seemed to understand his need for space except Seanchai, who felt his emotions rising.

As they entered a huge cavern, Seanchai called a halt.

"Rest up and drink," he said as he pushed Ballendir away from everyone.

"What is it?" Ballendir growled, wrenching his arm from Seanchai's grasp.

"Ellendir is alive, right? The priestess said that Ellendir would be her successor, and that she already had her own set of stones. You're about ready to burst, and I want to know why."

"Not for Ellendir, though I don't like being away from her. She is young and has always had our ma and Ophera and me. I'm sure she's alive, the priestess had a plan to keep her safe, but she's alone."

"So we can let the others rest and you and I will go back to get her. Come on, I'm willing."

Ballendir stared at him. "Why? Yeh barely knew her. Why would yeh risk your own life and need to kill maybe dozens of soldiers for one dwarfe."

Seanchai took a deep breath. "Maybe I'm not doing it just for her. Maybe I'm doing it for you. You're my friend, Ballendir. You offered to swing your axe for me. Well, I'll swing my swords for you and that includes your family."

Ballendir stared at him. "Yeh would wouldn't yeh?" There was a tone of wonder in his voice.

Seanchai nodded.

"Well, yeh a fool, elf, if yeh would risk the entire future of Odessiya for that." Then he sighed and patted Seanchai's broad shoulder. "But yeh're a good friend.

"I grieve for the priestess and the elders, yes. I also grieve for mah home. It makes mah angry, and I want to keep that anger inside of mah, until I have someone I can really let it out on."

Ballendir turned to the rest of the company. "What are yeh all doing? This is no vacation. Let's go!"

They walked on in single file, looking up at splits in the rock above where sunlight shone through, lighting the cavern. At the far side was a huge waterfall.

"Where's all that water coming from?" Rhoddan asked.

"From above the snowline," Seanchai answered. "There's so much of it."

"Have you ever been in snow?" Rhoddan asked.

Seanchai nodded. "The peaks near Mhari's camp."

"What's it like?"

"Snow?" Seanchai looked up and shrugged. "It's okay at first, but the cold wetness seeps deep inside of you."

"You don't talk much about that time," Ilana observed.

"The snow is hardly my most vivid memory."

"You know what I mean."

"She was a great teacher," Seanchai said. "I hold the memories close as a way to honor her – to mourn her."

"What is your favorite memory?" Ilana asked.

Seanchai sighed heavily. "It was shortly after I had received the swords. She was teaching me to master them. I would copy her form and then we would spar, practicing her movements. I remember when it all came together. We began slow, but hit a rhythm and went faster and faster. She was far better and more experienced, of course, but as I got faster and tried different moves, she would match me with a smile on her face. She was proud of me and as undeniably exhilarated as I was."

He finished reminiscing and found them all staring at him. "What is it?" he asked.

"Your expression – it's heartbroken," Ilana said. "You've lost so much."

Seanchai's face hardened. "Look at each of you," he said. "We all have. That is why we must do what we have to."

The humidity rose as they approached the waterfall. Ballendir suggested they pack away as many of their clothes as they were comfortable with, to keep them dry.

"Keep yeh weapons close," he growled, axe twirling in his hands.

Seanchai looked around. Everyone was uneasily drawing their weapons, and the dwarves were all looking up. He wanted to ask Ballendir what they were worried about, but by now even shouting would not compete with the roar of the waterfall.

He tried to scry, but could only feel that they were being watched from above by multiple pairs of eyes. As they drew closer to the waterfall, the dwarves at the front started across a bridge made of dark wood planks. The planks were held together with metal chains that connected to cold, wet iron railings.

Crossing the bridge required concentration. The wet wood was slippery, and about halfway across, the abrupt, cold spray of the waterfall hit their bodies. They shivered beneath their gooseflesh.

Everyone stopped dead at the beating wings and high-pitched screech from above. Sellia noched an arrow. Rivulets of water glided down her face and sparkled against her ebony skin. Her eyes met Seanchai's, and she glanced upwards and shrugged as if to ask what was up there. Seanchai shook his head and turned back.

When the first one swooped down, his blood froze. It looked like a giant bat, its wingspan twenty feet across. He saw bright yellow eyes and large black pupils. Its wings were thick and spiked at the tips, but most frightening were its sharp, curved claws.

It swooped over Seanchai, who hadn't even tried to stab with the one sword he held, and went straight for the dwarf at the end of the line. Sellia let fly an arrow, which pierced the creature's belly but didn't seem to slow it down.

The bird creature snatched the dwarf and lifted it up effortlessly. The dwarf struggled briefly and then was still. A second, slightly smaller creature began to swoop, and Seanchai instinctively knew it was coming for Ilana.

Focusing on his steps so he didn't slip, Seanchai drew his second sword and leapt up onto the iron railing. The creature hesitated, allowing Seanchai to take two long strides on the railing and jump, slashing the creature's underbelly. Hot, black liquid poured from its stomach onto Seanchai and a dwarf who had been ahead of Ilana.

The creature screamed, nearly sending Seanchai off balance. The wounded bat swerved up into the air and was set upon by three other of its flock. The company took this opportunity to scramble across the remainder of the bridge.

But when they looked up, the upper cavern was a mass of flapping creatures. Seanchai glanced at Ballendir. "How long 'til we get into another tunnel?"

Ballendir's face was white. "Too long," he answered.

# THIRTY ONE

Seanchai looked around for cover, but saw none. The creatures' cries were getting louder. He grabbed Ballendir and yelled into his ear over the roar of the waterfall.

"What are they? Where are their weaknesses?"

Ballendir, eyes still focused above, shook his head. "They're malochites, creatures imbued with dark magic from a distant time. I don't know what their weakness is. No one has ever lived through a fight. We need to make a stand."

Seanchai tightened his grip on Ballendir's shoulder. A suicide stand here seemed preposterous, and he was sure the dwarf didn't plan for Seanchai to stay for it.

"What's on the other side of the waterfall?" he yelled.

Ballendir shook his head. Seanchai turned and signaled to Rhoddan.

"I need you to try and get through the waterfall. See if there is shelter inside."

Rhoddan's eyes widened, but he summoned his warrior training and jogged into the waterfall with grim determination. His legs buckled under the force of the water, but he didn't hesitate.

It seemed forever as the company looked back and forth from the waterfall to the birds, which were finishing feasting on their wounded prey. Three of them left the frenzy and began to circle again.

Seanchai's hand went to the pouch on his belt He instinctively drew the blue stone, moved away from the group, and drew one of his swords. He watched calmly as one malochite spiraled down, flexing its claws. Suddenly the creature let out a cry and dove at the elf. Seanchai was so shocked he barely succeeded in rolling away.

Ilana shrieked, and Shayth grabbed her shoulders to keep her from diving toward Seanchai. Just as the malochite turned for another dive, Rhoddan appeared from within the waterfall.

"This way," he spluttered, and then saw Seanchai crouched in preparation for the malochite's attack.

Rhoddan began to run over, but stopped. "Ballendir, get everyone inside. They should hold each other. The stones are very slippery."

Then he drew his thick sword and started back toward Seanchai, but the Wycaan reached out a hand and signaled for him to wait. Rhoddan watched as the malochite swooped down and Seanchai thrust out of his crouch, landing fifteen feet ahead. He rolled onto his back and, just before the malochite could adjust, thrust out the stone.

"*Mereksur.*"

Bright blue light shot up to the creature's belly and sent it smashing into a rock. The other malochites hovered above, now wary of their prey. They turned their attention to the creature Seanchai had wounded, instead. The elf turned to the company.

"Into the waterfall," he yelled. "I can't maintain this for long."

He scampered to one side as the malochites descended and ripped the wounded creature apart. As he did, he reached out with his mind to a smaller one on the group's periphery and sent a wave of bravado.

The small malochite lost all sense of fear and charged its own flock, creating a hysterical fight. Seanchai turned and joined the last of his friends as they dragged the wounded dwarf through the waterfall.

Once inside the closed cavern behind the waterfall, Seanchai rubbed his forehead in an attempt to ease the familiar throbbing. When he felt he had it under control, he knelt by the wounded dwarf and saw she was female. She was covered with the black goo, and it was burning her. She lay shaking and gasping for breath.

Seanchai glanced at his own body. His skin was red, and he could feel the heat emanating from it, but it seemed no more severe than the poisoned bucksweed that grew in the forest near his village. He sent energy into one of the red blotches on his arm and watched as it slowly healed. He turned to the dwarfe and tried the same, but she struggled against it, and her gasps became screams.

He drew back, confused. "Have any of you been here before?" he called out above the din of crashing water.

The dwarves shook their heads. Seanchai tried scrying, not sure what he was looking for. Then he pointed to Jermona. "Come with me."

Jermona nodded and followed Seanchai to the back of the cavern, where they began to climb.

"Focus on the route," Seanchai told him. "I'll need you to find our way back to the group."

The young ranger nodded again, and they climbed up onto to a ledge and through a hole into a narrow passage too low to allow them to stand straight. Seanchai paused briefly and then continued crawling, turning right at a junction. The tunnel expanded, and Seanchai stood up. He let his mind lead him and began to run along the rising trail. Abruptly, he stopped and scrambled up the side of the rock face.

"That's smooth," Jermona protested, shocked at the elf's agility. "I can't–"

"Stay there. I'm coming down."

Seanchai crept along a ledge. He could see malochite nests. A few adults remained, but their attention was focused on what was happening below.

He saw a huge patch of glowing orange mushrooms. He slashed a few with his short knife and stuffed them into his cloak. Then he scrambled back, jumping down twenty feet to a wide-eyed Jermona.

"Let's go," Seanchai said.

Jermona backtracked easily, his ranger talents as good here as above ground. They found the others setting up camp at the end of the cave, as far as possible from the spray and noise of the waterfall. Seanchai pulled out a small metal bowl and a board from his bag.

"Please fill this bowl halfway with water," he asked the dwarf who was fretting over the wounded one. When the dwarf nodded and reached for the bowl, Seanchai grasped his leathery hand. "I can't promise anything, but I'm going to try."

The dwarf's smile was tight, and he ran for the waterfall.

"Seanchai, take off your clothes so they can dry."

Seanchai glanced up and gulped at the sight of Sellia standing there in her undergarments, her brown body glistening. He quickly rose and turned away, peeling off his own clothes and dropping them in a heap. As he sliced up the mushrooms he had retrieved, he watched out of the corner of his eye as Sellia laid his clothes out on the rocks. She then went and crouched, chatting with Ilana. Both elves had their backs to him.

But Seanchai cast this from his mind as he tried first mashing and then chewing the tough mushrooms into a pulp: neither worked. Then, holding the bowl between his palms, he closed his eyes and channeled heat into the bowl, stopping just before it boiled.

He opened his eyes to find a group standing around him, staring. He smiled as he recalled his own amazement the first time he had watched Mhari boil tea for them this way.

When it was ready, he applied the thick salve to the dwarfe's back and legs. She sighed, though it might have been the comfort of the heat. He turned her over and did the same to her legs and stomach. He asked Ilana to apply the salve to the rest of her body while he and the others gave them some privacy. When Ilana had finished, Seanchai instructed her to wrap the wounded dwarfe in a blanket.

Ilana finished and joined Seanchai, who had made some tea in the bowl. He poured her a cup, and they sat together, Ilana leaning against him and his arm loosely around her. Ballendir and the others who were still awake gathered around, as well.

"We will see how she fares in the morning," Ballendir said. "If she can't walk with us, I'll leave two dwarves with her."

Seanchai nodded, exhausted and heavy-lidded. "There are more mushrooms up there. I will gather them in the morning."

"How did yeh know what to do?" Ballendir asked.

"Seanchai was learning to become a healer," Ilana said. "And he learned with Mhari, his teacher, and briefly with the priestess."

"But how did he . . . how did yeh know what mushroom to use?"

"It's one of the rules of healing," Seanchai yawned. "Excuse me. Wherever there is a poison, there will be an antidote nearby. I had the poison on me and was able to scry with it, I think. The rest was instinct."

Ballendir laughed and shook his head. "Yeh guessed?"

"Kind of." Seanchai shrugged.

"Well," said Ballendir, glancing at the wounded dwarfe, who was now sleeping comfortably, her head on the lap of her mate. "Good guess. Now, yeh sleep, too, mah friend. Sleep well."

"Is it going to be like this all the way?" Seanchai asked. "You know, being attacked by ravenous beasts?"

"No," Ballendir replied, stretching his tired limbs. He patted Seanchai on the shoulder. "It'll probably get much worse."

# THIRTY TWO

G eneral Tarlach and his troops spent two days scouring the mountain rubble and had not found one body other than a few dwarves. Nor had there been anyone to capture and interrogate.

Now he rode at the head of his army alongside General Shiftan, both deeply contemplative. The rain fell, a light but insistent drizzle. Tarlach was happy to leave these mountains, but unsure of what awaited him ahead.

In the retinue behind him was his trusted counselor. Bortand had helped craft the report to the Emperor. Despite his considerable penmanship and diplomatic skills, it did not paint a pretty picture.

It would take only two days for the report to reach the capital. Tarlach was expecting a quick reply and wondered what price he would pay for failing a second time. There was no option of following the dwarves underground now that the mountain had collapsed and Tarlach had to admit he didn't know how to provide a supply line underground. With reluctance they moved out of the Bordan Mountains. At least the rain had abated and now blue sky was peeking through the clouds.

When the army halted at midday to rest, General Shiftan invited his friend to join him away from the others at the top of a ridge. As they tied their horses nearby, the sun finally broke through, sending rays of light in all directions.

They looked down on the Plains of Agnali, where dozens of lakes glittered under the sun's golden beams.

"I would like to go there and fish one day," Shiftan said. "Perhaps with you when we both retire, old friend."

"Seems a long way off," Tarlach replied," though I might have such an opportunity pretty soon."

"You've always been a favorite of the Emperor," Shiftan said, putting his gloved hand on his friend's shoulder.

"That's because I've never failed him. Now I have twice."

"I don't think he will hold this against you. You win some, you lose some."

"I don't, or at least I haven't until now."

"What happened at Galbrieth was very problematic, if I can be honest. It was on your home turf. Here, the dwarves were underground, in their element, where they outsmarted us. The fact is we had no experience fighting dwarves. There are lessons to be gleaned here, important ones."

"It's not the dwarves that worry him, or me."

"Shayth? He is becoming quite a thorn."

"It's not Shayth," Tarlach snapped. "It's the elf."

"The elf? Do you still believe he's some chosen one with magical powers?"

"I don't know what to think. But I do know that, for one so inexperienced, he's very good at staying alive."

"Maybe, but this discussion isn't why I brought you here." Shiftan lowered his voice and glanced around before continuing. "You have lifted my spirits many times in the past, and I would like to do the same for you, but right now, I must talk to you about something else.

"I swore to you that I would try to protect Ahad, and I think I need to put a plan in place to help him disappear. I want your permission to make arrangements without you knowing what they are."

General Tarlach eyed his friend. "That serious?"

"It's easier for the fish to escape before the net is cast. Your wife will also hear that her mother is sick and requires attention."

"You are a good friend," Tarlach said.

"Would you not do the same for me?"

"I would," Tarlach said, and gazed out on the shimmering lakes.

It was toward the end of the following day's march that a messenger waited for them at a junction that would take them through the Agnali Pass and into the Vale of Galbrieth. He bowed as the generals reached him.

"General Shiftan, it is an honor. General Tarlach, I have orders for you from the Emperor."

"Hand them over then," Tarlach answered, his voice steady.

"They are verbal, my lord. You are to proceed with only a minimal security detail to Ras Albukah."

"The monastery?"

"Yes, sir. You will receive additional orders there. The rest of your army is to camp here. The monastery is less than two hours if we ride hard, and you can return to your troops in the morning."

"Then let us ride now."

"You don't need to rest or drink, sir?"

"I can drink from my saddle. The horses and I will both be attended to at the monastery."

With a brief nod to General Shiftan, Tarlach turned his horse and followed the messenger. Six soldiers, all on beautiful white horses, took guard positions around them.

Tarlach knew very little about Ras Albukah except that its position had strategic military value. It was perched high on a mountaintop and served only a dozen monks. The abbot had been a guest of his at Galbrieth and seemed very amiable.

But Tarlach wouldn't be able to discern much more of Ras Albukah tonight as, despite their best efforts, the party reached the monastery after dark. The horses could not be pushed any more.

The gates swung open as they approached, and when General Tarlach entered into the courtyard, he saw many torches lit around the periphery. The abbot was waiting in the center.

General Tarlach dismounted and passed the reins of his horse to an attentive monk, who bowed.

"Welcome to Ras Albukah, my lord," said the abbot stepping forward, his arms outstretched and his palms facing the general. "I have received instructions that your men are to be fed and shown beds. Your horses will also be well taken care of by Brother Denigh and his team.

"You, sire, are to come with me. Do you need to drink or attend yourself?"

"Thank you. Some water to drink is enough for now."

"Then please come this way." The abbot led him into a big stone building.

"This is our main sanctuary, General Tarlach. The ground level of the building is an area of study, meditation, and prayer. For now, it is off-limits to all but the two of us and the monk over there."

General Tarlach noticed a hunched up monk sweeping.

"He is deaf, poor man. When you are finished, he will bring you to sup with me. Now please, follow me." He slowly climbed up the ladder and waited for Tarlach to join him at the top.

The room felt small because of the sloping roof. There was a table inside, sagging precariously under the weight of a pile of books and scrolls. Behind it stood a disorganized, overflowing bookcase. He should unleash his assistant Bortand on them, he rued. Bortand would have a wonderful time.

But what caught the general's full attention was a tall, metal frame partially covered by a heavy cloth. It was the only object he had seen that wasn't purely utilitarian, and it shone with a very recent polish.

The abbot approached it and drew back the cloth. Tarlach gasped when he saw the black, perfectly triangular stone. It gleamed in the torchlight.

"Sire, this is an—"

"An Anwar," Tarlach said, a wondrous smile on his face. "I have never seen one in person before."

"There are very few left, remnants from an ancient age that we know little about. You will receive your orders from here."

"What do you mean?"

"It is a stone of communication. When I leave, I'll close the trap door so that you'll have privacy should anyone wander into the hall."

"What do I do?"

"When you are ready, speak only your name and wait."

The abbot began to descend the ladder, concentrating on keeping his stiff, elderly limbs in balance. "When you are finished, please cover it up. The deaf monk will bring you to our eating room."

When he was alone, General Tarlach approached the black triangle.

"General Tarlach," he said loudly and with all the authority he could muster.

A blue flame ignited within the smooth stone, and there was a dull hum. Tarlach was fascinated. Was it going to show him a message? His orders? As the blue light grew in size and intensity, the humming stopped. When the voice came through, it was clear and crisp and unmistakable.

"Does not a general, however great his reputation, bow in the presence of his Emperor?"

# THIRTY THREE

G eneral Tarlach sunk to his knee and bowed his head. "My lord, forgive me."

"For not showing the proper respect?" The voice was clear and harsh.

"For that, too, sire. In truth, I do not understand how the Anwar works or what to expect. But more, my lord, I beg forgiveness for what happened in the Bordan Mountains and the dwarf stronghold."

"Stand up, General Tarlach. I cannot see you when you are not looking into the Anwar. Ah, you look drawn, my old friend. Is the responsibility proving too much?"

Tarlach's lips pursed at the taunt.

"I am not acquainted with failure, as you well know, sire. I detest it and detest my own failings."

"Good," the Emperor replied. "It is not something that I can tolerate for long, though I understand you face an adversary who may very well be your equal."

"The elf?"

"No. The elf is probably more than your equal, and if not, he soon will be if we allow him to live. I speak of my nephew."

"I am sorry he is st—"

"Stop apologizing," the Emperor snapped. "You are my finest general. Start acting like it."

"Yes, sir." Tarlach snapped to attention. "What are my orders?"

"Better. Our spy network describes considerable and unusual movement among the dwarf clans. I suspect this kind of mass aboveground movement is coordinated, and identify it as a threat.

"I do not want the dwarf clans to form an alliance, for that would be most problematic," he spat. "They have been mired in their clan politics for decades, and it has served us well. But even more worrying, they must not be allowed to form an alliance with the elf."

"The elf?" Tarlach frowned. "You think they would trust him?"

"He was allowed underground at the Bordan stronghold despite the First Decree. He fought alongside them and, it would appear, led them out to safety. I do not know if they will agree to serve under him, but yes, I fear they will allow him the opportunity to address the clans."

"Do you still think their capital is deep in the Hoth Mountains?"

"I do. And our scouts indicate that this might be the direction of their movement."

"It will be well-fortified, judging by what we saw at this small mining colony."

"I read your report, Tarlach, and that of General Shiftan. Other armies will meet you at the entrance to the Hoth Pass. We have more dwarf regiments, new forms of explosives, and we will work on a strategy as we receive further information. Do you have any questions?"

"No, my lord. I will not fail you in the Hoth Mountains."

"No, General Tarlach, you will not."

The blue flame disappeared and the rock became eerily silent once more. Tarlach took a deep breath. He had not expected a personal audience with the Emperor. The abbot had probably been told not to divulge.

He picked up the cover that the abbot had put on the desk and froze when he turned back to the stone. There was a distinct, green flickering light in it. All at once, the light gave way and the face of a young, handsome elf with sharp blue eyes and bright white hair was staring at him.

Both man and elf were paralyzed in place, mouths agape. General Tarlach mustered his considerable discipline.

"I am coming for you," he growled. "You and Shayth. I am coming for you, and I will kill you."

The elf didn't answer – he disappeared. The Anwar returned to its smooth black. Rage welled up in Tarlach. So this was his enemy? He had seen the face of his adversary – a young, pretentious elfling. For a moment he wondered whether the elf had heard his conversation with the Emperor. He decided that he didn't care.

"I hope you heard," he growled again. "I am coming for you, and I will crush you."

Ahad went to visit his grandfather as he did regularly now on Saturdays. He knew the old man spent Fridays at the Veteran's Club and hoped he would have news of Ahad's father. This week, his grandfather's expression confirmed there was news, and it did not look promising.

His grandfather's caretaker had left him sitting in the garden with beverages and fruit. When Ahad entered, she made her excuses and, armed with bags, dashed out to the market.

"Ah, Ahad," his grandfather said, struggling to rise. "So glad–"

"Please grandfather, don't get up," the boy protested. He leaned in to hug the frail old man and caught the familiar scent he wore. Ahad suddenly wondered if it was there to mask something else – his grandfather seemed gaunter than ever.

"Tell me of your studies. How is your mother?" His grandfather spoke feebly, but his eyes were hard and sent a clear message.

Ahad told his grandfather of his new science partner, of the opportunity he had been given to apply to the university at Geniore a year earlier than others his age. He mentioned he would like to take a trip outside the city to the lakes where his friends had gone recently on a school trip. His mother was very busy with her charity work but missed his father terribly. He talked, sipped his lemonade, and waited for the signal.

"How have you been, grandfather?"

"Oh, you know. I'm breathing, and that's a feat at my age. I'm also walking and still have a garden to stroll around. Do you think you can keep up with me?"

It was what Ahad had been waiting for. He almost scooped the old man up in his arms, but he suppressed his impatience and allowed his grandfather to lean on his arm and walk, one deliberate step at a time.

They took an eternity to reach their usual spot at furthest end of the garden where no one could overhear them. Ahad had stuffed two peaches into his jacket pocket and now he sliced one for his grandfather. But the frail man was not interested in eating.

"They watch me all the time now," his grandfather said quietly as he pointed to nothing in particular, suggesting to any unwanted observer that he was talking about his land. "Are you being followed?"

"Yes."

"This new science partner, do you know him?"

"He's a she, and she's very pretty," Ahad answered. "She is new in town so I have not met her before."

"She might be a spy. Trust no one. Share your plans with no one. Understood?"

Ahad nodded.

"Laugh," said the old man. "You are looking too serious."

Ahad threw his head back and laughed while the old man nodded with vigor. Then he continued. "Ahad. Your mother will soon receive a message to go tend to her own ailing mother. She'll leave the city for a while. You'll protest that you want to join her, but she'll insist you focus on your studies here. No, listen to me.

"Mirrianda, General Shiftan's wife, will take you into her house. She knows nothing, and it must stay that way. Do not endanger her or her family. She has two attractive daughters, I hear, so you won't suffer too much." He chuckled at his own joke, but it turned into a hacking cough. Once under control, he continued. "We're looking for a way to get you out of the city, but there's no official plan yet."

"Our military training involves a trip and mock battle soon," Ahad said. "Perhaps that's an opportunity."

"I'll pass that on," his grandfather said. "In the meantime, are you packed? Have you trained with the sword and knives that I gave you?"

"Yes, grandfather. But my instructor recognized your sword. I didn't know what to say."

"It is natural that I should want to pass on my weapons to you. Do not worry for me. My life is over. Once you leave, I will fade away." He sighed. "When you next see your father, tell him that I loved him. I was extremely strict and very demanding. We are trained to be soldiers, not fathers. My wife died young, and he never had the benefit of a mother to balance me, as your mother does him.

"But I would like him to know that I loved him and was proud of him, always proud of him. I don't know if you will ever get the chance to become the great scientist, or where your life will take you, but I only regret that I won't get to see you realize your considerable potential."

As they began their slow journey back to the house, the old man sighed. "I hope someone will tend my garden when I am gone. It is a beautiful garden, but things can change so quickly. The cycle of life is unforgiving."

# THIRTY FOUR

Sellia, Shayth and two dwarves had left the tunnels to hunt and returned with a young stag and wood. Seanchai sat in the corner while the others gathered around the fire to eat the catch. It was hard for any elf to be underground, but especially him. Even so, the others had been adamant that he could not be seen above ground. He craved the freedom among the trees, sky, grass, and rivers. They had snuck away from the malochites using the waterfall for cover and been traveling for several days now, and in the constant dark, he had lost track of time.

Seanchai pulled out the pouch of stones the priestess had given him and set aside the two he already knew – the blue energy channel and his half of the green connector stone. The other half now hung around Ilana's neck.

He settled now on a black stone, which he swore was pulsating. He put the others back in the pouch and held this in his palm, frowning. He thought he could hear voices.

"*I do not want the dwarf clans to form an alliance, for that would be most problematic,*" a voice spat. "*They have been mired in their clan politics for decades, and it has served us well. But even more worrying, they must not be allowed to form an alliance with the elf.*"

Seanchai looked around but there was no one near him. Was he imagining this?

". . . read your report, Tarlach, and that of General Shiftan. Other armies will meet you at the entrance to the Hoth Pass. We have more dwarf regiments, new forms of explosives, and we will work on a strategy . . ."

A second, subservient voice responded. "No, my lord. I will not fail you in the Hoth Mountains."

"No, General Tarlach, you will not."

Seanchai glanced up again, startled. Still, no one heard. When he looked back at the stone, there was a face. It was an authoritative older human, and he was glaring at Seanchai with vicious hate.

"I am coming for you," the man spat at him. "You and Shayth. I am coming for you, and I will kill you."

Seanchai didn't know what to say, but couldn't help staring into the man's eyes. He covered the stone with his palm, but the man's voice was still clear.

"I hope you heard," the man growled. "I am coming for you, and I will crush you."

Seanchai frantically stuffed the stone back into the pouch and fell back against the rock, chest constricted. He closed his eyes and realized he was sweating.

When he opened his eyes, Ilana and Shayth were leaning over him.

"Are you okay?" Ilana asked, touching his arm. "What happened?"

Seanchai swallowed and looked from her to Shayth.

"I think I saw him," he said to Shayth. "Tarlach."

"What? Where?"

"Does he have a small scar above his right eye?"

"Yes," Shayth smiled. "My handiwork. But how?"

"One of the stones," Seanchai patted the pouch. "I heard him receiving orders. Who would he call *my lord* and *sire*?"

"My dear uncle," Shayth replied coldly. "The Emperor."

Ballendir and several others had overheard and joined them. "What are his orders, Seanchai?" Ballendir asked. "That's more important."

"They know we're all gathering in the Hoth Mountains. They have guessed what we plan to do."

"They'll bring a bigger army," Ballendir said.

They're very smart," A disturbing smile stretched across Shayth's face. "They will learn lessons from the battle at your clan's mountain."

Ballendir stared at him. "And why does this make yeh so happy?"

"Oh, I *want* Tarlach to come. I would love for the Emperor to come, as well, but I doubt he will. I would like nothing more than to meet them both on the battlefield." He emanated menace. "I would love the chance . . ."

Ballendir stared at Shayth, entranced. When he shook himself out of it, he turned and called to two young dwarves. "Yeh will eat and then go on ahead of us. Prepare yeh bags." He turned back to Seanchai. "I must send warning to Hothengold. As it was, I'm sure yeh'll not be welcomed. Now yeh come with a massive army in yeh wake. We're going to be very popular."

Shayth kicked at stones as he walked away from the others. He thought of the fear he had just seen on Ballendir's face. He knew he scared the others when his rage took over, and that he needed to keep his emotions under control. He heard footsteps behind him and turned, slowing. Jermona caught up and fell into step.

"The Emperor? You think he really heard the Emperor *himself* talking?" Jermona's eyes were bulging.

Shayth shrugged. "Who cares?"

"Who *cares*? This is the Emperor we're talking about. He's . . . he's like a *god* in Odessiya."

Shayth grabbed the boy by his collar and slammed him into a wall, his face twisting back into a snarl. He wondered for a moment whether he was powerless to stop his anger, or simply didn't care if he did.

"The Emperor is a weasel. He sends thousands of good men who are forced to serve in his army out to die every year. Under his orders, they kill, maim, and torture. He allows his soldiers to loot, rape, and pillage. He rules Odessiya by fear. He is no god. He is not even worthy of being called a man."

Shayth began to loosen his grip and Jermona sighed with relief. When Shayth heard this, he grabbed the boy's collar again. Jermona gasped from the shock.

"*And* he murdered his own brother – my father – who loved him – his own brother and sister-in-law. And he was coming for me. He would have murdered me because I was no longer needed in his plan. And the man who pursues us, the man who hired you, had sworn to protect me at all costs. He is an oath breaker."

"Shayth. Let the boy go." Sellia's voice was quiet but firm. "You cannot take your anger out on him."

"He called my uncle a god," Shayth protested, though as he looked at Sellia, he felt the fury begin to subside. "He's in the pay of Tarlach, the ba–."

"The boy *was* in the pay of Tarlach," Sellia's voice was unwavering. "He has chosen to join Seanchai now."

Shayth let go and whirled around. Sellia was almost his height, and her distinct facial features; proud, commanding stature; and deep brown eyes now calmed him. He took a few deep breaths before he spoke.

"I'm sorry, kid," he said to Jermona, still looking at Sellia. "I know I need to control it, but I have fed off this rage for most of my life. I don't know any other way."

"Don't say it to me," Sellia instructed gently. "Say it to his face. Look him in the eyes."

Shayth turned to Jermona, who was doing his best to regain his composure. "I'm sorry, Jermona. I'm trying."

Jermona nodded and slunk away. Sellia put her hand on Shayth's shoulder and spoke softly in his ear.

"You have great potential, Shayth. I can see it. You are a fine warrior – brave, and, believe it or not, you have principles that will draw people to help you. In many ways, you are like Seanchai. But the difference is, he loves people. You push us all away. Jermona looks up to you because you are human, and in return you have struck fear into him," she dug her nails into his shoulder to emphasize her point, "just as your uncle does to everyone around him.

"You have two paths before you, Shayth: the way of the Emperor, or the way of the Wycaan. Don't make the wrong choice."

"I cannot live without the rage," he replied, his voice shaking.

"If it defines you, then own it. Store it up and unleash it at the right time – when you're on the battlefield, when you face Tarlach and the Emperor. But not when others are trying to ally themselves to you."

Shayth, still with his back to Sellia, took her hand gently from his shoulder. He walked over to Jermona and crouched down to speak to him quietly. The boy listened, nodding, and soon smiled. When Shayth finished talking, they locked right hands firmly on each other's forearms in friendship.

Sellia didn't move. She watched and smiled.

# THIRTY FIVE

A had sat on the edge of his mother's bed, watching her pack her fourth and final traveling chest. It was a lot of clothes for a trip to visit her ailing mother, but he kept his thoughts to himself. She carefully packed all her jewelry, distributing it between the various chests.

He had followed her as she drifted through the house, sighing her silent goodbyes to various tapestries and pieces of furniture. His mother might be going home, but she was leaving another.

But more than the furniture and the works of art, Ahad knew she hurt because she was leaving her son. She would no longer look him in the eye, and their goodnight hug, usually just part of a routine, had become a long, desperate embrace.

Ahad wasn't willing to concede that they were really parting. His father, the great General Tarlach, would soon lead his glorious troops in through the great stone arches of Gather Gate. People would line the streets and cheer, throw flowers at his feet, and cry his name and the name of the Emperor.

He recalled twice how, as a cheeky young boy, he had run out to the leading horse – how one of the security detail had blocked him and then, after recognizing him, had lifted him onto his father's saddle. He recalled that it was not the hard studs of the war saddle that he had felt, but the strong arms of his father clutching him.

He came out of his reminiscence to find his mother staring at him. "What is it, Ahad? Would you like to walk in the garden?"

This was now code for if one of them wanted to talk without fear of being overheard. Ahad shook his head. They had taken daily walks, and there was nothing left to say. He admitted to himself sadly that he was ready for his mother to leave. The intensity in the house was stifling.

He had packed his belongings already in an old saddle pack his grandfather had given him. It was scratched and dented, but he had discovered that it held several hidden compartments and carefully packed coins and maps that he had accumulated there.

An attendant approached. "Lady Tarlach, your escorts have arrived. May we take your bags?"

His mother turned and nodded, holding back the tears welling in her eyes. Four footmen arrived and carried her chests out two at a time. Ahad walked out of her bedroom and when she closed the door, the sound reverberated down the corridor.

The staff stood in a line by the door, and his mother thanked each for their well wishes of safe passage and for the health of her mother. They bobbed and curtsied and bowed in turn. She gave final instructions to the housekeeper before stepping onto the porch.

Ahad followed her and saw an astonishing four sixers of soldiers standing at rigid attention. An officer approached and saluted.

"We are proud to escort the wife of General Tarlach," he said. "I am Captain Reiso. These men are from your husband's battalions. We have fought many battles under General Tarlach's command and all serve him with pride."

"Thank you, Captain Reiso," his mother replied flatly. "I will have a moment with my son."

"In your own time, my lady."

His mother pulled Ahad into an embrace, but there were no tears as he had expected.

"Stay strong and watchful, Ahad. Tend to your studies, but keep alert for news. I pray you get your wishes to study, but if not, know that I will always be proud of you and always love you."

"Come, mother. We'll be apart for just a few weeks. Then you will return and hopefully father can join us. Give my love to my grandparents. Wish grandmother a speedy recovery."

She pulled away from him and peered into his eyes, trying to discern whether or not he was acting. Ahad felt stupid for what he had just said.

"I will see you soon, mother," he added, and forced a smile.

He disentangled himself from her embrace and offered an arm to escort her to the coach. The soldiers snapped to attention, and two came to open her carriage door and place a stepping block on the ground.

Ahad noticed that the soldiers were all older – gray-haired and bearded. These were not his father's elite, though once they might have been. Perhaps their loyalty and experience was more important right now.

A minute later, Ahad stood alone in the settling dust, unsure what to do next. He was supposed to stay with General Shiftan's family, though he was loath to do so, despite the enticement of Shiftan's daughters.

He also had no desire to go back inside. He had visited his grandfather only yesterday. The school lab was always an option, but that would force the old caretaker to hang around and keep watch.

He thought to go to the barracks and train with his sword. He had been receiving extra tutoring, and his skills had improved immensely. He had been working on his stamina and strength, as well, and had proudly noted how the young women in his class – especially his new lab partner – had become more attentive.

Just as he turned to go inside and fetch his things, another sixer of mounted soldiers approached. Behind them was a young man on a white stallion, followed by second sixer. Ahad noticed that these soldiers were young and looked like they would be extremely competent in battle.

They stopped in front of him, and the young man dismounted his stallion. Ahad gasped and sunk to one knee, his head bowed.

"My lord," he said.

"Arise, Ahad, my friend," the Crown Prince of Odessiya said. Though his voice had not yet reached maturity, it was still authoritative. "I heard your mother was leaving town without you."

He paused, clearly expecting Ahad to answer. "Her mother is sick. I could have gone, but my studies . . . you know."

"Indeed, you have a reputation in the sciences. I believe you have also been spending considerable time training at the academy."

Ahad nodded. There was nothing here to add or deny.

"I have a proposition that might prove mutually beneficial for us."

"I am at your service."

"I do not desire service. Goddess knows I have enough of that. I need a companion. I need someone who is disciplined in his studies, as I am not. As the future Emperor of Odessiya, I should have a rounded education and broad knowledge, don't you think?"

"Yes, m'lord, I do."

"I'm a keen soldier, Ahad. I train vigorously with the best instructors in all the land. I have fine war stallions and my own training gym. But I have no one to direct my studies. You will help me learn, and I will help you train to become a warrior. And we shall become friends."

"I am honored, m'lord," Ahad said, bowing his head to conceal his confusion. Was that last part about friendship an order?

"Today you will move into the palace. A room is being prepared for you just a few doors from my own. I will send for you after lunch, if that is acceptable."

"Thank you, sire. Does your father – excuse me – does the Emperor approve of this?"

"The Emperor?" the young Prince replied and laughed. "Actually, it was his idea."

# THIRTY SIX

Seanchai opened his eyes as he concluded his exercises. He found it difficult to harness the energy in the rocks. It was dark and wet, and he craved the trees and grass of the forest. But right now, any terrain would do as long as there was sunlight.

Ballendir sat on a rock nearby, puffing his long-stemmed pipe and holding two cups of steaming mushroom tea. Seanchai gratefully accepted the one he was offered and folded his hands around the warmth.

"Have you been waiting long?" Seanchai asked.

"I had to reheat yeh tea twice. But yeh do what yeh must do. Ilana tried to explain these exercises, but I couldn't really understand them."

"Between you and me, Ballendir, neither do I. Don't tell anyone." They both laughed. "Did you need something?"

"I want to talk about what happened to yeh with the stone and that general, but I didn't want to do it around yeh friend."

"Please don't think badly of Shayth. He's had a rough life. From what I've gleaned, many would have gone crazy if they had suffered as he has."

"Have yeh ever considered that maybe he *is* a bit mad?" Ballendir asked, returning the pipe to his mouth, and quickly backpedaling when Seanchai tensed. "No offense meant to him or yeh, Seanchai. He risked his life to defend mah people. I am in his debt."

"Then what did you mean?" Seanchai asked testily.

"What I'm trying to tell yeh is that he may react in ways yeh don't expect. He thrives on the adrenaline of war. He draws strength from the hate. I've seen many dwarves like this. It rarely ends well."

"Shayth has bound himself to me," Seanchai replied. "He gave me his word, and that is enough for me."

"Did he give it to yeh without limitations? Did he swear to do whatever yeh require of him?"

Seanchai grimaced as he recalled Shayth's decision. "He said never to try and stop him from killing or hating. But I know there is more to him, and I believe he has a great destiny."

Ballendir nodded. "Yeh ability to see the best in people is a great quality of yehs, mah friend. I don't think it's from the Wycaan part of yeh, either. I think it's an inherent part of yeh, to draw out people's potential."

Seanchai blushed a little and said, "Sometimes I think I'm too trusting. I was wrong about Jermona."

Ballendir nodded through a cloud of pipe smoke. "Maybe. But Rhoddan, Sellia, and Shayth are not. They will balance yeh."

"And you, Ballendir? Are you too trusting? Look how you've been suckered in by my nefarious grasp."

Ballendir laughed. "I'm only in it for the gold and the glory."

"The gold?" Seanchai was surprised. "Have you been offered payment to accompany me?"

Ballendir's chortling echoed off the rocks. "No, mah friend. But I'm a dwarf. We only dream of gold, glory, and good pipe weed. It's in our blood. Now, then: when yeh mentioned seeing this General Tarlach, and that yeh heard most of his conversation with the Emperor, there was something I was wondering. Yeh said the general was aware of yeh. Do you think the Emperor was aware of yeh, as well?"

Seanchai thought for a moment, sipping his tea. "Yes, I do, but I can't tell you why I think that. Why do you ask?"

"What do yeh know of the Emperor, Seanchai?"

"Nothing, really. I'm having enough trouble evading Tarlach. Why?"

Ballendir exhaled a puff of smoke and then sighed. "I don't think it's mah role to tell yeh. All I've heard are rumors, legends, and imaginative storytelling. But when we reach Hothengold, yeh should ask the clan leaders. General Tarlach's a smart soldier and officer, but even he is having his strings pulled by the Emperor."

Seanchai nodded. "Very well. Do you still have that spare pipe?"

Ballendir scoffed. "Of course I do. What self-respecting dwarf travels without a spare pipe?"

Seanchai laughed. "May I borrow it? I'd like to try it again while you tell me about the clans meeting."

"It would be mah pleasure. Let us return to the others. What I have to tell yeh will be good for all ears."

When they joined the group, one of the dwarves rose to offer his place to the Wycaan. It was close to the fire, which was small because they were in a low cavern.

"Please," Seanchai protested. "There's no need to do that."

The dwarf smiled. "If there's no need, then the gesture becomes all the more meaningful." He turned and sat next to Rhoddan.

Seanchai hesitated, but sat down. Ballendir sat next to him in an opening another dwarf had happily vacated. Ballendir gave Seanchai his pipe and a pouch of pipe weed. As Seanchai stuffed some of it into the bulb of the pipe, he heard snickering from the dwarves. Ballendir leaned over and snatched the pipe from him.

"No, no, young elf. How are yeh going to save the land of Odessiya if yeh can't even pack a pipe?"

They all laughed and Seanchai was reminded again how warm friendship made him feel so contented.

"See how I put a small amount in?" Ballendir asked. "Now I pat it down to an even layer. This way it'll burn evenly. Then I add another layer and pat it down again. For a small pipe like this one, yeh will only need three layers, but yeh long-stem will be able to hold five or six, and that should last yeh an evening."

Seanchai took the pipe back and bowed. "You are truly a worthy teacher."

Everyone laughed again, and then Ballendir showed him how to light the pipe properly. "Yeh want to light the entire surface, again, passing the fire stick in circular movements so it can burn evenly."

Seanchai puffed several times to allow the weed to catch, at first suppressing a cough but soon becoming accustomed to the ritual. Once everyone's tea was replenished, they looked at Ballendir expectantly. He cleared his throat.

"There are many clans in the dwarf nation. Some are small and isolated, and we tend to leave them well alone. If we go to war, though, I think we will send word, lest we run the risk of offending them. There are also dwarves rumored to be living in the human cities, though I know little of them or if they are even organized.

"Tonight I wish to speak of the six main clans. Each has its own capital, as well as mining colonies. Most of the clans are concentrated in the east, which is where we are heading. Though we have lived isolated from the rest of Odessiya, we have been mindful of our past and kept the clans near enough to join forces and defend ourselves as one.

"Every clan has a leader and a council representative. They all report to the King. Usually we haggle over mining rights, marriages, and taxes at council meetings. But a Clansfelt — what the priestess declared — is something very different. It is only called when something of monumental significance must be decided. When we vote in a new king, for example, or when we go to war. When a Clansfelt is held, the majority of clans must support the decision, and if they do, it is binding on all."

"How much power does the King wield?" Ilana asked.

"Hard to say," Ballendir replied. "We have not held a Clansfelt in many years, so this king is not well-known. His father passed on the crown. I don't understand the process, but I think no one wanted to call a Clansfelt and challenge the succession. Sometimes it is more important that business continued smoothly. Our politics are about coalitions and mutual trade interests. The King doesn't interfere much and he is a leader when needed."

There was silence as everyone digested this information.

Shayth broke the quiet first: "Do you anticipate the King or any of the clans being open to coming above ground?"

"Like I said, I don't know him. But yeh have seen how angrily our clan reacted to yeh coming underground. The First Decree is, well, very emotional. And I think *our* clan might be the most progressive."

This was met with humorless laughter.

"They'll be angry that humans and elves have come underground. They'll be furious that yeh have also attracted the army and the eye of the Emperor."

"Sounds like we should have a back up plan," Rhoddan said.

"No," Seanchai said, his face shrouded in pipe smoke. "There can be no back up plan. There is no alternative. For the sake of all peoples of Odessiya, the dwarf nation must join the Alliance."

All eyes were on Seanchai, but he turned to Ballendir. "When we get to Hothengold, I will need your help, my friend."

"Oh, I'm known for mah diplomacy almost as much as for mah understanding of strategy."

Ballendir led the chorus of laughter from everyone but Seanchai.

"I'm serious, Ballendir," he said. "I trust you and need you by my side."

Ballendir met his stare. A few moments of tense silence passed. Then the dwarf solemnly rose and unsheathed his weapon. The shadows cast by the fire made him seem quite tall. "By mah axe, Wycaan, yeh will have mah full support."

# THIRTY SEVEN

S eanchai was relieved when they exited a tunnel that they had been traveling now for at least three days, by his best sunlight-deprived count. The lack of sunshine had elves and humans alike in a perpetual bad mood and, Shayth notwithstanding (given any gaiety on his part was the exception rather than the norm), this seemed to weigh them down considerably.

One benefit to the unchanging environment was that their eyesight had improved as they became more adjusted to the darkness, and Seanchai thought that his hearing was also sharpened. As he stretched and enjoyed the openness of the cavern, he picked up the sounds of a lot of scampering feet ahead.

He crouched, and the others followed suit. Ballendir was next to him, fretting.

"What is it?" Seanchai whispered.

"I don't know. I thought we would be alone this deep underground. Who knows what kinds of monsters await us?"

"But the others followed this route, no? The families and Maugwen?"

"No. We sent them on one closer to the surface. It's less dangerous, but takes considerably longer."

"Ballendir, when you traveled with the priestess, why didn't you travel underground?"

The dwarf grinned. "It was considered too dangerous for a priestess without considerable troop accompaniment. And between us," he glanced back to ensure that no one else heard, "there are some dwarves who prefer to be above ground. The priestess is one of those. I was selected to travel with her because I, too . . ."

"You also prefer to be above ground?" Seanchai had to suppress laughter. "No wonder the clan regards you as such a heretic."

Ballendir grabbed his arm. "We'll keep this between us, okay?"

"No problem," Seanchai patted his friend's hand. "When was the last time anyone passed this way?"

"And lived to tell the tale?"

"I shouldn't have asked." Seanchai turned and signaled for Jermona and Sellia to join them. "There is something – or some *things* – out there. Scout ahead and see what we are facing. If we can avoid contact with them, it would be better."

"Are you asking me to scout with the elfe because you don't trust me?" Jermona pouted. "I am a fully trained ranger."

"In part," Seanchai replied. "But also this is not terrain you are familiar with. I value not only your skills, but your life."

"Come on," Sellia said to the young ranger. "Just try and keep quiet."

Jermona bristled until he saw her smile. Seanchai could relate. They disappeared into the darkness, and Seanchai called Rhoddan over. "We might be here a while. We should set a guard and have the rest of the company rest."

But they didn't have to wait long, after all. Jermona and Sellia returned, leading a group of six creatures armed with an assortment of heavy weapons, including curved broadswords and halberds. But they were not brandishing them, and Sellia had a grin on her face that contrasted nicely with the scowl on Jermona's.

"This is Seanchai, son of Seantai, the Wycaan that I spoke of," Sellia introduced. "Next to him is Ballendir, from the dwarf clan of Zu'Reising.

"Greetings," Scanchai rose and extended his hands in the universal sign of peace. Judging from the way the creatures stared; he realized it might not be quite so universal as those above ground thought.

One of the creatures stepped forward and bowed its head. It was the tallest of the party and stood at about five feet. "You have entered the kingdom of Saz'Saquat. To pass through, you must receive permission from our council. Or you may turn back, and we will forgive your trespass."

"I will happily meet with your council," Seanchai replied. He kept his voice steady, though he was excited at meeting a new potential ally. "Would you please escort us there?"

The creature nodded. "You may keep your weapons, but they must stay sheathed at all times. We have others watching with instructions to kill if they perceive any threat. Is that understood?"

"Clearly," Seanchai replied and turned to his company. "We come in peace," he said loudly. "Our only agenda is to pass through quickly."

The creatures led the group to their dwelling. As he passed Jermona, Seanchai patted the young ranger on the shoulder. "Good job," he said.

"It was the elfe who gave us away," Jermona muttered.

"Of course it was." Sellia smiled at Seanchai.

In route, Seanchai had an opportunity to observe his hosts. They were short and thin with disproportionately long arms. They were hairless and wore a light armor. He wondered whether this was for defense or to keep them dry from the ever-present moisture.

The group left the main path at a junction that took them around a bend. Up ahead, Seanchai was surprised to see a small town built into the walls all the way up the cavern on all sides.

They turned left up a path that had shops on either side. In the dim light, Seanchai couldn't discern what was being sold. He *could* sense a hum of energy that seemed to support these lights, though he couldn't track its source.

When they reached a plateau, there was a single stone building in front of them, supported by massive columns. Another creature stood in front of a solid-looking wooden door. This creature did not wear armor or carry a weapon. It bowed as they approached, and Seanchai and Ballendir reciprocated.

"Greetings, travelers. You have reached the hall of the council of Saz'Saquat. Three of you may enter. I strongly recommend that you choose a human, a dwarf and an elf, because your coexistence is what has intrigued the council since you were detected, and likely what has kept you alive.

"You must leave all weapons out here. The rest of your group may rest in the chamber over there. They will have food and drink. Who will enter?"

Seanchai and Ballendir stepped forward, and Seanchai turned to Shayth. "Will you join us?"

Shayth frowned. "You want me to represent my race?"

It was Sellia who responded. "Once, you were destined to hold the rank of such an ambassador. Perhaps it's time to see how you might have fared."

Shayth turned his head slightly, but Sellia did not smile or change her stoic expression. Their gazes locked for a few moments.

Then Shayth took a deep breath and stepped forward.

# THIRTY EIGHT

"The council of Saz'Saquat is in session," a loud male voice boomed. "Who stands before it? Come claim your rights and speak only truths."

Seanchai took a step forward. "I am Seanchai, son of Seantai. I am an elf and a Wycaan warrior. This is Ballendir, from Clan Den Zu'Reising. To my left stands Shayth, a human, of no family."

"You may step forward. In this hall, you will speak the truth and not be harmed for it. When you speak, the council will listen. When you are spoken to, we expect the courtesy returned."

Seanchai nodded his understanding. Another voice, a female, spoke.

"The tall ones from above ground cannot see us. We should brighten the chamber."

In the light, Seanchai could now see that they stood before a raised platform. Nine aqua green-skinned creatures, similar in build to those who had escorted everyone here, were seated in a semi-circle.

The female in the middle spoke.

"An elf, a dwarf, and a human," she observed, not trying to hide her curiosity. "We have been watching you since before you entered the far tunnel. We see that you are a close band, that no one is enslaved, and that you show each other respect.

"You are obviously on a journey of importance and haste, or you would not have come this way. Tell us the purpose of your journey. Know that we have spell casters among our council, and they can discern when you are not speaking the truth.

Ballendir stepped forward. "I am Ballendir, from the Clan of Den Zu'Reising. Our home was . . ."

Seanchai felt a presence in his mind. It was the old Saz'Saquatian sitting at the far end of the table staring at him. Its voice was clear in his head.

"*You have seen our people before, haven't you, white-haired one?*"

Seanchai tried to project his thoughts back. "*In my vision quest, I saw an aqua green-skinned race when the Great Alliance stood and when the great battle took place.*"

"*You seek to reforge that alliance?*"

"*Yes, I am on my way to . . .*"

Seanchai stopped, aware that everyone had fallen silent and was watching him and the telepathic council member.

"My apologies," Seanchai began.

"No," said the old Saz'Saquatian at the end of the table. "The blame is mine. I was scrying his mind, and he sensed me."

"Perhaps you can both allow the rest of us to participate?" the female said in a mixture of admonishment and amusement.

"I have seen your race before," Seanchai said, "in a vision when I was tested as a Wycaan. I am on a mission to reforge the Great Alliance and bring down the Emperor and his despotic rule. That is all we passed between us."

"But you did not intentionally seek us out?" another grayer green-skinned elder asked. "How, then, did you come by this path?"

"I was given directions from our priestess," Ballendir ventured, and it occurred to Seanchai that she might have intended this meeting.

The dwarf continued. "We are taking the fastest and least obtrusive route to the dwarf capital, Hothengold."

"You are being hunted by the Emperor's army?"

"Yes," Ballendir replied. "But I do not believe we're being followed here." He recounted the battle at Den Zu'Reising and the subsequent collapse of the mountain.

"Many, it seems, fall so that you might live." the female said to Seanchai. "Do you speak for all the elves?"

"No, my lady," Seanchai replied. "I am a Wycaan. My bond is to all races. It therefore falls to me to unite the races and bring about a new era of peace."

"That is interesting. You are young. Should you succeed to bring the Emperor's rule to an end, would you know how to rule fairly?"

"No, my lady, and in truth I have not given that much thought. Bringing Odessiya to that point in time sounds daunting enough right now." This brought laughter from the council. "From what I understand of our heritage, no Wycaan has ever held rule. We serve the rulers and the people."

"Are you the only Wycaan?"

Seanchai hesitated, and his voice wavered. "I hope not."

The female turned to Shayth. "And you, human. The Wycaan said you have no family. Is this true?"

"I was orphaned as a child. My actions and their consequences are mine alone," Shayth answered. His voice was cool and formal – a cadence Seanchai had heard often when they had first met.

"You are not, therefore, bonded to the Emperor in any way?"

"I chose to pledge my allegiance to Seanchai and Seanchai alone. Each member of our party has learned that the Wycaan is extremely adept at binding people to help him."

"You harbor much anger," said the telepath. "There is more that you choose not to reveal."

"It is of no importance," Shayth snapped.

Seanchai reached out a hand to calm him as the council tensed.

"Oh, but it is," the telepath replied. Then he turned to the council members. "I see much of what the human seeks to hide. It is important – very important – but of no consequence to our decision whether to let them pass through our territory. Should it become of consequence, either he or I will reveal it. Otherwise, we should respect his desire to not share his past with us."

"Please," said Seanchai. "Tell us who you are."

"We are the Aqua'lansis. Our people have traditionally lived in the great underwater cities in the seas around Odessiya and beyond. Our group here is a subspecies that has lived too long above the waterline and cannot return underwater. The dampness of caves is the best we can do. Our people came out of the water to join the Great Alliance and suffered in the same ways as the elves and dwarves. We are cut off from the rest of our people now."

Another from the council spoke. "It is told that the Wycaans can breathe under water. Is that so?"

"I can," Seanchai said. "My teacher could, and I have recently heard of another who was able to. I cannot speak for any others."

There was a murmur among the council members. The chief female interjected. "We will continue to talk without our guests. Rest and eat with your friends. We will call you back with our decision."

Seanchai felt as though he had just shut his eyes when he was woken and summoned to the great hall. One of his guards suggested that they stop for him to wash his face and wake up.

"Do I look that bad?" Seanchai asked.

The guard smiled. "Just fatigued. I saw how quickly you fell asleep."

The council was abuzz with anticipation. Seanchai noticed the telepathic elder point him out to an attendant, who approached Seanchai.

"Give him your mushroom pouch," the elder said to Seanchai. "He will prepare your drink. He is a healer and knows how."

"Thank you," Seanchai replied, handing over his pouch and turning to the council.

The elder began, her voice rich and pleasant. "Seanchai, son of Seantai, Wycaan warrior. The council grants you safe passage through our tunnels. Moreover, we will replenish your supplies and tell you of a shorter way to Hothengold. Our guides will accompany you partway. We will consider joining your alliance if the dwarves do, but our numbers are small and we need time to ponder this.

"In return, please consider this request: When matters have been settled at Hothengold and Odessiya is free, we ask that you join an expedition to Aqua'lania, the capital of our people. We believe we have created a system that will allow a delegation from here to go back underwater. It is a contraption that holds air and allows us to take it with us underwater. You will aid us in whatever way you can. Will you help us?"

Seanchai stood tall, his chest heaving with joy at this unexpected twist.

"I thank you for your generous offer and will fulfill your request if all goes well in our quest to defeat the Emperor. I would like to promise to help bring your people back to your nation. But I believe there will be a great battle at Hothengold, and I don't know what its casualties and consequences will be.

"However, I'm excited by the hope that your request brings me, both for reforging the Alliance and to show that the true role of a Wycaan is more than incessant fighting. Therefore, you have my word as a Wycaan that I will do my utmost to succeed in what you ask."

As one, the council rose to its feet. The leader addressed him with power and excitement.

"The promise of a Wycaan, Seanchai, son of Seantai, is good enough for this council. As we have kindled hope in you, so have you in us. Rest well, then, for a few hours. You will enter the great city of Hothengold in two days.

# THIRTY NINE

A had stared around his new room. He had always known comfort and luxury as the son of a leading general, but this was a whole other world. His room in the palace was huge. It had a balcony with a table and chairs, a private bathroom, and a cupboard that he could actually walk into. The valet who had brought his bags up droned on about how the room had been redesigned for a younger man.

He told Ahad how the Emperor himself had sent instructions to include a desk, a bookcase, and a second table where two could study comfortably together. The valet asked Ahad to sit at the table on the side facing the window, to see if his chair was comfortable and the correct height.

"What if the Crown Prince wants a view from his seat?" Ahad asked, amused.

"Oh, no. The Emperor wants no distractions for the Prince when he is studying. Also, that chair is custom-built to fit his height and posture."

Ahad turned to the bookcase, trying his best not to offend the earnest valet with a grin he wasn't sure he could suppress much longer. The valet, however, was relentless, and assumed that Ahad was checking out the books. The bottom two shelves had been filled with textbooks, but the upper ones were empty and waiting to be filled.

"If there is any other book that you or the Prince require, please let me know. Also, I was wondering which books you would require two copies of, so that you can both study together."

"Isn't the Prince a year behind me in school?" Ahad was confused.

The valet cleared his throat to signal he was on delicate ground. "The Prince, uhh, does not excel in his studies, though he has a fine mind."

"Then we shall have to find new ways to teach what he needs to know." Ahad found this challenge rather appealing.

"Spoken like a true tutor," came a voice from the doorway.

Ahad dropped to his knee, but saw that the valet only bowed.

"Ahad," the Prince corrected kindly. "You kneel before the Emperor alone. You need only bow to other royalty. Thank you, Steels. Should Ahad require anything, he will call for you."

"Yes, my lord," the valet bowed again and exited.

"My name is Phineus, Ahad. I don't like the name and will not suffer it in front of others. I tell you this as we will have a strange relationship. I am your Prince and yet you are my tutor. Perhaps one day we will also be friends. But not yet."

Prince Phineus walked around, surveying the room. He stopped by the table. "Which chair is mine? Wait, let me guess: this one, so that I am not distracted by the window. Am I correct?"

Before Ahad could answer, Phineus sat in the designated chair. "Ah, just the right height."

Ahad smiled and observed his new companion. Phineus was tall and thin. He had ginger hair, which Ahad assumed was from his mother's side, and freckles. Unlike other boys their age of such stature, however, he was not lanky or awkward.

"What are you thinking, Ahad? That I am petulant? Spoilt? The truth now."

"Actually, I was wondering if your military training is what gives you so much control over your movements. There are boys in my school who are tall and thin like you, but they are so . . . so ungainly."

"I will take the compliment, but please do not try to curry my favor by pandering to me."

"I was being honest," Ahad insisted.

The Prince frowned briefly. "I will teach you to be a better warrior by showing you no mercy in the sparring ring and gym. I expect you to treat me in kind when we study."

"I'm not sure it's discipline that you need," Ahad replied.

"Why?"

"You surely have that in you, just by way of your training and station. I thrive on the monotony of traditional study steps, but you might need . . ." He stopped and turned thoughtfully to the bookcase. He brought out a book on animals and turned to the insects. "Have you studied the skeletal differences?"

"Yes," groaned Phineus, "and I remember none of it."

"They probably showed you pictures and dead animals."

"And it was scintillating," Phineus yawned, and they both laughed.

"Let's go out riding," Ahad said. "I want to try something."

"See! You got all five correct," Ahad said as they sat on a rock while their horses grazed. Ahad felt very proud of himself. "It's much easier when you see them in nature. You can't tell the measure of an opponent you are fighting until you see him moving. Am I right?"

Phineus nodded. "And now I can remember the insects because I've been trained to see how an adversary holds himself. I like your approach, Ahad. Now, enough studies. Something for you, I think. Tell me a secret, a fear, an ambition."

Ahad thought for a moment. It occurred to him that this might be a trap, but if so, it was clumsy coming on their first day together. Still, he had to offer something.

"I worry about my father."

"Your father? General Tarlach's a great officer. I've studied his tactics in multiple battles. He has a brilliant strategic mind. My father thinks highly of him from what I've heard."

"Do you see the Emperor very often?"

Prince Phineus frowned. "Why do you ask?"

Ahad felt he had taken a wrong turn and redirected the conversation. "I miss my father. I wonder what kind of a relationship we would have if he was always close by."

Prince Phineus seemed to relax. "If you become a soldier and join his battalion, you could be near him."

"It would be different," Ahad answered. "He would always be the general and maintain that mask."

"Then you understand my relationship with the Emperor. Only we don't have the excuse of distance. He lives one floor above me and eats in the same wretched palace, but rarely at the same wretched table."

# FORTY

S eanchai and Ilana walked hand-in-hand at the back of the company.
Seanchai's friends had congratulated him on negotiating their
safe passage and were buoyed by the Aqua'lansis' shortcut. In contrast,
he had been brooding since they had left Saz'Saquat, apprehensive
because the shortened distance meant that he would face the dwarf
Clansfelt – and the next battle with this formidable general – quicker
than he had anticipated.

"Ballendir has continued to council you on dwarf politics,
Seanchai. Why are you so tense?" Ilana easily anticipated his fear.

"Ballendir is certainly a big help," Seanchai replied. "But it's been
more than half a century since the dwarves last met and a new king
took the throne. I'm not sure how accurate Ballendir's advice is."

"Just be yourself," Ilana said, squeezing his hand. "So far you've
done very well when you are just you."

"The first non-dwarf emissary, and I bring a huge army led by
General Tarlach to Hothengold as a gift."

"You just might have done them a favor. They were oblivious to
the fact that the Emperor has been studying explosives and training
a whole army of dwarves, Why was he doing that if not to unleash
them on the dwarves? Their whole defensive strategy has been
rendered useless. The Emperor would have had an army in front of

each clan stronghold and conquered them in days. They should be thanking you."

Seanchai laughed. "Perhaps *you* should represent me, not Ballendir."

The others had stopped ahead of them, and Seanchai let go of Ilana's hand. When they caught up with the group, Seanchai's mouth dropped open and Ilana gasped. Ballendir opened his arms excitedly.

"Welcome to Hothengold, capital of the great and ancient dwarf nation," he declared.

Seanchai shook his head in wonder. They had exited the tunnels and were on a ledge overlooking a gigantic cavern. It was so big, in fact, that he could not see its far side. This was truly a city – he could see houses, streets, and shops. The higher the ground, the more ostentatious the buildings became. Opposite them rose thick stone walls with towers and ramparts. No doubt this was the palace of the Dwarf King.

Everyone was looking at him, awaiting his instruction. He turned to Ballendir. "Master Dwarf," he said calmly. "We are in your hands. Please lead us into Hothengold."

"Mah pleasure," purred Ballendir.

A path unfolded before them as they made their way through the city. Their arrival had been anticipated, and hundreds of curious dwarves thronged the streets and leaned out of windows. Children and adults alike pointed and gawked.

Most of these dwarves had never been above ground, much less seen an elf or a human. How would Mhari have held herself? Seanchai kept his eyes ahead of him, trying to appear as regal as possible, but it was all a façade. He had to will his legs forward and muster all his discipline not to draw his hood over his head.

"You can bend your knees, you know," Rhoddan whispered from behind him, and the others snickered.

Seanchai relaxed ever so slightly. After a long while, shops replaced the houses, and the road widened considerably. Ahead was a thirty-foot statue on a stone pillar in the middle of a huge town square. As they came closer, Seanchai could see the statue was a dwarf with long, white hair. He gasped.

"Yeh needn't worry," Ballendir said. "We dwarves like our processions."

Confused, Seanchai looked in front to Ballendir. Waiting ahead of them was a contingent of dwarf soldiers, standing to attention. When they reached the soldiers, Ballendir stretched himself up tall, trying to look less nervous than he was.

"I am Ballendir, of the clan—"

"Your name precedes you, young dwarf," the captain intoned. "The dwarf who befriended outsiders. The dwarf who defied the First Decree and brought outsiders underground. Some call you a traitor; others claim you're a prophet."

"What do you think, Captain?" Ballendir challenged.

The captain stared at him for a moment and then smiled. "I think you would make an interesting companion for a night of quaffing ale and smoking good pipe weed."

Behind him, his soldiers laughed, and Ballendir relaxed. "Then I ask yeh permission to take mah party to the palace to prepare for the Clansfelt, Captain."

"Pass by us, you may not. We are so ordered to escort you ourselves." He addressed the entire group. "Our wise King has decided not to request your weapons. However, before entering the palace, you must each pass through the gate of fealty. Our spell casters have prepared it so that your passage through it binds you by oath not to draw your weapons against a dwarf of Hothengold unless in defense of self, the crown, or your party."

Seanchai and the others decided not to ask what would happen if the oath was broken. "We accept your terms, Captain," Seanchai said. "Please lead us on."

The captain turned and barked an order. His troops fell in line around the visitors, and they marched as a unit to the castle.

At the end of the square was a bustling market pouring out into the adjacent neighborhood. The road they followed led out from the center of the city and widened as it began its ascent to the imposing palace.

Along the roads were tall sculptures made of rock and shining stones. When they neared the thick stone walls surrounding the palace, a great iron portcullis was raised, the chains that cranked it rasping forebodingly.

Ballendir turned to Seanchai and spoke quietly. "I doubt that gate has been closed for many a year. They lowered it for yeh. Remember, dwarves are polite, but don't interpret their courtesies as trust. I'm very surprised that yeh've been allowed to keep yeh weapons. It may be that someone within our ranks is worried for yeh safety."

They entered a steep courtyard surrounded by smooth, tall walls and with four paths leading from it in each direction. The walls had narrow slits for archers, but there were none stationed for their arrival. In the courtyard's center stood another group of dwarves – soldiers and commoners alike. One dwarf stepped forward, clad in chain mail and holding a staff, but no weapons.

"I am Golthspere, diplomatic councilor to the King," he said. "Please consider me your host until the Clansfelt begins. We have three rooms prepared for you – one for the elfes, and one each for the male elves and humans. If this is problematic in any way, please let me know immediately. We do not know your customs. These attendants," he gestured to three dwarves nearby, "are at your service. You will have a chance to bathe, eat and rest."

"Thank you," Seanchai said. "This sounds great."

When he turned toward the attendants, Golthspere stopped him. "I have other instructions regarding you, Seanchai, son of Seantai." He pointed in another direction where a small dwarfe stood by an entrance, wrapped in a cloak. "You will please follow her."

Seanchai turned and smiled at his friends. "I'll see you soon," he said as cheerfully as he could manage around the pit in his stomach.

Ballendir stepped forward to accompany him, but Golthspere held out a hand. "He must walk alone."

Seanchai and Ballendir exchanged glances before the tall elf turned and joined his dwarfe guide, smiling. She bowed low and led him inside.

# FORTY ONE

Seanchai followed the diminutive dwarfe through several steeply descending corridors, each of which was considerably colder and damper than the last. Finally, they entered a small room connected to three others.

"Wait here, please," said the guide in a sweet voice. "I will be quick."

She disappeared into one of the adjoining rooms, and Seanchai heard whispers and movement. He considered scrying, but quickly dismissed the idea. He didn't want to offend them.

His hostess returned and smiled. "Please come inside."

Seanchai entered a small hexagonal room. In the middle was a fireplace with a low fire burning. The walls were lined with bookcases, and there were several scrolls on a desk. Three comfortable chairs were positioned near the fire.

A cloaked figure stood before him with his back turned, drinking from a goblet. All that Seanchai could make out was the shaking hand lifting the drink to his lips.

Seanchai glanced at the dwarfe who had escorted him. She hovered nearby, looking concerned. The figure put the cup down and took a staff from nearby. Leaning heavily on it, he shuffled around to meet his guest.

"Greetings, Seanchai, son of Seantai, Wycaan apprentice of the
late Master Mhari."

An unsteady hand rose to remove his hood. The dwarf that stood
before Seanchai was old and bent over, with long, white hair.

Seanchai gasped and then, recovering, bent low. "I had no idea
there were others," was all he could say, quickly adding "Master."

The old Wycaan dwarf moved slowly to a chair. The attendant
moved closer, but did not offer help.

"Sit, please. I have some tea prepared for you. It is not the danseng
that your Master preferred, but a mushroom with similar properties."

"Ruzakil?" Seanchai realized he was anxious to impress.

The dwarf stared at him for a moment, an eyebrow raised.

"When my own supply of danseng was growing low, I was given
a pouch of Ruzakil by . . ." Seanchai trailed off as he realized he was
speaking to the priestess' long-lost mate.

"How is she?" the old Wycaan asked.

"I'm sorry," Seanchai said, furious with himself. "I hadn't made
the connection."

"Always make the connection," the Master said sternly, and
Seanchai thought of Mhari. "You must measure your words at all
times, especially here at Hothengold."

"Yes, Master. The priestess brought down the Bordan Mountain
after she was sure we had escaped. I don't think she . . ."

The old one nodded. "According to dwarf mythology, we will
soon be together. I look forward to it. Did she pass on her knowledge?"

"Yes," Seanchai said. "Her name is Ellendir. She is the sister of Ballendir, the dwarf who offered to swing the axe for me."

The attendant brought Seanchai a cup of steaming Ruzakil, and he felt its restorative qualities on his first sip.

"Thank you," he said to her.

She bowed slightly. "Please give me your pouch. I will replenish and return it to you."

Seanchai did so, and then turned to find the old dwarf staring into the fire. He waited and, after a while, the old one sighed.

"Do you have a special someone? A mate?"

"I do," Seanchai replied.

"When did you last see her?"

"She travels with us."

The old Wycaan looked up at Seanchai. "That is good and problematic. She can be a great source of strength for you, but also your weakness."

"The old priestess counseled us about this," Seanchai said.

"Did she give you her stones?"

"Yes."

"The green ones?"

"Yes."

The old dwarf smiled. "It was a sad moment. I would not take my half. I tried to persuade her to find another mate who could reciprocate in a way that she deserved.

"She thought me cruel, even though she understood. What is the name of your mate?"

"Ilana."

"Have you thought of setting Ilana free? She is young. If she has aroused your heart then she must be special and so capable of finding a worthy mate, one who would be able to settle down and give her a good life."

"No. We have discussed it, but we won't give each other up."

"Seanchai," the dwarf's voice became stronger. "You condemn her to a life of waiting, a life of one-way sacrifice. She will spend her days wondering where you are, whether you are alive, if she will ever see you again. What kind of a life is that?

"You will not be able to travel together for long. Nature has demands upon our females. If you have offsprings, she will settle to tend them. Then you will be but a visitor, almost a stranger to your own children.

"And while you do travel together, she represents the weakest link in your chain. Is your relationship secret?"

"No."

The old dwarf shook his head. "Then she is a danger to you and a danger to those around you. If you ever have to decide between her life and your duty, will you be strong enough?"

Seanchai didn't answer, and from the look on the old Wycaan's face, he didn't need to.

"We have little time together, and I would like to pass on some of my own knowledge. Address me as Master Onyxei. How have you learned the stories, the words?"

"From Master Mhari, and from a book that she gave me."

"Do you have the book now?"

"Yes."

"You must learn it by heart. Never become attached to any possessions. Keep everything in your mind. What weapons do you know and carry?"

"I have the elf long and short knife. I can fire a bow, though I have not used one in combat. The Win Dao swords came to me during my transformation. Mhari taught me, but time was short, and I look forward to studying with a Master of such weapons."

"For now, prioritize the stories and words. Learning new weapons will have to wait, and I cannot train you. My death draws near.

"I was a prisoner of the Emperor, and I carry a poison inside my body that I have fought against in vain. The Emperor and his officers enjoy making and using new poisons. Be warned, for you might sometimes feel invincible. You are not."

The attendant appeared at the door. "Master? Excuse me. Minister Golthspere reminds you that Seanchai must attend the first hearing in a few hours."

"Will you not attend?" Seanchai asked, feeling the panic rising.

The old Wycaan shook his head. "I'm of no use anymore."

"But are we not meant to serve as councilors to our people?" Seanchai asked, his voice shaking.

"We are. But my people now have you to counsel them. A Wycaan who will lead them into the very battle for which they must prepare."

"But your presence," Seanchai continued, "would help to unite those who do not want to go above ground with those who do. It might help them see an elf before them if a dwarf stands beside him. You can help facilitate a smoother decision for the dwarf nation to create the Alliance."

The old Wycaan sighed. "Asserting my authority and then falling in the first wave of battle would be most detrimental for moral."

"What is important," Seanchai insisted, "is that a swift consensus is reached so that we can make the appropriate plans. The influence of a young, unmet Wycaan will not carry the weight you have. Stand with me before the council. Send a clear message that the Wycaan Order is united. Let them see dwarf and elf together, the races reuniting against a common evil. We are back to reforge the Alliance and lead all the peoples of Odessiya into a new age."

Master Onyxei pursed his dried lips. "That is a nice speech; remember it. I will consider what you have said. Now go rest and prepare."

# FORTY TWO

Seanchai was escorted to where his friends had settled. Rhoddan and Jermona were snoring contently; Shayth was awake and sharpening his blades. He looked up when Seanchai entered.

"What was that all about?"

Seanchai yawned. "Unfortunately, not something that's going to help us, it seems. I'll tell you later. Right now, I need to bathe and sleep."

"Give me your blades," Shayth replied. "I'll sharpen them for you."

"My blades don't need sharpening," Seanchai yawned proudly, "ever."

"Really? Cool, I guess. Sharpening weapons helps me relax and prevents me from losing my mind."

"We wouldn't want that, now, would we?" Seanchai asked, and Shayth smirked. "We've come a long way together, my friend."

"We have. You've changed my life, Seanchai, without even trying. Had you tried, I think you would have failed. Still, I need more blades to sharpen. Do you think I can take Rhoddan's without waking him?"

"Not a chance. Behind those rumbling snores is the sleep of a warrior. Here, why don't you work on these?"

He handed Shayth his elf blades: the long and short knife. He also took a dirk from his boot. Then he undressed.

"I didn't know you had that," Shayth said balancing the dirk in his hand. "It's a good blade."

"It was Mhari's. I have never used it, but it is . . . well . . . something of hers. You know?"

"Kind of," Shayth replied. "I haven't been that close to anyone but my parents, and I never got anything that belonged to my father." He paused and changed the subject. "Your swords need names. If you're going to change history, history will demand names for your blades."

Seanchai wrapped a towel around his body. "I've got enough to think about for now. You think on it, and we'll discuss it when we get a quiet moment."

They both laughed at the idea of a quiet moment.

"On our next vacation," Shayth said.

"How about Peacebringer and Justicemaker?" Seanchai asked.

Shayth laughed. "That'll strike terror in the hearts of our enemies. Why don't you leave this to me?"

Seanchai smiled and walked to their door.

"Seanchai?" Shayth regarded him seriously. "We've saved each other's lives in battle many times already. But you've saved my life in other ways. I want you to know I'm aware of this, and that I appreciate it."

Seanchai smiled, a little embarrassed. "Thank you," he said. "We all keep each other going. You, Ilana, Sellia, the mighty snoring warrior . . . it's like we feed off of each other. I cherish my relationship with each of you. We're like a family, and you're very much part of that family, Shayth."

"Me?" Shayth snorted. "Part of a family? Never saw that coming."

"It's the magic of the Wycaans," Seanchai laughed.

"No," said Shayth, his voice serious, "it's your own special magic."

When Seanchai returned from his bath, he found Ballendir sitting on Shayth's bed, smoking his pipe and describing a fierce battle that involved dwarf warriors' great heroism. He rose as Seanchai entered.

"Aah, here is the dwa- . . . err, elf himself. Come, Seanchai, I wish yeh to meet Rothendir, mah clan leader."

"Your clan leader? I thought that . . ."

"No," Ballendir replied. "Rothendir left our home with a few of the council before we even arrived. They were on their way back from surveying a potential mine further north and when they heard an army was approaching, they left for Hothengold to get help.

"The dwarf yeh met was Ethendir, another experienced leader, from mah own house. We wanted the enemy to think they had destroyed the clan leadership. I heard it was a very controversial decision for her to leave, and she was against it, but the clan overruled her. It was decided that the priestess and I would lead the fight. Some of the older warriors stayed, but many of the council left and came here."

"Why?" Seanchai asked. "How could they leave the others?"

"What happens here over the next few days will be critical for our clan's future. Dwarf clans constantly jostle for power, influence, and favor with the King. He decides which clan should mine a new area when gold or metals are discovered.

"The stakes are always high. I was worried when we arrived at Hothengold that Rothendir might balk at offering yeh open support if the King seems against yeh. Our clan has always been seen as a bit maverick, so it's important we make a good impression. What's so funny?"

"I'm sorry," Seanchai said, trying to suppress a smile. "I'm being counseled about fitting in by one who is seen as nonconformist in his own clan, and now discover that his clan is radical in comparison to the rest of the dwarf nation?"

"The first piece of advice I gave yeh was not to take council from mah. That was wise enough."

They laughed, and Seanchai looked around for his clothes. They weren't where he left them.

"Yeh'll have enough problems facing the high council without smelling badly. Yeh clothes are being washed. Try those on. They're probably too short for you."

Seanchai struggled into a long-sleeved, lime green v-neck tunic, which came halfway up to his elbows. The trousers were a thicker, brown material and hugged his legs. There was a rope to tie around his waist and a pair of thick socks. A brown waistcoat rounded out his outfit.

"How do I look?" he said, as he stretched out his arms. His shins were exposed from under his pants, and the seams at the shoulders tightened and groaned.

Shayth and the now-awake Rhoddan smiled as Ilana and Sellia entered the room.

"Don't you look dashing," Sellia said, embarrassing him as her eyes roved his body. "I think you've grown a bit since I last checked you out. Strapping lad."

Seanchai flew out of the room. "Come, Ballendir," he called. "We'll be late for our very important meeting."

His friends' laughter followed him down the corridor. Ballendir had to run to catch up.

"Nice retreat," the dwarf huffed, "but you're going the wrong way."

They stopped outside a doorway, and Ballendir spoke quietly with the two guards posted there. Seanchai could hear raised voices inside, and his elf hearing enabled him to pick up pieces of the argument. It didn't sound encouraging, and he sighed deeply as Ballendir led him inside.

The council sat around a table, their conversation curtailed into tense silence as their guests took their places.

"Welcome, Ballendir," said Rothendir. She was younger than her double had been, but held herself with authority. "Well met, Seanchai, son of Seantai. I've heard a lot about you."

Seanchai bowed. "I'm sorry for your losses and the losses of your clan."

She nodded. "Now is not the time to mourn our dead. I am sure they feast in the halls of our ancestors. But I thank you, nonetheless." She turned to Ballendir. "You made very good time."

"Our journey was eventful," Ballendir offered, "but those are tales for another time. Please bring us up to speed with what has happened here."

"The clans are angry," Rothendir said. "They're angry that dwarves have been conscripted to fight other dwarves. They're angry with us for allowing long folk underground. They're angry with Seanchai for the fact that a mighty army approaches. They're angry with the King for not making a decision yet. Other than that: business as usual."

"We heard arguing from outside," Seanchai said. "Is Clan Den Zu'Reising also divided?"

"It is," Rothendir said. "There are those here who blame you for the destruction of Mount Zu'Reising and the death of our priestess and elders. They feel any association with Seanchai compromises our position with the new king, and there are those who feel the time for hiding underground is over and would have been over even if you had not come along."

"How will you decide?" Seanchai asked.

They all looked to Rothendir. She sighed. "We have already decided. Clan Den Zu'Reising will help you gain the support of the other clans. But know we take a great risk and don't support you easily. We have just lost our home and mining base."

"Then why?" Seanchai asked.

Rothendir glanced to the red-haired dwarf who had opposed Seanchai at their first meeting at Mount Zu'Reising. He cleared his throat.

"We support you, Wycaan, because we know in our hearts that you're right. The empire is a threat to the dwarf nation. It must fall."

# FORTY THREE

A had sat across the table from the Prince. He had been in the palace for a week and had enjoyed riding the fine palace horses, honing his military training, and the intrigue of getting to know the Prince and the workings of the palace.

He had received access to the impressive royal library and had been allowed to take a number of books back to his room. His attempts to encourage his student to study, however, were often rebuffed.

That morning, Ahad was summoned before the Emperor. He dressed in his finest clothes and washed his face. But he was sweating, even in the comfortable spring air. He opened his bedroom door and found Phineus there.

"Going to see Daddy, I hear," the younger man spat, his face contorted by barely-suppressed jealous rage.

Ahad opened his mouth, but found nothing to say.

"Don't clam up," the Prince sneered. "He hates that. He'll do everything to intimidate you, and then get angry with you when he succeeds. Make sure you give a good account of our activities. He'll judge you in the end, not me. He is stuck with me."

"Hey," Ahad blurted out. "*He* summoned *me*, you know. How about a little support?"

The Prince winced and then stepped inside and closed the door to Ahad's room. "He's your Emperor. He holds your life in the palm of his hand. You can't be my friend *and* serve him. But remember, you're just a boy whose parents are in trouble with him, so you need to toe the line."

"*That's* your encouragement?"

"That's just the way it is."

Ahad glared at him. He felt as though he had been slapped across the face. "Excuse me," he said brusquely as he brushed past. "My Emperor awaits." He slammed the door behind him.

"What do I do?" Ahad asked the man who escorted him into a waiting room.

The man smiled. "You will not see him. He sits behind a curtain, though rest assured he sees you clearly. Kneel when he enters, and wait for him to tell you to rise. Then stand unless offered a seat. Answer his questions as succinctly as you can. He appreciates brevity and, of course, the absolute truth. Wait here."

Ahad gratefully accepted the glass of water he was offered. He sat and waited for what seemed hours before he was ushered into a room. A thick curtain hung across its middle. He saw a silhouette behind it and realized the Emperor was already there. He quickly dropped to his knee and bowed his head.

"Stand up, Ahad Tarlach," an icy voice said. "It's a pleasure to meet the son of my most accomplished general and revered friend."

"T-the honor is mine, my lord." Ahad rose and felt that his throat had constricted.

"I have spoken with your father. He knows you are here and is grateful. I also sent word to your mother, but I imagine her response will take several days yet."

"Thank you, my lord."

"How are you doing? Do you have everything you need?"

"Oh yes, sire. I-I appreciate everything you have provided."

"Good. Tell me, how is your relationship with my son?"

Ahad cleared his throat. "We're getting to know each other, sire. I hope we can become good friends."

"He needs a friendship such as yours. He needs your help to study. He is not, unfortunately, a good student."

"He's not receptive to conventional methods, my lord," Ahad said, realizing that he felt defensive for his new friend. "But if we can find ways that interest him so that he doesn't feel he is being forced to study, then . . . We went out on his horses and were watching insects while we rested. He picked up how to classify them really quickly by just seeing the insects move in nature. If he cou–"

"Enough." The Emperor cut him off. "I have little time, but I appreciate your diligence, Ahad. Show him kindness, knowledge, and friendship, and you will serve me well. Do you understand, lad?"

"Yes, my lord."

"Your father is on a difficult mission. He is used to defeating hoards of soldiers, but he seems unable to capture my nephew. What do you know of Shayth?"

"Very little, my lord. We played together when we were very young, so I am told. But once he came to live with us, he was a bit of a bully."

"Your parents were very kind to take the boy in. He betrayed their affection by running away. Then he embarrassed them by his murderous acts. Now he is betraying your father again."

Ahad didn't know what to say. He really hadn't much recollection of Shayth, but suddenly felt a wave of anger at how Shayth was hurting his father. The Emperor let this sit, and changed course.

"What would your father council if he was able to talk to you about being in my palace?"

"He would tell me to do my best to help the Crown Prince."

"What else? Remember, your father has a fine strategic mind."

Ahad blinked and thought fast. He felt the sweat trickle down his neck. "My lord, he would tell me that this is a fine opportunity for me to create a powerful ally. He would . . ."

Ahad's voice trailed off.

"Say what you were you going to say," the Emperor commanded.

Ahad swallowed hard. "He would remind me of his relationship with your brother. My father cherished his friendship with, with . . ."

" . . . with the late Prince Shindell. Yes, you are right. Do not falter. I demand your honesty, so reply as you must."

"I'm sorry about your brother, my lord – about his tragic loss."

"It's a terrible thing to lose a brother, Ahad. But there's nothing worse than losing a son."

Ahad thought that the Emperor was referring to a baby son he had lost. There had been much gossip for the Emperor soon married a concubine, who had already given birth several years before to Phineus. Some wondered if the baby had died a natural death for its mother was soon put aside for the former mistress.

Ahad's mind was racing. "Is the Prince in danger?"

"Not that I know of," the Emperor replied. "I am glad you are here with my son and in my palace. Thank you for your service. You may leave now."

Ahad bowed and left. He walked down the corridor behind his escort. What had the Emperor meant about losing a son? Maybe he wasn't even referring to the dead baby. Was it a threat to Ahad's own safety? Suddenly, he was afraid for his father and mother, and for himself. He badly wanted to talk with his grandfather, but wondered if he would even be allowed to leave the palace.

It suddenly hit Ahad. Was he already a prisoner?

His mind went to Shayth, that ungrateful, murderous bully. He hated him. If Shayth ever caused more damage to his father, Ahad swore that he would find and kill him.

# FORTY FOUR

Seanchai met with Rothendir and Ballendir the next morning in a small room reserved for Clan Den Zu'Reising away from the Great Hall.

The cave was plainly adorned with only a single shield on the wall. Seanchai noted the emblem of the clan: a black mountain going deep underground.

They settled around a small table on rock cubes. As soon as Seanchai sat down, an attendant brought him some of the mushroom tea in a thick ceramic mug, as well as a full pewter flask to refill from. The others were also served drinks. Only when the attendant left did Rothendir speak, her voice low as she leaned in.

"How did you sleep, Wycaan?"

"I slept well, thank you. It's been a while since I haven't had to guard or keep one ear open for danger."

She smiled. "You are not in immediate danger, no, but not everyone here is your ally yet. Keep your ears and eyes alert." She sipped her tea, allowing this to sink in. "What has Ballendir told you about the clan hierarchy?"

Ballendir went to speak, but the old dwarf raised her hand. "Let him tell me."

"I know there are six major clans here," Seanchai began, "though there are smaller ones that likely will not be represented at the Clansfelt.

I understand that four must agree for a decision to be binding to all, and I understand that we are unsure of the King's position."

"We?"

"Clan Den Zu'Reising is my ally, no?"

She smiled again. "We are. I was just surprised."

"That I said 'we'?"

She shook her head. "That I am so ready to accept it. Seanchai, you must prepare yourself to meet with the clans separately if we can arrange it. Clan Den Zu'Garten is the biggest and most powerful. They live here in Hothengold and the King is from their clan. I hope that you will meet with their council today. We must have their support.

"Clan Den Zu'Chantague lives in the south. They are very wealthy and can muster many troops, but will be wary of damaging the many assets and connections they have from their considerable business throughout the Empire. I am worried about them."

She paused again to drink. "Clan Dan Zu'Reiltan dwells in the north. They have been very isolated, like us, but for a very different reason. They are extremely devout to our religious ways and very traditional. They will be cautious about any change and certainly about having your presence underground. You will recognize them by their dark brown wraparound cloaks and hoods. Their priests wear the same in black, often with masks, as well. We will not waste time courting them.

"The two other clans are small, and we need to find out more about them. They both live in the central areas near here, so they're vulnerable and, I believe, will follow the lead of the two bigger clans, but we're trying to reach out and discover more.

"For now, we must focus on Clan Den Zu'Garten and Clan Den Zu'Chantague.

Like I said, we are trying to set up . . ."

She stopped abruptly as the attendant swept into the room.

"I said we should not be disturbed," she snapped, but the attendant just nodded.

"I have a message from the King, mi'lady. He wishes to meet Seanchai."

"When?"

"Now."

Ballendir and Rothendir exchanged worried glances that only intensified when the attendant stopped Ballendir from rising from his seat.

"The King requires only the presence of the Wycaan."

Seanchai stood up.

"Be careful," Rothendir said. "Do not assume you are alone even when no other is in sight."

Seanchai walked through a series of passages surrounded by four guards. They did not speak to him, and Seanchai noticed how the expressions on the faces of those he passed seemed to divide by age. The older dwarves seemed angry or suspicious of him, while the younger ones regarded him more with curiosity and anticipation.

They stopped to allow a procession of brown-clad dwarves spreading incense pass before them.

"Dan Zu'Reiltan?" Seanchai muttered, and one of the guards nodded curtly.

In the middle were four masked, black-clad dwarves like Rothendir had described. They stopped when they saw Seanchai.

One stepped forward, and the guards were hesitant about whether to give way or not.

"It's okay," Seanchai said. "Let him approach."

They moved aside and the masked face turned up to look at Seanchai.

"Greetings," Seanchai said, holding his hands out to his side, palms facing the dwarf.

The dwarf slowly regarded Seanchai's hands before lifting his mask just enough to spit on the ground.

"Your presence defiles our city and people. You should go back above ground with the other tall ones. Leave, or there will be blood shed."

"Blood will be shed either way," Seanchai replied, loud enough for all to hear. "There are thousands of troops marching to the Hoth Mountains as we speak."

"They come for you, not us. You bring them upon us."

"The Emperor seeks total domination. He already has thousands of dwarves in servitude."

"They went above ground and so lost the protection of the gods."

"You don't understand the intentions of the Emperor," Seanchai couldn't hide his frustration.

"And you do not understand the intentions of our gods," the priest snapped back. "Go back to where you came from, or the gods will send you by our hands."

Again, he spat on the ground, turned, and rejoined the others. The chanting and procession continued. When they had passed, Seanchai turned to his guards.

"What do you think of them?"

"They are priests," one replied, without enthusiasm. "We must respect them."

"Why?"

"They have the ear of the gods," another replied. "Please come, the King is waiting."

The path sloped upward sharply and leveled out onto a plateau near the wall of the great cavern with a simple stone garden, benches, and tall columns. All were decorated with carvings or gems. Sculptured rocks were arranged in various patterns. They approached a small group of dwarves who parted at their approach.

In the middle stood the King, crowned by a round band of gold that held several shining stones. He smiled at Seanchai, and then told his retinue to leave them.

"Your Majesty," Seanchai bowed. "I was not expecting to meet you so soon. I have not been counseled in how to address you, or your customs."

"Do not worry, at least when we're alone," the King replied. "These are pressing times, and we need to act fast. My people need a strong leader, and I must understand what is transpiring above ground. Please join me over at that bench."

As they walked together, Seanchai saw a diminutive figure on the bench. The King extended a hand. "I believe you've met my cherished friend and councilor, Master Onyxei."

# FORTY FIVE

"Master Onyxei," Seanchai said, and again bowed. The King settled on the bench next to the old Wycaan, and Seanchai knelt on the floor. Even in such a position, he was almost at head height with his two companions.

"Before I was crowned, I led a small group of dwarves to secretly learn more of the other races. This is how I met Onyxei."

"You rescued me, to be more accurate," Onyxei said as he stroked his white beard, "and you have taken care of me all these years."

"I went to Master Onyxei's chambers when you arrived, and we sat for many hours. He told me of your quest to reforge the Alliance and spoke of the Wycaans.

"I grew up with stories of when the races lived together in harmony, but never imagined I'd see the day one worked to unite us all again. And you come in such dire circumstances. Had you come here by yourself and without real cause, you would not have been received well. In fact, you may well not have been received at all.

"But there are two huge armies at your back with dwarf soldiers willing to raise their axes against their own. Our considerable defenses were never built to stave off other dwarves."

"They also come with explosives," Seanchai added. "I'm sure they'll have learned a few things from their attack on Den

Zu'Reising. Fighting underground makes you particularly vulnerable to explosives."

The King nodded. "You ask me to accept you and your friends underground, then you ask that we all join you above ground to fight a massive army of our own people? You aren't too demanding, are you?"

He laughed and Onyxei smiled, shaking his white beard. "For centuries, it has fallen to the Wycaans to bring bad tidings and warnings and Seanchai is a Wycaan. But we are often simply messengers. You knew the Empire would come eventually. The training of dwarves and the exploration of explosives as a means of war illustrates that this has been planned for some time."

The King nodded. "Still, it is a tough position. I must determine what's in the best interest of my people, not cater to my own sense of adventure. You know that, my friend. I need to know this is a fight we can win. If not, I must listen to those who counsel for negotiation. And do remember, I am only one voice on the High Council."

"But you are a powerful voice," Onyxei persisted, playing his part in a debate they had clearly been through many times. "Many don't know you as I do, but they will bind themselves to you when they do."

"Even Clan Dan Zu'Reiltan?" Seanchai interrupted.

"You have met them?" The King asked and frowned.

"I met a few of their priests just now on my way here."

"Did they roll out the welcome mat for you?" The King smiled wryly. "I met with them a few hours ago. It did not go well, but they will be bound by the council's decision."

"Even if it goes against their religious beliefs?"

Onyxei laughed. "Religions are like water, Seanchai. Despite their strong adherence to traditions, they cannot stand still and remain pure. Defying the council is an extreme step indeed. They would lose considerable influence and power."

"And could they try something violent?"

"Did they threaten you?" Onyxei's face was immediately serious.

"Yes, but I'm more worried about the King and any clan leaders who openly support us."

Onyxei spoke after a moment of contemplation. "To attack you, Seanchai, yes, I could imagine that. But to assassinate another clan chief or even the King seems very far-fetched."

"Yet not beyond the realm of possibility," the King admitted. "I am going to call the first council meeting tomorrow, Seanchai. You will be allowed to address us once, but only clan members may be present for the debate and proceedings. Know that I will listen closely to your words. You still have to persuade me, too."

"Very well," Seanchai said and bowed. "Thank you, Your Majesty."

The King turned to Onyxei. "Come, my friend. I will walk you back to your chambers."

Seanchai watched them slowly walk away and disappear into a tunnel. He headed back to his escorts. As he did, he caught glimpses of silver from behind pillars. The King was obviously keeping up significant security despite his dismissal of an assassination attempt.

But when he reached his guards, he gasped. All four lay crumpled on the ground, blood dripping from the sides of their mouths and from holes in their necks. Poison. Seanchai crouched and summoned wards to protect himself. He was still not used to creating such defenses but Mhari had told him they could deflect most arrows and darts, though not a broadsword or axe. Scrying the area around him, he discerned that there was no one nearby him.

He ran back toward the tunnel the King and Onyxei had taken, but realized he wouldn't know which direction to go if the tunnel split. A group of soldiers were standing at the edge of the park. Seanchai shouted to them. "The King is in danger. To the King."

They hurried after him. Inside the tunnel, he tripped over three soldiers' bodies, then veered toward the sound of a scuffle nearby. The tunnel opened into a wider cavern where the King and the Wycaan dwarf stood back-to-back in the middle. Menacing dark shapes circled them, and there were poison darts on the ground.

The Wycaan dwarf's wards were protecting himself and the King, but Seanchai could sense the energy in Onyxei's wards was weaker than his own.

He drew his swords and charged a group of dark-clothed dwarves, who fell swiftly under his whirling blades. A second group fled into a nearby tunnel. Seanchai started after them, but quickly realized his mistake and turned back.

A third group of black-clad dwarves surrounded Onyxei and the King, while a fourth group fought with the guards Seanchai had brought. One held a big iron crossbow. Seanchai knew its heavy arrow would pierce Onyxei's weakening defenses. The old Wycaan's head turned to Seanchai. His soundless voice was clear in Seanchai's mind.

"*The King, Seanchai. Save the King.*"

"No," Seanchai yelled.

"*I'm a Wycaan Master. I order you, student of Mhari.*"

Seanchai leapt at the same moment the crossbow released its arrow. Time slowed for him. While in midair, he saw that Onyxei had stepped before the King, putting himself in front of the crossbow. And out of Seanchai's grasp. The ancient Wycaan had made his decision. Seanchai could only save one.

"Nooooo," cried Seanchai once more, as he pushed the King to the ground.

The elf rolled and was immediately back on his feet, blue stone in hand. "*Mereksur,*" he yelled, and streams of blue light shattered the crossbow and sent all three dwarves flying.

Seanchai charged at one with his sword in blind rage, slashing the dwarf as he raised his head. He twirled and struck a second with his other sword. Before he could reach the third, he heard the King roar.

"Keep him alive."

Seanchai's swords froze, but his boot kicked the dwarf in the chin, sending him crumpling to the ground. Seanchai turned to find the King kneeling over the Wycaan dwarf. He ran over and put his hands over the teacher's wounds.

Onyxei sighed and shook his head. "It is done, young Wycaan," he wheezed. "Save your strength."

"I could have saved you," Seanchai whispered, still panting.

"No, you had to make a choice and it was the right one," Onyxei gasped. "Your duty is to the races and to the Alliance. I'm sorry. I would have been proud to teach you."

He struggled to breathe, and when he spoke again, his voice was fainter. "Seanchai, stand by the King. He is a dwarf made of gold, as we say. The dwarves will follow him into the Alliance. Stand by him in council and battle. Hothengold must not fall. Win this battle . . . and you will . . . bind the dwarf . . . nation. Stand . . . with . . . the . . . King."

The old Wycaan's body went limp. Seanchai rose and scooped the dwarf up in his arms. The King stood and gently closed the old one's eyes.

Seanchai's voice was cold. "Is the council in session? Now?"

The King nodded and looked Seanchai in the eyes, trying to discern what he wanted to do. "Follow me," he said.

Flanked now by a whole battalion of soldiers, the King led Seanchai down through the park and into a tall stone courtyard. The huge doors to the council building was made of heavy wood and held together by gleaming iron. Two guards sprang to attention and pushed open the doors.

The many voices inside instantly fell silent. Seanchai barely took in the huge ceiling, ornate carvings, or triangle of benches. The King pointed to a slab of rock in the middle, and Seanchai gently lowered the body of the old dwarf onto it.

The King walked to his throne but did not sit down. His voice was at once quiet and powerful.

"A group of dwarves attempted an assassination of the crown just moments ago in the corridors near the park. Some escaped, and a half dozen lie dead."

Seanchai noted that the King did not mention that one attacker was still alive and being interrogated at this moment.

"To attack a fellow dwarf is heinous; to attack a king, unthinkable. The dwarf nation is a race of noble blood. We will not descend into anarchy – not now, not ever. Tomorrow, the high council will convene and decide our actions on this matter and the case of the Emperor's approaching armies."

Then he turned and pointed to Master Onyxei, and his mournful tone resonated through the hall.

"But today we will mourn the death of the greatest dwarf to live among us. Behold! Here lies Onyxei, Wycaan Master. All his life he served the interests of the races and ever of the dwarves. Look upon him and bear witness. He died to save my life. His sacrifice will not be in vain. This council will not allow that."

A huge staff crashed down on the stone floor echoing off the stone walls and sending sparks into the air. As one, the dwarves bowed their heads.

"Bear witness. Here lies Onyxei, Wycaan Master," the King called again. "May he find peace and honor in the halls of our ancestors."

*And love*, Seanchai said to himself, thinking of Onyxei and Ophera's reunion. *And love.*

# FORTY SIX

A fter his meeting with the Emperor, Ahad wanted nothing more than to be left alone. He assumed Phineus would be waiting for him in his room, so he left the inner keep of the palace and wondered if he could actually walk out the main gate without being stopped.

"Maybe it's time to discover whether I really am a prisoner or not," he muttered to himself.

Ahad put his hands in his pockets and walked toward the gates, kicking stones as he went. He tried to whistle nonchalantly, but he was never very good at it and figured it a little too forced. There were two guards lounging at the main palace gate and a third was in an arch above the guardhouse. He was armed with a bow and arrows and could release the iron portcullis if his colleagues below couldn't.

Ahad shivered when he realized that all three guards were looking at him. He decided to pretend that it was because they weren't sure if he was a noble or not, and they were trying to decide whether they should stand to attention and salute.

"Hello," Ahad said as he approached. "Caught anyone trying to invade?"

"Not today, young sire," one replied, a bit uncertainly, as if the question caught him off guard. "The empire is safe and well-guarded."

"Very good," Ahad said, feeling that he needed a follow up.

"Not trying to escape, are you, young sire?" the second soldier asked.

"That's exactly what I'm trying to do," Ahad replied as cheerfully as he could muster. "I hate my homework."

The soldiers laughed, but stopped when a voice spoke from behind Ahad. "Steady up, men. This be the son of General Tarlach himself, if I not be very much mistaken. Master Ahad, isn't it?"

Ahad turned and nodded to the approaching soldier.

"My son be in your class at the school. Ruen says that you be the best student in the whole school. I bet you devour your homework. Just like your father, I say. General Tarlach is a very smart man. I fought under him in–"

"Now 'old on there, Javers. I doubt the young master 'as any interest in your battle stories. Run along, little sire. The Emperor's finest will 'old off the storyteller while you escape."

Ahad laughed as he thanked them and walked through the gate. The palace stood on a steep hill overlooking the capital. Ahad didn't want to walk down the slope because he would have to climb it on his way back. He walked toward the royal cemetery instead. The dead wouldn't bother him.

He entered through the huge iron gates and looked around. The cemetery was immaculately maintained, though he could make out which sections were older by the weather-beaten headstones.

He headed for a section of vaults out of sight of the entrance and sat down with his back against one. The smooth marble cooled his back, and he began to relax. He yawned and closed his eyes. It was hard to feel in danger here, with the warm air, birds singing and – his eyes flew back open.

He heard voices behind him. A man and woman were talking softly on their way to another part of the cemetery. He sighed. He was still tense, and now also wide-awake. He pulled a piece of grass and began chewing its stem while he waited for them to pass. His eyes wandered to the beautiful stone on the graves next to him.

*Prince Shindell, brother to the Emperor, loyal husband and father. Died in battle.*

Shayth's father? Ahad leaned forward and read the inscription of the tombstone next to his. Shayth's mother. He checked the dates. They had died within days of each other, and a quick calculation confirmed that Shayth had been six years old when it happened.

He leaned back against the marble again. That's why his father had taken Shayth into their home. He had been a close friend of Prince Shindell and probably felt responsible for his friend's child. His father was an honorable man. He had opened his house to the boy who now betrayed him.

"Hiding?" A voice said from above.

Ahad jumped. He looked up to see Phineus sitting on the vault and laughing at him.

"You look like you just saw a ghost," he chortled.

Ahad smiled. He was surprised to discover that he was happy to see his patron.

"So, what happened? Was Daddy appreciative of your efforts to reform me?"

"He seemed pleased with me," Ahad replied. "He understands the immense challenge I face."

"Hey! I'm the Crown Prince of Odessiya. You show respect."

Ahad stood up. "Is that the kind of relationship you want?" he asked seriously.

Phineus frowned. "No," he said, quietly chagrined. "It was a natural reaction, I guess. I'm not used to having real friends. I want you to sit up here with me. Please."

"Isn't that disrespectful?"

"No," the younger man smiled. "I'm sure Baron . . ." he twisted round to read the headstone, but the names were faded. "I'm sure the . . . the good Baron and his wife are honored that the Crown Prince and his friend are sitting here." He reached out a hand. "Come on."

Ahad let himself be pulled up.

"If we are going to be friends," Ahad said, "I want something from you. When it's just the two of us, I want to call you by your name."

"Hmmm," the Prince frowned. "Okay, you can call me Crown when we're alone." He burst out laughing. "Okay, okay," he said when he saw Ahad was serious. "You may call me, Phineus. Be careful how you use it, though." Again he laughed.

"Why are you so jolly? An hour ago you bit my head off."

"You got to see my father. I was jealous. Now that I can see it didn't go well, I'm happier."

"Why?"

"My father respects your father because he's an excellent general and therefore useful. But he doesn't trust him. Do you know why?"

Ahad shook his head.

"The answer, my dear brilliant student, lies in front of you."

Ahad looked at Shayth's parents' graves in front of him.

"That's right. Your father pledged fealty to mine, but gave his friendship to Prince Shindell. You can serve more than one master, Ahad, but you cannot be friends with two opposing rivals. Understand?"

Ahad nodded. "But now my father is paying the penalty with Shayth always escaping. I hope he captures him soon."

"I don't think he will capture him. Shayth is too good to be taken alive from what I hear. Do you know why?" He didn't wait for an answer. "Because Shayth knows no fear, only hate and rage. And that makes him too dangerous to be taken alive. Your father will have to kill him, and the question is whether or not the good general has the stomach for it."

Ahad stared at Phineus. "If he's been ordered to kill this murderer, then he will. My father has no fear, either."

The Prince smiled. "Very loyal of you. If the great General Tarlach doesn't kill Shayth, then he will die himself. But if he *does* kill the boy, then he will have to come here and face his best friend. Even with Prince Shindell dead and buried, it will not be an easy conversation."

Ahad frowned. "Do you think Shayth knows that?"

An evil grin crossed the heir's face. "I'm sure he does, but I doubt he even cares. If he's going to die, I think he'll want it to happen while he's fighting one of our fathers. What I wonder is, if he ever succeeds and kills the men he blames for becoming an orphan, what will Shayth have to live for?"

Ahad's face twisted. When he spoke, his voice was cold and menacing. "Nothing. He'll live in wait for me. I will kill him and redeem my father's honor. Shayth will not live if he slays my father."

"You? Shayth has left a long trail of dead warriors. What makes you think you can match him if your father can't?"

Ahad felt his anger rising. "Because you promised to provide me with the best military training in Odessiya. And you will take great pride in teaching me, because you crave the close friendship Prince Shindell had with my father."

The Prince nodded. "I like it. But many others who have fought him have had equal training and more experience – how will you rise above them all?"

"Because I come armed with the same weapons Shayth fights with and that my father apparently doesn't."

Phineus frowned, puzzled.

"Hate," Ahad said, "and revenge."

# FORTY SEVEN

"How could you do this?" Seanchai thumped the rock table with his fist, wincing at the pain. "Master Onyxei's body is still warm."

"But his soul is with our ancestors, not here with us," Rothendir replied calmly. "I must do what I think is best for our clan and the dwarf nation."

"You never asked me or—"

"I do not need your permission, elf. I am clan leader." There was an edge in Rothendir's voice.

"Seanchai," Ballendir said, "Rothendir is right. Yeh're grieving the Wycaan. Yeh're not fit to make such decisions. By agreeing not to bring Clan Dan Zu'Reiltan to justice, Rothendir has secured their vote. With the King implicated in this agreement, we probably have Clan Den Zu'Garten's support as well."

"What about justice?" Seanchai could feel the anger emanating from his flushed face. "Who pays for the slaying of Master Onyxei?"

"His life has not been taken in vain," Rothendir said. "His sacrifice, tragic though it is, might have just brought the clans together to act against the Emperor and help you build your alliance. Seanchai, I have been a friend of Master Onyxei for decades, and I think we both know that he would approve of my actions. I had to do what was best for the greater good, though I mourn him, too. You must understand me."

"Seanchai," Ballendir leaned over the table. "Tomorrow yeh must address the High Council. Yeh have to put yeh emotions aside and be calm and rational. If anyone tries to rile yeh, yeh can't respond in anger."

"And you must conduct yourself well during the debate, which will be long and tiresome," Rothendir added.

"The King said that I would not be allowed to stay after I've said my piece," Seanchai said.

"The King, wise though he seems, was not aware of a point of law. When Ballendir pledged for you, he essentially asked that you join the clan, and clan members may join the debate. It's a complex area of law, but I don't think anyone will argue with Clan Den Zu'Reising at this time."

Seanchai sighed. "I barely knew Master Onyxei and yet it seems like I've known him for years."

"I think there's something that binds yeh Wycaans," Ballendir said. "The way yeh speak of your teacher, Mhari, one would be forgiven for thinking that yeh spent years with her."

"It was barely a couple of months," Seanchai said, his voice scarcely more than a whisper. He wiped away a tear. "I must go and prepare for tomorrow."

"We are here for you should you wish to consult with us."

"Thank you, Clan Leader Rothendir. I know you believe in the path you have chosen. You are far wiser and more experienced than I in the ways of politics and leadership."

"Thank you, Wycaan. Though you lack experience, your heart is pure. That is your strength."

Seanchai woke and lay staring at the ceiling. He had not slept well; anger seeped into his dreams when he had finally drifted off. He rose while it was still dark and took his swords to an empty room.

There, he trained with the Win Dao swords, slowly parroting moves that Mhari had taught him before moving into a free flow. He lost track of time and his surroundings as his concentration fused with his movement.

When he was finished, he put the swords down and assumed the first standing position. But not long after he had settled in his stance, Seanchai heard dwarves bustling outside the room and was instantly reminded that he must attend the Clansfelt.

Resigned to the fact that he would not regain the serenity he needed, he turned to pick up his shirt. Ilana sat on the floor, hugging her knees.

"I love to watch you train," she said, suppressing a yawn. "You let down all your armoring, let all the tension leave you. It's beautiful to watch."

"I'd like one day to teach you," he replied. "It would be fun to train together."

"I'd like that," she replied, and handed him a cup of tea. "When I brought it for you, it was hot," she said by way of apology.

"It tastes great," Seanchai replied after the first gulp. The tea was bitter enough when it was warm, but even worse at room temperature. He took a moment to heat it with energy through his hands.

"Seanchai?"

"Yes."

"I've been thinking. There is a fair chance that at least one of us isn't going to come through this. No, listen, please. We've seen two Wycaans die in a short time. You're going to be in constant danger, and I'll be by your side. You remember the priestess' words."

"Of course I remember," Seanchai replied moodily. "Why are you telling me this?"

"I want us to make a bond; a pledge. If one of us dies, the other will go on living. As unfathomable as it seems, neither of us should be alone. I want you to promise me that if I die, you'll try and find someone else. I don't accept that Wycaans should remain solitary. It'll be a hard life for your mate, but she'll be honored to take on that role. Promise me?"

"Neither of us—"

"Promise me!" she urged. "You have great powers, Seanchai, but you are not indestructible and cannot make me so. You cannot decide who lives and who dies."

He touched her cheek tenderly. "There is no room in my heart for another elfe," he said quietly. "My heart is full. It would not be fair to her."

"You have a big heart. In time, you'll find a place. At least promise me that you'll keep yourself open to it."

Seanchai drew away and stared hard at her. "Why is this so important to you?"

"I believe the priestess was seeing something," Ilana's voice faltered. "There was a certainty in her voice that I feel inside of me. I would rest easier knowing that you will try to move on."

Seanchai thought back to the words of Master Onyxei regarding his relationship with the priestess. "If I promise, can we stop talking about it?"

"Yes."

Seanchai took her in his arms and held her tightly. "I don't believe I'll ever find someone who can come close to how I feel for you. But if you die, I promise to try and rebuild my life with someone else."

"Swear," she insisted in his ear, "in the ancient language."

Seanchai sighed. "*Ashbar*. I swear."

He released her and turned, quickly exiting the room.

Ilana stood there, hugging herself, tears falling from her eyes. "Thank you," she said, but only the ancient rock walls of Hothengold bore witness.

# FORTY EIGHT

The clan guards kept tight watch on Rothendir and Seanchai as Clan Den Zu'Reising paraded to the Clansfelt. Ballendir walked behind Seanchai, providing ongoing commentary.

Seanchai glanced at Rothendir as she walked by his side, impressed by her stride and the stature that emanated power and intention the likes of which Seanchai had not seen from her before. Clan Den Zu'Reising, though one of the smaller clans, had become a major force following its alliance with Seanchai and the assassination attempt. He could sense her resolute desire to win big today.

As they paraded through the center of town, the streets were packed, and, everywhere he looked, Seanchai saw worry and apprehension. The dwarves had enjoyed a long period of peace and tranquility while the Emperor's interests were engaged elsewhere. But Seanchai's presence and the calling of the Clansfelt was a sign that this time was at an end, whether they liked it or not.

The clan began their ascent toward the palace. An old dwarfe, heavyset and bent, left the crowd and stood in front of the delegation, glaring at Seanchai. The soldiers went to move her aside, but she put her fists on her hips.

"Wait," Seanchai said and walked over to her.

"Steady," Ballendir said, keeping close behind him.

"Do you want to say something?" Seanchai asked politely.

"Why did you come?" she asked. "Last time your kind walked among us, thousands of my people were captured, tortured, and killed in battle."

"As were my people," Seanchai replied. "I understand your fears. But what are the alternatives?"

"We have done a good job of protecting our own," the old dwarfe said.

"No, you haven't," Seanchai replied, projecting his voice for all around to hear. "You have done a good job of delaying the inevitable. The Emperor hadn't forgotten you. He won't allow anyone to stay free of his tyranny. Look how prepared he was for the fight at Zu'Reising. He has explosives and a dwarf army of his own. The time for hiding underground has come to an end." He stood up straight. "The only real choice to be made today is whether you will fight him alone or as part of the Alliance."

Seanchai surveyed the crowd as if challenging anyone to argue. None dared and he turned to Rothendir. "Let's go," he said.

"We're ready," Ballendir whispered, excitement in his voice.

"We are," she replied.

The Great Hall was a hive of activity. Dwarves milled around in every direction. Seanchai, grateful for his height, could make out a huge seven-sided table with a throne on one side. In the middle was a beautiful stone sculpture of a black and gold forest.

Each clan had a side of the table with six cube chairs in two equal rows. Clan Den Zu'Reising's side was facing the throne and the two most powerful clans – a strategic win by Rothendir. She sat in the middle of the front row, and an elder companion of Rothendir's sat next to her. Ballendir and Seanchai took two seats behind them. The third front seat remained empty.

"Who will sit there?" Seanchai asked.

"The clan's priestess would have," Ballendir whispered back. "Rothendir feels it is an appropriate statement to leave the chair empty."

"A powerful message," Seanchai agreed.

Next to Seanchai was one of the leaders who had fought at Zu'Reising. The dwarf gave him a curt nod. Seanchai turned to Ballendir, who leaned in.

"Not renowned as a smiler," his friend whispered, "but a very respected warrior."

Next to the throne was Clan Den Zu'Garten. Ballendir told Seanchai that he hoped winning over the King would concurrently win over his clan of origin, but judging by the stern faces staring at him, Seanchai wasn't too convinced this was likely.

On the other side of the throne sat Clan Den Zu'Chantague. They were the wealthiest of the clans and had no problem showing this. They all wore ornate capes sewn of fine materials and edged in gold over their armor. Two of them carried staffs bedecked with jewels. Clans Den Zu'Chantague and Dan Du'Reiltan took their places around the table, as well.

Clan Den Zu'Chantague potentially had the most to lose from a war with the empire. They had established trade routes and made much of their wealth through business with the humans.

Sitting next to the wealthy clan was Clan Dan Zu'Reiltan, the black and brown robes of the religious sect offering a sharp contrast to the opulence next to them. Seanchai realized there was nothing to discern behind the masks they wore.

The scholars of Clan Dan Zu'Ornagen and the artisans of Clan Dan Zu'Ulster joined the others. Rothendir had not been able to determine whether either had an army, or what their political stances were. One of the artisans turned to Seanchai as he sat.

"Welcome, elf," he said. "I wish we could meet under different circumstances. One day, I would like to travel to see the crafts of the elves."

"I would like that, too," Seanchai replied, wondering what art his people still possessed. He was suddenly struck by how truly uncohesive the elf races were, and how much was lost because of it.

Clan Den Zu'Reising, while not exactly opposite the King, were positioned facing the throne and the two most powerful clans. Rothendir had fought vigorously, from what Seanchai had heard, to receive this seating arrangement.

The pounding of a thick, metal-edged staff brought him abruptly from his reverie. All fell silent and a deep voice boomed. "Rise up. Rise up, mighty dwarf nation. Your King walks among you."

In unison, those around the table were on their feet, though Seanchai thought he saw resentment on a few faces. The King entered, wearing his crown and red velvet robes. Two bulky warriors stood on either side of him in shining armor, holding glimmering pikes.

Once all were again seated, a huge banner unfurled behind the throne. On it was a shield with a crown on top and two ornate axes beneath. The King was going to great lengths to ensure a regal presence, and Seanchai conceded he had been successful thus far.

The dwarf by the door with the huge staff banged it again on the floor twice. His deep voice boomed out. "Behold, the Clansfelt meets. Let all who seek council with the dwarf nation come forward. Speak only with truth and honor." Again the huge staff banged down on the stone floor twice.

The Clansfelt had begun.

# FORTY NINE

Seanchai rose brusquely from his chair when break was called on the second day and was out of the conference hall before any dwarf had even moved. Ballendir shuffled after him and caught up in an adjacent corridor. He put his hand on the tall elf's arm, and Seanchai spun around.

"Don't say anything here," Ballendir said, bringing his finger to his lips. "Come with mah."

He led the Wycaan through a maze of corridors to a room designated for their clan. Once they were behind closed doors, Ballendir spoke again.

"Okay, Seanchai. Let it out, mah friend."

"We have just sat for a whole day and . . . and everyone's just introduced themselves. This isn't supposed to be a common gathering. There's a huge army out there coming this way, fully bent on destroying us all. Pleasantries!"

He stopped mid-rant when he noticed Ballendir watching him, arms folded across his chest, and smiling.

"What?" Seanchai asked, "What is so amusing?"

"Yeh, mah friend. I told Rothendir that yeh had been warned and, in truth, yeh had. This is not an easy process. Everything's delicately balanced. The clans have not met in half a century, many are new leaders, and most are unfamiliar with the King. Statuses and circumstances have changed as some have got richer, others poorer. Everyone is dancing around, trying to work out the pecking order, and until they do, they will not vote."

"But there are ten thousand voters getting closer," Seanchai snapped. "They are each armed and determined to destroy Hothengold. Apart from Clan Den Zu'Garten, who lives here, no one has brought an army with them. They will need to be sum–"

"Seanchai!" Ballendir's rebuke was sharp, and his hands moved to his hips. "Do yeh really think these leaders are stupid? No clan will bring their troops too near the Clansfelt, as that might be interpreted as an aggressive power move, but they're nearby. We aren't fools, Seanchai. We have lived underground all these years, but we have not ignored what's been happening above ground."

Seanchai turned around and took a few moments to compose himself. He poured himself a cup of water from a flagon on a table and offered Ballendir some.

"Bah, I need something stronger," the dwarf said, producing a pewter flask from his hip.

"So it frustrates you, too?" Seanchai smiled.

"Of course it does. I wouldn't even be allowed near the Great Hall if it wasn't for yeh. I have vouched for yeh with my axe. Rothendir's under the impression that if anyone can control yeh, it's mah."

Seanchai laughed. "She's probably right. When are they going to start addressing the issue? When am I going to be offered a chance to speak?"

"Very soon, young elf. But yeh must control yeh emotions. Yeh shuffle in yeh chair, pick yeh fingernails, stare at dwarves who are not speaking. Yeh need to show interest, and yeh cannot jump up at breaks and charge out like yeh can't hold your bladder."

Seanchai laughed.

"Seriously, Seanchai. Yeh need to take yeh time before leaving. Allow other dwarves to approach and talk with yeh. Yeh need to gain their trust. Whatever yeh story, if yeh can't count upon their trust, yeh're lost," Ballendir took another swig, "as are we all."

"You're worried, Ballendir?"

"Aye. I told yeh I'm not one for all this politicking. But don't depend on mah observations. There's so much posturing, so much pride. I have listed everyone as being against us at some point."

"But we already have an agreement with Clan Dan Zu'Reiltan, don't we?"

"We do," Ballendir said. "But they have their pride just like the rest. We must allow them to vote in favor because they have no choice if that 's possible."

"I don't understand."

"If we can garner enough votes without forcing them to openly support us, they will be doubly in our debt. And though this agreement is a secret, all the other clans will see how benevolent we are. Bah! I hate this, too."

"You say the armies are nearby, Ballendir. Is anyone making plans for the battle?"

"Good question," the dwarf answered. "Yeh have to assume that Clan Den Zu'Garten has plans to defend its own city."

"Plans that can deal with explosives and trained dwarf regiments?"

Ballendir frowned. "And cave trolls and probably other monsters."

There was a knock on the door. A young dwarf poked his head around the door. "Rothendir requests that you join the council to eat."

"Thank yeh," Ballendir replied. "We'll be along shortly." The door closed and Ballendir turned to Seanchai. "Play the game, Wycaan, and take deep breaths."

The dining room was huge. When Seanchai entered, he saw Rothendir glare at him and tried to put a permanent smile on his face. A dwarf approached him.

"My lord Wycaan," he said. "Would you do us the honor of joining Clan Dan Zu'Ulster at our table?"

"Thank you," Seanchai beamed. "I would be delighted."

They moved to an l-shaped table, and one young dwarf rose and offered his place at the angle.

"I couldn't," Seanchai protested.

"I saved you the seat," the young dwarf said, pointing to his setting. "Look, I haven't eaten. We all want to be able to hear you, and this hall is loud."

Seanchai thanked him, sat down and spooned some fish and vegetables onto his plate.

"Elves don't eat meat?" A big dwarf with intricate metalwork on his armor asked.

"Most elves do, I think," Seanchai replied. "But Wycaans prefer fish. It's how I've been instructed."

"I've never seen a plump Wycaan," one exclaimed, patting his considerable stomach. "Perhaps I should ask to join the order."

They all laughed, and Seanchai felt himself relax. "You have met other Wycaans?" he asked hopefully.

"I must admit that there are several flaws in my argument," the dwarf replied. "Not least is that you are the first I have met. But I have seen many fine pieces of art depicting Wycaans. My name is Ruffminsk. This fine dwarf is Dugenminsk, our clan leader."

Seanchai nodded to each. The rotund Ruffminsk had a huge beard that flowed down over his ample stomach. Dugenminsk, the dwarf in the ornate amour, had a shorter red beard and blazing locks to match.

They plied him with questions about elves and Wycaans. He would admit when he did not know an answer, and it didn't seem to bother anyone. He had not met that many elves outside of those in his own village, and his training was not complete. Seanchai smiled at the acceptance he felt.

The young dwarf who had given Seanchai his seat sat near the end, but constantly rose to bring more bread, cheese, and fish for Seanchai. He beamed each time Seanchai protested and thanked him.

When the meal was over, many of the dwarves at the table rose and left. Seanchai stayed behind with Dugenminsk, Ruffminsk, and a priestess who didn't speak.

Ruffminsk leaned forward. "Our people are apprehensive. We are not a big clan in terms of heads or weapons, but we neither are we poor or unarmed. Our metalwork," he caressed the lip of his chest plate, "is not only beautiful, but tough.

"We'll not be the first to cast our vote. We'll listen to you and the bigger clans and see which path they decide upon."

"Why?" Seanchai asked. "The size of a clan is irrelevant. The armies that the Emperor can muster will claim everyone, whether they stand with the Alliance or alone. Perhaps what the Clansfelt needs is for a smaller clan to take the initiative. Maybe you can create a momentum of inevitability that will stop the clan posturing. There is little time."

The dwarves glanced at each other.

"You have a keen mind, young Wycaan," Dugenminsk said. "We'll consider your request. But we want to hear what you have to say to the Council first."

"That's fair," Seanchai consented.

"Good," Ruffminsk replied. "We have three gifts for you." He signaled to the Seanchai's young dwarf admirer, who approached, beaming. "This is Thorminsk. He is a promising apprentice, taught by our greatest artisan. Please accept these gifts made from his hands."

Seanchai opened the first. It was a pipe, long, in the fashion of the elves, but buffeted with intricately carved pewter.

"The pewter will protect your pipe when you travel," Thorminsk said, his pride clear.

"Smoke it during breaks at the Clansfelt," Dugenminsk said, and gave him a pouch of pipe weed. "This is a very earthy weed and has three different mushrooms in it. We say it will help you grow your beard."

They all laughed.

"This is our second gift," Thorminsk said, offering another small pouch.

It was a beautiful hip flask, and Seanchai gasped.

"Thank you," he said.

"Note that it is full," Ruffminsk said. "You can't smoke the weed when you get frustrated in the Clans meetings – yes, we've seen you fidgeting – but you can steal a swig from this. It will help keep you calm. You'll have to wait for your third gift."

"Thank you; thank you all," Seanchai said. "I don't know what to say."

"It's what you will say when you return to the hall that is important," Ruffminsk said.

# FIFTY

Much to Seanchai's disdain, Rothendir asked no questions about his lunch with Clan Dan Zu'Ulster as they took their seats in the Great Hall. Ballendir, however, was thrilled at the lunchtime events and excited when Seanchai discreetly showed him the gifts.

"That's a fine pipe, mah lad," he whispered. "But please don't smoke it yet in public."

"Are you worried how others might interpret the gifts?"

"No. I'm worried yeh'll inhale once and disgrace our clan by coughing yeh guts up." Ballendir chuckled to himself, and then patted Seanchai's arm. "Well done, laddie."

Though the King had not joined every session since the Clansfelt had begun he entered this time, waiting until all were settled, prompting them to rise in acknowledgement.

"No, no," the King protested. "Please be seated."

This made Seanchai smile and Ballendir leaned over. "I see yeh're getting the hang of dwarf politics," he whispered.

When the King was settled, all eyes turned to Ruffminsk, from Clan Dan Zu'Ulster, who was holding up the small, ceremonial axe that indicated his wish to speak. Suddenly, there was a feeling that the Clansfelt was about to really begin.

A few seconds passed as all stared at the magnificent axe. Its handle was intertwined metal strands, and the head arched beautifully. Small stones, reflecting the torchlight, gave it life and vibrancy. The King broke the spell by clearing his throat.

"Forgive me, Clan Leader Ruffminsk. The artisanship of Clan Dan Zu'Ulster is legendary throughout our nation, and thus we are all dazzled by the beauty of your axe."

Ruffminsk bowed his head. "Your Majesty is most kind. Clan Dan Zu'Ulster indeed prides itself on our craft. But, unfortunately, today we must speak of war, not artistry.

"The Clansfelt has spent time thus far introducing our leaders and this is most important. We have updated each other on our economies and growth since we last met a half-century ago and this we all know to be necessary.

"But time is of the essence. An elf sits in our midst despite the First Decree. Yet we have not questioned it thus far because these are not ordinary times. One of our clans has been attacked and driven from its home, an attack the likes of which has not been witnessed in our generation. A large imperial army approaches with conscripted dwarves among its ranks. These are indeed not ordinary times.

"My fellow dwarves: our clans have given us their trust to lead them in the light and the dark. They have given us their allegiance to make the right decisions at the right time. That time is now.

"With your permission, my King, let us call upon the elf. It has been fifty years since the Clansfelt has met and much longer since a Wycaan has addressed us. That time, also, is now."

Seanchai noticed that, as Rothendir turned her head towards the King, she held the faintest of smiles. He wondered how spontaneous his lunchtime invitation had been. Perhaps Rothendir sent Ballendir to keep Seanchai from the dinning hall while she spoke with Ruffminsk?

Ruffminsk bowed his head respectfully toward the King and sat down. But the King did not get a chance to reply, as a tall priest of Clan Dan Zu'Reiltan rapped his black speaking axe on the table. The King looked at him emotionlessly.

"Your Majesty." The deep voice was muffled behind the mask. "Think well upon your next move. The gods hold their breath and wait. We have heeded their words and forbidden any other than dwarf to come beneath the ground. This is the First Decree. Look what happens when dwarves defy the gods and move above ground. They become slaves in our enemy's army and will surely suffer for their sins while alive and in the hereafter.

"Clan Dan Zu'Reiltan has held its tongue until now, but know that you tread upon a thin piece of rope – you and the entire dwarf nation."

The King turned to the black-robed dwarves and looked on for a moment. Then he raised his own axe, a beautiful long-handled weapon, laden with gold and jewels.

"The presence of the elf worries me too, Clan Leader. I do not have the ears of the gods, though if I did, they would find me a humble servant. So until their will is revealed directly to me as the High King, I will make the best decisions I can for our race based upon the facts as I understand them.

"The best decisions require we hear all views and weigh the information offered. That an elf walks among us – and humans too – is a sign of changing times. That one of these is a Wycaan is a sign indeed that we must listen. It is our duty to hear and consider his words.

"Wycaan: are you ready to address the Clansfelt?"

Seanchai's legs went to jelly, and he wondered whether he could summon the strength even to rise. He took a deep breath, drawing energy from the earth to pull him up and give him strength. Then he turned slowly to the High King of the Dwarves and spoke.

# FIFTY ONE

A had was surprised when the letter arrived, though it was more because it signified that a month at the palace had passed without him noticing. His growing relationship with the Prince was unpredictable. They could be thick as thieves one moment and the next, Phineus was argumentative and antisocial.

Oddly, when Ahad pushed Phineus in his studies, the Prince was appreciative, even when he was frustrated with his own learning difficulties. In weapons training, Ahad was the willing student, and, though he smarted from several bruises and bumps, he knew the Prince was making him fitter, stronger, and a far better warrior.

He could tell from the handwriting that the letter was from his mother. He took it to a hammock in the nearby courtyard and put it to his nose, disappointed to find that it didn't smell like her. He glanced around, certain he was being watched, and opened the letter.

*My dear Ahad,*

*How I miss you. It has been only a short while since I left to take care of my parents. I don't even remember how long it has been since your father, you and I spent time together. Perhaps when he brings this current campaign to its end, we shall take some time as a family and travel.*

*My journey was uneventful, and I am grateful for that. My mother is weak, but carries on. Her stoicism makes it difficult to truly know her condition. My father is a bit lost, and his memory is weak. I am happy to be among my family, but miss you, your father, and the capital.*

*Please send my regards to your grandfather. Take care of him and visit often in my absence. He will be lonely and have need of your company. Let him tell his stories even if they do not always make sense.*

*Study hard my son. I know I have no need to tell you this.*

*I love you.*

Ahad read the letter again more carefully. The final paragraph confused him. His mother never visited or even acknowledged her father-in-law. There had been some argument when Ahad was young. She was never disrespectful toward him and never denied Ahad a visit, but neither had she ever encouraged it.

Ahad folded the letter and rose from the hammock. He jumped when he found Phineus standing almost exactly where Ahad's feet touched the ground.

"A letter, my shadow?" the Prince asked. Shadow was the nickname he had given Ahad because they spent so much time together.

"From my mother," Ahad replied. "All is well."

"I hope she doesn't plan to return too soon," Phineus said and then blushed. "What I mean—"

"Thank you," Ahad said sincerely. He could feel a bond growing between them and appreciated knowing Phineus could, too. "Do you have need of me?"

"No, I was just wondering what you were doing today. It's Sunday, so don't suggest studying."

"Ha. I was actually planning to visit my grandfather. It has been too long."

"He lives in the city?"

"No," Ahad replied. "Just outside. May I borrow a horse?"

"Of course. Maybe I should join you."

Ahad hesitated. If he said no, then Phineus might get suspicious. But if he came, Ahad would not be able to ask what he really wanted to know.

"Sure – my grandfather would be happy to have someone else to give history lessons to. He likes to tell long stories of the campaigns he fought in. He often repeats himself and sometimes dozes off mid-sentence. But I know he would be glad for more company."

Phineus shuffled his feet. "I'll ride with you but won't come inside. I shouldn't trouble your grandfather to host royalty. I'll ride on from there. Please join me at the waterfall when you finish."

"What kind of a friend are you to leave me to face my grandfather alone?" Ahad protested with a smile.

"Oh, I will be your friend, Ahad. I dream sometimes of you and me fighting side-by-side in battle. And right now that seems more attractive than sitting through a senile old man's war stories."

Ahad arrived at his grandfather's house and began their usual routine sitting in the garden, sipping lemonade. His grandfather read Ahad's letter and commented loudly how nice it was that Ahad's mother worried about him.

They walked to their usual spot at the boundary of his grandfather's property, Ahad noticing once again that the old man's health had worsened.

"Without wishing to open old wounds, grandfather, why would my mother suddenly take an interest in you?"

"Your mother wrote that letter," his grandfather turned slowly and smiled, "but she did not send it. It was prepared before she left to get you here if we felt you should come talk with me. And look, it worked."

He laughed. "It was my idea. Your mother and I don't enjoy each other's company, but we both care about you and have collaborated together regarding our situation. I needed you to come visit."

"What have you heard?" Ahad asked. "Is father alright?"

"Your father is well. News reached the officer's club yesterday that he leads a massive army to confront the dwarves in their capital city and believes the elf and your old friend Shayth are trying to rally them to form an alliance against the Emperor."

"They don't stand a chance against the might of the Emperor's army," Ahad declared, "especially with my father at the helm."

"Perhaps you're right. But unity is a powerful weapon, and the dwarves know they will be enslaved if they lose. It is their capital. They have nowhere to run to. Shayth and the elf have also proved quite adept at eluding your father."

"My father will kill Shayth," Ahad snapped, immediately embarrassed.

"Maybe," the old man replied, observing his grandson curiously. "If, that is, he is willing to."

"If not, I'll have no problem doing it for him. I'm training hard. I'm fit and ready."

"Ready?" his grandfather replied. "Good. Be ready. Be ready to flee the city. Do you know where you will go?"

"Yes," Ahad replied without hesitation. "To find the traitor Shayth. Wherever he is, I will track him down and kill him."

# FIFTY TWO

"My Lord, High King of the Dwarves, Clan leaders, and trusted advisors. I understand how hard it is for you that I, Seanchai, son of Seantai, an elf of Markwin Wood, stands before you today, and that my friends including Shayth, a human, are underground. I am aware of your history. I am aware of the First Decree. I am aware of your history.

"Centuries ago, your ancestors, a brave and noble people, stood on the Plains of Mirylyn. They marched into a battle against tyranny together with the rest of the free nations. When thousands of brave dwarf soldiers lay slain and strewn across the sweeping valley, King Hothen took the survivors underground to protect themselves. Your rich culture and tradition tell us that their souls sit to this day in the great hall of your ancestors, feasting with your gods."

There were murmurs around the table. Even Clan Dan Zu'Reiltan's priests nodded their heads in agreement. Seanchai put his hand on his long knife and took a breath.

"Now, you have discovered that this strategy which has kept your people safe since that great battle will endure no more. You have discovered that many of your people are already slaves to the will of the Emperor. Worst yet, he has trained them to fight against you, to spill the blood of their brothers and sisters. At the battle of Mount Zu'Reising, they struck with axe and sword, dwarf against dwarf. You know this to be true. You have heard the words of Rothendir, Clan Leader of Den Zu'Reising."

A wave of comments passed around the hall. Seanchai paused to allow the crowd's murmurs to cease.

"And they came with effective and well-thought-out ways to destroy your defenses. They have learned from the conscripted dwarves how to use explosives to break seam lines and widen tunnels. This allows them to attack with pictorians and cave trolls. All this, you now know to be true.

"The Emperor has not known the bitter taste of defeat and will not take kindly to it. For too long has he ruled over man, abused elves, and disclaimed the dwarves. For too long he has wielded his power for evil.

"But this will be his undoing. Some among you say that this army was sent not to attack you, but to capture and kill Shayth, his brother's son, and myself. But consider this: The Emperor murdered Shayth's father and mother – his own blood – and, though he seeks to wipe this branch of his family from the face of the earth, he would not send out an entire army when an assassin would be more appropriate.

"He fears me. The Emperor understands history and knows that in times of darkness, the races have always looked to the Wycaan Masters for direction, for protection, and for moral guidance.

"Moreover, he knows that the only way the races can cast off their bonds is to unite. Only a Wycaan can achieve this."

Seanchai stopped and sipped from a flagon of water. He wiped his mouth on his sleeve and stared around the room.

"Do not delude yourselves into thinking that the Emperor and his general are not preparing to attack you. It took time to conscript, train, and dominate dwarves so that they would fight other dwarves. It took time to experiment and learn how to use explosives. And it took time for General Tarlach and his armies to find where you were. I did not lead them to you – I just gave them a reason to get here faster.

"What I say to you is disturbing. What I say is uncomfortable. But you know in your hearts that I speak the truth. I am a Wycaan – not a Master like Master Onyxei – but I am trained, I am young, and I am determined."

Seanchai paused again and reflected on the steely reserve in his voice as it echoed back from the stone cavern's walls.

"As a Wycaan, I am committed to reforging the Alliance, to bringing the free men together with the Tutans from the Southern Desert, the Aqua'lansis, the elves of Odessiya, and the Shanrea – the elves of the West."

"Ha!" the bark of laughter came from the far end from Clan Dan Zu'Ornagen.

The King looked over and frowned. No one had asked permission to speak. One of them stood up.

"My apologies, Your Majesty," he bowed and then turned to Seanchai. "To you as well, Wycaan. I should not have interrupted. My clan is one of great scholarly practice and I myself have dedicated my life to studying the ancient races. I have read about and seen these antiquities you speak of, but never beyond the pages of storybooks and legends."

He sat down, and Seanchai pondered how to respond. He wanted to secure the vote of Clan Dan Zu'Ornagen, not alienate them with a cutting reply.

"What is your name, sire?"

The dwarf stood again and bowed his head. "I am Ziskagen, at your service."

"And you are a scholar of the history of our land, of Odessiya?"

"Of history, yes, and of cultural customs and ancient civic law."

"Are you regarded within your clan with great academic respect?"

The dwarf puffed out his chest. "I could provide a list of my research and my scrolls. Many have been copied and reside in the libraries of my fellow clans."

Seanchai smiled. "I hope one day to have the opportunity to study them and learn more of Odessiya from you."

The dwarf beamed, but Seanchai held his gaze. He was not finished.

"As an expert in the lore of this land, are you also acquainted with the social rules surrounding the Wycaan Order?"

"Indeed I am," Ziskagen replied. "I was honored to learn and write from the first-hand accounts of Master Onyxei. I recorded many of the vision quests that he went on after he came to live here in Hothengold."

"Then answer this for me, Master Ziskagen. From all your studies of the rich history of Odessiya, from all the stories and the legends of the great races, has a Wycaan ever stood before the peoples of Odessiya and not spoken the truth?"

The question was posed in a soft, respectful tone, but what it lacked in volume, it made up in intent.

Silence descended on the Great Hall. Seanchai kept his gaze on the scholar as his mind churned through his massive memory. At length, the King turned to Ziskagen.

"Master Ziskagen, of the most learned Clan Dan Zu'Ornagen, the Clansfelt awaits your reply. In your considerable recollection, has a Wycaan ever lied to the peoples of Odessiya?"

The scholar turned his gaze to the king and cleared his throat. In a deep, measured voice that resounded through the Great Hall, he said: "No, Your Majesty. A Wycaan has never lied when called to address the races, never in the history of Odessiya."

A buzz of voices broke out around the room. The King leaned back and waited, fleetingly locking gazes with Rothendir. Then he brought his heavy axe down on the stone table. Sparks shot from its handle, and the sharp thwack brought the clans instantly back to decorum.

But the priest of Clan Dan Zu'Reiltan held his black axe in the air. The King sighed and nodded, and Ballendir gently tugged Seanchai back down to his seat.

"Your Majesty. This is a momentous decision. I request that the Clansfelt adjourn and allow the Clan Head Council to sit and debate."

Seanchai felt his brow tighten. He turned to Ballendir, who signaled that he neither speak nor react. Instead, Rothendir raised her silver axe.

"I will second that," she said, "as long as it is clear to all the clans that the vote happens here in the full Clansfelt. There shall be no secret casting of ballots."

The priest turned and nodded. The big dwarf who stood behind the King with the thick staff pounded it twice on the floor and proclaimed:

"It is so ordered. The Clansfelt adjourns. All save the clan leaders and the King will leave the hall. The doors will be locked. You will be summoned by the blow of a horn when his Majesty calls the Clansfelt back to session."

The staff cracked down on the stone floor twice and the room erupted in debate. Seanchai looked to Ballendir and opened his mouth to speak, but Rothendir whirled round.

"Ballendir," she hissed. "Get him out of here. Now."

# FIFTY THREE

B allendir's iron grip led Seanchai out of the hall. Once outside, Seanchai turned and opened his mouth, but the dwarf cut him off.

"Not here, Seanchai. Wait until we're in our clan's quarters."

Seanchai took a deep breath, and, together, they walked through the bustling corridors away from the Great Hall. Outside of the huge stone building, Seanchai looked around. A path opened up in front of them as dwarves scurried out of their way, glancing furtively.

The facial expressions seemed harder than they had when the delegation of Clan Den Zu'Reising had made their way through the streets on the way to the Clansfelt. Then, he had felt anticipation. Now as the Clansfelt had dragged on, the dwarves not privy to the discussions had found plenty of time to hypothesize on and become afraid of what was transpiring.

Seanchai tried to walk taller and more purposefully, smiling at those he passed. He received the occasional smile back from young male dwarves and curt nods – if he was acknowledged at all – from everyone else.

He glanced at Ballendir, who was looking straight ahead and clearly anxious to reach their quarters. Seanchai tried to replay the actions of those last few minutes of the Clansfelt.

Had he alienated the scholarly Clan Dan Zu'Ornagen? There had seemed no way at the time to let Ziskagen's comment pass. Seanchai shook his head as he walked. At some point, a Wycaan needed to lead and not just request and respond. The exchange with Ziskagen had been that defining moment, but he had not been allowed to continue. What would Master Onyxei have done? Would Mhari, his own teacher, have approached it differently?

No. He would not apologize or agonize over what had been. The wisdom of the Wycaan Masters was not accessible anymore, and he would have to trust his own judgment and listen to the advice of those around him. A sense of calm descended over Seanchai. He had done his best, and his teachers would have agreed.

They turned into the Clan Den Zu'Reising compound. In the central square, Rhoddan, Sellia, and Ilana sat in a corner. Rhoddan and Sellia were both sweating. Ilana looked anxious and was talking animatedly. When they saw Ballendir and Seanchai enter, they sprung to their feet.

"Have they decided already?" Sellia asked with no preliminaries.

"They have gone behind closed doors," Seanchai replied, suddenly sullen.

"Meaning?"

"I don't know," Seanchai said, taking Ilana's hand. "What do you make of it, Ballendir?"

"Let's go inside and talk," Ballendir said.

"Where's Shayth?" Seanchai asked.

"He and Jermona went out with a dwarf scouting party," Rhoddan replied. "I would have joined them, but Sellia needs to learn hand-to-hand combat before we engage Tarlach's army."

Sellia smiled. "Show Seanchai your ribs."

Rhoddan lifted his shirt and revealed a bruise that closely resembled the sole of a boot.

"Beautiful colors," Seanchai said as he leaned down. "You have an artistic streak, Sellia."

"Yes," she replied. "Let me know if you want one to match."

Seanchai felt himself calm being with his friends, despite the tension and danger that surrounded them. They entered a small room with a stone table, and Ballendir brought in a flagon and glasses. They each poured some ale and gathered around the table.

"The lad did well," Ballendir said at last. "I think he struck the right balance between asking for our support and establishing his role leading the races." Ballendir relayed the exchange with the scholar of Clan Dan Zu'Ornagen and also of Seanchai's lunch with the artisans of Clan Dan Zu'Ulster. Seanchai showed them the flask and pipe. Then he turned to Ballendir.

"I still don't understand why the clan chiefs closed the meeting. What happened?"

"Most likely, there was a shift in alignment within a clan," Ballendir said. "In other words, one clan had pledged a certain way and now wants to rescind its support to whichever side they chose. If so, that clan will need to be frank with all concerned, and this is best achieved with as few ears as possible."

"You think I lost the scholars?" Seanchai asked.

"Possibly," the dwarf took another long drink. "Or maybe they weren't on our side from the beginning and yeh won them over in scholarly debate. I think that might count for more than if yeh had drawn your swords and slain a couple of their delegation, though I like that idea better. Anyway, all we can do now is to trust in Rothendir."

"I'm going to go rest," Seanchai said suddenly and turned to leave.

"No," Ballendir said, his voice sharp. "Don't do it. If they find out, yeh will have betrayed their trust," he walked over to Seanchai and stared hard into his eyes, "and mine."

Seanchai stared back and then bowed his head. "You're right," he said. "I apologize. Let's go sit in the courtyard and imagine some blue sky."

"What were you going to do?" Sellia asked as they walked outside.

"Scry," he replied.

She feigned disgust. "You dog," she said. "How could you even think of it?" Then she put a hand on his shoulder and turned to Ilana. "There's hope for him yet."

Ilana rolled her eyes. It was a wonderful expression, Seanchai thought.

# FIFTY FOUR

Rothendir, Clan Leader of Clan Den Zu'Reising, was the first to enter the small room adjacent to the Great Hall. It had nothing more than a small table and several stone cubes. They were identical save the King's, which was slightly taller.

She chose the seat directly opposite the King. She would need his help here, she feared, for whatever shift was about to occur. She would need to respond quickly and flawlessly, and she was about to discover what kind of king sat upon the throne.

As the room filled, the King's own clan leader, Renggal, sat next to him, but to the other side of the raised chair sat the leader of Den Zu'Chantague, the clan of traders who stood to lose the most. To his other side sat the black-clad priest of Clan Dan Zu'Reiltan. If this was indeed a coalition, it was a powerful one.

Dugenminsk, the leader of Clan Dan Zu'Ulster sat between the priest and Rothendir and Ziskagen, the leader of the scholar clan sat on her other side. The priest immediately held his axe up, but the King signaled for him to lower it.

"Let me speak first, clan leaders," the King said. "I address you all as one. In this room, we sit as equals and will talk without formalities. Time is of the essence and with each hour, our options narrow. Speak your mind and hold your tempers. This might not be the most foremost of our abilities, but we must rise to our responsibilities." This was met with polite laughter.

"The enemy nears, if enemy they are. We have two choices: to negotiate or to fight. Allow me to lay out both options as I see them. If we negotiate, we show weakness in the face of an approaching army. This is no respectful diplomatic delegation coming to open exploratory talks.

"We may be able to barter by handing over the Wycaan and Emperor's nephew. But they will insist on taxation and might even demand back taxes. And I believe they will demand to patrol our cities and force us to lower the defenses designed to keep them out.

"To follow this route feels painful, but would save much bloodshed. Be mindful that Hothengold might fall and that Clan Den Zu'Garten has the most to lose if this happens. If we stand together, then it must be everyone and the support must be a permanent coalition, no matter what.

"It is hard to imagine the capital of the dwarf nation being patrolled, taxed, and subjugated. It is not our way. We are a proud and independent race. Moreover, the presence of the Wycaan reminds us that once so were the elves. I look to their broken villages and shudder. If we open our gates without a fight, I fear for our future.

"If we fight, we must immediately create a war cabinet with the clans' best military minds. There, we'll devise our strategy. We shall go around the table and each clan will speak in turn."

He turned to his own clan's leader. "Dear Renggal, it is your right as host and representative of the largest clan to speak first."

But before Renggal could speak, Rothendir struck the table with her axe. As the only dwarfe in the room and the leader of the clan that had called the Clansfelt, she needed to take control. All eyes went to her.

"Your Majesty, with the greatest respect, you said that we sat here as equals, so clan size and host city should not dictate speaking order. In the end, each clan's vote counts the same. I called the Clansfelt, but my own kingdom could not host since the Emperor's army destroyed it. And so I invoke the *Shingalla*, the right of first address."

The King stared at her, and she questioned the wisdom of her move. Renggal, however, turned to the King. "I concur, Your Majesty, and freely yield to Clan Leader Rothendir."

The King's smile was tight. "So be it. Speak your mind, Rothendir."

The dwarfe leaned forward and put her hands on the stone table. Its coolness and solidity offered purpose and comfort. It occurred to her that Renggal might be relieved that he would now not have to reveal his position so early.

"Thank you, Your Majesty, and to you, Renggal, for your graciousness. My lords, you have already heard my account of the battle at Mount Zu'Reising. True, Tarlach's forces were tracking the Wycaan and the Emperor's nephew, and that, had Seanchai not saved our priestess, our clan's existence might have remained intact.

"But also remember how quickly a trained and ready force was assembled, one fully equipped to attack dwarves underground. This must have been in the works for a long time. There was no offer of negotiation, no hesitation, no mercy. Why should we expect any of those things now?

"I, also, believe we have two options. We can stay and fight here, leveraging the defenses of Hothengold against Tarlach's army to cost him mightily. This would be my preference.

"Alternately, we can lead them away. They have come prepared to siege Hothengold. We don't offer them this opportunity. We attack them as they enter the passes to this mountain range, and we force them to follow us away from this city and its people. If the Wycaan and the Emperor's son are with our forces, Tarlach will surely follow them. I want to be clear, however, that I do not believe this will distract them from Hothengold forever.

"But, my dear King, do not consider negotiation. In this situation, it is just another word for surrender or massacre. Even if they do not attack this time, it would only be so they can even better prepare to take Hothengold. They will take their time so that they can attack with an entire army of dwarves, backed by better explosives and more than the three cave trolls they brought to our mountain. Mark my words: they will come. You can postpone bloodshed, but not avoid it. And if we do not join the Alliance now, when the Emperor's armies return, we will fight alone."

Rothendir sat down. There was a heavy silence in the wake of her speech, and each clan leader was deep in thought. Here, behind closed doors, there was no more posturing. It was the head of the trader clan, Den Zu'Chantague, who broke the silence.

"I came to Hothengold intending to prevent a war, to persuade the Clansfelt to negotiate, offer some ground in trade, accept taxation. If the dwarf nation goes to war, the loss of trade with the empire will change everything for my people. But as I listen to Clan Leader Rothendir, I begin to realize that it is not so simple. I cannot vote *for* war because of what this means for my clan, but neither can I vote *against* a war that in my heart I know is coming." He stopped a moment and cleared his throat. "Clan Den Zu'Chantague will, for now at least, abstain."

# FIFTY FIVE

M ore than a day had passed since the Clansfelt had withdrawn to a council of the clan leaders. There was no word about how things progressed. If the clan chiefs had broken during the night to sleep, no one knew. Ilana felt the tension descend all around her, a sense of heavy foreboding. Seanchai had been so insufferable that even she had decided to give him space.

He passed the time training with swords and exercising to build his strength, endurance, and store of energy. Without his standing exercises and the sword training, she wondered if he might have lost his mind.

Shayth, Jermona, and the other dwarf scouts returned late into the night, and the report that they brought was chilling. The three units of dwarves they had seen at Mount Zu'Reising had now grown into a full-fledged battalion. Jermona had crept as close as he could to General Tarlach's camp without being detected by the rangers he had left behind.

Along with this battalion of well-armed and highly disciplined dwarves, there were two battalions of pictorians and a number of cave trolls. Shayth mentioned that it seemed the cave trolls were craving a fight and didn't care too much who they were fighting.

Shayth's ultimate conclusion was this: There were a lot of them, and they were two days from the pass that entered the mountain range.

This increased sense of urgency only served to darken Seanchai's mood even more. Shayth tried to alleviate it somewhat by offering to spar with him. While Rhoddan, Ilana, and Sellia were all solid swordsmen, only Shayth could push Seanchai enough to make him feel that he was getting a good workout. Seanchai in turn forced Shayth into sparring at his highest level.

Without shirts they soon each wore a sheen of shiny sweat on their muscled bodies as they took turns to attack and defend. They trained in the courtyard of Clan Den Zu'Reising's housing and soon attracted a large crowd. Word spread outside the courtyard, and young dwarves scrambled onto the walls of the surrounding houses to watch.

Ilana also watched, mesmerized, both with the art of the duel and Seanchai's drastic transformation from the scrawny wood elf she had first known. She glanced over and saw that Sellia was watching with a similar intensity. She moved closer to her friend and took her hand.

"Please, a word in your ear." She guided Sellia to a stone bench nearby.

"You trying to stop me from staring at your boyfriend?" Sellia taunted, flashing her beautiful white teeth. "How do you know I'm not salivating over Shayth?"

Ilana, despite her heaviness, laughed. "How well you know me, Sellia. We've been friends for as long as I can remember."

"We grew up as the only two elfes in Uncle's camp without wrinkles and with all our teeth. How could we not?" Sellia grinned.

"Then we are fast friends?"

"Yes," she replied, but Sellia was not smiling anymore. "What is it, Ilana? Are you really threatened because I flirt with Seanchai and make fun of him? I do the same to Rhoddan; only it's not much of a challenge since he blushes if I just look at him. Your elf is more of a challenge, but I know he's *your* elf."

"I trust you, Sellia," Ilana said, tucking a loose strand of hair behind a pointed ear, "and this is why we're talking. Are you really attracted to Seanchai?"

"Do you think there is an elfe with two eyes who wouldn't be?"

"Seriously."

"Okay," Sellia sat up straight. "Yes, I'm attracted to him. How many elves have you seen pursue me to be their mate? I have lost count, as have you, probably. Dyrovas was a special elf, and I lost him. He could have been the one. I wait for someone who is just as formidable."

"Dyrovas *was* special," Ilana agreed. "I grieved him even though I was still young and already grieving my mother."

"We have lost many good elves," Sellia sighed.

"And we have survived because we find new partners and move on, always seeking to go beyond survival and live in happiness."

Sellia turned and saw the tears brimming in Ilana's eyes. She put an arm around the younger elfe. "What is it, little one?" she whispered.

"I want you to do something for me," Ilana said, her voice going quiet. "If I die—"

"Ilana!"

"No, please listen. The old priestess saw something when we were with her. It's possible – very possible – that I will die before this is all over, maybe here."

"Okay," Sellia said warily.

"If so, I want you to mate with Seanchai, if that is something you both desire. My death mustn't be an obstacle. If I die, you have my blessing and my wish. Seanchai is strong with his blades and powerful with the energy, but he's weak and sensitive at his core. He can't be alone. He craves his friends and he craves love."

She turned to Sellia and grabbed her arm, fingernails digging into Sellia's dark skin. "If I die, will you let him find comfort in your arms? For me?"

"You're really worried by the priestess' premonitions, aren't you?"

"I am."

"Ilana. You have to focus on the present. You need to play your part supporting Seanchai in the approaching battle. You cannot allow something like this to distract you. That, my dear friend, is what might kill you."

Ilana didn't hesitate. "Then help me not be distracted. Tell me that you'll take my place if I die."

Sellia stared into her friend's eyes, searching for a sign that this was a joke or paranoia. She saw only sadness. "Okay. I'll let Seanchai find solace in my arms and, if he is so inclined, I shall willingly be his mate."

Ilana's eyes welled, and her body tensed. When she spoke, her voice was but a whisper. "Swear to me. Bind yourself in the ancient tongue."

Sellia looked at her friend, concerned. She grabbed Ilana and pulled her into a fierce embrace. They held each other tightly as silent tears fell down both their cheeks.

"*Ashbar*," Sellia whispered, and Ilana's body relaxed.

They loosened their grips and stared into each other's faces. "Thank you," Ilana said.

She took Sellia's hand in hers, put something in the palm and closed her friend's fingers tightly. When Sellia opened her hand, she held half of the green stone fastened on a leather cord.

"Ilana," the dark elfe's voice quivered.

"That stone will enable you to find him if you are separated," Ilana said, smiling with relief. "He carries the other half."

Before Sellia could respond, a mighty horn trumpeted from the palace, filling the entire cavern. The Clansfelt was ready to vote.

# FIFTY SIX

General Tarlach was furious, and his soldiers were well aware of this. They avoided him like a plague, and when his officers were summoned for meetings, they came with pits of fear in their stomachs.

Their progress had been slower than planned. A storm had stalled them, as wagon wheels got stuck in the mud. The rain also seemed to irritate the pictorians, even though they lived in the north. Truth be told, it didn't take much to anger a pictorian, and Tarlach was aware that the dispositions of his troops' various backgrounds could easily lead to friction, a hair-breath stage from violence.

The incident with the cave troll had been unfortunate, even though it had worked out. General Tarlach didn't know how the fight had begun, but when the raucous cries had reached his ears, it didn't matter. It wasn't a question of who was right, but who was standing.

He took his time as his guards pushed their way through the crowd, but when he arrived, everyone froze. Tarlach saw that a pictorian and cave troll were fighting. The pictorians maintained a discipline and order, whereas the cave trolls were wild individuals. The pictorians were an integral part of his army, but the cave trolls a luxury. He quickly made up his mind.

In one swift movement, Tarlach drew his sword, propelled himself up off a rock, twisted in midair and decapitated the cave troll. The giant's head rolled off and its severed neck spurted a fountain of yellow blood.

Landing smoothly on his feet, Tarlach addressed the pictorian most engaged in the fight.

"Where is your commander?" the general ordered.

A huge pictorian pushed through the ranks, a massive, double bladed axe strapped across his back. Tarlach turned to him. "First Boar Umnesilk, I will not tolerate fighting among soldiers within our camp. Given that cave trolls can be difficult, I will overlook your indiscretion this time. I trust you will make this clear to your boars?"

The pictorian officer met his gaze, but General Tarlach didn't flinch. Understanding crossed the huge boar's face. In one smooth movement he released his double bladed axe from his back and swung at his soldier. The flat side of the axe smashed into his soldier's face with a sickening crush of bone. Tarlach noted that even in the cloudy light, the axe glistened and the sound as it cracked the bones of the soldier's face echoed around the camp.

The boar went down in a heap. Tarlach didn't know if he was dead or not. Frankly, he didn't care. As he began to walk back toward his command center, he purposely veered closer to the other cave trolls. They slunk back and stared from him to their headless comrade, blood still bubbling out of its neck.

Message received, Tarlach thought, but waited until he was back in his tent to smile.

Ahad left his grandfather, wondering, as always, if this might be the last time they would see each other. He mounted his horse and began to ride back to the palace before remembering that Phineus had invited him to the waterfall.

Ahad hesitated. He wondered, as he often did, whether this invitation was actually an invitation, or an order. It was unclear more often than not. He turned his horse around. If he did not join Phineus, there might be some suspicion concerning his visit to his grandfather.

It was an easy ride to the waterfall. He left his horse with the Prince's escort and walked through the trees. Already, the roar of the waterfall was helping him to relax. He found the Prince and his retinue near the bottom of the thirty-foot wall of water. Other people picnicked further down from the waterfall, kept away by deference to the Prince, as well as two burly bodyguards.

There were two young women with the Phineus. The one not in his arms was from Ahad's science class. His grandfather had been suspicious of her, thinking she might be a spy. Ahad had never had the chance to find out, but her presence, despite her beauty, was now disconcerting.

When Phineus saw Ahad, he waved him over. "Come, Ahad. We have wine and fruit here, though you will need to earn them. Ginette and I have been in the water. You and Tarica have not. No wine for Tarica, as yet."

The Prince wanted a show? So be it. Ahad continued on his way, unbuttoning his loose shirt and throwing it on the ground near the Prince. He was suddenly proud of his hardening body, a result of the intensive military training he was receiving. Still walking, he awkwardly managed to take off his boots and socks, determined not to flinch at the sharp pebbles under his bare feet. He unzipped his breeches and stepped out of them at the water edge. Then, only in his undergarment, he strode out into the water.

It was freezing, and he had to struggle not to turn and run out. Finally, he got up the gumption to dive under the water. When he surfaced, he turned and began to swim back. He wasn't sure whether the water was warmer than he thought or his body was numb.

Tarica was waiting for him near the water's edge. She was in the river, with the water up to her thighs. She wore undergarments and a tight, white shirt that exposed her stomach and arms. Ahad couldn't help but notice her curves and felt a thrill of excitement.

When he reached her, she put her arms around him and shivered from his cold body. Unsure, he put his hands around her waist. Her body was deliciously warm. She gasped from his touch.

"Here's the deal," she whispered in his ear. "I want to drink wine, but I don't want to die of hypothermia. You're going to help. Do you understand?"

Ahad stroked her lower back and nodded. He didn't trust himself to say anything, lest his voice crack. She continued.

"If my body goes under the water, it will turn from smooth to pimply and would be cold and unwelcoming, as will I toward you. Believe me?"

Ahad nodded. "That would be a tragedy," he whispered.

"Good," she said. "Now, insist that I leave the water with you. Hold my hand and drag me out. I'll make it worth your while."

"How?" Ahad regretted the words as soon as they left his mouth.

She rolled her eyes. "I'll tell you about this mineral that was found near the Shorian cliffs. It has amazing properties, and you don't know about it."

Ahad laughed. She wasn't just super-cute, but also super-smart. He deftly scooped her up in his arms and walked out of the water, back to where Phineus was lying with the other girl.

"Hey," the Prince objected. "Someone didn't get wet."

"My fault," Ahad interjected. "I kind of enjoy her warm."

He dropped down on the huge blanket and poured a cup of wine. He passed it to Tarica, who joined him and laid her head on his thigh.

"How was your visit? How is General Tarlach senior?" Phineus asked.

It was the way that Tarica turned her head to listen. Everything about her up until now had been so relaxed and lazy. This subtle but obvious movement had not.

Ahad was glad he hadn't started drinking. So Tarica really was too good to be true. He wondered if she was working for the Prince or the Emperor. Was there even a difference? The net was closing, and he felt snared.

# FIFTY SEVEN

When Seanchai and Ballendir entered the Great Hall, the room was already bustling. The galleries were packed with spectators, the rows behind the clan delegations were filled, and anticipation permeated the air.

All eyes turned to Seanchai when he entered. He had insisted that Shayth, Ilana, Sellia and Rhoddan be present. He was determined that this time he would have his own delegation. Ballendir couldn't understand the reasoning, but Seanchai wanted to show that he was bringing more than just himself to the table.

As everyone took their seats, Shayth and the elves stood behind Seanchai. He hoped that their height standing added to his seated would emanate power.

When all were settled, the master of ceremonies entered and struck the ground with his thick staff. Seanchai was used to the sparks that shot off the floor, but struggled to keep a straight face at Rhoddan's awe-filled, whispered, "cool."

The King entered and regarded Seanchai and his friends as he walked around the other side of the great stone table. When he sat, the other delegations resumed their seats. The King looked over at the elves and humans.

"Seanchai," the King said evenly as he sat. "I wish to know the names of your companions so that I may welcome them to the Clansfelt."

Seanchai stood. "High King of the Dwarves, this is Ilana, Rhoddan and Sellia of the Elven Resistance." He turned to Shayth and let tension build momentarily. "And here stands Shayth, son of the late Prince Shindell."

A murmur went through the crowd and Shayth obliged with his best scowl. Seanchai wasn't sure for whom the scowl was intended. He rather suspected it might be for him.

The King smiled. "Welcome, then, Ilana, Rhoddan and Sellia of the Elven Resistance. Welcome, Prince Shayth." This title only served to deepen Shayth's glare, but the King had looked away. "Dwarves of Hothengold, delegations of the Six Clans, we have debated at length with regard to the dilemma before us. We have debated publicly and in clan council.

"The armies of General Tarlach approach our mountain range. Two options have I given the council. I asked them to decide whether we should attempt a negotiation, or whether we should stand and fight. A diplomatic or war council will decide the parameters of either negotiation or war. The clan leaders will each cast a vote for their people. If there is not a two-thirds majority, either I will add my vote to decide, or we shall begin discussions again. But I warn you, my fellow dwarves. We do not have the luxury of time to conduct further debate. Let our decision be quick, and may the gods judge it to be correct."

With that, the King raised his majestic axe and thumped the stone table with the handle's hoof. He turned to Renggal, head of Clan Den Zu'Garten.

Renggal sighed deeply before he spoke. "Your Majesty. My council has weighed our options carefully. Here, in the heart of our mountain, in our great city, the battle will take place. We recognize the grave danger facing us and everything we stand to lose. Nonetheless, Clan Den Zu'Garten votes for war."

A buzz went around the room. Seanchai had thought their vote was already with him, but a glance between Rothendir and Ballendir suggested they had not been quite so certain.

The master of ceremonies banged once with his heavy staff, on the stone floor and an expectant silence descended. The King turned to Renggal. "Your wisdom is great and known throughout the six clans, Renggal. I am sure this decision was not taken lightly." Then he raised his voice. "I call upon Clan Den Zu'Reising."

Rothendir rose slowly. "My clan has already felt the steel of the Emperor's rule. Many brave dwarves from our clan feast in the halls of our ancestors because of the attack unleashed by General Tarlach's armies. Clan Den Zu'Reising cries out for revenge. We vote for war."

The King turned to his other side.

"Lord Natague, what say Clan Den Zu'Chantague?"

"Your Majesty." The stout, well-dressed dwarf leaned forward and cleared his throat. "Your Majesty, our council has debated long. We maintain good relations with the Empire and believe that, as long as we can be strong in trade, we can protect our independence. We would, of course, extend such influence to protect all clans.

"Clan Den Zu'Chantague therefore votes against war. We put our trust in negotiations."

Seanchai felt a wave of panic. Clan Den Zu'Chantague was extremely wealthy and would surely influence the other clans. Again, the master of ceremonies banged his staff on the stone floor, silencing the murmurs.

The King turned to Clan Dan Zu'Ornagen. "Master Ziskagen. What say the scholars?"

Seanchai had to resist biting his nails. He was about to pay the price for bettering Master Ziskagen before the Clansfelt.

Ziskagen rose and bowed to his King. "Your Majesty. Our council stayed up all night. We evaluated the history of our race and tried to discern relevant patterns. As such, we believe that the dwarf race cannot defeat the Emperor's army. Clan Dan Zu'Ornagen votes against war and for negotiation."

He sat down heavily, staring at a ripple in the middle of the stone table. Seanchai felt that Ziskagen was not proud of his council's choice. The big elf squeezed the arms of his chair. He had counted on the scholars to offset the traders and religious zealots. Ballendir patted Seanchai's arm, but couldn't help his other hand from twisting his long beard in frustration.

"Master Craftsman," the King said without emotion. "Dugenminsk, what say Clan Dan Zu'Ulster?"

Dugenminsk rose from his chair. He looked defiantly around the table. "An artisan cannot pursue his craft in servitude. Only in freedom can we aspire to the excellence we strive for. Clan Dan Zu'Ulster votes for war and freedom."

Seanchai sighed with relief. He had feared that the smaller clans would side with the traders, especially given that they needed to sell their wares to survive. But perhaps there really was more to dwarves than the pursuit of wealth.

"The vote stands at three to two. We turn now to those who serve our gods. High Priest Zu'Altan, what does Clan Dan Zu'Reiltan say?"

All eyes fell upon the tall masked priest as he gripped the table and pulled himself to his feet. Seanchai could tell that the mask was staring in his direction.

His breathing sounded labored, or maybe, Seanchai thought, he was struggling with the decision his clan had made. There was a deal in place, an agreement not to expose the assassination attempt on the King. But with the opposing side holding a three to two advantage, he could renege on the agreement and claim that any accusation was just bad blood on the accusers' side.

"My King. You and Clan Dan Zu'Reiltan hold similar roles, for we lead our people in different ways. The priests guard against any intrusion from above, not in defense of our lives, but in defense of our race.

"We have seen the destiny of those who went above ground and mingled with the long-legged. They are now slaves, sacrificing their souls and slaying good, gods-fearing dwarves at the whim of a despotic leader.

"Lessons should be learned from what happens when one strays too far from the path laid out by our gods. Therefore, we call upon all dwarves to defend our races at this dire time, so that we may secure not only the lives of our people, but also the destiny of our race. In service to the gods, Clan Dan Zu'Reiltan votes for war."

A cry went up as the Great Hall erupted in a cacophony of discussion and surprise. The master of ceremonies allowed this to continue a few moments before bringing his staff crashing to the ground once, twice, three times until the will of the people died down and all eyes went to the King, who stood up and stared around the Great Hall. Then he turned to Seanchai.

"Rise, Wycaan Warrior," he said, and Seanchai rose to his feet, though he could barely control his breathing. "Many centuries have passed since a Wycaan stood before the Clansfelt and pleaded with us as you have.

"Now, as High King of the Dwarves, I give you our answer. Dwarves are the most ancient of races. Our history is rich with tales of honor and great battles fought for freedom and dignity. Too long has the land of Odessiya been bound by the hate of man, of callous dictators such as the Emperor and his nefarious ancestors. Too long have the dwarves stayed underground.

"It is fitting that a Wycaan comes to raise the banner of freedom for dwarves, elves, and men. It is right that you stand in this, the Great Hall of Hothengold, and rekindle the flame of the Alliance.

"Therefore, I respond as is the will of this noble council. In the weeks to come, many of our finest will die and feast in the great halls of our ancestors. They will be grieved, but they will go to their fate with pride, knowing that when Odessiya cried out for freedom, the dwarf nation answered with one resounding voice."

He turned to his people and raised his golden axe. His voice rose and filled the cavern. "We will honor the oaths of our ancestors. The Wycaan has called and the dwarf nation answers: THE ALLIANCE STANDS ONCE MORE: FOR FREEDOM AND THE ALLIANCE OF ODESSIYA.

"TO WAR!"

"TO WAR!"

"TO WAR!"

# FIFTY EIGHT

Seanchai maintained his stoicism even as the Great Hall erupted in chants. He noticed that even dwarves from the two clans who voted against war were cheering. Now that the decision was taken, the dwarves did indeed speak with one voice.

It took him awhile to leave the hall. Everyone, it seemed, wanted to shake his hand and clap him on the back. Finally, together with his friends and the delegation of Clan Den Zu'Reising, he made it back to their residence and only there did he let his emotions show. He hugged his friends and thanked Ballendir again and again. When Rothendir entered the compound, all stopped and turned to receive her. Seanchai pushed forward.

"I don't know how to thank you, Clan Leader Rothendir," he said, bowing.

"Thank me?" she replied, her voice was hoarse from debating and her eyes swollen from lack of sleep. "I serve the dwarf nation and Clan Den Zu'Reising. My clan was attacked, and we grieve the loss of our priestess and many elders. You have nothing to thank me for, but you can repay me by doing all that is in your strength to bring us victory and revenge. For now, go rest. You will soon be called for."

"Called for?"

"Yes," she replied. "Did you think we were just going to wait and see what General Tarlach sends our way? There is a war council. You and Shayth will be there."

"Me?" Shayth asked.

"Yes," Rothendir turned to him. "You're a human and have a relationship with the general. It makes perfect sense."

Seanchai saw Shayth turn red and was about to intervene when Sellia appeared at the human's side.

"Remember your destiny, Shayth," she whispered. "If the dwarves say they need you, you must answer their call. Go to the council and help with the battle plan. Go as a free man, and as one who turned his back on the Emperor's ways."

Seanchai received his summons the next morning. Ballendir would also be joining them. Shayth was brooding and didn't say much as they ate breakfast, but Seanchai bombarded the dwarf with questions about Hothengold, dwarf defenses, and the surrounding countryside.

"Do yeh have some ideas?" Ballendir asked on their way to the palace.

"I do," Seanchai said, "but I want to listen to what others think before I make any suggestions."

"Very wise," Ballendir said. "But don't wait too long. We need to organize this considerably faster than the Clansfelt."

"Otherwise," Shayth added, "we risk forfeiting our decision to Tarlach."

When they entered the hall of the war council, Seanchai stared around him. These were not the dwarves who had sat around the table in the Great Hall. They were bigger, rougher, and more muscular. The politicians had stood aside for the military to take over, and Seanchai was impressed.

In the middle was what looked like a sand box, elevated two feet above the ground and resting on a huge slab of stone. But what impressed Seanchai was the model inside of it, an exact replica of the mountainside and the surrounding area. In various areas, the walls were cut away to allow an inside look.

"There are more," Ballendir said and pointed around the room.

Some were of adjacent areas, and one was Hothengold itself, split in half so that both sides could be examined from the inside.

"This is amazing," Seanchai whispered. "Who does this?"

"A team of sculptors is employed to maintain their accuracy. Impressive, huh?" He had turned to Shayth.

"Indeed," Shayth replied, though his tone did not back his words. They both stared at him. "I have seen the halls that my uncle maintains, each for a different state within the empire. They are intricately detailed."

A large dwarf banged a nearby table. His voice was deep and authoritative. "Come, everyone, and sit. The time to talk is over. Now we plan."

As they all took seats, Seanchai noted that there were no clan divisions or preferential seating. The only dwarves he recognized were Dugenminsk from the artisan clan of Dan Zu'Ulster and Ziskagen, the scholar he had bested, from Clan Dan Zu'Ornagen.

"Have you had a chance to burn in the pipe?" Dugenminsk asked, leaning forward.

"I'm frightened to let him try," Ballendir answered. "It might end up a cinder, he's been so uptight."

There was a round of relaxed laughter. This was going to be far less formal than the Clansfelt, Seanchai thought. The large dwarf dragged a piece of slate over. It was covered in Dwarvish with arrows connecting and crisscrossing.

"My name is Rus'ik Armsgarten of Clan Den Zu'Garten," the big dwarf said, stroking his large black and white beard. "I have trained and led our army for three decades. The King asked me to bring you together and form the war council."

"Looks like you already have a plan," Ziskagen said, pointing to the board.

"I have been planning the defense of this city for many years and, while the Clansfelt was politicking, I was receiving intelligence and adapting my original plans. After we vote in a War Council Chief, I request the opportunity to explain this, though I admit it is an insufficient strategy for what we face."

Dugenminsk turned to Seanchai. "With respect, Wycaan, I believe that the War Chief should be a dwarf."

"I agree," Seanchai replied.

"Then," Dugenminsk turned back to everyone, "I propose that Rus'ik Armsgarten be the head of this council. He has more experience than most of us and this is his clan's capital."

"Seconded," Ziskagen said. "Let's not waste any more time."

There were murmurs and nods of agreement around the table.

"Thank you," Armsgarten replied. "I'm honored by your trust."

He launched into a long explanation of the writing on the slate board, pointing out how the city had been built with a number of layers, each of which would provide an opportunity to kill many soldiers without unduly exposing the dwarves.

As he continued, Armsgarten glanced more and more frequently at Shayth, whose expression was darkening by the minute. Finally, Armsgarten stopped.

"What is it, Prince Shayth? Speak your mind."

"I am no prince," Shayth growled. "I have renounced my connection to the royal house. The only ties I want with them involve my bow or broadsword."

"I mean no offense," Armsgarten replied. "But your body language suggests this is not the reason for your anger."

"I live and breathe by my anger," Shayth replied. "In a few days, you will be happy to see how I express that rage. But you are correct: my problem is with your plan. It is meant to wear down an enemy too powerful to meet on open ground. That would make sense, but Tarlach won't care how many soldiers he loses. He will not be worn down. He will never submit. He will throw more and more soldiers until we exhaust our arms, our options, and our soldiers."

"And we have not begun to discuss his use of dwarves or explosives," Seanchai added. "Rus'ik, is there a good place away from here? Can we engage their army and lead them through the mountains?"

Everyone was looking at him.

"Dwarves do not ordinarily excel above ground," Ballendir answered.

"They have as many dwarf soldiers as we do," Shayth replied, catching on to Seanchai's idea. "The trolls are slow, and the pictorians, while deadly in combat, are little more than large targets from afar."

"But where could we lead them?" Rus'ik asked, beginning to come around to the idea.

There was silence for a while, and then Ziskagen spoke. "To the Fog Marshes of Oblinzt."

This was met by a murmur of either excitement or fear – Seanchai couldn't tell which.

"What are the Fog Marshes of Oblinzt?" he asked, turning to Ballendir.

Ballendir sighed. "They are a good place to die."

# FIFTY NINE

S eanchai watched as the warriors in the room transformed from hopelessness to excitement. Led by Rus'ik Armsgarten, the group moved from model to model, expounding on how the enemy could be engaged at different spots along the way.

Seanchai gathered that it would take only two or three days to reach the Fog Marshes of Oblinzt, and that there were several points along the way where they could engage the enemy with guerilla hit-and-run tactics. Once in the swamps, it would be a very different battle.

"We can only send our youngest and fittest troops," Rus'ik Armsgarten said. "It will be hard moving and fighting on such terrain."

"Older, more experienced troops can help in the beginning," Dugenminsk suggested and pointed to the areas he was suggesting. "We can help engage at this, this and this point, and then double back to either secure Hothengold or to attack from the rear. But only the fittest will last all the way. It will be very dangerous for them."

"I will be with them," Seanchai said. "And the elves and Shayth are better suited out in the open than fighting in narrow passages underground."

"Also, if we are to ask the young troops to go and do so much, let them see Seanchai leading them," Shayth replied.

A look passed among some of the dwarves.

"What is it, Rus'ik?" Seanchai asked, suddenly alarmed.

Rus'ik shuffled his feet and searched for the right words. "I'm worried how it will be perceived," he said, clearly choosing his words. "You come here and urge us to fight, bring a large army in your wake, and then you leave."

"I will be with the youn–"

"He doesn't trust you, Seanchai," Shayth interjected. "We could all just run off and leave them. The war goes badly, and we cut our losses and flee. Is that right, Rus'ik?"

"But . . . I gave you my word," Seanchai said, hurt.

"It's a matter of perception," Rus'ik answered, folding his beard furiously. "I'm not good at diplomacy. I'm a soldier, not a politician."

"Maybe your mate could stay and help defend the city?" Dugenminsk said. "We have seen the love that exists between you. If she stays, the dwarves of the city will be assured that you'll not forsake them."

Seanchai stared at him. "But then Tarlach will come after her and the ones left here, won't he?" he said.

"I think it's safe to assume there'll be some sort of assault on the city," Rus'ik said, "even if you succeed in leading them away."

"But we can make it look like an evacuation," Seanchai suggested. "Have some dressed as women, older dwarfes, and younglings, and give them packages to carry."

"Don't underestimate the tenacity of our elders or our females." Ballendir growled. "Shayth? Will the general commit all his forces to the chase?"

Shayth shook his head. "No, he will want to see Hothengold buried."

"You can't be serious?"

At this precise moment, Seanchai would have rather faced a hundred pictorians than Ilana this angry and hurt. "You agreed to this?" Her hands were clenched into tight fists on her arched waist.

"I said I would talk to you about it," Seanchai replied. "I don't like it any more than you do, but . . ."

"But what?" she demanded.

He sighed. "I understand why they're requesting it. Look, I hate to be away from you. I don't want to ever again feel how I felt when you languished in a dungeon at Galbrieth, but I think there is something to their request. You can give inspiration and hope to the people penned in here at Hothengold. They have not seen combat, and you are skilled at being amazingly calm one minute and a ferocious warrior the next."

Ilana looked at his earnest expression and suddenly burst out laughing. "Is this how you woo a young elfe?" She moved closer and hugged him tightly. "You will come back?"

"Of course," he whispered in her ear.

"And if I manage to help repel the troops sent here, I'll come after you."

"Not by yourself," Seanchai gasped.

She laughed. "I love you," she said and pulled him even closer.

"I will ask Sellia to stay with you," Seanchai said. "You shouldn't be the only one left here."

Ilana abruptly pulled away. She was frowning and fiddling with strands of her hair.

"What is it, Ilana?" he asked, recognizing the signs.

"I want Sellia to go with you," Ilana said. "She is quick and more experienced in guerilla tactics than any of you. Maybe Rhoddan could stay with me. I'm comfortable with him, and he'll make a better fighter close up."

Seanchai examined her face. She was holding something back and he was tempted to scry, but stopped himself. Rhoddan was a good fighter in any environment, but Ilana had always been closer to Sellia.

"Please," she said, and Seanchai thought he saw tears beginning to well in her eyes. "Don't question me. I agree to stay behind without arguing, but you allow me to keep who I choose."

Seanchai stroked her cheek and twisted her hair behind her pointed ear. "Okay."

The spy was quite adapt at leaving Hothengold and even more so in penetrating the guards of the Emperor's army. Wrapped in a dark cloak, he made his way to the tent that he recognized from past visits to the general.

Two tall sentries stood outside the tent, and the spy could see silhouettes of a number of figures inside. The spy retreated into the shadows, waiting for the meeting to end. He was cold and hungry, but he could wait. He wouldn't reveal himself to any more than the two who knew him.

After a half hour, a small, rotund man exited with a pile of scrolls balanced precariously. The spy followed him and waited until no one else would overhear their conversation.

"Well met, Master Bortand," he hissed.

Bortand jumped and promptly dropped several scrolls in the wet dirt. When he looked around, there was no one there. "Very funny!" he called out. "I'm sure General Tarlach will want to know how his paperwork got dirty."

"I think General Tarlach has more important things on his plate right now," the voice whispered from the darkness between two tents. "Please inform the general that he has an uninvited visitor."

Bortand stared into the darkness, but saw no one. He hesitated for a moment before returning to the general's command tent. When Tarlach saw him enter, he detached himself from the officer standing around the model of the mountain.

"Gentlemen," he announced after Bortand had whispered the message. "Enough for tonight. Please leave me. We shall resume at first light tomorrow."

The tent quickly emptied. Continuing their discussions as they left the tent, no one noticed the hooded figure only two feet from them.

When the tent was empty, Tarlach came and stood outside the entrance between the two guards. The spy appeared before him, fully cloaked and hooded.

"Let him pass," Tarlach said and returned inside.

The figure followed and closed the tent flaps. Then he turned to the expectant general and removed his hood.

"Jermona," General Tarlach said, showing no surprise. "You have returned. I thought you might have changed your colors."

The boy's eyes flashed. "I'm a ranger, general. A ranger before anything."

"And you bring information so that I'll forgive your indiscretions?"

"Oh, yes," Jermona replied with a smile. "Valuable information."

# SIXTY

When General Tarlach's officers reconvened the following morning, they found their commander considerably more upbeat. The general had called them in well before dawn, but had breakfast waiting for them. He watched with satisfaction as the officers piled up their plates with great enthusiasm.

A couple of younger officers sidled over to where the general stood.

"Thank you, sir," one ventured, raising his plate.

"Are we celebrating something, sir?" another asked.

Tarlach nodded. He had barely slept after his meeting with Jermona. Having imparted the information that the general craved, Jermona had asked to rejoin the general's personal staff as his chief ranger.

Tarlach had been impressed with the young man's ambition, but somewhat puzzled by his request. This was not ranger behavior. But then, the boy was young and definitely talented.

He had sent Jermona back to Hothengold despite the young man's protests. Once the fighting began, he could slip away and join the general during the mayhem of battle. "Lay low," he had said. "You have disappeared without reason. You will need a story. Keep it simple and sullen."

Now the general turned to his officers. "Gentlemen," he said, "to business."

They gathered around the big model.

"Last night, I received more information. The dwarves are divided about what to do. Most do not want to stay and fight underground after what we did to the Zu'Reising clan and their miserable mountain.

"Many will try and leave. They plan to move all their gold and treasure from Hothengold. One might assume they will rename it, simply, Hothen."

The officers laughed.

"They plan to evacuate their old and young first in small groups. We suspect they have already begun to leave. The main body will be leaving with most of their military. The extremists will stay and hope that either we will not bother to attack them, or will allow them to negotiate a surrender."

"Probably the traders," one soldier suggested. "Will we let them live?"

"No," General Tarlach replied, his voice firm. "There are many other dwarf colonies that do not yet know the true potential of the Emperor. These dwarves must be made an example of.

"Tomorrow morning, we will enter the Hoth mountain range and leave a company of dwarves, cave trolls, and explosives masters.

"The men and pictorians will circle behind the mountain range to confront those who are escaping. They must be leaving through an exit on the other side of Mount Hoth, or else we would have noticed. But I also want to be ready to attack their army when they do choose to leave."

There was nodding and murmurs of assent. Several officers started discussing different points of the mountain. General Shiftan, however, was standing to one side, detached from the excitement. Tarlach walked over to him.

"What is it, my friend?" Tarlach asked.

General Shiftan turned away from the other soldiers. He took a plate and threw on a piece of bread, some cheese and eggs. But he was clearly not hungry. Then he sat at a small table at the opposite end. Tarlach sat opposite him.

"Are you sure about your source?" Shiftan asked quietly, forcing General Tarlach to lean forward.

"My spy? Yes. Why?"

"Do you remember the dwarf officer that I had with us at Mount Zu'Reising? Let me bring him in here and explain what we have discovered. I will only inform him of the facts, but I want to see his reaction. I think he may have a different idea of what's happening."

"Very well, my friend," Tarlach said. "But while we wait for him to come you should eat. That food is hot."

Shiftan smiled. "How many times have you and I eaten cold food in the field." He turned and signaled to one of his younger officers.

Five minutes later, as General Shiftan finished his last forkful of eggs, the dwarf appeared, wearing his gold leaf on a cloak. He saluted both generals. Much to Tarlach's annoyance, General Shiftan sent the dwarf to fill a plate for himself.

The dwarf returned with a heaping plate. "Eat while it is hot," Shiftan said, "but listen carefully while you do. I want to share some secret information that we have just received and gauge your reaction. You should feel free to speak openly with us, but say nothing once you leave this tent. Understood?"

The dwarf nodded. He could do little else since his mouth was full.

"We understand that the dwarves of Hothengold are divided. Most are leaving and taking the gold, and only a small fanatical contingent is staying to defend the capital."

The dwarf was frowning around his huge bite of food. Tarlach reached over and stayed the next loaded fork on its way to the dwarf's mouth.

"Steady on. Why are you frowning?"

"Sir," the dwarf said after swallowing his food and wiping his mouth on his sleeve. "It's been a long time since I lived in dwarf society, but yeh story sounds a bit suspect. Begging yeh pardon, sir," he added quickly to Shiftan.

"I ordered you to speak freely," Shiftan replied.

"Very well, sir. There hasn't been a Clansfelt in fifty years, but . . ."

"Wait. This gathering of clans is a Clansfelt?"

"Yes sir. Like I said it's very rare. The laws surrounding it are ancient and strictly observed. Once a decision is reached, all clans must adhere to it. If they're splitting their forces, it must be part of a plan.

"I also can't believe they'd abandon Hothengold, It's the capital, the heart of the dwarf nation. It's beautiful and steeped in history. Also there're many old and young living there. The march out would be treacherous and destroy the people's moral.

"And there is something else, sir," the dwarf scratched his long, wild hair. "They couldn't possibly move all the gold and precious metals stored in Hothengold, and dwarves never abandon their wealth."

"Where are the elves and Shayth going to be?" Shiftan asked. "Are they staying or going?"

The dwarf scratched his beard. "I'd expect them to be leaving. They are faster and used to fighting on the run, I reckon."

"But if we are wrong as you say," Tarlach said, "and they will leave a large force to defend the city, or using this ploy of running to distract us, then wouldn't the dwarves demand some of the elf's party to stay?"

"Makes sense. The dwarves are helping the elf and he goes off. Seems like sound business to demand collateral, if yeh take mah meaning."

General Shiftan sipped from a cup of steaming chicory. "If some of them are staying, then there's an expectation to hold Hothengold. From what we've seen of this elf, he's soft when it comes to his friends. He will lead their army out but will plan to return."

"So what do you suggest?" Tarlach asked.

"We must follow the elf," General Shiftan said. "He poses the biggest threat. If we can discover where he is, we send our main forces there."

Tarlach nodded and dismissed the dwarf. When he was alone with Shiftan, he leaned forward.

"At Galbrieth, I tried to lure the elf by capturing his friends. It worked in that he came. This time it will be different."

"How?"

"I plan to be there to confront him myself. This time there is too much at stake, and I must make sure we succeed. It might also be that only I can defeat him." Tarlach ripped a chunk of bread from a loaf and squashed the soft dough in a fist. "Shayth too must die."

"I will try to take Shayth out for you as I promised."

"We must succeed." Tarlach hissed.

"We will, my friend, but all the same, let me move Ahad."

"You doubt me?"

Shiftan stared back at his old friend. When he spoke, his voice was steady. "No one is infallible."

"And if I succeed? What will happen to my son if it is known he fled the palace after the Emperor has been so kind to him? No. There is only one way. I must not fail."

# SIXTY ONE

Seanchai completed a strenuous practice routine with his Win Dao swords and was panting and sweating. His body ached satisfyingly from the effort. Rhoddan had been practicing, as well, though they did not spar. According to Ilana, Rhoddan's ego could not take being beaten too often. Seanchai went and sat next to his friend, who was sitting nearby, sharpening his own blades.

"Didn't I see you sharpening these yesterday?"

"Uh-ha," Rhoddan confirmed, "and probably the day before that and the day before that and the day before that . . ."

"Why so often?" Seanchai wiped away sweat with his shirt.

"It's the waiting," Rhoddan answered. "I'm ready to fight. It's what I've trained for all my life. But you can't train for the waiting."

Seanchai nodded. "Thank you for staying with Ilana to defend the city. I regret to say I think it will require more waiting."

"Do you think they'll even attack here, once you've engaged them?"

"I don't know," Seanchai replied, "But Shayth is convinced they will. He says Tarlach will feel a need to destroy the city, no matter what. He'll want to send a message to all the dwarf clans."

"Shayth is hardly objective," Rhoddan said.

"Totally not objective," said a human voice from behind them. Shayth's eyes were coal-black as always when the rage rose. "My fear is that he'll lead the forces here and not in pursuit of us. If you get the chance, Rhoddan, kill him without hesitation. I might never forgive you for getting to him before me, but strike as soon as you can. And remember, he is very, very good. He trains as much as you and I, and he has a lot of experience."

A small group entered the room with Ilana and Sellia. "You have guests," Sellia announced.

Seanchai turned to see the stout, red-haired dwarf, Ruffminsk, from the artisan clan, Dan Zu'Ulster. Behind him, Seanchai recognized the young dwarf who had made him the pipe and flask. He was carrying a large package wrapped in burlap.

"Welcome, Ruffminsk and Thorminsk," Seanchai said. "To what do we owe this honor?"

"Well met, Seanchai, son of Seantai," Ruffminsk said and bowed. "We come with a message from our Clan Leader, Dugenminsk. He regrets to send us in his stead, but the hour is near, and he prepares our troops."

Seanchai nodded. "What can I do for you?"

Thorminsk set the package down on a flat stone and began unwrapping it while Ruffminsk spoke.

"When you dined with us during the Clansfelt, we said we had three gifts for you. Pipes and hip flasks are not what are required in times like these. Thorminsk is one of a very few who specializes in King's Mail. He uses intricate techniques to create a thin but powerful mail that fits close to the body. It is capable of repelling most blades and even fire. It will never rust or lose its suppleness. Parents hand these down to their children for generations. It is very slow work and takes years to create a single suit.

"Thorminsk has been working on this for some time. This morning, he finished it, and we request that you honor us by wearing it into battle."

They all looked upon the blushing Thorminsk, who held the long tunic up. "This might be too long," he said, and Seanchai noticed his slim hands were shaking.

Seanchai stepped forward and took the mail. "Thank you," he said. "It's . . . wow! It's so light."

Everyone laughed.

"Don't let its weight fool you," Ruffminsk said. "The King's Mail is the mail of monarchs. Most dwarves can only dream of owning one, for they are beyond value."

Seanchai slipped it on. Indeed, it was a bit big, but Thorminsk approached with a set of tools and began adjusting it. Seanchai noted how he carefully saved every link, and then something occurred to him.

"Thorminsk, if you have been working on this for some time, how come it is not shorter and wider to fit a dwarf?"

The young dwarf reddened. "If you were an expert in our craft, Wycaan, you would notice that this is a fusion of two mails, each of a subtly different mixture of metals. It is very unprofessional, but given the time constraints, I had little choice. If we all come through this alive, I would be honored to finish your mail as it should be made."

"I think the two-tone adds character," Ilana said.

Thorminsk grimaced, Seanchai smiled, and Sellia rolled her eyes. But Seanchai then had another thought.

"If these King's Mails are so rare, where did you have another to combine with the one you were making?"

"It is of no consequence," Thorminsk said. "I am honored to have the opportunity to create one for a Wycaan. As a child, I heard the stories, and I dreamed that one day I would make the armor of the Wycaans."

Seanchai looked at him, and the dwarf glanced away and met Shayth's gaze. Shayth shook his head. "Let me guess. This specialization is something that has passed through your family?"

Thorminsk looked to Ruffminsk for help, but found none forthcoming. Shayth continued. "Your family probably owns a King's Mail of its own, an heirloom. Did you combine the mail of your family?"

Thorminsk looked like he was about to bolt. Seanchai didn't help by immediately trying to take the tunic off. "I can't accept this from you. It is your family's most prized possession and source of wealth. I—"

Thorminsk spun round and his voice, though high, was sharp, and there were tears brimming in his eyes. "What good is wealth if we are all dead? What good is a family heirloom if no one from the family lives? Tomorrow, many of my people will sacrifice their lives for our freedom.

"I have little talent on the battlefield, but in the craft of the dwarves I have no living equal save my teacher. When the battle is over and victory assured, the legends told by my clan will remember that the victorious Wycaan led us to freedom wearing a coat of arms made by Thorminsk, son of Dorenminsk, of the Clan Dan Zu'Ulster. You dishonor me by not accepting my gift."

Seanchai took a deep breath.

"I accept this fine work of King's Mail, Thorminsk, son of Dorenminsk. I am honored that Clan Dan Zu'Ulster sees fit to let me wear it into battle. And I like the two-tone, as well."

Everyone laughed, and the red in Thorminsk's cheeks deepened even more as the powerful elf swept him into his arms. "Thank you,

Thorminsk," he whispered into the dwarf's ear. "May I be worthy of your skills and your sacrifice."

"You will, Wycaan," the young dwarf replied. "I know you will."

At that moment, the great horn of Hothengold was blown. One long, rich note hung over the entire city. Seanchai straightened and surveyed his friends.

"It is time," he said, and picked up his Win Dao swords.

# SIXTY TWO

G eneral Shiftan led a battalion of humans and pictorians up into the pass under cover of dark. The goal was to establish a stronghold on the high ground to protect the main body of the army as they entered the mountain range.

Though he was confident that he would achieve this by going up at night, he had nonetheless employed a large convoy of troops. His own soldiers were battle-experienced and disciplined. He believed the pictorians were a wild card, but General Tarlach believed in them, and he had faith in Tarlach.

As they moved through a steep, walled section of the path, however, General Shiftan learned abruptly that this was not going to be as easy as he thought. Darkness was a double-edged sword. He heard the whistles of arrows long before he saw them, followed by grunts and cries from his soldiers as they fell.

"Circle," he yelled, and his troops fell into a tight ring, shields interlaced above them to provide protection. "Umnesilk, move the pictorians to the cliff walls.

The first boar cried a guttural order and the pictorians moved slowly, holding shields absurdly small for their huge bodies. But Shiftan observed that no pictorian fell, though a few limped to cover.

"First Archers, fire with brands," he called. "Second Archers, shoot on sight."

A wave of flaming arrows flew into the air, illuminating the sky. The general could discern nothing, but his second wave of archers instinctively shot a wave of arrows up to the ridges above them.

"Advance together. Umnesilk, bring your troops along the walls."

The army slowly advanced. Occasionally, a soldier fell as an arrow slipped through, but the shields quickly closed. The walls of the ravine narrowed, and suddenly, it was not arrows, but large rocks and boulders that were raining down on them. As a few of his soldiers staggered and fell, General Shiftan halted the advance.

"Soldiers, kneel. Brace against your shields," he shouted. "First Boar Umnesilk, secure the heights."

Shiftan surmised that the pictorians had engaged the rebel dwarves several minutes later when the rockfall ceased. He ordered the army to lower their shields and sent one company up to aid the pictorians on either side.

As he did, a horn was blown. Dwarves swarmed down to the ravine floor, and the battle became hand-to-hand. Shiftan felt the surge of adrenaline as he cried out to his troops to fight. He raised his sword and cut into the closest enemy dwarf.

How long passed, he could not tell. How many dwarves fell to his sword, he did not count. Shiftan was a battled-hardened veteran, and his body and mind entered an automatic state of fluid consciousness.

Then, through the dust, he saw a taller warrior. The figure approached him. *My dear friend Tarlach, this one dies for you.* "Come meet your sentence, Shayth, you traitor," Shiftan yelled, though he doubted the boy heard over the melee.

Shayth reached him and swung his sword. The general deflected it with his shield and locked swords on the follow through. He gasped as the deep blackness of Shayth's eyes.

"You aren't Tarlach," Shayth growled. "Where's the worm?"

"You're not worthy of meeting him in combat," Shiftan spat back.

Shayth suddenly spun their blades and sent Shiftan off balance. With one swift movement, he kicked the general's knee and sent him to the ground. His blade immediately pressed against the older man's throat.

"I won't kill you, General whoever-you-are, but take a message to Tarlach. Tell him I'm waiting. Tell him this time, we finish it."

With that, he kicked hard into Shiftan's thigh, deadening his leg. Shiftan almost passed out from the pain. He was aware that his troops had surrounded him and that he was being lifted. He heard the voice of his second-in-command shouting orders.

"Get him out of here," the officer barked.

"No," Shiftan rasped. "Where is he?"

"The boy has fled, General Shiftan, sir," the man supporting him said. "They all have, the cowards."

Seanchai had not been involved in the first engagement with the Tarlach's army, but he led the second wave. Rus'ik Armsgarten had anticipated that the pictorians might get past the first ambush. He was right.

Shayth's company gradually retreated uphill into another tight gorge. As Shayth gave cover, fighting furiously with the two lead pictorians, his group fled through the narrow corridor. A whistle from above was the signal for Shayth to spring back. As he did, a huge boulder rolled down and crushed one pictorian.

The other pictorian, unharmed, hesitated when he realized that he was alone. His pause was fatal, as Shayth's big broadsword plunged though the side of his armor.

Shayth quickly followed the dwarves. The boulder would not hold back the pictorians for long. When they broke through, they rushed in single file through the tight corridor. A few more fell to boulders, but a dozen made it past.

A small complement of archers, led by Sellia, waited for them. Following her instructions, the archers aimed at the pictorians' exposed throats and sides. They held their bows until all twelve were assembled.

The pictorians stared at Seanchai, who stood alone about thirty yards from them, smiling broadly, with his arms folded across his chest. Slowly, he drew the Win Dao swords from their sheaths and even in the dull dawn light, they flashed their challenge. The Wycaan made a few practice arcs with his swords and the whoosh of the blades cut the air.

One pictorian yelled a response and began to run forward, swiftly followed by the others. The archers were ready instantaneously and released their arrows, felling ten pictorian soldiers before they could reach Seanchai. One of the two that made it through did so with three arrows protruding from his body.

Seanchai dodged him, pushing his own weight to speed the giant's momentum into a rock. The huge, horned creature toppled over, and Shayth removed his head with a double-handed blow of his broadsword.

The other pictorian was more measured in his approach and exchanged a few blows with Seanchai. Though large, at least seven feet in height and just as broad, he was agile but every move was matched by the elf. Seanchai could probably have finished him quickly, but knowing that many dwarves were watching, he wanted to show them that he could deliver. Finally a blur of sword blades descended on the retreating pictorian, and one connected with the great creature's throat.

The pictorian went down slowly onto its knees and stared at Seanchai, who whipped his swords in two quick circles before sheathing them.

"Well fought, pictorian. You meet your end with honor."

Seanchai didn't expect the pictorian to understand, but even so, the beast looked relieved and nodded as it toppled and gasped its last breath.

A cheer rose around the canyon.

"Come, my friends," Seanchai called. "We're just beginning."

# SIXTY THREE

T he Emperor's army continued to fight for a foothold in the mountain range throughout the next day. Dwarf resistance was met at every point, as heavy casualties rose for those trying to ascend into the pass.

But gradually, General Tarlach's superior numbers began to tell, and the his army made ground. As the sun descended, a horn blasted a signal, and Tarlach knew he had won this round. The fighting became sporadic and then ceased.

He ordered his troops to create a defensible net and set up temporary camp. Word went out for officers to report to a hastily established central command. Auxiliary supplies were brought up throughout the night. By the end of the next day, Tarlach planned to begin building his base camp in full view of Hothengold.

The reports from his officers offered little. This was the dwarves' terrain, and they were expected to mount an intelligent defense. But the sheer numbers of the Emperor's army could wear them down. This war was going to prove costly, but Tarlach was willing to pay the price.

General Shiftan limped in and sat heavily on a chair. "What happened to you?" Tarlach asked his old friend. "Did you get too close to a mule?"

"He was a stubborn ass, to be sure," Shiftan said and relayed the encounter with Shayth. "He's good, my friend. I saw him dispatch several of my troops, and when I reached him, he finished me off quickly."

"Perhaps you should listen to him and let me meet him," Tarlach said.

"No," Shiftan winced as he stretched his leg. "I underestimated him. And there's something else, something you should pay heed to. There is something about him that draws you into his rage, like a tornado sucking you in. I'm sure you can better him, Tarlach, but only if you stay detached, and that might not prove easy for you."

Rus'ik Armsgarten sent dwarf units to assail the Emperor's army throughout the night. Every hour or so, another intrusion of missiles, burning arrows, or dwarves with hand weapons would attack from one side or another.

The plan would not inflict serious damage on the huge army, but was meant more to deny them a good night's sleep. Recognizing this, General Tarlach withdrew a number of divisions to sleep in the center of the camp and stationed auxiliary forces to maintain a defensive perimeter. When dawn broke, the dwarves withdrew.

It was at least five hours into daylight before the empire's forces began to advance toward the capital once more. As the day progressed and the troops were met with no more than a few skirmishes, Tarlach began to wonder whether he would see the main force of the dwarf army emerge.

One of General Shiftan's riders galloped toward him, bringing his horse to an abrupt stop and jumping down. The man saluted badly, too excited for military etiquette. They were in a battle now. Tarlach would overlook such ineptitudes.

"General Tarlach, sir. I bring news from General Shiftan. His troops have intercepted a group of fleeing dwarves. They have them pinned down and will block additional exits within the hour."

General Shiftan had taken a large part of the army during the early part of the previous evening around the southern side of the mountain range to cut off the escape route of the fleeing dwarves. The plan was to attack from both sides. If dwarves were indeed fleeing, Tarlach didn't intend for more than a few to get through.

"Go refresh, man. We'll tend to your horse, and then you'll return to your battalion."

The man saluted and disappeared. Tarlach went to eat, satisfied that things were going as anticipated. But before he finished his meal, another messenger burst into the eating area. Tarlach's guards sprung up, but the high-pitched voice of the messenger carried.

"I have urgent news for General Tarlach. Let me pass."

Tarlach stood and walked over to the man. "What is it?"

"General Shiftan requires reinforcements. He instructs me to tell you that his forces have been attacked by two more groups of dwarves led by the elf and the traitor. His troops are pinned down. He requests the pictorians."

Tarlach turned to one of his officers. "Find First Boar Umnesilk. His units are in the advance. Tell him to prepare his troops to move out with haste, and for him to come here."

He turned back to the messenger. "Come, sit, and tell me more."

"We found about fifty of the buggers in the mountains," the soldier told him. "All ages – male and female. But when we surrounded them, they quickly closed in formation and produced weapons.

"Surrounding them laid our lines thin for an attack from behind, and they were waiting for us, hiding in small caves, I think. I saw the white-haired one with the two curved swords, my lord. He attacked from one side. Archers were waiting for us on the ridges above, and the traitor led an attack from the right.

"There were also the dwarves in the middle. There weren't many, but they were very disciplined, very competent."

Tarlach nodded. "Go find the other messenger and tell him to be ready to return with the pictorians. He should take another horse if he thinks it necessary. You take care of your horse and eat. Be ready to relay a message at any time."

The soldier stood up and saluted. He wheeled round to go and banged straight into the eight-foot mass of First Boar Umnesilk. The pictorian didn't flinch, but the man fell back onto the table. He jumped to his feet and drew a short sword, but froze when he saw whom he faced. Umnesilk hadn't moved.

"Steady man," Tarlach said. "We have enough fighting on our hands."

"My fault," growled Umnesilk, raising his massive hands to the side, palms facing the man.

Though he was signaling the universal sign of peace, the pictorian could just as nonchalantly have snapped the man in half, Tarlach thought.

The man nodded and scuttled away. Expressionless, Umnesilk turned to Tarlach. "You send, General?"

"How soon can your troops move out?"

"Now. We have weapons, need nothing more."

Tarlach smiled. "How quickly can you make it to the other side of the mountain? The paths are rocky and steep. It is about twelve miles. At a brisk walk, how long will it take you?"

Umnesilk frowned. "If urgent, why walk? Pictorians run. Sun move little in sky."

"I need your boars to arrive ready to fight. They can't rest when they get there."

"Rest? We see battle, we roar."

"A messenger of General Shiftan's unit will lead you there."

"He slow us," Umnesilk replied.

"He'll ride a horse," Tarlach smiled again. "The elf and the Emperor's nephew are there. If you can finish them off, do so, but make sure they're dead. I need to be sure."

"We rip off heads. Bring them. That good?"

"That works," the general replied.

# SIXTY FOUR

Seanchai took a brief respite and surveyed the battle. Tarlach had not sent as many troops to this side as he had hoped. Rus'ik Armsgarten had sent small groups to draw soldiers away from the main army that was descending on Hothengold, but it seemed that the general was focused on the capital. He grimaced; Shayth had been right.

Ballendir came up to him, breathing hard and covered in blood. Seanchai looked closely, trying to discern if any belonged to Ballendir.

"I'm fine, laddie. Having a great time. But look: I nicked mah axe on some idiot's helmet. No respect for a dwarf's weaponry."

Seanchai smiled. He was happy with how the battle had gone, but the way the dwarves reveled in the bloodshed was unsettling.

"What's wrong, son?" Ballendir asked, sensing Seanchai's unease.

"I'm worried that there aren't more troops here. It means there are more bearing down on Hothengold."

Ballendir surveyed the fighting. "You're right. But they'll hold until we get back. Don't worry. She's a tough lass, even if she isn't a dwarf."

Seanchai smiled. He was caught. Ballendir knew him well. They heard calls, and Shayth came running up with a breathless dwarf.

"Pictorians," Shayth said. "Tarlach has dispatched two regiments, at least. We need to move on."

"But we can finish this," Ballendir protested.

"They're fast," Seanchai said. "We won't get to the fog marshes before they catch up to us."

"Blow the horn," Ballendir said to a dwarf that kept close to him. "We head for the swamps."

The dwarf brought the horn to his mouth and sent out two short blasts, followed moments later by another two. Seanchai watched as the dwarves began to move off, and then turned to Shayth.

"Find Sellia and the archers. Take them up onto the ridges. They might need to slow the pictorians down."

Shayth nodded and moved off. Seanchai turned back to Ballendir.

"How far to the marshes of Oblinzt?"

"Four miles."

"Let's move," Seanchai said. "Tell the wounded to hide in the mountains and return to Hothengold when they can."

Seanchai put his ear to the ground to try and hear the pictorians' pounding feet, but with the battle still raging below him, it was not possible. He sighed and shook his head. He had been underground for so long, wanting only to come above ground and now he desperately wanted to get back underground to Hothengold. He wanted to get back to Ilana. It was that simple.

The army of General Tarlach did not attack Hothengold with waves of soldiers. Instead, the first detected intrusion was a dozen conscripted dwarves and scouts laying explosives.

Rus'ik Armsgarten was furious with himself. He had been bracing for a full frontal attack. His guards had not detected these incursions, and now he wondered how many explosive devices had been hidden already. He was in command. It was his responsibility to maintain a defense.

The older dwarves, the sick, and the young had been taken deep inside the mountain. There was a good chance that there would be no way out for them now that the Emperor's army was also on the south side.

He looked down at the city from his balcony in the barracks. It felt so empty, so foreboding. Here and there, a couple of dwarves walked, carrying arms or supplies, but this was a far cry from the bustling marketplace it had been.

He turned and saw Rothendir approaching with the two young elves. He had met the Wycaan's mate briefly, but not the other. He was well built and carried an array of swords and knives. Was he her bodyguard, the war chief wondered?

"Greetings, Rus'ik Armsgarten."

"Well met, Clan Leader Rothendir. How may I help you?"

"We've been discussing the enemy's explosives. Rhoddan has an idea."

The big elf stepped forward.

"Well met, Master Rhoddan," Armsgarten said and bowed.

"Likewise," Rhoddan replied with a nod.

"Alas, we've no time for pleasantries in these uncivilized times. What are your thoughts, elf warrior?"

"I was wondering whether Hothengold has defensive explosives planted as Rothendir's clan did at Mount Zu'Reising. I'm guessing you do. Why not detonate them now? Collapse the entrances and deny the Empire the chance to detonate theirs."

"It would deny us an option to leave," the old dwarf general said, but his tone suggested that he was considering it. "And it would deny Ballendir's troops the opportunity to come to our aid."

"But at the same time, it'll buy us more time to hold out until that aid comes – *if* it comes."

Everyone stared at him with varying degrees of coldness, but Rhoddan stood firm.

"We need to consider every option," he insisted.

Rus'ik Armsgarten tugged his massive beard. "I was hoping our explosives could take out many of the Emperor's troops. If we use them now to slow them down, they'll dig their way through, or lay siege. If Ballendir cannot get back, we're trapped and we're dead."

"We have to assume they'll succeed and get back to us," Rhoddan answered. "It would be better for them to engage Tarlach's army from the other side."

Armsgarten shook his head. "I don't like it." Then he turned to Rothendir. "But we should suggest it at the war counsel this evening."

Rothendir nodded. "Let Rhoddan join us and address the council with his thoughts."

Rus'ik didn't answer. His eyes moved to the roof of the cavern, where they could hear fighting above them. Then came the first explosion. It was a deep rumble that shook loose little more than a few shards of rock, but it resonated throughout the city.

Then they heard a slow, persistent beating.

"What is that?" Ilana asked, seeing fear in the dwarves' eyes.

"The Hiyenmut," muttered Rothendir. "Dwarves bang their axes on their shields before charging into battle."

"But it's coming from outside," Rhoddan said.

"That," Rothendir replied, "is why we're so shocked."

"The battle of Hothengold has begun," said Rus'ik, and he brought a huge golden horn to his lips.

# SIXTY FIVE

Seanchai stopped to sip from his flask. The bitter liquid was potent, and he felt his muscles reinvigorate. He looked behind him and with his sharp elf eyesight could make out the dust being kicked up by the pictorians.

There were two traps set for the army chasing them, in addition to the archers. None were going to be particularly effective, but Seanchai needed to buy them time to get the dwarves into the marshes.

He wondered about the Fog Marshes. It was unclear to him how they would fight once there. Was the place big enough? Was it foggy enough to conceal them? Would they scatter?

Shayth joined him. "You okay?"

"Yes," Seanchai said. "Listen. When we get to the swamps, stay close, okay."

"Sure." Shayth looked at him waiting for more.

"If it looks like we're winning and everything becomes scattered, I might make a run back to Hothengold."

"I'll be with you," Shayth said, patting his arm. "But make sure that Ballendir knows. Come with me now. They are hoping to trap a few pictorians in that crevice. The dwarves call it The Three Crags."

"You know where to go?" Seanchai asked.

"No," Shayth replied. "But that's never stopped me yet. Come on."

They ran together for another half hour and found a dwarf to take them to the place. They hid away from the path and rested. Two more dwarves joined them, one of them Seanchai recognized as Thorminsk, the young craftsman.

"How're you doing?" Seanchai asked.

"I'm good," Thorminsk answered after he had caught his breath. "I've had a few close calls, but it seems there's always someone around to save my skin. Still, what's important is that *you* survive long enough for me to fix that King's Mail. You can't have two separate metals in it. It's just not done. I'm so embarrassed."

Seanchai laughed. "I like it. Not done? It's one of a kind, like me. But if that's what'll keep you going, so be it."

"Shh," Shayth hissed from ten yards away.

They heard the heavy pounding of pictorians meet the cries of attacking dwarves. Seanchai and the others crept up to join Shayth.

One giant pictorian led the group. He wore a gold leaf and swiftly dispatched three dwarves.

"That's probably their leader, their First Boar," Shayth whispered. "See the gold leaf? It would be great if we could take him down."

At least three sixers of pictorians followed the dwarves up the path of the Three Crags, roaring with rage. An explosion rocked them and was met with more roars and the battle cries of dwarves.

"Come on," Shayth said and jumped down to the path.

They hid behind rocks and pillars of stone as the pictorians approached beneath them, snarling to each other. Six had survived, and, as they passed, Shayth and Seanchai jumped down and tackled the two bringing up the rear. Seanchai then felled the two closest to him with his swords, instinctively seeking their necks or their sides, both vulnerable despite their thick armor.

Feeling a growing sense of urgency, he reached for his blue stone as two more pictorians decapitated a dwarf each and turned to him. Seanchai saw behind them that Thorminsk was suddenly alone and facing the massive pictorian officer. He had to help his friend.

Holding the blue stone, he cried out *"Mereksur."* Blinding blue light smashed into one of the pictorians, and, as the other watched in amazement, Seanchai leapt with deadly speed and with one blow sent his head rolling. The body remained standing, while its thick, purple blood spurted up like a fountain.

The First Boar also stared as Seanchai confronted him. Thorminsk was lying on a rock within striking distance of the giant boar.

"Leave him," Seanchai roared.

The pictorian smiled. "You Special One? Must take head to general. Show you dead."

"Who are you?" Seanchai snarled, "So I can say your name as I kill you."

"First Boar Umnesilk. Am ready to die, always ready."

"You know," Seanchai said as he drew his second Win Dao sword, "that pictorians once fought for their own freedom. Do you know who came to their aid? It was the Wycaans, the special ones. Look into your legends, First Boar. You were once a proud and free people."

"Still proud," Umnesilk replied.

"No, you're not. You're the hunting dogs of the Empire, sent far from your tribes to do the bidding of an evil leader. You kill those who crave the freedom that you, too, have lost."

Seanchai thought he saw a flash of doubt crossed the First Boar's face, but then the giant roared and leapt at Seanchai with amazing speed. A lesser elf would have been crushed, but when Umnesilk landed and swung his huge axe, Seanchai was gone. Umnesilk reeled round in surprise and saw that Seanchai had sheathed his swords.

"Why?" Umnesilk taunted.

"Because I want you to live. I saw on your face that you know my words are true. Go back to your tribes, reconnect to the proud race you were, and join the Alliance as we fight for everyone's freedom, including yours."

"You rebels hate pictorians."

"Of course we do. You kill and maim many freedom fighters: human, elf, and dwarf. But you can change that. You're First Boar."

The pictorian stared at him and then charged again. Seanchai moved out of his way and held out a palm, sending the huge boar flying into the rock face. Shayth noched an arrow and pulled his bowstring taut.

"No, Shayth." Seanchai approached the pictorian, who was struggling to stand. "Remember my words, First Boar. I won't kill you because you know I'm right. Think upon my words. Be the one to free your own people."

Seanchai leapt into the air and smashed a boot into the back of the pictorian's head. The great boar collapsed to the ground.

"We should kill him," Shayth yelled, hate spewing out with each word. "He's First Boar."

"No," Seanchai swung round. "There's a Second Boar, and a third, and a fourth. This one's intelligent. I saw on his face that he was listening. I saw that he knew his people's legends."

Seanchai turned as he heard a groan and ran to Thorminsk, whose breath was now a wheeze.

"Easy there, my friend," Seanchai said, cradling the young dwarf's head in his arm.

"Might not . . . get to . . . fix your . . ."

"You will," Seanchai said, trying not to show his concern. "You're going to be okay. We . . . we'll come back for you."

Thorminsk shook his head. "Back snapped . . . heard it. Fight on, Wycaan. Show them . . . my greatest work . . . Please. My tools go to Orenminsk."

"Who's that?" Seanchai asked, confused.

"My son . . . will be . . . great . . . crafts . . ." the dwarf broke off, wheezing. He struggled to continue. "He's three. Give him . . . my tools. Tell him . . . I died well."

Thorminsk took a long rasping breath and then went still.

"No!" Seanchai cried out and hugged the limp body. He rose, shaking his head, and drew one of his swords. "You didn't need to kill him," he yelled at the First Boar, who was awake and watching with a glazed expression on his face. Seanchai advanced on him. "He wasn't even a warrior. He was a craftsman. Where is your honor in killing him? He wasn't even a warrior."

Seanchai swung the sword down to split the pictorian's head. But Shayth's sword blocked him only inches from the horn of the First Boar. Seanchai staggered back, and Shayth moved in front of the helpless giant.

"Let me kill him," Seanchai screamed.

Shayth raised his sword, and when he spoke, his voice was quiet. "I'll kill him for you – sever his head if you wish. But remember what you offered him when you spoke as a Wycaan. He's First Boar. This could help the Alliance. It's more important than your personal need for revenge. It won't bring Thorminsk back."

Seanchai glared at Shayth, struggling for a moment to control himself. "That's coming from you?" But he turned his back on the pictorian and heard Shayth speak to Umnesilk in a clear, emotionless tone.

"Remember this moment, First Boar. Witness the difference between the Emperor and the Wycaan." Seanchai turned to watch as

Shayth pointed his thick broadsword at the elf. "He'll put the freedom of Odessiya before his personal desires or his personal grief. You killed his friend, but he's sparing you because he serves a higher purpose. Remember this for as long as you live."

There was no fear on the face of First Boar Umnesilk. The pictorian looked from Shayth to Seanchai and nodded.

# SIXTY SIX

The battle for the outer entrances of Hothengold had been intense. Having to face other dwarves in battle was a first for all but Rothendir's clan and it infuriated them. It was not just about defending the capital, and the King. They took the assault by conscripted dwarves as a personal affront, and the sparks flew from axe blades.

When the fight was between dwarves in the narrow corridors, then the conscripts seemed less committed, and many fell as a consequence. However, when the battle took place in exposed passages, it was hard for the defenders as they faced more humans.

Ilana and Rhoddan were critical at these moments and constantly in the thick of the fray fighting the human soldiers. Rus'ik Armsgarten soon realized the value of sending them to where the fighting was most desperate, and soon both elves were exhausted and carrying multiple wounds.

A horn blow was followed by a huge explosion that rocked the great cavern. Rothendir walked past and stopped when she saw Ilana.

"We have collapsed the outer entrances," Rothendir said, wiping away a tear. "It is Mount Zu'Reising all over again."

"But this time we have a solid plan and the numbers to defend the city," Ilana replied.

Rothendir stared at her and noticed her bandage. "Are you okay, Ilana?"

"Just a scratch."

"I'm told the priestess said you were special. We all see your strength and courage. You're a worthy mate of the Wycaan."

Ilana smiled, and watched Rothendir leave. When she pulled her eyes away from the Clan Leader, she saw that Rhoddan was staring at her.

"What is it?" he asked. "You look so down."

"I don't like war," she snapped.

"But you've been fighting all of your life. What makes it different?" Rhoddan countered.

Ilana shrugged, holding back the growing certainty she felt that she would never see Seanchai again.

She didn't have a chance to respond as another enormous explosion had all the dwarves staring up. Its lack of preceding horn indicated it was the enemy's work. It was followed by several more. The blasts seemed concentrated on the far end of the cavern, where Ballendir had led them in.

A strained silence followed and then they heard a sickening, drawn out crunch, and the far wall began to buckle. The dwarves screamed and gasped. They were attuned to the rock's voice. Now they heard its pain, and it was a terrifying sound.

Huge slabs fell onto the wide floor of the cavern where most of the dwarves lived. The side of the mountain had been breached. Hothengold was exposed as sunlight poured in. They heard the cheers coming from the far side and watched in stunned silence, as troops made their way in over the rubble.

Then Rhoddan jumped up and turned to a dwarf with a horn.

"Blow your horn. Sound the alarm." He drew his sword. "To me," he cried and, sword held aloft, he stoically walked out of the castle to meet the enemy.

The horrifying cries were amplified by the clash of thousands of dwarves and humans. Rus'ik Armsgarten led his troops into wave after wave of enemy soldiers where, at first, they held their own. But, as the tunnels were widened for the cave trolls and more seasoned human soldiers, the dwarves of Hothengold began to retreat.

A long horn blast signaled for the dwarves to retreat inside the walls of the palace. The King, himself, led out a chosen regiment that momentarily pushed the Tarlach's forces back, allowing most of his dwarves to enter inside the palace before its iron gates clapped shut. The echo of the iron smashing onto the rock grounds reverberated off the rock walls and sent shivers of finality down the dwarves' spines.

"What now?" Rhoddan asked as a healer from Clan Zu'Reising dressed his wounds.

"We try and hold on for as long as we can," Rothendir replied. She sat next to him with a nasty gash across her forehead and down her cheek. "We hope that Ballendir beats the army out there and returns in time."

"Do you think it's possible?"

The elderly dwarf leader looked at him and, for a moment, her expression told the truth. But she rallied. "There is always hope, young elf. And as long as there is hope, we are not beaten."

There was a lull in the fighting with the gates now closed. Rhoddan stood and went to the walls. A massive army was assembling in front of them, and trolls were busy leveling the houses to allow room for siege engines.

"High King of the Dwarves," a voice boomed suddenly. "You have six hours to bury your dead for they fought valiantly as have all your people. There's no shame in your actions. But take that time to consider surrendering Hothengold to the Empire. The Emperor is generous and compassionate. He will give mercy to those who deserve it."

No response was given.

Rus'ik Armsgarten called for the war council to meet, and the Great Hall filled with dwarves. Rhoddan had not specifically been invited, but he entered alongside Rothendir without anyone questioning his presence. In fact, many dwarves packed the great hall, though they left a respectful distance around the large stone table for the delegates. When all members of the war council were in attendance, Armsgarten stood up to address them. Though he was clearly wounded and exhausted, he held himself erect and his deep voice carried for all to hear.

"My friends. I'll not try to suggest that the situation is good. But this keep and the surrounding walls were built for just such a situation. We have water and food supplies. Many fine warriors stand among us determined to defend our walls.

"Our objective remains: to hold out for as long as there is a dwarf who can still raise his axe. I'm confident that Ballendir's soldiers will succeed, but I don't know if there will be enough time for them to regroup and return here in time.

"In the meantime, it falls to us to kill as many of the enemy as possible, so that when Ballendir's forces engage them, their chances will be better served by our sacrifices."

Rhoddan looked around the room. The dwarves who sat here were bruised, bloodied, and battered. Yet fire still burned in their eyes. They accepted their destiny with dignity, and Rhoddan felt a surge of emotion.

Without planning, he stood and looked at Rus'ik Armsgarten.

"What is it, Rhoddan, elf-friend of the Wycaan? You have fought valiantly and inspired our troops with your own courage. Your reaction when Tarlach's army came through the hole was critical. You have earned the right to speak."

Rhoddan swallowed hard, not sure what he wanted to say. "I'm much younger than any of you and not as skilled at underground combat. In my short life, I have faced too many battles, and fought alongside the finest elves and humans of the freedom fighters in Odessiya."

He paused and sighed. "I . . . I just wanted you to know . . . that I'm proud to fight alongside such courageous dwarves. If we are to die here, well . . . I die in the company of great warriors. It's what I always wanted."

He sat down. Ruffminsk, the big, red-bearded dwarf from Clan Dan Zu'Ulster, raised his bloodstained, battle-scarred axe. His presence around the table meant that Dugenminsk, their clan leader, was either wounded or dead.

"Well said, young elf. If I die, my only regret will be that I never got to fight alongside other noble elves such as the Wycaan, Ilana, and yourself, and that I never lived to see the reformation of the Alliance."

Other dwarves nodded in agreement and then fell into silence. Ilana rose to her feet.

"You are wrong, Ruffminsk. This battle has been fought with dwarves, elves, and humans side-by-side. You rue never seeing the formation of the Alliance, but it's you, Ruffminsk and all of you," she swept her arm around the hall, "who created the very Alliance itself. It's here; we are the Alliance. You did not bear witness to history. You all have *made* history."

Rus'ik Armsgarten slammed the base of his axe handle on the stone table and roared. "Then let us give history itself a mighty tale that will pass on from generation to generation and be told for ten thousand years!"

A mighty cheer went up that echoed through the great cavern. It reached the ears of the human, dwarf and pictorian regiments. It reached the ears of General Tarlach.

*Alliance! Alliance! Alliance!*

# SIXTY SEVEN

Seanchai and Shayth loped silently together toward the Fog Marshes of Oblinzt. The original plan was for Seanchai and Shayth to be at the head of the fleeing resistance, and now the detour with the pictorians had diverted them from the chase. Enemy troops could be in front and behind them.

They moved with caution through a narrow area, and Seanchai's acute hearing picked up some scuffling around a blind bend. He signaled to Shayth, and they both slid to the closest wall, silently drawing their weapons. Seanchai went first, crouching as he edged around the corner.

He stopped and stood up. "It's okay, Shayth. We have no chance against such noble warriors."

Ballendir was sitting cross-legged on a flat rock, nonchalantly picking some dirt from under a fingernail with his knife. Sellia stood a few yards above him, her bow ready, but not taut.

"Nice to see a couple of cute guys out for a stroll," she said, and Seanchai couldn't help but feel a thrill at her words.

"Nice of them to turn up, yeh mean," Ballendir added. "I think they just got winded, Sellia. Now are yeh boys ready to start fighting?"

Seanchai couldn't help himself, and he gave the dwarf a strong hug. When he looked up at Sellia, she poked the tip of her bow into

his chest. "This is strictly business, you big chump. I've only waited for you this long because he's the boss." She nodded at Ballendir.

Come on," said Ballendir. "I don't want to be late for the party."

Several dwarves materialized out of the shadows, and the group began a gradual downhill jog. Sellia trotted alongside Seanchai. "You okay?" she asked quietly. Seanchai nodded and Sellia squeezed his shoulder. "She's tough, Seanchai. She's a survivor."

A half hour later, there was a sudden drop in temperature. Seanchai looked over at Ballendir.

"We're close," the dwarf said. "Everyone spread out. Be prepared."

Even as the words came out of Ballendir's mouth, Seanchai wheeled round. "Horses," he hissed, and the company faded into the shadows. But Seanchai knelt to the ground and then stared at Sellia to get her input. "It's just one horse," he said, confused.

Sellia bent down and listened for a few moments. "One horse, but there are others on foot."

Seanchai and Sellia dissolved into the shadows with the others. Minutes later, a horse galloped up. Sellia had an arrow ready, but Seanchai stopped her.

"A dwarf," he whispered to Ballendir.

"Being chased by humans and pictorians on foot," Sellia said, and shot an arrow.

It sailed by the dwarf and wounded a pictorian who grunted, yanked the arrow out and threw it to the ground, before continuing.

"Shoot the humans!" Seanchai cried, and Shayth and Sellia began taking them down in rapid succession. Seanchai ran out past the horse. Two pictorians fell swiftly to his Win Dao swords.

Another heaved up a heavy javelin and, as he launched it, Seanchai raised his palm. The spear left the pictorian's hand and dropped to the ground, where he stared at it in disbelief. It was the last sight he ever saw as a second blast of Seanchai's energy sent him careening into his friend behind him. Both fell and were swiftly dispatched by Seanchai's double blades.

Two humans had turned and ran away. Seanchai thought to chase them, but let them go, hoping they would bring Tarlach's army with them and away from Hothengold.

He turned to the others, who were all around the dwarf they had just rescued. Ballendir turned to Seanchai.

"Nicely done," he said, though Seanchai heard concern in his voice.

"What is it?" Seanchai asked.

"Shayth was right. General Tarlach is attacking Hothengold. He has a huge army there: all the dwarves, the cave trolls, and more humans."

The messenger wiped his beard on his sleeve. "They blew out the entrances. They have been infiltrating and laying explosives for days. When we collapsed the north side, they came in from the south.

The company began to talk among themselves, but the messenger interrupted. "There's more," he said. "Tarlach has sent troops after you – maybe a hundred humans. He's hoping they'll keep you busy while he focuses on the assault of Hothengold."

"Why?" Seanchai kicked a stone in frustration. "Why won't he come after me and Shayth? He must know we're here."

There was a moment's silence. Then Shayth replied. "He doesn't need to. He knows you'll come back to the capital."

"How does he know that we'll . . ." Seanchai trailed off into thought. "Ilana," he gasped.

Shayth agreed. "As long as Ilana is holed up there, he knows you'll come to him."

"How does he know . . ."

"There's no time for that now," Ballendir snapped and turned to two of his dwarves. "Go into the marshes and find out how many dwarves we have here. We meet at the first staging." He glared at Seanchai. "All of us."

"Ballendir," Seanchai pleaded.

"Once I know how many dwarves I have here, I'll decide who returns and when."

"But Hothengold could fall," Seanchai objected.

"We'll fight at the first staging, Seanchai. With you and Shayth, we can kill most of the humans. Then we'll leave a token force, dwarves who know the marshes. They'll lead the humans around and pick them off. The rest of us will head back with yeh."

Seanchai shook his head. "I think—"

"Yeh swore to fight under mah command," Ballendir boomed. "I don't need yeh to think right now."

"But Ilana is—"

"So are a few thousand of mah people. So are mah clan and my King. Do yeh think I don't want to run back? But I'll not expose our troops to fight above ground like that. We'll be of no use to Hothengold if we're dead."

Seanchai glared at Ballendir, his chest heaving, but Sellia firmly took his arm. "Come on," she said. "Let's do this quickly," and she led Seanchai into the Fog Marshes of Oblinzt.

# SIXTY EIGHT

General Tarlach paced along the platform erected against the main south wall of the giant cavern, watching the city of Hothengold being systematically cleared through the middle. Everything was being demolished to create a straight, wide path to the walls of the palace keep.

The army's siege machines were being assembled inside the mountain – Tarlach's experts had warned not to risk enlarging the hole they had made. He didn't want to collapse the mountain altogether – not yet. He would raze Hothengold to the ground from inside, but he needed Shayth and the elf, dead or alive. He was now convinced his family's lives depended on it.

The general watched as more troops were called in to help assemble the siege engines and clear the roads. They had been working non-stop now for two days and he was anxious to begin the attack. His soldiers growing fatigue could prove costly, but he had enough troops to ensure victory.

He knew that Shayth and the elf were not here. He had pulled back troops from General Shiftan's chase when he had realized this. He wanted them to return to Hothengold. He wanted to time it so that victory was at hand, but not complete. If he already held Hothengold, they might not come with such a small force. He had to allow them to think they could make a difference.

This morning he had received news that dwarf troops were at a basin of marshes and that the battle there would be slow due to a thick fog in the area. He had withdrawn his pictorians so they could lead the charge against Hothengold together with the cave trolls to give his soldiers a short respite before they joined the fray.

He wanted to capture the King. It would be as important a signal as destroying the capital to both the dwarves and the Emperor. He would break the King quickly, he was sure of that.

"General Tarlach, sir. The officers are assembled," a soldier said, snapping to attention and saluting.

"Thank you," Tarlach said. He took one last look at the siege engines and then turned around.

The command tent was situated just outside the mountainside. A hasty model of the city had been assembled as they continued to receive better intelligence. General Shiftan, though still limping, was ready to brief on the attack. It would begin at dawn and, by darkness, the city would fall.

Tarlach watched his friend give orders to their officers. There were three pictorian officers, including the replacement for Umnesilk, who had not been seen since he had engaged the enemy on the way to the marshes. If he had encountered the elf, the first boar might have bested him. But a strong instinct told Tarlach that the Wycaan still lived.

"General Tarlach," General Shiftan said. "Would you like to add anything?"

Tarlach walked slowly to the model. He turned and faced his officers. One of them had his shield strapped across his back. Tarlach gestured to it. "May I?"

He took the man's shield and examined the strong, thick metal. Then he swung round and obliterated the model of Hothengold.

There was a muted gasp from around the room as they all stared at the flattened model.

Tarlach returned the shield to the stunned soldier and then faced his officers calmly. "Have I made myself clear?" he asked.

The officers, released from their spell, let out a cheer that carried through the camp.

When all had quieted down, General Tarlach cried out, "Then let the battle of Hothengold begin!"

General Tarlach watched the siege engines hurl rocks, and then firebombs, at the fortress walls, though the lack of wood in the dwarf city made flames less effective.

The dwarves also had catapults and burned four siege engines in quick succession.

"Impressive," General Shiftan said from alongside him. "They're proving tough little fighters."

"Have you fought any of them hand-to-hand?" Tarlach asked, not looking round.

"I have. They match our human soldiers' skill with their perseverance, but they're no match for the pictorians."

"You didn't mention how they fare against the dwarves under our command."

Shiftan smiled. "I think they do particularly well because they hate them so. The idea that dwarf would raise axe against another dwarf like this has them frothing."

"Are you worried at all?" Tarlach asked, after glancing round to see that no one else was within earshot.

"No," his friend replied. "But it'll be tough hand-to-hand. They're worthy opponents. And . . ." his voice trailed off.

"And what?" Tarlach turned to look at him.

"Well, it would be better if we had the upper hand before the Wycaan and Shayth return."

"You don't approve of my refusal to send reinforcements to those marshes?"

"I don't." Shiftan was one of only a few who would dare to question Tarlach's decisions, but he had earned that right. "They could succeed and return here too quickly."

"And we'll have conquered the city," Tarlach replied. "I need to be the one to face the Wycaan, and have my best troops and pictorians to take care of Shayth if I can't. We need to trap them where they cannot escape and take them down."

"Did the Emperor not express his desire to take them alive?"

"Only if possible, but either way, he wants it to end here. I'm beginning to doubt they can be taken alive, but I'll try if the opportunity arises."

He got up and took a deep breath. "I'm going to take the pictorians and cave trolls in at the head. When I'm gone, send in our troops. Once the walls are breached, the dwarf regiments are to spearhead the attack."

With that, General Tarlach strode away, calling to the cave trolls, who pounded forward in front of him. He resisted the urge to look behind him. He could hear the three units of pictorians marching behind. As they came within arrow range of a wide area of smashed palace walls, he drew his huge broadsword, raised it high, and cried: "Charge!"

# SIXTY NINE

Seanchai peered through the ground-hugging fog. This was an amazing setting. As far as he could see, there was a crisscross of hidden paths bordered by deep muddy pools. He wondered how big the area was.

The fog was constantly changing. One moment it was wispy and thin, and the next, thick and soupy. He was glad for his sharp elf hearing here, discovering approaching soldiers and discerning how many they were, long before the soldiers were aware of their presence. He was grouped with Shayth, Ballendir, and an old dwarf who clearly knew the marsh very well.

There were several such groups, each led by an older guide. Ballendir had promised they would lead the Emperor's army into the marshes, lose them, then double back and head for Hothengold, leaving their marsh guides to "clean up" as Ballendir put it.

Seanchai crouched at the sound of several soldiers' voices. He signaled this to the old dwarf who drew a map in the sand, showing Seanchai where the path went. The map probably covered about thirty feet in front of them, but it was enough.

They all braced themselves as the soldiers neared.

"This is crazy," one soldier moaned. "We don't know where we're going, who we're fighting, nothing."

"Quiet," said another from behind him. "They say the White Demon has magical hearing. He could be right in front of you, and you wouldn't know it."

Seanchai rose out of the fog, his two swords flashing, and proved the soldier right. When he finished "cleaning up," he rejoined the others and the old dwarf turned to Seanchai.

"Is it true?" he asked, with a look of wonder on his face.

"Is what true?"

"Do you have magical hearing?"

"No," Seanchai replied. "Elves have good hearing—and we always keep our ears clean."

Their laughter echoed in the fog.

"White Demon?" Ballendir said from behind him. "I like it. Maybe I can be the Bearded Demon."

They continued for a short while and reached a round area of ground where other dwarf companies had collected. All reported encounters with soldiers, and Seanchai stared eagerly at Ballendir as the dwarf assessed how many soldiers had been killed. He estimated that at least a hundred had entered the swamp, and half were dead.

"Please, Ballendir," Seanchai pleaded quietly. "Let me return to Hothengold."

Ballendir stared at him for a moment, considering, and then turned to the older dwarf. "I have two more of mah groups out here. Can one of yeh people find and guide them out?"

"Yes," the dwarf answered. "No need to wait for them. We'll send them along and make sure there are no soldiers left." The guide squeezed Seanchai's arm. "Come, White Demon. Let me lead you out of the marshes."

Seanchai was itching to keep the group moving once they reached the edge of the marshes and continued on without a sound or a wave to his dwarf companion. Ballendir called to him, obviously annoyed, and glanced at their guide.

"Thank you for your help," Seanchai said, chagrined, bowing to the old dwarf.

The dwarf grinned. "The honor was mine, White Demon. Go, now, and save my city."

Ballendir nudged Seanchai forward. "So, what're we waiting for? To Hothengold."

The group set off at a steady jog, Ballendir constantly calling Seanchai to pace himself with the others. "We must be fresh when we arrive," he repeated again and again.

A few minutes later, Seanchai stopped and crouched, looking toward the mountain to his left. The rest of the company followed suit until they saw movement and recognized a dwarf.

Ballendir rose to meet him.

"I have six wounded, and thirty healthy," the dwarf said. "After we drew the pictorians and humans into the gorge, we waited as you instructed to stop reinforcements reaching the marshes."

"Why did you not tell them to come help us?" Seanchai asked.

"I didn't want us confused who was behind us," Ballendir answered. Then he smiled. "And I wanted some fresh troops for the battle ahead."

He turned back to the dwarf. "Leave an older dwarf with the wounded. The rest will come with us."

Seanchai estimated they were now had nearly seventy dwarves, and this number increased as they continued. A few hours later, they reached the gorge where Shayth and Seanchai had fought the pictorians. He called over to Ballendir.

"I'll catch you up."

Ballendir rolled his eyes, but signaled to Shayth to follow the Wycaan.

In the gorge, they found numerous corpses of dwarves and pictorians. Most had already been picked over by scavengers. Seanchai found Thorminsk, wrapped his body in a cloak that he took from another dwarf, and covered the body with stones.

When he finished, Shayth touched his shoulder. "Let's go. We'll honor his death at the right time. He would want you to go and save his people."

Seanchai nodded and turned to leave. "He was a good dwarf," he said. "And he left a son behind, one who won't even remember him when he grows up."

"We must go," Shayth insisted. "Many have fallen who shouldn't have."

"And some still live who should be dead," Seanchai replied, his voice bitter.

Shayth grinned. "You're beginning to sound like me."

As they began to leave, Shayth stopped.

"What is it?" Seanchai asked.

"The First Boar," Shayth pointed to a rock, "He was lying there. He lives still."

"We should have finished him when we had the chance," Seanchai muttered.

"Come on," Shayth said, resting a hand on the elf's shoulder. "You really are beginning to sound like me, and it's getting weird."

They set off at a brisk pace, and when they caught up again with the main party, Seanchai gasped. There must have been more than six hundred dwarves.

"This isn't a company," Seanchai exclaimed. "It's an army."

"Then let's make a difference," Ballendir cried. "With me"

They set off at a brisker pace but as they neared the Hoth Mountain, Ballendir stopped. "We rest," he said.

"What?" Seanchai said. "But we're so close."

"And we aren't going to walk into a trap," Ballendir snapped. He called two dwarves and sent them into a concealed entrance that Seanchai hadn't seen.

When the scouts returned, Ballendir called his troops around him and spoke quickly. "Our forces have retreated into the palace. There's an army of men attacking the keep as we speak. There are also reinforcements resting where we will enter the cavern. We're outnumbered about two-to-one, so let's surprise them and take them out fast. We'll regroup and continue together. Remember, the main force is at the walls, so no one runs ahead. Is that clear? *No one* runs ahead." He glared pointedly at Seanchai, who nodded.

They walked quietly through the tunnel and descended on the resting battalion with a vengeance. Seanchai was possessed. Legends would later tell how half that battalion fell to his Win Dao swords. But the Wycaan wasn't counting; his mind had become numb, focused on one goal. He only wanted to reach the keep, defend the King, face off with Tarlach, and most of all, find Ilana.

They advanced smoothly, but as they approached the outer wall, they faced at least a hundred pictorians.

Ballendir swore and turned to organize his troops, but Seanchai stepped past, sheathed his swords and marched toward the biggest boar, who met him halfway.

"Umnesilk, First Boar of the Pictorians," Seanchai cried, and his voice carried to all who were gathered. "Now is the time. Now is the moment. This is when the once noble pictorian race decides its destiny."

"We decided, Wycaan," the First Boar's voice was deep and traveled well. "We not fight you, but not fight Emperor. Not now; not this way. Give safe passage and we leave battlefield. We return to homeland in north."

Seanchai bowed. "I applaud and respect you, Umnesilk, First Boar. When we meet again, let us meet as friends." He turned and called out. "Ballendir, let them pass."

The dwarves moved aside, and the massive pictorians lumbered out of the keep.

"Now," called Seanchai, drawing his swords and holding them high. "To the King. To the King."

# SEVENTY

It had taken three hours for General Tarlach's troops to secure the outer walls, and the dwarves had retreated to the first of two inner walls. He surveyed the ground between them. It was a hundred yards, and there was nothing to protect or shield his men.

He sent the dwarf regiments to attack first. He wasn't about to waste the pictorians – they were big targets, anyway – or his elite forces, soldiers trained for close quarter fighting. They would be critical in the next stage. He also had once thought that Hothengold dwarves having to kill fellow dwarves might be debilitating to their morale, but he wasn't so sure anymore, given the ferocity he had seen from the rebels.

Three waves of conscripted dwarves attacked and were repelled by arrows before they could so much as plant a ladder into place. He pulled them back and signaled to General Shiftan to bring in troops, who formed a shield cover and moved in. Under the shields were dwarves armed with explosives.

As they neared the first of the two inner walls, rocks rained down on them, followed by burning oil. The echo of screams inside the cavern made even the seasoned General Tarlach cringe.

Two groups reached the walls and stood firm, despite losing many to the burning liquids. Their hasty retreat was met with cheers from the dwarves on the walls, but massive explosions drowned them out. The first inner wall was breached.

Tarlach sent the dwarf battalions in to take control of the ramparts. The fighting was intense, and when Tarlach saw that the free dwarves were holding their ground, he sent in the pictorians. The line broke and Tarlach, flanked by his elite guard, walked through the wall.

The final stretch up to the keep was only fifty feet away and surrounded by a second wall about the same size as the one they had just leveled. They made it through at a heavy cost. The dwarves on the walls, having seen what happened previously, threw everything they had to prevent the human shield reaching the wall. When Tarlach stepped forward, he had to negotiate piles of bodies. He had lost many soldiers, but he had two regiments of special forces itching to be unleashed. And he still had the pictorians.

Inside was a grassy knoll and path that led into the gateway of the keep itself. Organized regiments of dwarves met them on the grass fighting desperately and bravely. Tarlach was in the thick of the action and he wielded his broadsword with great speed and skill. More than once his warrior energy surged through his body and he let out an unbridled roar. The soldiers around him raised their heads and yelled in response.

Gradually the dwarf defenses were pushed back and General Tarlach's forces finally infiltrated the keep. The fighting scattered into the narrow streets and alleyways. Many dwarves and men fell as each building was furiously defended. Tarlach kept his guard close by and moved toward the palace and the Great Hall.

Here they met their strongest opposition, and Tarlach caught glimpses of the King fighting alongside his fellow dwarves. He was about to head toward the King when he spied two elves.

He paused. Though he had seen them only fleetingly, he was sure these were the two elves he had captured in Galbrieth. The male was a very competent swordsman and the female . . . was she the mate of the Wycaan? Tarlach felt a thrill rush through him. He called his honor guard around him and charged toward the two elves.

The fighting was intense and erratic. The elves retreated through alleys and corridors, entering into one side of a building and exiting a doorway on the other side.

Seeing an opening, Tarlach circled the fighting and climbed nimbly up a wall. He jumped over a crowd and landed facing the elfe. She didn't hesitate, attacking with her long and short knife with some skill. Tarlach was impressed, but comfortable. He could wear her down.

But he didn't get the chance. The male elf hit him from the side and sent him spinning into a wall. He recovered quickly and engaged the male with blows fast and evenly matched. Sparks rang from the clashing of the two heavy broadswords and, for a moment, Tarlach was pinned back.

They sparred from one building to another, separating from the main battle. Tarlach was vaguely aware that it was just the two of them as he jumped onto a low wall, and the elf followed. He was surprised to find a steep drop on the wall's other side.

If this fazed the elf, he didn't show it, but steadily advanced. Suddenly a great horn, deeper than that of the dwarves, was blown. The elf froze, and Tarlach took the opening. He feigned to the right but hit from the left. His blade slashed into the elf's shoulder, sending his sword over the edge.

"You were a worthy opponent, elf," Tarlach said. "I will spare your life this day and let the Emperor do with you what he will."

The elf was holding his shoulder, but he never flinched. "I would rather die a proud warrior than submit to the indignity of captivity."

"Very well," Tarlach replied, feeling a begrudging measure of respect for the elf. "Let me at least know your name."

"I am Rhoddan," he replied evenly, "close friend of Seanchai the Wycaan, he who has reforged the Alliance to set Odessiya free from your oppression."

"A fine warrior, but a misguided fool nonetheless. Die well, Rhoddan, Elf Warrior." Tarlach raised his sword, but Rhoddan just smiled.

"I will die by my own hands," he said, and jumped from the wall.

Tarlach was momentarily stunned as he stared down into the darkness. He heard a thump, but no cry from the elf. He quickly regained his composure and ran back to where the battle had centered. He looked around and saw the elfe and a few dwarves retreat into a small hall.

When he entered, he saw a dozen of his troops in a stand off with three dwarves and the elfe. He strode up between them, his boots clicking on the stone floor.

"Lay down your weapons. It's over. I have you . . ." he stared at Ilana, ". . . again."

Ilana jumped forward to stab him and with amazing speed, he sidestepped and smashed his fist into her face. She flew across the floor and lay there crumpled.

"Kill the dwarves but I want her kept alive. Bind her and keep her here in this hall." The soldiers nodded and Tarlach turned to one of his guards. "Bring my healer here and tell him to bring the black demendina poison – he is to force enough inside her to keep her alive for another day, but no more. He is also to bring a vial of antidote and hand it to me personally."

It suddenly dawned on Tarlach that the fighting outside the hall had stopped. "Where are the pictorians?" he asked as an officer burst into the hall.

"That horn we just heard, my lord," the officer was panting, his eyes bulging. "The pictorians have gone."

# SEVENTY ONE

S eanchai's arms ached as he wound his way through the narrow streets. His Win Dao swords were in constant motion, plowing into wherever the enemy congregated. He paused for a moment and rubbed his arms.

Shayth, always close by, checked for enemy troops and then spoke to Seanchai.

"You're getting tired, aren't you?"

"Of course not," Seanchai replied. "I could continue for another week." His smile was more of a wince.

"Seanchai." Shayth put a hand on the elf's arm to stop him. "Where are the stones the Priestess gave you?"

Seanchai pulled out the small leather bag. He put his hand in and pulled out the red one. He stared at it. Then, instinctively, he cupped it in both hands and immediately felt waves of heat moving through his body. Swiftly, the fatigue became a dull ache. He nodded to Shayth. "Okay. Let's keep going."

As they began to move, a cheer rose up from behind them and a hundred dwarves swarmed out from a corridor to their right. At first Seanchai feared they were conscripted dwarves, but he saw their coat-of-arms was a shield with a crown on top and two ornate axes beneath the shield and sighed in relief. They were soldiers of Hothengold.

Suddenly, a cry came from an alleyway to their right. "Seanchai! Shayth!" Sellia appeared, glistening with sweat and bleeding from a nasty gash on her cheek. "I need you. Come."

Seanchai turned to Ballendir. "You have enough dwarves to reach the Great Hall. We'll join you there."

They ran after Sellia, who dashed through an alley with a high wall to one side. Seanchai gasped as they reached the broken body of Rhoddan and nearly shoved past Sellia to drop to his side.

"You've been enjoying yourself," Seanchai said, his voice breaking.

Rhoddan lay awkwardly, limbs jutting in impossible directions. His cuts had been hastily dressed with strips of cloth. When he spoke, his voice was hoarse.

"Ilana," he said. " . . . the small hall . . . above here." He tried to move his head.

"Is she okay?" Seanchai asked, his heart beating in his ears.

Rhoddan shook his head. "Don't know . . . Tarlach. I think . . . he knows she's your . . . I pushed him away . . . I couldn't . . ."

"It's okay," Seanchai said. "Shayth and I will go. Sellia, stay with Rhoddan." He pulled out the pouch and took the red stone. He wrapped Rhoddan's hands around it. "Hang on to this. I'll be back."

"Seanchai." Rhoddan tried to grab his arm. "Tarlach . . . he's very good."

"Yes," Seanchai snapped back. "But if he's touched Ilana, he's dead."

Rhoddan looked at Sellia.

"I'm going with you," Sellia said. "It's what Rhoddan wants."

Rhoddan nodded ever so slightly. "Let me . . . keep . . . my honor."

Seanchai began to argue, but Shayth grabbed his arm. "Come on. There's no time."

ALON SHALEV 401

They ran up back through the alley and up the other side. At the door, four guards braced themselves to fight. But Seanchai was in no mood and reached out his hands. "*Mereksur,*" he yelled, and blue light left his palms and smashed the guards and the door to smithereens.

Through the dust and debris stepped the Wycaan warrior; the beautiful black elfe with her bow noched on one side; and the Emperor's nephew, broadsword held at the ready, on the other.

More blue light shot from Seanchai's hands, and two more soldiers fell and lay still.

"That's enough," Tarlach's strong voice boomed. "I have her. I can hurt her."

Seanchai stopped. He saw Ilana, sitting against a wall, shivering and hugging herself as waves of pain shot through her body. Seanchai's voice became a growl. "You've lost, Tarlach. You've lost before, and you know you've lost again."

"I don't think so, my young Wycaan," Tarlach's voice was steady and patient, as if he had all the time in the world. "You never completed your training. In fact, you barely even started. Your teachers have a nasty habit of dying, I hear.

"Allow me to teach you a basic lesson that any soldier learns: Know your enemy. What you fail to know about me, young elf, is that I have no heart, no conscience. I'm the epitome of the human warrior. I was born to command, to conquer, and to win."

Tarlach smiled before continuing. "I studied my enemy and know that he has a soft spot for his friends. This weakness lured him into my trap at Galbrieth, from which he barely escaped. He has a conscience, which is why he allowed a couple of his friends to remain in this living tomb. And, most of all, he's in love, and will do whatever he must to save his mate.

"Well, I'm going to give you that opportunity. Even now, poison runs through her body, and only I have the antidote. Come with me to the capital. Meet the Emperor. He is looking forward to meeting you."

"What about Shayth?" Seanchai felt that the words leaving his mouth were not his own.

"Forget about me," Shayth hissed. "Let me . . ."

Seanchai put out a hand to stop him.

"Seanchai," Sellia said but got no further.

"What about Shayth?" Seanchai repeated.

Tarlach shrugged. "Again, he is for the Emperor. Shayth is family. Family is always so complicated."

"And the dwarves?"

"They become subjects of the Empire. It will end the bloodshed, Seanchai. You have the opportunity to end the violence here and now."

Seanchai's gaze went from Tarlach to Ilana. She looked up at him, her pale skin dripping with sweat and tears. She summoned all her strength to rise haltingly.

"You made me a promise, Seanchai," she said, her voice barely a whisper. Tarlach began to silence her, but stopped. "You promised to love me forever," she continued. "You swore to be my partner in all I am, all I believe in. You promised never to betray me or do anything to destroy my dreams. You swore in the ancient language."

She slid back to the floor. Seanchai couldn't take his eyes from her. His chest was heaving; his sweaty palms clenched the Win Dao swords.

"You heard her words," Tarlach said, oozing false sympathy. "You can fulfill her dreams. You can make her very happy."

Seanchai wrenched his eyes slowly from Ilana to Tarlach. He stared at him.

"Ilana," he said after a few moments. "I love you, more than anything in the world. You know that, right? I must hear you say it."

"I know, Seanchai, and I love you too. I'm sorry it must end this way, but this is why the oath is binding. You must keep your word."

Still staring at Tarlach, Seanchai continued. "You are my soul mate, and I'll make good my oath. I keep all my oaths." He turned slowly to Shayth, his voice breaking. "Tarlach is yours."

Seanchai looked at Ilana one more time and turned around. He heard Ilana cry out, "Sellia! Keep your oath, too, and I die in peace."

Seanchai felt Sellia's arm around him as they walked out from the hall. Victory was theirs, but it felt so very hollow.

Shayth slowly drew his broadsword and stared at Tarlach. "I've waited for this moment for most of my life, craving the opportunity to kill you. But I'll let you live, Tarlach. Give her the antidote, and I'll spare you."

Tarlach smiled. "You've become soft, Shayth. I wouldn't expect you to care about a she-elf. What have they done to you?"

Shayth stared back. "Done *to* me?" he sneered. "It's what they've done *for* me. They gave me what you took away. The Emperor took my parents from me, but your cowardice stripped me of all hope and humanity. The elves and the Wycaan gave these things back to me, and I like how it feels."

"I did not harm you," Tarlach replied, and Shayth was surprised to hear sadness in his voice. "I took you into my house. I grieved your father's death. I even tried to free you in Galbrieth. You know it was I who had worn the black garb. You saw the wound on my forehead when they brought you to my office afterwards. So you see, my dear Shayth, I do care."

"Not enough. You let the monster who killed my father live," Shayth's voice rose. "And you continue to this day to serve him. You denied your best friend the justice he deserved."

"You cannot bring your father back, you idiot," Tarlach spat. "Prince Shindell was my best friend and a great man. I never got over his death. I never forgave myself."

"Then we have something in common," Shayth said taking a step forward. "For I have never forgiven you either."

"You kill me, then she dies, too."

"I understand."

"So you would deny the life so dear to your best friend?" Tarlach sneered. "Where is *your* humanity? Are you so different from me?"

Shayth hesitated a moment and glanced at the crumpled Ilana. She raised her head, straining with the effort, and he saw the plea in her eyes. At that moment, he had his answer.

"There is no similarity. My father died because of worthless palace intrigue. Ilana will die to set Odessiya free. Don't you dare compare yourself to her or Seanchai. You're not worthy. Maybe I'm no better than you and that saddens me. But somehow, Seanchai, Ilana, Rhoddan, and Sellia have allowed me to think I still have a part to play: that I can put things right.

"And unbelievable though it seems, I offer that same gift to you. Put down your sword and give her the antidote."

Tarlach stared at him, and then smiled. "You're a foolish boy who follows another foolish youth. You can't comprehend the Emperor's power, and you underestimate mine."

Tarlach leapt forward, and their broadswords clashed. Faster and faster the swords flew, and Tarlach pushed Shayth back, but then the youngster ducked, rolled to one side and took the upper hand. They parried back and forth, neither giving way, sparks flying from their blades. Shayth, despite the growing fatigue, felt exhilarated. He became engulfed in the moment, and years of rage erupted from his heart into his arms and legs. He dueled faster and faster, finally forcing Tarlach to retreat.

The general back stepped around the room, blocking Shayth's blows. On the defensive, the experienced swordsman barely held his own. As he retreated past Ilana, she found enough energy to stick out a foot. Tarlach stumbled, giving Shayth the chance to leap forward and drive his blade straight through the general's heart.

Tarlach fell to his knees. He reached for the small vial in his pocket and smiled at Shayth. Then he smashed it on the ground, the antidote seeping into the cracks of the stone floor. He stared at Shayth as blood poured from his chest and his lips.

"You once a-asked . . . me a q-question that . . . I-I never answered. I don't know . . . if I would . . . have . . . let them . . . t-take you . . . from my house." He wheezed, struggling to take in more air. "I don't know, but . . . I hope . . . I would . . . have stopped them."

"And that," Shayth replied, drawing his sword out from the general's body, "is why I side with the Wycaan. You *hope* you might have come to my defense. He *knows* he would have."

Tarlach stared into Shayth's black eyes and then collapsed to the ground. Shayth bent down to Ilana. He scooped her up in his arms. Her skin was cold and clammy.

"Shayth," she whispered. "I want to die above ground . . . to see the sky . . . one last time . . . with Seanchai."

Shayth, hugging her limp body, charged from the hall. He saw
Seanchai and yelled for him to follow. They ran through the palace
and out through the northern entrance to a peak on the western side.
Seanchai sat on a flat boulder, and Shayth rested Ilana on his lap. As
the sky blazed red, Seanchai held her close.

"Do you see the sun setting, Ilana?" Seanchai asked, tears falling
from his eyes. "It's beautiful."

"No," she whispered, her eyes now closed. "I . . . see . . . a new . . .
dawn . . . rising . . . over . . . Odessiya. It's beautiful. D-do you see it?"

"No, but I will," Seanchai replied holding her tightly, his voice
breaking. "And I swear, all of Odessiya will see it, too." He stroked
the hair from her face. "*Ashbar,*" he whispered, sealing his oath in the
ancient language.

And Seanchai drew her close one final time.

# EPILOGUE

A had walked numbly through the palace corridors. His father, forever invincible in his eyes, was dead. Reports were confirming that Shayth had murdered him, killing the great man who had once taken the young orphan into his house.

Ahad had seen the Emperor only once before. Then he had approached in terror. Now he felt nothing. He didn't care what the Emperor had to say. He wanted only to leave, to track down and face his father's murderer.

He waited in the anteroom without looking at the art or the books. He didn't touch the beverages or fruit. He didn't care how long he waited. It was irrelevant.

When he was shown in, he went down on one knee as instructed, but didn't bow his head. He assumed the Emperor, hidden behind the veil, noticed, but he didn't care.

"I am sorry for your loss, Ahad. Your father was my finest general and served me well. You follow in his footsteps. You have helped my son and became his friend. You are a trained warrior. I am glad to take you officially into my service."

Ahad didn't respond.

"Usually," the Emperor continued, clearly affronted, "I am thanked for such a gesture. Why do you not show appreciation?"

Ahad cleared his throat. "My lord. If you wish to reward me, free me from your service. Give me a sword, a horse, and your blessing."

"Where would you go, Ahad?"

"To track the scum who murdered my father."

"And when you find him?"

"I will kill him and the elf that rides with him."

"You might be a match for Shayth, but not for the Wycaan."

Ahad felt his temper slip. "How do you know?"

Through the veil, he saw the Emperor stand.

"Ahad. I will grant you your wish in time. But first you will receive special training so that you can go forth and avenge your father's death. Kill my nephew. But you will not fight the elf. Only one person lives in Odessiya who can now best his Wycaan skills."

"And who is that?" Ahad snapped before he could stop himself. In a quieter voice, he said, "My lord, excuse me. Let me serve the one who can kill the elf."

"I grant you that wish, too," the Emperor said, "and in doing so, I reveal a secret that only a handful in this land know."

With that, the Emperor pushed the veil back. Ahad stared into the face of his ruler – it was smooth, his muscles tight, and as he removed his turban, Ahad saw long, snow-white hair.

"All Wycaans have white hair. Now you know, Ahad. Only a Wycaan Master can defeat a Wycaan. When you find him, you will have the ability to summon me. I will unleash the full force of a Wycaan Master, and the Wycaan elf they call Seanchai will die. I swear this to you in memory of your father.

"*Ashbar.*"

# AUTHOR'S NOTE:

Dear Friend,

If you are reading these words, you have hopefully come through these many battles relatively unscathed. I hoped you laughed and cried with these characters, as I have. We share a common bond as those who fight side-by-side for a common good always form, and I hope you will join me and continue with them into the third book, *Ashbar*.

There are many great epic fantasy novels to choose from and I am honored you decided to read *The First Decree*. Please consider leaving a brief review if you purchased this book online. Feel free to contact me at anelfwriter@gmail.com or sign up for my weekly blog post at http://www.elfwriter.com. I also tweet at @elfwriter.

Thank you, again,

Alon

# NON-FANTASY NOVELS BY ALON SHALEV:

*Unwanted Heroes* *(Three Clover Press, 2012)*
*A Gardener's Tale* (Three Clover Press, 2011)
*The Accidental Activist* (Three Clover Press, 2010)

*The story continues:*

# WYCAAN MASTER, BOOK 3: ASHBAR

by Alon Shalev

ISBN: 978-0-9884428-7-0 (paperback)

Tourmaline Books, Berkeley, California

Coming out in 2013

*"Hear my words and hearken to my warnings. For I have seen a vision of the future and it will surely come to pass.*

*The Age of the Alliance will end with such blood spilt that will flow down the sides of the mountains and collect into a river of despair, flowing from the battlefield into extinction. And it shall be that when all civil society collapses, so too will the destiny of many races, but none will fall so low as the elves.*

*Many of our people will lie still forever, decomposing among the weeds and those who live will become a pitiful people, a social underclass. Dignity will be lost, hope forgotten and the Elf Code only a myth, the rambling of fools.*

*The Age of Man will be upon the land, it values forged by iron and weapons, greed and power. And the humans will waxen and spread throughout the land, taking all that they need and desire, leaving their scraps for the survivors of the other races to carve out a humble existence.*

*So hearken to my word, proud elves, for you are the most ancient of peoples, the founders and custodians of the Great Alliance. Take your sons and daughters and head into the West, to the great forest of Markwin. Fortify its magical boundaries and close yourselves off from the madness that will erupt.*

*Preserve the Elf Code, learn and develop the magic of the earth. And wait. For though many of the Wycaan warriors will fall in defense of the Alliance, there will be those who survive and pass on the teachings.*

*Wait and be patient, my people. For I have seen that one will come from the East, a Wycaan of our own ears, pointed and proud. But he will be young and unstable, ready to fall by the way. Teach him then our heritage and ways. Train him to find his inner core, and provide him with the foundation he will need.*

*For it falls to him to reforge the Alliance and he must not fail. For his failure will be the end of the elves, and the dwarves, and all the races save those of man. Then all that will stand between man and his greed will be the earth itself and the earth will not be subjugated. Life as we know it will end . . . forever.*

*Wycaan Master Tansu*
*From the Book of Prophecies.*